CONNIE MONK

Rachel's Way

FONTANA/Collins

First published in Great Britain by
Judy Piatkus (Publishers) Ltd 1989

First published by Fontana Paperbacks 1990

Copyright © 1989 by Connie Monk

Printed and bound in Great Britain by
William Collins Sons & Co. Ltd, Glasgow

Rachel's Way

Chapter One

Appearing out of the fading dusk, a bat swooped low, then soared overhead to be lost beyond the garden, going on its wild way. There was no other movement, no sound. The air was still, heavy with the scent of flowers. Listening, Rachel's ears were tuned to the first sound of John's carriage on the lane. Anticipation was a physical thing; in her chest a thousand butterflies fluttered.

'Mama!' she heard. A hopeful call.

Momentary irritation made her bite her lip.

Then it came again: 'Mama!' This time louder, more demanding. It was Patsy. She'd been christened 'Patience', a misnomer if ever there was one!

'What is it, Patsy? I'm outside in the garden.' Even so she started back to the house. A straggling rose caught at her wide skirt as she passed and, when she stooped to disentangle it, another tore at her wrist, the scratch drawing blood. Sucking the wound she went up the stone steps from the lawn to the terrace.

From above in Patsy's room she could hear movements, a chair being dragged to the window. Then the little girl's head appeared, hardly more than a dark shape.

'I'm hot. Boiled hot.'

'Throw off your covers, just keep a sheet. You'll soon be asleep again.'

''Course I'm not 'sleep. I'm waiting for Papa. Listening.'

'You'll see him in the morning. Jump back into bed. It's late.'

'Papa will want to see me. Tonight — not in the morning.'

The four-year-old had no doubts. 'Need a drink. Drink, Mama.' Then in a voice Rachel couldn't refuse: 'Please, can I? Just a tiny drink. Te'bly thirsty.'

'I'll come up. You get back into bed and I'll bring you one.' Rachel imagined Patsy's face, wide-set blue eyes, large and pleading; her dark curls tousled from her tossing and wriggling in the feathered nest of her bed. How could she expect her to want to sleep when any moment John would be home? For nearly a month he'd been away in Cornwall, to Patsy it must have seemed endless. Yesterday had come his last brief letter:

I shall be home on Wednesday, sometime during the evening. Until I see you I'll tell you no more than that. Suffice it to say that it has been a most eventful few weeks, weeks that I am confident have set the seal of success on many future years.

He'd gone to Cornwall to see the progress on an engine he'd designed that was being built there for a mining company. Nothing unusual in that, only in the length of time he'd been away. Usually he would have been home within a week. The engine must have led to other work. She'd never been to Cornwall but she knew the extent of the mining industry there. No doubt John was pleased with the way things had turned out; and, if he was, so of course was she.

With a candle holder in one hand and a glass half full of water in the other she went up to Patsy's room.

'What woke you? I peeped in earlier and you were fast asleep.'

'Jus' 'tending. Snorted, I 'spect – like this.' And to demonstrate she gave an excellent imitation of a grunting pig, and dissolved into peals of merriment at her own cleverness, rolling on her bed, her feet kicking excitedly towards the ceiling.

'No wonder you're too hot! Come on, you scamp, have a sip of water then we'll turn your pillow to the cool side. Just look at the mess your bed's in, all rucks and creases!' Rachel smoothed the sheets, then steadied the glass so that the water wasn't drained in one draught.

'Let's have a story, shall we? Let's have the one 'bout when

2

you were little, Mama. You know, the one 'bout when you lost your boat on the lake. Please, Mama.' Oh so sweetly, a tiny smile playing at the corners of her rosebud mouth and the dimple deepening in her left cheek. 'Please, let's have umpteen 'gain, shall we. . . ? It was her childishly muddled understanding of what she'd been told that was impossible to resist. 'I've told you umpteen times.' It was that, and her smallness, her innocence, her hope — and her trust. Rachel had no power to refuse her, any more than she had to resist bending to rub her face against the tumbled curls. She was rewarded by a mighty hug, then Patsy lay down and waited for the tale she must have known almost by heart.

They were well into it when in one movement the little girl sat bolt upright. 'Sshh!' Her small finger shot up. 'Wait! 's 'im! 'Tis, it's Papa. Hark!'

They both listened. A carriage had stopped . . . the front door was opening . . .

'Lie quietly. I'll see he comes up.'

'Me's going down. He'll 'spect me.' Already Patsy was out of bed and half way across the floor, her nightgown held high so that she could run.

They made a picture, the little girl scooped up in his arms, a wriggling mass of ecstatic joy held high above him, stretching down to rain kisses on whatever part of him she could reach. John, as dark as she was herself, the same curly hair, the same laughing blue eyes, the same dimple. As Patsy had so surely said: 'He'll want to see me.'

From half way down the stairs Rachel watched them then, as she came down to the hall, John held one arm to encircle her. So the three of them stood locked together under the gaslit chandelier.

'Missed me? Been behaving yourselves?'

'What kept you away so long?' Her gingery brown eyes were answer enough to questions so unnecessary.

'I'll tell you all about it.' Then, tossing the laughing Patsy into the air and catching her: 'But first I'll see this young lady back to her bed.'

Custom of the age decreed that it was a mother's responsibility to bring up a family. The father might make the discipline, even see that his offspring were taught the route of

3

a path that was straight – and very often narrow, too – but wiping away tears, kissing bumps and bruises, teaching the skills of throwing a diabolo or bowling a hoop, these things were considered beneath him. But not John.

He was some time despatching Patsy just as Rachel had known he would be. But he was home and tonight she could tell that there was a repressed undercurrent of excitement in him, just as there was in her. Let Patsy have these few minutes; her time would come. For now she was content to wait. More content than Mrs. Trump, the housekeeper, who listened from half way up the back stairs, anxious to get the meal dished up.

'Serve them right if it's done to a cinder,' she grumbled to Doris, the housemaid, clumping back to the basement kitchen. 'He's up there with young Patsy, could hear 'em from right down here. Got her that excited, she's laughing fit to bust. And just look at my nice dinner if you please. Never a care for what time we'll be getting to our beds!'

Doris was young. Her life was made up of dreams.

'He's been away so long, Mrs. Trump, they must be that glad to have him home.'

'Time you learnt to stand up for yourself, my girl. Let them think they can treat you anyhow and they'll walk right over you. Well, I'm telling you, if this dinner's beyond eating they've got no one to blame but themselves. Can't help getting home late, I dare say, but there's time enough for games tomorrow. Well, if they can't get their forks into their roast potatoes it's no fault of mine.'

Doris's romantic heart had no room for roast potatoes.

Upstairs John sat on the edge of Patsy's bed. They both knew the rules. First a game – and tonight it had been a wild romp that had brought forth the shrieks that Mrs. Trump had heard. But when Patsy was told: 'In you hop,' she knew they'd reached the next stage and in she'd hopped.

Now he bent to kiss her. 'Sleep well. God bless you.'

'Oh! 'Minds me! Wait!' Up shot the little finger. 'Something else –' and out she wriggled to kneel by the side of her bed, hands together, eyes shut so tight that her face was screwed up, the pink soles of her still-baby feet tugging at his heart-strings. 'Dear God,' she whispered earnestly, 'thank

4

You for bringing Papa back. He'd been gone such a long time.' She opened her eyes, then as another thought struck her, shut them again: 'Oh yes, and thank You for making me be awake when he got here. Amen.' That to her Maker, and to her father as she crawled back between the sheets: 'I'd done the rest when I came to bed. That was extra.'

Just as Rachel had earlier, John found it quite impossible not to bend over her, rubbing his face against her rumpled curls.

At last from where she waited in the drawing-room Rachel heard him coming down the stairs.

'Fancy her managing to stay awake,' he chuckled as he came in. 'Now I'll tell you —' But he didn't. She wound her arms around his neck and raised her mouth to his. A quickening of response from him and her pulses raced. Hadn't she felt that repressed excitement in him earlier? Her mouth moved hungrily under his.

A tap on the door and he pulled away, pushing her from him. 'Come in,' he called. 'Ah, and here's Doris. I know what it is, Doris. You've come to grumble at us for keeping dinner waiting, is that it?'

'Sorry, sir – beg pardon, ma'm – but Mrs. Trump sent me – it's cos she's feared it'll spoil, see.'

Rachel came to her rescue. 'I was just going to ring, Doris. Tell Mrs. Trump we're on our way to the dining-room now.'

'Yes 'um.' And with a half bob somewhere in John's direction, she fled. Her interruption had extinguished that momentary flame in him and it had seemingly put from his mind that he'd been going to tell Rachel about his trip. It wasn't until the meal was served and they were alone that he referred to it.

'Raise your glass, Rachel. We are going to drink a toast.'

'To your coming home?'

'I'll explain in a moment. First, raise your glass. I give you,' he paused a second, there was something of the actor in John, timing was important, then: 'Treddinock!'

Treddinock? But that was where he'd been to see his engine. She was prepared to trust his judgement; if he gave his blessing to the place, she was prepared to believe it should be blessed. But it wasn't in her nature to follow blindly.

'You mean we're drinking to your engine?'

'More than that, Rachel. Much more. I've taken a stake in Harding and Ross, the firm who are building it. Invested in the company. Edward Harding was the brains, he was the engineer. I'd met him several times, had great respect for him. He died earlier in the year, just after work was started on this engine I'd designed for Wheal Dovey. Albert Ross is married to his daughter. He must have been taken into the firm for her sake. No doubt he knows something about finance — well, if he doesn't his contribution is nil, for he doesn't pretend to be an engineer. Not impressed with the man at all. Even in these months the company is going downhill. No right-minded mine owner is going to put his work to Albert Ross. The share price has plummeted, I bought in at excellent terms. What's more Ross should be glad to have me there.'

It was impossible not to be carried along on the tide of his enthusiasm. He never talked about his work, his life was kept in two separate compartments. This only added to Rachel's awareness that this evening was different.

'A partner in the business. I'll drink to that. Treddinock.'

'More than a partner before I'm through. If old Mr. Harding was prepared to carry Ross, I certainly shan't be.'

'But surely he has shares.'

'What?' He seemed surprised at her words. She'd stepped out of line. Her role was to listen, to applaud. He frowned. 'Shares, perhaps, but no knowledge of the trade, no concern except for the income to be derived from it. Harding, Ross and Treweek. The new name will turn the tide. A Cornish name, eh! Treweeks will be known the length and breadth of the West Country — Treweeks of Treddinock.'

And not for a minute did she doubt him. He was a successful engineer. He'd been well on his way towards his goal when she'd met him. A weekend with an aunt in Shropshire, a dinner party to welcome her and John invited as a guest. That had been over eleven years ago, in the spring of 1870. By now he was thirty-five and still a good-looking man, a strong face — despite the dimple in his left cheek — a face that instilled trust. But eleven years ago, at twenty-four, he'd been almost too handsome; and eighteen-year-old Rachel had been ripe for romance, had fallen in love with him with all the violence of first love. By autumn of that same year they'd been married. His climb up the ladder of success had never faltered and neither had his confidence. She was sure he enjoyed his work but he never discussed what he did with her. In that he was no different from most other men of their acquaintance, indeed most other men of the time.

This evening she saw a new John. She may not have understood what he was saying, she had no conception of the working of an engine. It wasn't *what* he said that held her, it was his manner, his zeal, his buoyancy.

'The whole design of the boiler is different from the ancient one being replaced at Wheal Dovey. That was fire around water. Not any longer. Water around fire.' He must surely know she didn't understand, she'd never seen an industrial boiler. 'The rams in the pump will be sixteen inches in diameter,' he held his hands apart to illustrate. She knew just what sixteen inches looked like; but what did a ram do? 'That shaft will carry eighty tons of water upwards at any one time. Eighty tons, think of that.' She did. She nodded appreciatively, but he probably didn't notice. Still he talked. He'd designed engines enough in the past but she'd never known him like this. 'It's the biggest to come out of Harding's — hah, Harding, Ross and Treweek. Treweek's engine. It'll bring orders. I tell you, we're at the start of something big.'

She wanted to reach out and touch him, she wanted to feel him draw her into his fervour. But the width of the table was between them. And in her heart she suspected he was talking 'at' her, not 'to' her. Any audience would have served. Yet, even if that were true, she was excited by what he was doing — and by what it was doing to him. They'd travelled comfortably in the same groove for so long, now suddenly it was John who was branching to a new route. With shining eyes she watched him.

Later they went outside into the warm summer darkness of the terrace.

'Smell the air, John. Isn't it beautiful.' She spoke quietly. On a night like this, so still, the moon just rising over the top of the elm trees in the lane, it seemed wrong to break the silence.

'Umph.' But she knew he wasn't thinking about the scents of summer.

'More than fourteen years I've lived away.' He might have been thinking aloud. 'I've been back, a day here, a day there, but only visiting, not to live amongst them like I did this time. I believe I was growing to be as much a foreigner as the rest of you.' He was holding a lucifer to his tobacco, drawing on his pipe between each sentence. 'The Cornish, we Cornish, are a race apart.'

She forgot the stillness of the night. 'What utter nonsense! Whatever difference to a man can it make which side of the Tamar he's born on!'

'I can't explain it to you, but it's the truth. Going back there I felt it — my country — my people. That's why I'm so positive about what I'm doing.' Still drawing on his pipe, it was the voice of contentment. 'A stake in my own land. I've put pretty well all I have into this, you know. It's the most important thing I've ever done.'

In the darkness he exhaled a cloud of tobacco smoke, masking the fragrance of the night-scented flowers. Pipe smoke was synonymous with John in her mind, the familiar smell of it was reassuring. She wasn't prepared for what he said next, his tone businesslike: 'For the first year or two I intend to be there a good deal, I want to keep an eye on how things are shaping. Not just the work for Wheal Dovey; new orders. That fellow Ross has no idea.'

Silence. She forced her mind into action. 'Foreigner', 'a race apart', 'start of something big, something important', 'a stake in my own land'. All around her his words echoed. And all the while that his life was full, what about her? Was she supposed to wait here, live for the days he'd spare to come back and see them? While he was becoming more and more involved she and Patsy would be outside the orb of it all, not even able to picture this place Treddinock, somewhere they didn't know, somewhere they'd be 'foreigners'.

'We'll shut up the house. One year, two years, as long as we're all of us together does it matter how long?'

The idea was new to him. And quite out of the question.

'You've not seen it. Treddinock isn't what you'd think of as a village. It's just a small working community, the works are

8

on the edge of it. There's not a house there fit to take you and Patsy to.'

'Then John, we'll find one that isn't and we'll make it fit. Do you think we're going to wave you goodbye and send you off to somewhere not fit to live in all by yourself? Anyway,' she hit below the belt, 'from what you said just now I thought you were so proud of this splendid country of yours, I thought you'd want to show it to us.' Her voice teased. Pipe or no, she moved close to him, nestling her face against his neck. 'We belong together, all three of us. Don't we?' She saw the glow of his pipe as he laid it on the low wall of the terrace.

Only for a second did he picture the cottages of Treddinock. Joy leapt within her as her lips clung to his.

Upstairs at the top of the house in her stiflingly hot attic bedroom Doris snuffed out her candle then pushed her window as wide as she could. Her day was over. Only a slight sound, but enough to recall John from where Rachel was leading him. Even so, he still held her.

'And I never saw it.' He rubbed his cheek against her hair. 'The one cloud in the whole thing was having to live in the inn, leaving you and Patsy here. I'd have come home, my life would have been filled with railway journeys. And I didn't even consider shutting the house.' The full impact seemed to hit him. He pulled himself back from her. 'I say, Rachel, you're a marvel. There won't be anywhere in Treddinock, but I'll look in Helston or even Penzance.'

Houses could come later. Tonight Rachel craved just that he needed her, now, at Treddinock, always. He felt her fingers caressing the back of his neck, then his spine; her moist lips teased his. He kissed her lightly.

'You're a clever girl. Of course, that's why I married you,' he told her with a soft laugh.

She rose to the occasion and laughed too. 'There! And all these years I've been thinking it was for my beauty!' It was a consciously light-hearted retort, born of disappointment. But his reply banished all that. He held her at arm's length, his hands on her shoulder.

'Brains or beauty, whatever the reason — I'm glad I did. You know that, don't you?'

She groped in her mind for something grand and beautiful

to answer him but found nothing. Anyway her voice seemed to have died. So she leant against him and wordlessly nodded her head.

'Time to go in,' he whispered.

Uninvited came the image of those moments earlier in the evening, the bat swooping out of the dusk then disappearing just as swiftly, all around her the stillness and peace while she'd been alive with some inner excitement. Memory had already taken over, rejecting the sharp dig of the rose's thorn, holding just what was good. She remembered only for a moment as they moved back into the house and bolted the door against the night.

'You go on up,' he told her. 'I'll not be more than a few minutes, there are just some papers I want to glance at.'

'Come soon.' She reminded herself of his words . . . 'whatever the reason — I'm glad I did.' John had never been a man for empty endearments.

Glancing at his papers seemed to her to keep him a long time. She didn't get into bed. Instead she made excuses to herself of things to do: sorted out her lace collars, tidied the box where she kept her hair combs and pins, gave her hair an extra hundred strokes of the brush. Then she heard him come up the stairs and go into the communicating room to get ready for bed. He'd be a few minutes yet, she knew his habits exactly. He always hung away his clothes, put his boots on trees. Still she waited. The night stretched long ahead of them, longer if she was still not in bed when he came in.

Carefully she examined her reflection. Next month she'd be thirty. The face that looked back at her still had the expectancy that belongs to youth. It must be the flattering light, she told herself. Tawny hair, not curly like John's and Patsy's, yet not quite straight either; eyes the exact shade; high cheekbones. By the standard of the day she wouldn't be called beautiful, her eyebrows were too positive and her nose was peppered with freckles, especially this time of year. Still no sign of John, still she waited. The examination went on. Undoing the buttons of her nightgown she slipped it off her shoulders and let it fall to the ground. Too thin, she could see her ribs and her hip bones. As if to prove it she ran her hands up and down her lean body, then held them to her breasts.

Nearly thirty. Still the same size as she'd been at eighteen — yet she wasn't the same. She pulled her nightgown up from the floor, feeling the caress of the smooth silk as she slipped her arms back into the sleeves. In the communicating room she could hear John moving about. In twelve years she'd learnt to recognise each sound. Reaching up she turned off the gas tap, putting the room into darkness, then opened the curtains and the window. She heard the door; he was coming.

'No gas?'

'It's light. Come over by the window.' Instinctively she whispered, even though Patsy never stirred once she was sleeping. 'I can see you clearly.'

'The moon's full.' He came to stand behind her. She leant against him. He could feel the warmth of her and pulled her closer against him.

She knew no rules of a relationship. Until she'd met John there had been no man in her life. Whether all men, all husbands, behaved as he did she had no idea. Tonight she was sure they would make love, every pulse in her strained towards it, and yet, because she was sure, she wanted to move slowly, to savour every touch.

'Let's just lie on top of the bed.' She held his hands to her, hands that were warm. 'You've been away so long ...' And when she said it she believed it must have been the month apart that made her feel like this, her and him too. But it had to do with more than four weeks' separation; perhaps it was the hot night, perhaps it was the exhilaration of the new venture. In truth John's sexual drive had never been strong, even in the beginning. But then, Rachel had no means of comparison. Tonight, though, she had no doubt. Tonight his need was plain. And that's when she said: 'You've been away so long ...'

Her words triggered off a memory. Still holding her affectionately he chuckled. 'That's what young Patsy said,' and he proceeded to tell her the incident of the 'extra' prayers. Then he dropped a light kiss on the back of her head and turned away to pull the covers off the bed, draping them over the end rail. 'We can pull them up afterwards,' he said.

She was ashamed of the inexplicable disappointment she felt. What had she hoped for? What had she wanted? So much

11

more, yet she didn't know what. In the moonlit room he saw what she was doing; her nightgown fell on the floor around her ankles. Gently he pushed her on to the bed, then lifting his nightshirt eased himself above her. Where now was the long night? Beneath him her movements were wild. She had no will except the force that drove her. She'd longed for every unknown avenue to be explored, but now she rushed towards her goal . . . nearer . . . nearer . . . Too soon and without warning she was left, suspended in the middle of nowhere; John jerked himself free of her and rolled to the bed at her side. For him there was no turning back, no stemming nature. She could feel his movement as he brought himself to climax.

'Damn you, damn you,' she sobbed, not knowing what she said or what she did as with her back arched her nails dug into his leg that was still lying across her. In that moment she hated him.

She felt him wiping the warm wetness from her side. 'Sorry,' he gasped, misunderstanding her, 'had to finish — couldn't help it.' He pulled the covers from the bottom rail then turned her to 'sit in his lap', his arm across her in the same companionable way they always slept. 'Missed you. Good to be home.' His voice was full of contentment, already he was drowsy. 'Have to be extra careful about all that, Rachel, mustn't risk any more family now, with you and Patsy coming with me.'

Not very likely, she said silently. Took us seven years to manage to get Patsy. And in her present mood she wasn't fair-minded enough to remember that it was because of the difficult time Patsy had given her that the doctor had advised them: 'Wait a while before there's another.' And what other way was there but 'finishing like a gentleman'?

John wriggled closer, pulling her towards him so that they slotted together like two pieces of a jig-saw puzzle. 'Umph,' he grunted, somehow saying it all.

Long after he slept she was still awake. The hollow disappointment only gradually gave way to affection. Dear John. Her own satisfaction must come from knowing she'd made him happy. As he slept she lifted his hand to her cheek, a cheek still wet from her tears.

*　　*　　*

It had sounded so simple when she'd said it. 'We shall come with you.' In broad daylight they could see the hurdles. Certainly she and Patsy couldn't go in the first instance. John had arranged to stay at the Copperhouse Inn, just as he had for this last month. It would be impossible to take them there, especially Patsy. So he returned to Cornwall on his own, leaving Rachel to arrange to close the house while he found somewhere as near to Treddinock as he could so that they could join him. In a year or two they'd be back; even John with his newly appreciated Cornish roots didn't envisage a lifetime in a backwater like Treddinock.

In the month he had stayed there it had been general knowledge that it was he who had designed the engine that was going to be installed at Wheal Dovey and that he was the new partner at Harding and Ross. Now, within hours of his return, there was hardly a household up or down Fore Street where the latest news hadn't travelled; he was looking for somewhere to bring his wife. That was on a Tuesday. It was the following Sunday as the congregation flocked out of the Wesleyan Chapel at the end of that same street that old Mary Bovis heard the first whisper of it from where she sat on a wooden bench in her front porch.

'A dear man he is, and such a smile,' she heard. 'Natural enough he's wanting his wife with him and the child too. Not short of a shilling from what I can see. Well, stands to reason he can't be, folk are saying that he's put up more than half for Harding's. 'Course, you know how stories get about, and far be it from me, coming out from the chapel here, to spread tales. Perhaps he has, perhaps he hasn't, likely the tale's been given a stretch. Still, not short of a bob, for that I can vouch. See the fine boots I polish up for 'un.'

Mary recognised the voice, it was Fanny Boles from the Copperhouse Inn. The group of women were gathered right by her gate. Who was this dear man with the smile and the quality boots? There was only one way to find out.

'Fine morning, Fanny. Come and tell me all your news. Days since my bones have let me walk down the street. Unless a body stops by my gate there's never a soul to have a jaw with.'

''Morning, Mrs. Bovis. I was just saying about Mr.

13

Treweek, him who's taken a stake in Harding's. Stayed all last month at the Copper with Bert and me, then home to see his missus for a day or two, and back to us again. I was just telling them, he's after somewhere here so that he can bring them. His wife and Patsy — that's his little girl. He talks a lot about Patsy, apple of his eye, she seems to be. But nothing in Treddinock for his sort. He talks of going over to Helston tomorrow. Rent or buy, seems he'll take either.'

'A man like that would need somewhere with space for a servant or two,' another woman put in. 'I dare say there'll be a place in Helston, or around Redruth or Camborne way.' Then having dealt with the Treweeks' problems: 'Not been too good this week then, Mrs. Bovis. A nice sit in the sun'll do you good.'

So John was forgotten. Or was he?

That same evening a message was brought to him. Mrs. Bovis at Mulberry Cottage wanted to see him. Old she may be, crippled with rheumatism too, but there was nothing wrong with Mary Bovis's brain. For months her daughter had been trying to persuade her to move out to live with her and her family in Truro, but she'd fought to hang on to her independence. Thinking of the guineas she might get from this well-to-do man who was pining for his wife, she made a decision. With the sort of money he'd be prepared to pay for Mulberry Cottage there would be no loss of independence. Indeed there wouldn't. She chuckled wickedly to herself. She could just imagine how Egbert, Vi's husband, would dance attendance on her! She'd make sure they knew how much she'd got — but she'd make sure too that she'd be the one to hold the chest it would be locked away in.

She met John's eyes unflinchingly as she named her price. He knew it was more than the cottage was worth; she knew it too. But when a man wants something badly enough he'll pay what he can afford, not what it's worth, or that's the way she bargained. Fine looking man ... missing his wife ... no doubt about it, she'd get her money. That would make Egbert sit up! And of course she was right.

Treddinock was a working community, cottages built in terraces around the turn of the century, granite and slate, functional — if a kitchen and one room downstairs with two tiny bedrooms above can be called functional. One or two were older — Mulberry Cottage one of them — one or two were bigger and stood in their own small gardens. Mulberry Cottage was detached, three rooms downstairs and three up, with a stable for a pony and room for a trap. Of these 'better' houses there were four others: the manager of the smelting house lived in one, so too did the Captain of Wheal Dovey, the Master Assayer and the schoolteacher. These were the 'silk hatters'. Coming down the social scale there was the cooper, the carpenter and the chandler. But most of the dwellings in Treddinock were miners' cottages, built in terraces fronting the street, small, grey and dingy. Years ago, before Mary had been widowed, her husband had been Captain of Wheal Dovey. If the time had come for her to give up Mulberry Cottage, who better to have it than the man who'd designed the great engine which was being installed there? Only last week she'd watched from her gate as the enormous cast-iron beam had been moved slowly on its way to the mine. And no doubt the other thing that tipped the scales was the thought of the ninety-five guineas she'd carry with her to Truro.

Straight away John wrote to tell Rachel the news. It wasn't the sort of home he'd intended, but it was close to the works. For the time being they would just bring enough to furnish it, leave the rest of their home under dust sheets. Later was soon enough to think of the future.

Mulberry Cottage, Treddinock. The picture it conjured up was almost rural. Who would have expected the two-storey granite house that stood beneath its slate roof next door to the Wesleyan Chapel on Fore Street? Its name had become attached to it quite naturally over the years as the two mulberry trees planted in the narrow strip of front garden had matured. They weren't great specimens, just large enough that in summer their leaves kept out what light the small casement windows at the front of the house might have let in.

Rachel watched each day for news of when Mrs. Bovis would be gone and when at last she sent for the van to take her furniture they were already into September. By the end of that same week dust sheets covered the furniture that was to be left behind; Mrs. Trump had been welcomed with open arms at the vicarage where a domestic crisis had left the vicar at the

15

mercy of his sister, with the prospect either of pangs of hunger or of dyspepsia; Doris had moved back to Birmingham to live with a cousin and find work in a factory.

The journey to Cornwall was long. There are limits to how long a four-year-old can find a train ride entertaining. Patsy fought tiredness, determined not to give way to sleep as though she were still a baby. But at last it was over and they climbed down on to the platform at Redruth Station.

'There's him! There's Papa!' Pulling free of her mother's hand Patsy darted to hurl herself into John's outstretched arms.

The last stage of the journey was by road, shut together inside the coach while the driver rode aloft and their last minute packing was loaded onto the back step. With her nose almost pressed to the window Rachel took in everything. Everything? The scene opened before them as they covered the miles, a scene with little variety. She'd grown up amongst the hills of Shropshire; in the years since her marriage she'd become accustomed to the gentle beauty of Warwickshire. There had been nothing like this. A mist hung over the barren landscape, not dense enough to be called fog, yet giving the clusters of buildings grouped at the head of each mine a ghostly appearance.

'You'd never believe riches could come out of land like this,' she spoke her thoughts aloud. She hadn't expected an answer; which was as well for neither of the others seemed to have heard her. Patsy was on John's lap, snuggled against him, sniffing appreciatively. One little hand was raised to touch his face, then her fingers started to 'walk' around it. A giggle bubbled up from her very depths as he tried to snap them between his teeth each time they passed his mouth.

From somewhere in the distance a dog howled. It was a melancholy sound.

'Mrs. Boles from the inn arranged for a woman to come in,' John told her when Patsy's attention had turned to measuring her hands against his, and he had his face to himself again. 'She's got the furniture in place and will be there with a meal ready for us.'

'What's she like?'

'Mrs. Boles assured me she's reliable. I've not really taken much notice. She's worked hard there, I believe, done her best with the place.'

'Is it much further?' She was still watching the unchanging scene.

'We're about half way.' Already dusk and mist were merging together, promising an early end to the day. 'See this garden wall we're just passing? That belongs to the Hardings. Old Mr. Harding used to live there. It's his daughter's now, the one who is married to Ross.' And very grand it looked. But Rachel couldn't imagine why anyone should have built it here, in the middle of nowhere!

Another couple of miles or so and they came to a copse. As copses go it was very average, but the sight of it on such a dreary evening was cheering. It put her in the right frame of mind for her first sight of Treddinock. No one could possibly have called it an attractive village, it hadn't a single building of note. 'A working community,' John had told her and she could see he'd spoken the truth. Not two stones put together for the sake of beauty. And, unaccountably, she felt her spirits lifting. It was as if this complex of workers' cottages, the cooper's yard, the inn, the chapel, the group of women standing talking outside the grocer's shop, all these things gave a meaning and purpose to the lifeless headgear of the mines they'd passed on their way. All across the region there must be villages like Treddinock, each one playing its part, collectively making up an industry that spread its tentacles all across the world. 'No greater miners than the Cornish,' John had told her in his newfound ancestral pride.

Outside Mulberry Cottage she climbed from the carriage. This was to be her home. She looked down the straight of Fore Street, the first early lamps each casting their own pools of mysterious light from cottage windows. A group of men passed them, their hobnailed boots noisy on the cobblestones, their voices as strange to her as the rest of the scene.

'They'll be men coming home from the day core,' John said. She didn't understand him but neither did she question. Time enough. Their heavy footsteps were like the heartbeat of the village. She would become part of it — and she was glad.

Patsy was already in the small front garden. In great leaps she was measuring the distance to the front porch. 'That's three,' she announced, 'I did it in three. See! One, two, three,' and back to the gate.

The front door opened and they were greeted by a young woman in a plain grey dress and white apron, presumably the one who had got the cottage ready for them. Even in that moment when all Rachel's natural eagerness was to see inside her home, yet she was held by the loveliness of the girl. Girl? Woman? Hard to tell, for she had the clear, translucent complexion of a child, and yet her expression had the sort of serenity that has to be won. And John had said he hadn't noticed! She didn't doubt the truth of his words; they told her much that she already knew and in those few seconds salved the hurt his seeming casualness had so often inflicted.

'A race apart' John had called them and, the following morning, Rachel wondered whether after all it had been such nonsense. Her revised opinion stemmed from a visit to Mr. Traherne's grocery shop armed with a long list to stock the cupboard. A group of women were standing talking in what might have been a foreign language, yet as the doorbell clanged to announce her arrival they were silent, staring at her with open curiosity.

'Yo'm Mrs. Treweek,' the grocer greeted her. It was a more promising beginning than the women's sudden silence had led her to expect.

'That's right, Mr. Traherne.'

But having let her know that he'd noted she was there, he turned back to the gathered assembly.

A short, dark-haired woman in a hessian apron picked up the story she'd been telling when the bell had interrupted: 'Yu gurt vule, I told un, wad'ee wanna lit thicky aul vire ver? Canna zee I jes 'anged out m' clane claws!'

'I zaw un. Maakin a prapper dirty aul smitch,' another answered sympathetically.

It was lost on Rachel. On that first morning she couldn't guess at the bonfire that had blown its smoke over 'the hessian lady's' washing.

'Wad'ee wan t'day, Maud?' Mr. Traherne had let them have their gossip, now he set the pace. It was time for business.

18

'Jes gimme a vu bits o'bacon. Nuff vor a raw tiddy vry.'

After Maud had gone two more were served. In Mr. Traherne's shop there was no hurry. Perhaps what they found to talk about was no more than Rachel might have heard anywhere, but it seemed so as she listened, understanding only the occasional word. Yet she was sure they weren't meaning to be unfriendly; their smiles didn't exclude her and probably neither would their words if only she could have understood them.

'An' now, Mrs. Treweek, I'll sar'ee.' At last the grocer turned to her. By this time someone else had come in and was waiting but nothing hurried him, Rachel had seen that already. As she read out her list he piled the goods on the wooden counter. Her first lesson in interpreting the tongue came when she asked for eggs. From a great earthenware tub he counted them out, putting them carefully into a basket. One was cracked. He set it aside, muttering: 'Thicks naw guid – ers scat.' She understood. Whether to be 'scat' was cracked, broken or simply not up to standard she had yet to learn, but it was Lesson No.1. And when he came to the end of her list, without ado he called to someone upstairs, 'Sar fer a wee whail, Mary, will'ee? I'm jes gwain t'gie Mrs. Treweek a liff wi' hair gouds.'

And Rachel understood *that* too. She even held the shop door open for him as he carried the large box before him, and again the kitchen door at Mulberry Cottage.

''Morning, li'l maid,' he beamed at an aproned Patsy who was kneeling on a wooden chair, her hands plunged into some sort of pastey mess in a bowl. It seemed the vernacular presented no problem to her if her answering smile was anything to go on. 'Mrs. Caldecott,' he acknowledged 'the someone from the village' Mrs. Boles had found for them.

Dulcie Caldecott was the name of the girl who'd had the cottage ready to welcome them last night. Cold light of morning did nothing to detract from her loveliness. She was standing at the kitchen table kneading a pan of dough. Her dark hair was taken back into a sleek coil from its centre parting; her features were neat, her teeth even and startlingly white; her velvety brown eyes were fringed with the longest lashes Rachel had ever seen. Last night she had said she was a

19

widow, her husband had died last winter leaving her with a stepson. That and the fact she would gladly come each day to work at Mulberry Cottage was as much as she'd said.

'It was his lungs,' she told Rachel when, the groceries put away, she went back to her kneading and the conversation resumed from where they'd left it the previous night. 'It's the disease of the mines. More die from lung trouble than any other way, you know. And can you wonder!' All the while she talked her hands were working rhythmically and Patsy, by her side, was trying to do the same. 'He always vowed that Toby would never be a miner.'

'Toby's your stepson? I suppose he's at school this morning?'

'No, Toby's been finished with school a long time, he's coming up to sixteen now. When we can get the money together he'll go to college. He works for Mr. Dowty, the Master Assayer. Richard used to tell me that right from when he was eight and old enough to do a job, he used to run home from his lessons each day so that he could be off to help the assayer. Not much use in those days, probably, but Mr. Dowty could see he was bright and he taught him. He gets five and eightpence a week now; he'd not do that in the mine. One of these days he'll be a Master Assayer himself. But no matter how much Mr. Dowty teaches him, it'll be necessary for him to qualify at college.'

Rachel listened, but it wasn't Toby who interested her as much as Dulcie herself. The more she talked the more apparent it was that her background was not that of a servant. Gently spoken, no trace of the brogue of the locals. What had brought her to Treddinock, to a life amongst the miners?

'Dulcie, you don't come from around here?'

'I've always lived in the West Country, but not always Cornwall. I've travelled all over the place, doing the circuit with my father. My mother died when I was quite young. He was a preacher. I expect as a child I was an encumbrance to him. There was no love in him.' And none in her voice, either, as she spoke of him. 'He reared me to read aloud from the Good Book. He harangued sinners with threats of hellfire.' She stopped pummelling the dough and looked at Rachel, her dark eyes puzzled. 'He never liked me, never loved me — or anyone, I don't believe. Is that what it's all about? Surely there's another side – love, tolerance, forgiveness. Not always threats, always hellfire.' The dough was given a vigorous pounding. 'Then I met Richard. Gentle, kind; he lived all the things I believed. My father tried to make me feel guilty for wanting a life of my own – guilty for contemplating marrying a man who earned his living going down the mine. He thought he'd brought me up to serve that God of vengeance he puts such store in. For a so-called holy man he was the most dreadful snob! There, now this is ready to prove.' She shook out a clean cloth and covered the dough. She was as deft and matter of fact in her movements as ever Mrs. Trump had been. She took the pan and put it on the rack high above the range.

'And mine.' Patsy passed her small bowl containing a hard grey lump and there was nothing in Dulcie's expression to suggest it was anything less than perfect as she slipped it under the end of the cloth.

'I'm going to tell Hodgkin what I've made.' And off Patsy went stamping her way up the steep stairs to consort with her toy bunny. Without a word Dulcie raised the cloth and pulled an elastic piece of dough from the already spongy mass in the large pan and replaced the hard grey dollop.

Rachel decided that, preacher or no, her father must have been a singularly stupid man.

She welcomed the fact that everything about life in Treddinock was different. They were here until John saw the business back on its feet – one year, perhaps even two, but certainly not a lifetime. So the contrast to the comforts they'd taken for granted added to the flavour as far as Rachel was concerned. Never had she lived in a house like Mulberry Cottage. The front door opened to a dark passage which, in turn, led to a shadowy stairway, steep and narrow. To the left of the passage two steps led down to the stone-floored kitchen and beyond that to the scullery. To the right of the passage was the sitting-room and behind that the dining-room. It was the sitting-room that suffered most from the mulberry trees, planted only feet from the small casement window. Up the stairs were three bedrooms, one over the sitting room, the second leading off from it, and a third over the kitchen, its window looking down on to the roof of the scullery.

Rachel anticipated no welcoming callers with visiting cards and invitations for her to take tea. But in that she was wrong, or at least partially wrong. Elizabeth Ross certainly called, she even announced herself by sending in her card, but there was no welcome in her manner and no invitation for Rachel to visit the house with the walled garden John had pointed out to her on the way to Treddinock.

As straight as a ram rod, Elizabeth sat on an upright chair, her very attitude making it clear she didn't intend to waste time on what was a duty visit. Her costume was fitting for fashionable society but not for this little sitting-room. Her gown fitted tightly over her thin, corseted figure, the exaggerated bustle set at ninety degrees from her waist and on her head a bonnet topped with a tall crown of ostrich feathers. Such a striking outfit might have flattered a beautiful woman; for her it did nothing. Worse than thin, she was boney, her hands like claws and her complexion sallow. It wasn't her fault that nature had used her so meanly, but only she was responsible for her expression. Was it the stained yellow teeth or the sour breath that surely went with them that pulled the corners of her mouth into that droop?

'I can't believe you'll make your visit long. You must find it trying to be so cramped.' It was plain what her opinion was of Mulberry Cottage.

'I've no idea how long we shall be here, but John was so fortunate to find us somewhere right in the village. We shall be very comfortable.' Rachel was quick to defend her new home – and surprised at how much she resented Elizabeth's critical tone.

Tea was offered and refused. After a few more minutes Elizabeth rose to leave. It had been an uncomfortable visit, void of warmth. And yet to get here she'd been driven more than five miles when she needn't have bothered to come at all.

'It was kind of you to call and welcome me,' Rachel said as she escorted her back to her carriage, to be answered by no more than slight nod of the ostrich plumes. She knew the point scored had been hers but it gave her no pleasure; the visit left her with a feeling of failure.

22

Rachel hadn't been prepared to acknowledge it, but the rooms *were* cramped. In those first weeks they were all aware of it, even Patsy whose bedroom wasn't much more than a cupboard with a small window. But with the onset of autumn and the shorter days there was something very cosy about the cottage. Rachel wanted to savour the intimacy of living at such close quarters. Another year and it would be no more than a memory.

At Wheal Dovey the great cast-iron beam was already installed, protruding from the second storey of the new engine house. It was early in November when she stood at her bedroom window, with Patsy and Dulcie, as slowly, foot by foot, the cylinder of the new pumping engine was dragged by. It was anchored to a frame of timbers, four wheels on each side and chains holding it steady. John had told her when it would be coming, 25 tons of cast-iron in a cylinder whose diameter would dwarf any man.

'Are they putting the cylinder in today?' she asked him next morning at breakfast. 'I thought we'd go and watch.'

'Patsy? You mean you'd take Patsy to that minehead?'

'Why, yes. We won't get in the way.'

'That's not what I mean. You'd need eyes everywhere. Have you any idea of the harm she might come to — lifting wheels, tramways, crushing gear, the shafts.' He looked at Rachel in disbelief that she would be so foolhardy. 'There are plenty of other places to go. Keep her away from the mine.'

He was right. There were plenty of places, places Patsy found more fun than going to Wheal Dovey. The favourite, as the trees shed a carpet of gold, was the copse on the outskirts of the village. On the far side of it they discovered a lake, so of course Patsy had to have a boat to sail.

'Like you did, Mama.' She clutched it proudly as they went off for the launching. To her it was a sign of progress towards maturity. Rachel remembered the much-told story of her own childhood; she remembered the night John had come home with the news that had brought them to Treddinock; she remembered the summer evening, the scent of the garden. Already it was long ago and far away.

One afternoon when the mist was very nearly fog and the air cold, she left Patsy at home with Dulcie and walked by herself to the mine. John's engine wasn't in use yet, the beam was still. The tall chimney by the boiler house seemed to lose itself in the mist. Nothing broke the perpetual rhythm of the stamps that crushed the ore, nor the creaking of the wheel that drove the Man Engine that brought the men 'to grass': up to the surface. As she stood looking at the scene a young girl hurried up the hill. A slightly built girl of perhaps twelve or thirteen, shabbily dressed, her honey-brown hair smooth and straight. As she passed Rachel she gave her a shy smile. What an enchanting little creature; old and outgrown clothes couldn't disguise her charm. It had nothing to do with being pretty, it was something more striking than that. What was there about her that put Rachel in mind of a fairy child, an elfin creature? She didn't slow her pace, but went on her way to wait near the head of the Man Engine Shaft.

Then Rachel heard something else. She stood very still and listened as the sound grew louder. Men's voices, deep and musical. She recognised the tune of a hymn (living next door to the chapel she was familiar with it), louder and louder as they neared the surface.

'Still let me prove thy perfect will,
My acts of faith and love repeat;
Till death thy endless mercies seal,
And make the sacrifice complete.'

Even the words were clear now. Deep, full, rich, male voices rejoicing in the chill winter afternoon that waited for them as they came from their hole in the ground. Through a haze of tears she saw them. Not tears of sadness, nor yet pity; it was some emotion she hardly understood. Each man's face was thrown into eerie relief by the shadow cast by the light of the stump of candle he wore attached by clay to the front of his hard hat. Dirty, wet from the water that dripped constantly from the rock, grimed from the dust that filled the still air down there. And yet they sang. This was the morning core. She knew what it meant now. At six o'clock, while she'd been warm and comfortable in her feather bed, they would have been a hundred or more fathoms under the ground. From six until two they'd worked and then had come the long climb back. It was nearly three now when the Man Engine brought them up the final shaft. And still they could sing.

'It makes one feel very humble.' She hadn't realised anyone was near her but the voice didn't startle her, it was part of the mood of the strange scene. She nodded and turning to see who had spoken recognised the tall figure of the mine doctor. Dulcie had told her that's who he was when they'd seen him in Fore Street. But he hadn't come to stand and watch. Already he had gone on towards the buildings. Now the men had reached grass. The moment was over.

She saw 'the elf' move towards one of the men. Rachel watched the way he put his hand on her shoulder as she walked with them to the drying-room where, once again, she waited, this time while he changed his clothes. It must be her father. The waiting child was part of the scene, only *she* was an outsider.

So often it's the small things that leave a lasting memory — a snatch of music, a whiff or scent, the feel of a door handle, the squeak of a gate, the wild swoop of a bat. But Rachel knew even now that these moments had been important, as if she'd been guided to the mine for a reason on this foggy afternoon. 'Humble' the doctor had said. Had it been humility that moved her so?

Chapter Two

Rachel's understanding of the local tongue must have been a gradual thing, building from that first morning when the egg was 'scat'. In the early days she was consciously groping in the dark but before long she ceased to think about it, part understanding and part guessing. It was a week or so before Christmas when she realised what a long way she'd come; and again it was when she was in Mr. Traherne's shop. Patsy had been anxious to stay at home, her world was full of secrets shared only with Dulcie until 25th December, secrets that Rachel pretended not to notice. At any other time a visit to Mr. Traherne couldn't have been managed without her, he was her firm friend.

'Zo where's t' li'l maid z'morning?'

'I slipped out without her. Mr. Traherne, have you any little things to fill a sock?'

'Zo 'tis Vathir Kirsmis business yo's cum 'bout. I cun vind 'ee one or two li'l bits, yu be sure on't. I kip a vu odds in t'drowar.'

It was then that it occurred to Rachel that not so many weeks ago even if she'd understood him she would have made her own mental translation. Now she waited expectantly for the one or two little bits to be brought from the drawer where he kept a few odds. Mr. Traherne wasn't going to fail Father Christmas. A small naked doll which he suggested could be 'trigged up easy nuff', a wooden rocking horse not more than three inches long, a uniformed lead drummer boy (not so long ago she would have puzzled to hear it called 'a vine saujer' but now, she nodded in agreement, it was a fine soldier indeed), a few marbles, a tin whistle and a gob-stopper to put in the toe. Enough to give Patsy's Christmas morning a touch of magic.

''Tis chillin we need 't aum ver Kirsmis, socks to vill jes like you dwain ver li'l Patsy. Enjoy it, Mrs. Treweek, time runs on zo quick.'

For so many reasons this Christmas had to be something special. They had no one but each other. Good or bad, it would be what they made it. Determined that it would be all that Patsy dreamed, Rachel and John built their day around her. When she was safely tucked in bed the two of them banked up the fire and sat at the hearthside.

'She enjoyed it all, didn't she?' John smiled, remembering Patsy's starry eyed excitement.

'It was the best Christmas we've ever had, John.'

'What! Doing your own cooking! And very well you did it too. Ah well,' he stretched out his feet to the warmth, 'all over for another year.' She could almost feel his contentment. She moved to sit on a footstool, her crossed arms resting on his knee, her head on her arms. The day had been full of harmony; she needed to hang on to it, as a physical thing she needed to know it wasn't finished with Patsy leaving them. Then he reached to take a sheaf of papers from the top of the low bookshelf by the fireplace.

'John! You're not working!'

'Umph? No? Did you want us to talk about something?'

'Nothing in particular. But this isn't any ordinary evening, this is Christmas. You can work every other — and usually do!'

'Poor Rachel,' he put the papers on his lap, 'I'm not much of a companion, am I?'

'Yes you are, of course you are.' She knelt now, forcing his legs apart so that she could come between his knees. 'But it's only half-past seven, people will still be dressing for the evening. Once you start working our day is all over.'

'Silly girl,' he chuckled affectionately at her earnest expression. 'I'll put it aside until tomorrow if that'll please you.'

Her glance fell on the papers. A report of the accounts at Treddinock mine.

'What have you to do with Treddinock? Except for putting the new engine in?'

27

'Actually I have put a little money in it. Ross recommended it. He's no fool when it comes to finance and he's had an interest in the mine here for years. It's he who lent me these accounts – not just this year's, these go right back. They were bringing rich ore out of it, they'd found a seam such as is an adventurer's dream. They were at the two hundred level when there was a landslip. It was about two years ago. Quite a disaster at the time. The level hasn't been worked since. Of course, it's flooded now. That's where my engine comes in. The seam is lost, but the mineral is there for the finding. There will be exploration, they'll find it. There was no indication that it was worked out. Copper, ten per cent mineral in the ore that was being raised.'

She sat back on her heels.

'Albert Ross ... you say he told you. But I thought you didn't take to Albert Ross.'

'He's no engineer, but he doesn't profess to be. I believe I misjudged him. I imagined old Mr. Harding had taken him into the company as a passenger simply because he'd married his daughter, a form of dowry. Be that as it may, he has his own talents – and finance is one of them.' Unexpectedly he laughed. 'His others seem to relate to his success with the ladies.'

'What is he like? To look at, I mean?'

'Much like anybody else.' John laughed. 'What funny things you do ask! I suppose if I think about it he's something of a dandy. I dare say you ladies would call him handsome, I don't know.' He bent forward and dropped a light kiss on her forehead. 'And now, Ma'am, just for ten minutes, please may I read my accounts?' It was worded as a question, but it was no question. What John meant was: 'I am going to read my accounts.'

'Imagine it! You've got a stake in the mine. What is it they call investors? Adventurers, isn't that it? My husband is an adventurer!'

'Not to any great extent. But I have faith in my engine, and when that level is forked out exploration will start again on the lode. Now is the right time to buy in. Once they start lifting copper it'll be too late, the share price will rocket.'

'But I thought you had all your resources in Harding's?'

For a moment he hesitated, undecided how much to tell. Then: 'Money put into Treddinock Mine will pay us back a hundredfold. There's a meeting at the count house early in January to discuss the latest figures, tell the venturers their profits and, in this case, warn them of the expenses ahead when it's possible to open beyond the two hundred level. Like sugar on a pill, they put on a dinner. I remember when I was a boy I used to hear about those count house dinners. In those days they'd get the business over with in the first hour then spend the rest of the day eating and drinking. It's not like that any more. The accounts for the last quarter will be presented, the estimates given for the next. I tell you, Rachel, any money I could invest in Wheal Dovey would more than repay me. There's a great wealth under that rocky ground. And –' again he hesitated – 'you may think me quixotic, foolhardy even, but it's a sign that I have faith in what the engine will do.' And there spoke the John she knew. All this talk of count house dinners, gambling his last penny on the chance of winning wealth – that was alien to his nature. But here he came to the crux of the whole thing: he would stake all he had on the engine that had been a creation of his own brain, built in his own workshops.

She leant forward and wound her arms around his neck.

'Dear John. Of course you're right. The mine is – is – it's like the pulse that gives Treddinock life.' She could see that such flowery language made him uncomfortable, so she went on, more practically: 'I'm glad you've taken a stake. It gives us the right to belong here.' Adding with a teasing twinkle in her ginger eyes: 'I'm not such a foreigner as you expected.'

'Good girl.' For a moment she believed he was going to say more, but this time he thought better of it and picked up his papers.

Perhaps the atmosphere of their 'homely' Christmas had relaxed him; perhaps his confidence in the wealth that would come to him from Wheal Dovey set his vision on the years ahead; or it could have had something to do with Rachel clutching at the right to belong to Treddinock. On the other hand it might have had nothing to do with any of these things, been simply that for once his needs had matched her own. As the early weeks of 1883 went by she became certain there was

29

to be another child and certain, too, that it had been conceived on Christmas night. A temporary move to Treddinock had prompted the ever careful John to resolve he must be doubly certain that this shouldn't happen. Yet when they realised that she was pregnant they both knew the time was right. This time it must be a boy. Fervently she prayed that she would have a son, somehow never doubting it. This child was a pointer to the future, a male heir to follow in John's steps, someone for him to teach the things he cared about. Even to herself she wouldn't acknowledge that no second daughter would ever find a place in the heart that belonged so firmly to Patsy. What was between her and her father was something very special.

The engine went into use at the end of January, a mild misty day in a mild misty winter. John decided that such an occasion merited relaxation of the rules and, driving them in the dog-cart, he took Rachel and Patsy to the head of the mine. Patsy was impressed — she understood him well enough to know that's what he wanted. She stood up in the cart, her head back as she peered upwards at the tall engine house. The beam — or 'bob' as the men called it — was rocking, its steady pace never varying.

'Looks like a big giant nodding his head,' she chuckled. 'Won't it get tired?' Her own head moved in unison, down, up, down.

'Never,' John told her. 'When you're tucked up in bed it'll still be nodding — and when you get up in the morning.'

Still her own head bobbed, up, down, up, down. Then, with a deep sigh, she squeezed onto the seat between John and Rachel. ''Straordinary,' she observed sagely. It was the latest addition to her vocabulary. In the last few days she'd found much in life extraordinary.

There was little wonder John had put the mine out of bounds for her. In the dogcart she was safe enough, but the area was full of pitfalls.

'Everyone seems so busy,' there was something akin to envy in Rachel's voice, 'they understand the whole picture. I wish I did.' She took in the wild scene, the machinery, the steady rise and fall of the stamps and the rocking of the smaller Cornish engine beam that drove them, the never-ceasing activity. 'Where are you pumping from?'

'It's a complex layout. This shaft here, Lugger's Shaft it's called, goes down to some two hundred fathoms. Across there where you see the tramway, that's the entrance to Pearson's Shaft.' Looking at it she remembered the voices of the men who'd came out of it into the autumn afternoon. 'Pearson is diagonal following the seam. Then horizontally from the side of the hill and intersecting them both are adits for drainage. Over the way to the right you can see the gear at the head of Marston Shaft, that's on the Kinsley Lode. There's a labyrinth of tunnels below ground, the adits cut from grass right through Pearson, Lugger's and Marston. The deepest point is at the bottom of Pearson where it's flooded. These rocks are riddled with natural springs. That's where the landslip occurred.'

'So there are three shafts?'

'Three that come right to grass and are used for lifting. But it's not as simple as that. Except for Pearson nothing goes straight down — and even that isn't really straight, it bends, slopes, widens into a gallery, then perhaps into a narrow passage down again. Every tunnel or shaft grows out of the natural circumstance. Follow a seam and work it, probably a narrow seam; but if not, if it's rich, then that's how a gallery is formed, a wide expanse, the roof supported by timbers such as you've never seen. Three shafts, you say. Actually there are more, for ventilation, from the top vertically downwards to circulate air.'

'Just imagine it, John. Right down there with no air except what can be brought in through chimneys in the ground; that's what they are, chimneys in the ground.' Rachel shivered.

'It's a living and the tributers always hope to strike a rich seam. Look at you, you're cold. I must get you home.'

Already, just as a spectator, she'd learnt more about the mine in this short while than she had about his engines in all their years. Looking back over her shoulder as the dogcart started for home, it was the people she watched. Some of them she recognised; people from Treddinock.

'Patsy needs new boots. I'm taking her to Helston today, Dulcie, we'll make the most of the blue sky.' For this morning

31

the incessant mist of the winter had cleared. They had woken
to a high, clear sky. To look from the kitchen window it might
have been the herald of spring.

'It's beautiful. But don't be misled by appearances, it's
treacherously cold. There's ice on the horse trough up the
road.'

'We'll put a rug over our legs. And we shall be home before
the sun goes down.'

Fine words, spoken with confidence.

They left home full of excitement. Until they'd come to
Treddinock a shopping expedition had meant no more than
ten minutes' drive. This was their first day out together; today
their relationship was taking a big step. Patsy was aware of it,
for it carried a wonderfully heavy responsibility; she and her
mother were on an outing, like two grown-up ladies. She sat
very straight, tried to wear a sober expression as befitted an
adult, or so she believed; somehow though her face kept
forgetting and smiling! Rachel was aware of the importance
of the day too.'My daughter and I ...' This was what the
future would be like!

Helston came up to their expectations. Patsy was fitted with
a pair of red boots, soft leather hugging her calves, each one
fastened up the side with no less than twenty buttons. Sitting
on the chair with her legs stuck straight out in front of her she
watched as, with the speed gained from years of experience,
the elderly shopkeeper hooked each button through its hole.
Catching Rachel's eye all she could do was nod her head,
words failing her. By now she'd lost all hope of that serious
grown-up countenance. Her mouth was set in a half-opened
beam showing two rows of pearly milk teeth.

'Let's pack her old ones, then she can keep them on,' she
heard her mother say as the last button was pulled through.
Her joy was almost beyond bearing.

Outside in the street surely everyone must have noticed. As
far as she was concerned she couldn't take her eyes off her
scarlet-clad legs. It was dreadfully difficult to hold herself in
check and remember her grown-up manners, but she made an
effort – such fine footwear demanded that she should. Then
back in the dogcart, they drove on up Wendron Street to the
coaching inn where they had their lunch. Still the sky was

clear, but the wind had freshened. It was lovely to sit by the log fire and be plied with warm food.

By the time they came out the wind was no longer merely fresh, it was bitingly cold, seeming to cut their faces. It blew from the north east and the clouds were banking overhead. There was a strange light, a hint of yellow in the gathering gloom. Wrapping the rug well round Patsy and covering her own legs, Rachel took up the reins and started for home.

A return journey never seems as long; she was pleased with the way they were covering the miles. By now it was a race against the weather. There was something odd about the way the cart was running, it wasn't smooth, Patsy's side didn't seem to pull with hers.

'Peep over the edge, Patsy. Have we got something caught in the wheel?'

Patsy peeped. 'No, only the wheel. 'Spect it's all right, just wobbly.'

'Wobbly?'

'Bit funny. Come and look.'

But of course by the time they'd stopped and Rachel walked round to look there was nothing to see. To her it appeared a perfectly normal wheel. Perhaps they'd imagined the trouble. Certainly no good could come of standing here looking at it. The only thing to do was to get home.

'Walk on.' The pony obliged.

'Wobbly, still wobbly, Mama.' Patsy made progress reports her responsibility and repeated them at frequent intervals. But in between times she gave her attention to her beautiful boots and stuck her feet out from the rug so that she didn't lose sight of them. So passed another two or three miles.

Then two things happened.

'Look, Mama, snowflakes! Can you see them? Do you think we'll have real proper snow?'

'Not before we get home, I hope.'

That was the first. The second hardly needed Patsy's progress report, Rachel was pulling in the reins even before she was told: 'It's dreadfully wobbly, bending over and it's ...' Patsy was lost for the right words and anyway it was too late for it to matter. Her mother had stopped the cart and was climbing out.

33

The wheel was at an angle. A few more revolutions and it would have been off completely.

'Sit very still and keep wrapped up in the rug. It's quite safe as long as you don't wriggle about.'

'But how are we going to get home if we sit still? Will we walk?'

'Perhaps there's a house somewhere. If I could borrow a hammer or something I might get the wheel on straight.'

'Could we ride on Dancer? Come back tomorrow with a hammer?'

Whatever they did, they certainly must do something and do it soon. Snow wasn't so much falling as billowing in the wind, a foretaste of what they could expect. Rachel unlaced her boot and took it off, balancing on one foot as she tried to hammer the wheel back into line on the axle with her heel. Patsy leant over the edge, watching. And all the while the wind gathered strength.

'You seem to have trouble. Can I help you?' How the trap had approached without either of them hearing she didn't know, the sound must have been lost in the howling wind — in that or her hammering.

Still on one foot, her boot in her hand, Rachel turned in relief. 'Why! You're the doctor from the mine. I've seen you in Treddinock.'

'That's right. Giles Derwent. Your boot will do more good protecting your foot than knocking that wheel. I'll drive you home with me, then come back with my man and we'll look at it for you. It's no distance.'

'If I could just make it safe enough to drive slowly home . . .' She gave it another smart rap.

'You'll do no good while the weight is on the axle. Hold my shoulder while you put that boot where it ought to be.' It was evident Dr. Giles Derwent was used to having his orders obeyed.

She wriggled her foot back into her tall boot, managing without the help of his shoulder. He held his arms up to Patsy who all this time had been holding the still pose of a statue, more frightened than she would admit.

'Now then, young lady, just stand up and I'll lift you out.'

Two complete strangers at the head of Pearson Shaft on a

misty November afternoon, and for that one moment they had clearly read each other's hearts. She told herself that her sense of disappointment had nothing to do with the fact that he apparently didn't recognise her, probably didn't even remember the incident at all. And where now was his humility? His manner was arrogant, he took their obedience for granted. She had no choice but to do as he said. The snow was already settling on their clothes, blowing like fine powder along the dry surface of the road.

They left Dancer, her reins hanging in front of her. Even if she tried she'd not get far with the wheel like that. Another hour and it would be dark. Already at Treddinock Dulcie would be watching for them.

Rachel had believed the area devoid of houses; even when she'd suggested trying to find somewhere to borrow a hammer she'd had no faith in the idea. Yet hardly more than half a mile along the road from where they had been picked up they turned into a tree-lined lane and not far away she could see houses. In the summer the leafy trees would have hidden them; even at this time of year they were shielded by evergreens. Not just one house, but three or four, perhaps more. At the gate of the third Dr. Derwent turned into the drive. Perleigh House was very different from the granite and slate buildings of Treddinock. It was red brick, with grey brick ornamentation, tall sash windows and a twin gabled roof. It couldn't have been more than a few years old. A model of modern design, Perleigh, and its neighbours too. Giles opened the front door and ushered them into the hallway; more than a passage, less than a room, but large enough to accommodate the hatstand and a table.

'Are you there?' he called. 'I've brought visitors.'

A second or two of silence then a rush of footsteps, first on the linoleum from the second floor to the first, then muffled by carpet as they came on down. Three children and behind them a woman.

'Miss Huntley, this is Mrs. Treweek. Mrs. Treweek and . . . ?'

'Patsy,' Rachel supplied.

'Ah. And Patsy. I'm leaving them for you to look after for a while. I suggest you give them some tea while I taken Perrin with me to see what we can do to their dogcart.'

Miss Huntley smiled prettily at the doctor. Rachel had the impression that whatever look she cast in his direction she would be sure it was cast prettily. But that was only a passing thought. Mostly she was surprised that he knew who she was, curious whether he remembered the afternoon at Wheal Dovey.

'The children are having tea up in the nursery,' Miss Huntley was saying.

'Excellent. I expect Patsy would prefer that. I'll leave you to look after Mrs. Treweek.'

'It's very good of you,' Rachel started. But he didn't wait for her thanks. Saying something about daylight soon going he went in search of Perrin and the tools.

She'd seen him about in Treddinock, for one brief moment that afternoon at the mine she'd felt she knew him. But until now she'd never imagined him against a background of home, children, this fair-haired young woman and, presumably, somewhere a wife. She'd known him to be a man somewhere in his forties, tall and made taller by the silk hat he invariably wore, a boney face – hawklike, she'd privately thought, although now that she looked more closely, she wasn't sure why. Today she added to her first impression. His eyes were brown, his hands well kept, his hair dark and smooth, brushed back from a widow's peak. Not a handsome face, it was the alertness in his expression that was arresting.

'Set another place at the table and look after your guest,' Miss Huntley told the children, then opened the drawing-room door to usher Rachel in. Just for a second Patsy looked to her mother for support, then she gathered up her courage and followed the others up the stairs. It was the sight of her red boots that gave her the confidence she lacked; she held up her skirt to expose a few more inches of their scarlet beauty.

Miss Huntley pulled the bell cord and ordered tea to be brought to the drawing-room. She seemed very much at home, she must be a family guest.

'What happened to your dogcart? Where is it?'

Briefly the story was told. Then as Rosalind Huntley poured the tea, Rachel asked: 'Do the children belong to Dr. Derwent?'

'Yes. I care for them. Their mother died more than three

years ago. We were dear friends, Anna and I. There's Oliver, he's ten, Trudie is nine and Peter just six.'

'And you've been here ever since she died?'

'Oh, before that. It's been my home for ages. Anna was a sort of heroine to me since I was small. We lived near each other, our parents were friends. She was a few years older than me and so beautiful. I would gladly have been her slave. When she and Giles married I was her Maid of Honour. I often used to stay here, help with the children when they were babies. Then, after Peter was born, she was so poorly; she never seemed very well. You'd think a doctor would be able to cure his own, wouldn't you? In the beginning of the winter of '79 she had pneumonia, there was no fight in her. I was with her right to the end and, of course, I stayed on. Giles needed someone to look after the children, someone who really loved them. It's almost as if they are my own. But there, that's enough about us. Tell me about you. You must be new to the district, for I've never seen you.'

'My husband took a partnership in Harding's the engine builders and he wanted to be on hand there for a while. So Patsy and I came too and we've a cottage in Treddinock. When John feels the time has come, we'll go back to Warwickshire.'

'You'll be glad to go home I should think! Treddinock's a dreary place, isn't it?'

'No.' Rachel spoke thoughtfully, looking at the truth that until now she'd not put into words. 'We've only been here since September. John said a year or perhaps more, so I'd not thought yet about going home. But I shan't be glad. I believe the people have accepted me. John is a Cornishman — anyway he gives work to some of them and understands the industries down here — but I'm just an outsider, a foreigner. I bring nothing. They could so easily have made me feel like an interloper but they haven't and I'm grateful.'

Rosalind was looking past her and she realised she could feel a draught. Someone had opened the door from the cold hallway.

'It's snowing hard now.' She turned at the sound of Giles Derwent's voice. 'I shall drive you home. At least we can raise the hood and keep some of it off you. Your pony and cart will be safe in my stable for the night.'

It wasn't until they were almost back in Treddinock that he said: 'Never believe you bring them nothing in this village. You bring them colour and interest, you and your delightful daughter; you let them see a graciousness that their own lives lack, and yet you give them friendship.'

'How can you say that? You didn't even know us until a few hours ago.'

'Oh yes, but I did. You may not remember me, but I saw you at Wheal Dovey. More than that, though. I visit houses in Treddinock, I talk with the people.'

She didn't answer him directly, only after a silence and apropos of nothing: 'Life plays strange tricks. Everything seemed set for ever for us in our old home — I remember thinking something like that on the night John told me he'd gone into the business here. I would never have guessed that we should be here — or that it would seem so right. You can never be sure of what the next hand you get dealt will bring.'

As soon as she'd spoken she wished her words back. What a tactless thing to say to a man who'd lost his beautiful Anna.

He must have sensed her discomfort.

'Very often it's not what we would choose. But who are we to think we know best?'

'You believe there's a predestined pattern?'

He turned to look at her, his boney features transformed in a smile. 'I believe, Mrs. Treweek, we are getting out of our depth with only a hundred yards to your front gate.' Then, turning to look down at Patsy: 'And shall I tell you something too, young Patsy?'

'Yes please.'

'I do believe that's the prettiest pair of boots I've seen all the winter.'

She nodded her head vigorously, holding up the parcel she'd been nursing. 'They're new. These are my old ones in the parcel.' To him it might have just been childish chatter, but not to Rachel. All the way home Patsy had sat with her feet stuck out before her, her boots had been at the forefront of her mind. So when they were remarked on, her answer summed up what filled her innocent world.

And by then even the last hundred yards had been covered. They were home.

38

'I'll make sure the cart is back with you tomorrow. Either I'll drive over in it and ask Rosalind and the children to come in and meet me or Perrin will bring it.'

'You've been so kind. If you hadn't come along —'

'If I hadn't come along, someone else would have. So I'm glad to have been first on the scene. One of these days we'll continue our talk. I hope one day soon.'

He declined her invitation that he should come in to the cottage, and having helped them down he drove off into the snowy evening. Dulcie had the front door open as they came up the short front path; she must have been watching for them. In her red boots Patsy felt quite beautiful! And following behind her Rachel not so very different.

It snowed all that night, while the wind howled. When the men went past on the way to Wheal Dovey to start the morning core their heavy tread was muffled, and by the time daylight came their footprints lost in a fresh covering. So it continued all that day. When the snow clouds finally moved away there was no hint of a thaw. The wind dropped — and with it, the temperature. Water froze in the pump outside the back door; the thin branches of the mulberry trees hung low, weighted down with frozen snow, like a white lace curtain outside the sitting-room window. But indoors the cottage was a haven of comfort. Fires burnt in every grate.

'Toby tells me the boys have been sliding on Whems Pool,' Dulcie told them.

'Where's Whems Pool?'

'You know it. It's where Patsy sails her boat.'

'Can we go and see it, Mama? Today, can we go? Please can we?'

For two days they'd been indoors watching the swirling snow. Rachel was as keen as Patsy to get out. By early afternoon they were on their way to the copse.

'Hope there's boys there sliding like Dulcie said,' Patsy chattered as she alternately skipped, hopped, jumped or strode out manfully. The ground was crisp, each step leaving a deep imprint. Rays of sunshine slanted through the leafless branches, sun that seemed to give no warmth. Rachel stood still.

'Come on, Mama, why are you standing?'

'Just looking at it, Patsy.'

'Oh.' The idea of just looking was new. Patsy stopped and looked too. She gazed up through the snowy branches to the clear sky. She stood quite still, she listened to the silence.

'It's like magic . . .' she whispered.

Rachel nodded. It was more than magic. The beauty of the silent wood was only a part of it. It was Patsy's growing understanding, her awareness.

The moment was shattered by the sound of voices, children shouting.

'There's boys.' Patsy's scarlet shod feet were firmly back on the ground. 'Come on, let's hurry.' And when they reached the lake and she saw them, big boys — and girls too — skimming across the icy surface, of course she wanted to try it for herself. A month or two ago Rachel would have taken her. It was seven weeks since Christmas and, even though she felt well and had suffered none of the ailments associated with early pregnancy, she had no doubts. Dearly she would like to have tried her own skill, but she wasn't prepared for the consequences of a fall.

'I'll take her on if you like, Mrs. Treweek. The ice is quite safe.' It was the elfin girl Rachel had seen that afternoon at the mine.

'You know us?'

'We've seen you sometimes. Toby told me who you were. I live next door to him.'

'And you'll take care of Patsy? She's never been on ice before.'

'Whems Pond doesn't usually freeze like this, it's the first time for most of us.' (Actually, although Rachel no longer noticed, the child called it 'vreeze' and said it was the 'vurst' time 'vor' most of them.)

And how Patsy loved it! She had no fear, she screeched as loudly as any and skidded as far too, although her new friend didn't let go of her hand.

All the way home her chatter was non-stop. It was Dulcie who told them about the elfin child with her honey-brown hair and dark eyes, her clearly marked straight dark eyebrows and pointed chin. A face not easy to forget, gentle yet lively.

40

'Richard always called her Toby's sweetheart,' she laughed. 'They've always been the same, since they were tiny. Sally Pendleton's her name. One of these days they'll grow up and one of them will get hurt, when they discover there's a big sea to swim in and plenty of other fish in it.'

And at the pond Rachel watched them and understood what Richard had meant. There was a oneness in the two youngsters, she saw it clearly, yet they probably took it so for granted they hardly noticed.

At the time Rachel's interest in Sally was that she could be trusted to take care of Patsy. And it seemed she could. The next day was Saturday; again they went to Whems Pond. Still the sky was clear, the air crisp and cold.

On Sunday they woke up to a change. Still the sun shone but the crystal brightness had gone, a gentle breeze blew in from the west. Except for the carpet of white it might have been spring.

'We could show you the ice, Papa. Will we take you?' Patsy asked hopefully as Rachel tied her bonnet and re-buttoned her coat that she had managed to fasten with the buttons in the wrong holes. Sunday belonged to the family; either John drove them out in the dogcart or they walked together.

'It'll be thawing today,' he told her. The snow that still clung to the branches was wet, there was the sound of steady dripping. 'But we'll walk that way if that's where you'd like to go.'

Strange that on a day when there was the first hint of warmth in those rays of sunshine the magic had gone in the wood. The paths had been well trodden over the last few days. Where the snow was hard-packed it was wet, slippery.

'Don't think the boys are there. Nor my friend Sally. I can't hear them.' Patsy was disappointed. She too could sense that the glory of those few days had gone.

'It's Sunday. They won't be out playing on the Sabbath,' John told her.

But they were wrong. Sally was there, and half a dozen or so more, one of them the slightly built dark youth Rachel recognised to be Toby. They'd come hoping to slide but the thaw was too rapid. Now they were split into two teams, each busily scooping up handfuls of snow and building an arsenal of missiles. Any moment battle would begin. Patsy saw them and ran ahead.

'Patsy!' John called, 'Keep away from those snowballs.' With snow as wet as this they could be dangerous.

'Going to,' she answered, still running. Sally was the first to realise what she meant to do.

'No, Patsy, don't go on there. You can't slide on that ice.'

Patsy laughed. How silly Sally was. Of course she could slide. The ice was shining, lovely and slippery. Fancy wanting to make snowballs when the lake was just waiting to be slid on!

John and Rachel realised too. It wasn't to the children that Patsy was running but to the edge of the lake, and when she reached it she didn't hesitate.

Oh, the joy of it! No one to hold her hand, the soles of her new boots skimming so fast over the ice that was wet. She threw back her head, stretched out her arms. 'Whoosh!' Like steam being let out of a boiler, she must screech or burst with triumph.

'Patsy! Come back! Come back I say!' Ahead of Rachel John didn't see her slip. Perhaps it was a protruding tree root under the melting snow that caught her foot, or perhaps it was simply that she slipped on wet ice. To fall takes only a second, but it would haunt her for the rest of her life. She saw the water lapping over Patsy's feet, joy wiped away by sudden terror. 'Mama!' she heard ... Her own foothold was lost, the tree trunk rushing at her. Mercifully she didn't see any more, didn't hear the last frenzied scream as the icy water filled those beautiful boots and pulled Patsy down.

The tree trunk hit her temple. She was mercifully spared the next few minutes, perhaps not even that. Time had no meaning for any of them.

'No, sir, don't. You're too heavy. I'll go. I'll try.' It was Toby who tried to push in front of John, but John gave no sign of hearing him. Some of the bigger boys were tearing at the frozen branches thinking they might make a platform, or at least something to grasp. No one knew what should be done; they all had to do something.

Lying full length on the ice John moved towards where the rippling water spoke of movement under the surface. His face was contorted. 'No ... no ... dear God, no ... don't ... no ...' His mind was stripped of everything except that he must reach her quickly. She was there, only a few yards from him, she must know he was coming. His own anguished cries, the children at the lakeside, Rachel − for him none of them existed. Toby was on the ice now, trying to move in from the other side, the boys sliding branches out to him in a vain attempt to give support.

Rachel opened her eyes, lifted her head − and remembered. A trickle of warm blood ran down the side of her face as she struggled to her knees and then to her feet. The scene had changed in the minutes she'd lost, changed and moved on, and yet she'd seen it all as Patsy had cried out to her. That John was on the lake was just part of the same horror. Of course he was. He couldn't leave Patsy.

She felt sick. 'Sick with fright' − wasn't that what people said? She stood straight, breathed deeply as if to find her own control was to help him. He would never fail Patsy. Oh, her face! 'Mama!' 'Please ... please ... let John find her, let John reach her ... please ... please ...'

Chapter Three

The gap in the ice was widening. Rachel watched him flounder, every natural instinct making him fight for a hold on it. There was no other way for him, he must do what he did, how else could he reach her and bring her back? In her mind Rachel saw beneath the grey water; but not for a second did she doubt him ... she couldn't. To doubt him would be to face the alternative. She was vaguely aware that some of the older children had run for help. She heard them calling to each other, one was to find someone to bring a trap, they would need blankets, the doctor ... here her mind baulked. To be fetching the doctor meant they expected someone to be hurt. But John would bring her out, of course he would ... The boys were making a platform of branches they'd torn from the trees, something for him to hang to.

Seconds ticked by. He was coming to the surface, she saw a movement, a hand; ripples on the water as he went down again. He was raising her! Yes, he had her! Clearly Rachel saw Patsy's head above the water, John's arms holding her. Then, down again ... ripples spreading out until they touched the ice ... the boys pushed a long branch right across the gap, a hand-hold for when he came up again. They all watched ... watched ... the ripples were still ...

The sun was going down in a glow of amber glory; after a day that had promised that spring was waiting in the wings, the night was going to be cold again. Rachel wasn't aware of it, she was numb but her chill had nothing to do with the fast-falling temperature.

'Fetch Dulcie,' Toby had told Sally as soon as the melting ice had sunk under Patsy's red boots and without waiting to see more she had done as he said, running all the way to the village.

One look at her was enough to tell Dulcie there was trouble.

'Toby says please come,' Sally gasped breathlessly, and before her words were out Dulcie was pulling her cloak from its peg. Only as they ran back side by side was the story thrown at her in breathless gasps.

'She didn't understand.' Sally's elfin face was pink from exertion but she didn't let her pace slacken. 'Ice looks safe — they'll get her out, won't they? They'll save her — won't they?'

A pony and trap was coming towards them. At any other time Sally might have been surprised at the familiarity of the driver's greeting and of Dulcie's response. But this afternoon the encounter simply meant that they could get back to Whems Pond more quickly.

'Dulcie! You're not going somewhere?' he sounded surprised.

'It's Patsy! Patsy Treweek. She's gone through the ice on Whems Pond.'

'Get up, both of you.' And almost before they'd squeezed on to the seat with him the driver had put the pony into a brisk trot back the way he had come.

'Are her parents with her?'

'Yes, both of them. Albert, she'll be so frightened. I didn't stop to think, I should have brought a blanket to wrap her in.'

It was Sally who answered that they'd soon wrap her in their coats.

'Yes, of course. And with the trap we'll soon get her home.' Even Dulcie didn't seem able to face any other possibility.

Only Albert Ross, taking her hand in his, said: 'Pray God you're right. If the ice is thin enough to give way under a small child, I don't see . . .' He didn't finish his sentence. He didn't need to.

But none of them were prepared for what they found. When Sally had left the pond John had been on the bank shouting to Sally to come back. They needed no blankets. There was no one to wrap in their discarded coats. Rachel stood as if she were rooted to the churned up, slushy snow where such a short time ago the children had been making their missiles for a fight. She'd seemed not to notice as most of them had run off, frightened by what they'd seen, wanting to fetch parents as if grown-ups could do what they couldn't. Minutes had gone by, how long she didn't know. Then Dulcie was with her, Dulcie and a man.

Not the time for introductions but when he told her: 'I'm Albert Ross,' for a second she took her attention from the patch of dark, still water and looked at him. She was back by the fireside, kneeling in front of John. The little room was full of the scent of the Christmas spruce. 'What's he like?' she'd wanted to know. Now, looking at him, she remembered John's laughing: 'What funny things you do ask! Something of a dandy. I dare say you ladies would call him handsome.' She recalled the warmth of the fireside, the smoky smell of his tobacco. Standing here alone she had been numbed, so shocked that nothing had held reality. But the vividness of memory brought her face to face with what was happening.

'No – ' Involuntarily she flinched. 'They'll get them out. They've broken the ice away – see – over there. They'll get them out.'

'Them?' Dulcie asked.

'Them? You mean John too?' The truth became clear to Albert.

'He had to go to Patsy, of course he did. And he's found her. I saw them. He's got her, he's holding her.'

Toby Caldecott had come to join them. 'Let them take you home now, Mrs. Treweek,' he said.

'Come.' Dulcie nodded and put an arm around her.

Rachel looked from one to the other. She seemed lost, bemused. 'We only came for a walk.'

'Come home.' Albert took her arm. 'The men will do what they can here. John wouldn't want you to be here.'

There were other voices too. Men as they hit the ice trying to clear it from the pond. 'Zuns not been on't over thi' zide.' 'Get a boat on't 'morrow.' 'Ah, if i' doan't vreeze over agin a'vore morning.'

'How long ago did it happen?' Albert asked Toby. 'Mr. Treweek, I mean.'

'Almost the minute Sally set off. Must be more than half an hour ago.'

'Come home,' Dulcie pleaded.

'Nawt we gan do till morning, Mr. Ross. Be dark a'vore we cun vetch a boat,' someone was saying.

Rachel heard the men making arrangements. A party would come with a boat and poles. But not tonight. Already the long shadows of the trees had fallen across the pond, behind them the wood was gloomy in the fading light.

'Just a few minutes more — let me stay. I can find my way back to the lane. You go.'

Albert didn't argue and neither did Dulcie. Everyone was leaving the pond and they did the same. But they waited in the shelter of the trees where they could still see Rachel. Neither of them voiced their fear. Now except for Rachel there was no one by the pond; and except for them there was no one in the wood.

Dulcie's whisper was barely audible and yet it rasped. 'That God my father preaches about — did He do this to them? Little Patsy —'

Albert took her in his arms, his hand cradling her head as he pressed it to his shouder.

'Why, Albert, why? They were happy. Is that it? Is that why? Was that their sin? He'd like that, Father would. He'd say it was her punishment, she'd loved them more than she had God, so now she has nothing.' She clung to him like a drowning man to a raft — a drowning man — a drowning child. He felt her tears on his neck. 'She was just a baby — she hadn't had a life.'

Wet snow muffled the sound of footsteps; it wasn't until he was almost on them that they saw someone coming.

'Where's Patsy? Have they got her out?' Giles Derwent wasted no time. Even though the farmer's son had ridden for him and he'd come straight away, he lived some way from the village. Already too much time had been lost. As he asked the question he hoped to hear that someone had taken her home.

'Neither of them, Giles. Her father tried to save her and I'm afraid he's gone too,' Albert told him. 'There's nothing more they can do now, the light is almost gone. There was nothing they could do right from the start.'

'Poor little love,' Dulcie wept. 'She must have been so excited to bring him to the pond. She told me yesterday:

"Tomorrow I'm going to show Papa how I slide." Poor little love.'

'Take her home, Albert. Leave Mrs. Treweek with me.'

All this time Rachel hadn't moved. To turn her back on that dark water was to accept. When she became aware that someone was approaching she looked round; then quickly back again as if in that second of taking her attention from the pond she might have missed a movement. That it was Giles who came to stand by her side didn't surprise her; but then surprise required reason. She started to speak, blurting out words in short, jerky sentences.

'He's found her. I saw them. He's holding her. He won't leave go of her. Lifted her right up. Her head was out of the water. She's lost her bonnet. Her hair's got green weeds in it. Lost her bonnet.' She heard her voice, shrill, getting louder; she knew it was but couldn't control it. 'He's holding her. When they slipped back her hair floated on the water as they went down. Her face went under the water. I watched her face go under the water. Her hair stood up. I could still see her hair.'

She turned to look at Giles, her gingery eyes wide with pain and yet there were no tears. '"Will we take you to the pond?" That's what she said to him. "Will we?" She's got her red boots on. "Will we ..." Always she said that. She'll be saying it now. "Will we have to stay here? Will we?"'

Rachel started to sob — hard, tearless crying. 'It's not fair. She's not had a chance. Every day she learnt something new. She can't be gone. I don't believe it, I don't believe it. She hadn't had long enough to know about living.'

'What can I say to you?' Giles knew so well that the path she had to walk must be walked alone, there was no side tracking it. No one could help her. 'Come.' He put his arm around her shoulder.

'But supposing —?' How she trembled, a combination of shock and cold.

'No.' He shook his head. 'If you can find comfort in anything it must be that they're together.' But he didn't hurry her. They'd leave the pond when she gave the signal, not before.

For a while she stood silent. He wondered whether she'd

48

understood, or even heard, what he'd said. When she did speak he knew that she had. 'They needed to be together.'

'How did you hurt your head?' For the blood had dried on the side of her face and already a lump was swelling on her temple.

'I slipped. She was on the pond."Swoosh!" That's what she shouted as she slid. "Swoosh!" John called to her to come back. We chased after her. That's when I fell. I don't know how. There was a tree. She screamed. The water was lapping round her feet, over her red boots. "Mama" − oh, her face − so frightened. And I fell, I couldn't get there. She called me and I didn't come −' She pulled away from Giles, crying now, blinded by tears, turning first one way towards the wood, then the other back to the pond. She seemed lost, running away from herself.

'She's not frightened any more. The pain is yours, not theirs. It's over.'

'Yes, it's over. It's all finished."I can count to twenty-seven," she told us this morning. Twenty-seven! She never got to twenty-eight ...'

The fight was gone from her. She let herself be led through the twilight of the copse; she didn't question when he helped her into his trap. Her storm of tears had left her drained. As they drove towards the village she sat with her head bowed, her eyes closed. She might have been asleep.

Albert was still at the cottage with Dulcie, but it was Giles who took control. When he asked Rachel what relatives she had she mumbled something about John's father being in London and his brother in Winchester. She said she had a sister. Then, as if her concentration wouldn't hold any longer: 'There's a book of addresses in the bureau. Ask Dulcie.'

He did. With Dulcie he went through the book, making notes of names and addresses. 'She may want to write letters herself, but whether she does or not, I'll send to each of these. And I'll see to all the arrangements that have to be made.'

Then, returning to Rachel, he opened his doctor's bag. 'You're to take this small draught I shall mix for you, then Dulcie will see you get straight to bed.'

He felt her staring at him. It was as if she was seeing him for the first time, he was some sort of specimen she'd not noticed before. 'You're a very bossy man,' she observed. It wasn't said offensively, it was as if she was telling him something she felt it only right he should know. 'I didn't expect you would be. But I noticed it the other day when we – when we –' he was forgotten, bossy or no.

'Here,' he clicked his bag shut and passed her the promised draught, 'it'll help you sleep.' Tomorrow would be soon enough for her to set out on that lonely path that lay ahead of her. 'Dulcie, I want you to go upstairs with Mrs. Treweek, help her into bed. I shall be here first thing in the morning.' Then as another thought struck him: 'She's not to be alone. You don't live here, do you?' Dulcie shook her head, about to say that nothing would make her leave Rachel tonight, but he didn't give her a chance to speak. 'Then make arrangements to do so, at least for the present.'

Rachel 'knocked back' the mixture he'd given her, involuntarily pulling a face. 'There's no need for Dulcie to stay. I'm quite all right.'

But he ignored her.

'Of course I shall stay,' Dulcie answered them both, 'I wouldn't dream of going home. Mr. Ross has already gone to tell Toby.'

Rachel was standing up now, making a gallant attempt to clutch at some sort of dignity, not for dignity's sake but to help her find her courage. Soon the door would be bolted for the night – Patsy and John the other side of it – gone from the house – gone – this very minute they were beneath the cold, still water – water in their eyes – water in their ears – water – She stood as tall and straight as she could.

Giles took her hand. 'Go to bed, my dear. Try not to think, try not to question. I'll be here first thing in the morning.'

Dulcie helped Rachel undress and saw her into bed. 'Would you like me to sit in here with you?'

Rachel's eyes were closed. She whispered that she wanted just to sleep, quite sure that she would lie awake all through the night. How could she sleep? Would their eyes be open? Water in their eyes . . . Dulcie took the candle and crept from the room.

It must have been the potion that Giles had given her for within seconds Rachel was drifting towards oblivion. What made her slip her hand under John's pillow? Her fingers touched his nightshirt. She rolled over and buried her face where his should have been. All these hours, even from the first moment, it had been Patsy who had torn at her heart. Now she wept for John. She wept that he could have been taken from her and her anguish for Patsy had overshadowed everything. She moved his pillow aside and laid her face against his nightshirt, folded so precisely, just as he left it each morning.

The sleeping draught was winning. In the morning she woke with a crick in her neck as well as an ache in her heart.

The family came. Hewlett Treweek was first to arrive. Rachel had never known her mother-in-law but had always supposed John must have taken after her, for he certainly bore no resemblance to his father. A slightly built man, small hands, small feet, narrow shoulders. There was about him a touch of the innocence of childhood. Although now she did see for the first time that John had inherited one thing from him, that dimple in his left cheek.

'They'll all be here — and they'll all think they know best what's good for you, m'dear,' he said almost in the same breath as his first expressions of grief. 'There's only one person to listen to — and that's yourself. Vincent and Clarry will want to sweep you off to Winchester, you see if they don't. And they'll mean well. Then there's your Muriel, she'll say you'd be better off to go back to where your roots were. It's your life, just remember that. In a pickle at the moment, but time — time and will-power — will see you in the clear again. Don't let them live it for you. John gave you a good home up in Warwick, my advice would be that you go back to it. But there I go, I'm as bad as the rest of them will be. Pity you ever came down to this place, pity John ever did either. None of this would have happened.'

'I've not thought about the future yet.'

'No, my dear,' his cherubic face puckered in concern, 'I don't expect you have, I don't expect you even want to. But take it a day at a time. The days add up, you know. If things don't hold any interest for you, never admit to it, put on a show, eh? And somewhere along the line y'know, without you being sure when, tomorrow'll find a meaning again. Don't mean to preach at you, dear me no, not what I came for at all.'

It was Tuesday night. Hewlett had come within the hour of Giles' letter reaching him. For the two days since the accident Rachel had felt she was watching life through the wrong end of a telescope; unconsciously she clung to the feeling. Dulcie had been with her; Giles had come two or three times both days; Albert Ross had been to the cottage too, and Toby; but none of them had aroused any answering emotion in Rachel. She'd seen Mr. Traherne come through the gate, but she'd stayed in the sitting-room, left Dulcie to talk to him as he'd unashamedly wiped away a tear for the li'l maid who'd been his friend. Now John's father touched a chord in Rachel, perhaps because he *was* John's father, Patsy's grandfather.

'Go to Winchester? Or Shrewsbury? Why, that's nonsense, why should I do that? And you're not preaching. I know what you say is right, I know I must make sure it's right.'

'Good girl.'

'A man has his work but what is there for me? It's just so empty. You say be interested — so empty . . .' For a moment she must have turned the telescope, the enormity of the emptiness was almost beyond bearing.

'Dear, oh dear, yes. You've friends of course in Warwick. It won't take you long to pack up here. That little person who helps you — very personable I thought. Umph, indeed she is.' He rubbed the nails of one hand against the palm of the other, examining them as though he'd never seen them before. 'How did you come by her, I wonder? Seemed out of place working in the kitchen. Umph. Personable, indeed she is.'

'John engaged her before I arrived. She's a real friend.' And again he'd broken through her barrier of reserve. She recalled John's answer when she asked him about Dulcie: 'I've not really noticed.' It seemed that this was a field where John and his father differed.

'She's found me a bed at the inn, so she tells me. So, m'dear, I'd better go and make myself known there or they'll be wanting to bolt the door and I'll be the wrong side of it.' With the agility of a far younger man Hewlett stood up from the low fireside chair. 'Yes, just you wait and see, m'dear, they'll all have your life mapped out, they'll all think they

52

know best. If you care to — and I'm not saying a word to persuade you — you'd be welcome to travel back to London with me, give yourself a change while that pretty little woman closes up the place and sends your things back to Warwick.'

'When the time comes perhaps that's what I'll do, come up and stay a while with you, Father. I've just not thought ahead yet, not to Warwick — and certainly not to Winchester or Shrewsbury!' Rachel added with the hint of something that was almost a smile.

The elderly man had offered advice to her, age and experience gave him the right. As she held his coat for him to put his arms in the sleeves, their positions seemed reversed. It was a heavy garment, it reached nearly to his ankles and had a wide fur collar. In it he looked overdressed, swamped.

'Goodnight, m'dear,' self-consciously he gave her a peck, 'another day gone, don't y'see? One at a time, good or bad, they none of 'em last but a few hours.'

'Yours has today, Father. You'll be glad to get to bed. I'm truly grateful to you for coming so quickly.'

'Had to. Wanted to be first in the field, before the others got their oars in. Owed it young John, don't y'see, to give you a bit of support.'

The next day Vincent and Clarry Treweek arrived from Winchester, followed an hour or so later by Muriel Hamblin, Rachel's sister. Muriel had been a widow for seven years; she felt that of all of them she was the one whose advice should be heeded. After all it was based on first hand experience — and even if it hadn't been she would still have been convinced that no one knew better than she did.

Hewlett had helped Rachel more than he realised on that evening of his arrival. There was one occasion when Muriel was in full spate about early roots being the strongest, the roots nature intended; across the room Rachel's gaze met his, she could have sworn he winked! Her mouth twitched into what was almost the flicker of a smile.

'. . . stay with me while your house is sold – in this place, of course, not that this can be worth a fortune. I'd help you find somewhere. We'd welcome you into our circle. You're not the first woman to be widowed young, I wasn't so much older myself. I'll help you find your feet. We have a pleasant enough way of living. John was doing well, you won't find yourself poor.'

'It sounds an empty, idle existence,' Clarry Treweek put her oar in, ready to steer the boat her way. 'If I know anything about Rachel she'd rather feel herself being useful. With six children I'm run off my feet; and dear Harold needs more time than I can give him.' Harold was her third child, ten years old now, with a mental age of about three. 'But I do agree with you, Muriel, it's family she needs.'

Dulcie came into the room carrying a large tray laden with tea.

'All right?' she mouthed silently, her brows raised in enquiry, to be answered by a barely perceptible nod. Of them all only Dulcie knew the happiness they'd found in this little house. The others talked of widowhood, of getting away from Treddinock; even Hewlett saw the cottage as a mistake that should never have happened. It wasn't surprising that Patsy figured as a secondary loss, they'd none of them seen her since she was a baby. Only Dulcie knew that it took three huge leaps from the porch to reach the iron gate by the road; it was Dulcie who'd taught her how to make a 'P' for Patsy, how to roll pastry, how to stick a needle through a piece of canvas to make a cross stitch. It was Dulcie who'd found Rachel yesterday in the small bedroom staring blindly at the heaped toybox.

'I ought to sort them out,' Rachel had said, but she'd made no move to do it.

'Leave them. I'll do them. There's plenty of time.' Since the accident Dulcie had slept in Patsy's bed but she'd not touched anything in the room.

'Some children have nothing. We ought to give them away.' Rachel had picked up Hodgkin, the bunny, Patsy's special friend.

'I think she'd like that. But not yet – can't we wait?'

'It won't get any easier. Dulcie, I'm frightened. I'm so frightened that if I cling to her things, that's all my memories will become. A room full of unused toys and clothes. We'll give them to that little girl in Howard's Lane, the cripple child, she's about Patsy's size. She'd like her to have her things.'

Dulcie nodded. But still they'd not made a start on sorting them out.

'Will we do that, Dulcie? Will we?' How often they'd heard Patsy say it. Rachel's voice had been a pathetic echo; she'd needed to bring Patsy close yet when she had it had been more than she could bear. Together they'd cried.

Those were the things she'd shared with Dulcie. The family were outside it all.

It was Friday, the day after the funeral. Muriel had intended to return to Shrewsbury today, she'd not expected such shilly-shallying from Rachel. Of course, the girl had always been pig-headed. But whatever she decided about the house in Warwick she might just as well leave Dulcie Caldecott to keep an eye on this place until it was sold.

Vincent and Clarry had gone this morning. And quite right too! To suggest that Rachel would spend her life looking after that poor mooney son of theirs! Now, in Shrewsbury there were musical soirées, needlework meetings, tea parties, the theatre ... Oh well, she'd give her one more day. It was quite right that old Mr. Treweek should have gone to Helston to attend to John's business with the solicitor, a man's place to do that; and natural enough that Rachel had wanted to go with him. John had done very well, she'd find herself comfortably placed. Hark! Yes, that was the carriage, they must be back.

She sat very straight despite the low fireside chair, poised to hear the results of their visit. The rain was beating a gentle tattoo on the window pane, washing away any last traces of snow from the spots shaded from the sun.

'Take off your coats and come by the fire. I've instructed Dulcie to listen for you and bring the tea as soon as you come.' It seemed she had put herself in charge. 'I take it that he left everything in order? John was always a very tidy and methodical person.' Praise indeed!

Rachel nodded. The journey appeared to have done her good, she looked brighter, wide awake. She must have found herself better placed than she'd anticipated.

'I'm going to sell the house in Warwick, Muriel.'

'Very wise too. I've told you you're welcome to come to me

while you look for something else. I know the area, I'll help –'

'I mean to stay here.'

Her words seemed to echo in the silence that suddenly fell on the room. It was Hewlett who broke it.

'Your decision, indeed, yes. But this is no place for you, m'dear. How can it be? Not once the shock has dulled. In Treddinock you'd find no social life,' ('And make no second marriage,' he added to himself) 'no friends –'

'Father, I have friends. Didn't you see the people at the cemetery yesterday? They weren't there out of duty, they'd never been guests at our dinner table; I don't go to their chapel, join in their hymn singing on Sundays. They were there because they loved Patsy and respected John. They are my friends.'

'You're talking rubbish!' Muriel stood up, her extra two inches giving her authority over Rachel, that and her ten years' seniority. 'You're letting grief and sentiment cloud your reason. As if people of their sort could ever be your friends!'

'Muriel, I didn't know what I meant to do. Didn't know? Didn't care would be nearer the truth. Then this afternoon I learnt just how our affairs stood, John's and mine. It was like a pointer showing me the way. He'd raised money on the house to invest in Treddinock Mine. I shall sell the property outright, repay the debt.'

'He'd mortgaged your home!'

'Yes. And I'm glad. He did it for the mine. I can see now it's where I must invest. We'd talked about it ...' her voice trailed away.

'You must do no such thing! What a mercy I didn't rush off home today! You must do nothing, nothing at all, until you've had time to get over the shock of all this. It seems to have unhinged you! You'll squander anything there is – if he hasn't done it already. Mr. Treweek, can't you make her see sense? I'd never have believed it of John, to raise money on his family's home on the chance of taking a profit from some mine.'

'When I heard what he'd done it was as if he was telling me ... We'd talked about it, don't you see? He knew how I felt

56

about the mine. It's as if I can suddenly see the road ahead of me.'

'An uphill one, my dear.' Hewlett was less certain.

'And I'm glad about that too. You can only be comfortable on a silk cushion if you have contentment in your heart. I need an uphill climb, one with a goal at the top. Or, in this case, one with a beam engine at the top, John's engine. Like a nodding giant, Patsy called it.' Saying her name, associating her with John's engine, helped to put Rachel on course.

Muriel opened her mouth with some retort but thought better of it and it was Hewlett, sounding more confident than he felt, who said: 'Each day will be a step forward. Sometimes a big step, sometimes hardly a step at all. A stride today, eh, m'dear! Good girl. If it's the way you want to play your hand then play it.' But he couldn't stop himself adding: 'You can always change your mind by and by, sell out of Harding's and of the mine too.'

'That's no way to set out up a hill, Father.' Brave words, far braver than she felt. Tomorrow Muriel and Hewlett would both be gone. She was certain Muriel considered her only one stage short of mad to stay here; it was likely her father-in-law did too, but he was a high-principled man. After counselling her to choose her own path he wouldn't criticise her choice. Even now there was one thing she didn't tell them, something only she and John had known and now the secret was her own. She intended to keep it that way, too. 'I'm expecting a child!' What a stir the announcement would make! She couldn't face the scene that would follow, Muriel's insistence that she mustn't be left here alone. And there was something else she couldn't face; she couldn't bring herself to think about the coming baby. Despite her fall in the woods her body relentlessly held on to this new life. Only her heart rejected it. Until last Sunday she'd looked at her figure eagerly anticipating the first change. Now she shrank from it. All the maternal love in her clung to that other baby, from the first day she'd cradled her to her breast, to the horror of the scream for a 'Mama' who hadn't answered.

She said nothing. Hewlett had told her to put on a show, that was the way through her days. And he was right. That way would put a superficial gloss over her emotions, a gloss she could skim over ... oh no! ... no, not that ... She wanted her visitors gone, she wanted to bring down the curtain on the show.

By mid-day they'd been driven away to Redruth, sharing the same carriage, and she was alone with Dulcie. The show was drawing to a close, she had only to act out the last scene. In the kitchen she found Dulcie pressing clothes, one flat iron in use, two more keeping hot on the top of the range.

'I want to get back to normal now they've gone, Dulcie. The house isn't big enough for visitors even though they slept at the Copperhouse.'

'I think they were comfortable there,' Dulcie said. 'I'll put a stitch in this hem for you, you must have caught your heel in it.' It was just something to say. Rachel's talk of getting back to normal defied answer.

'You must go home to Toby. I'm perfectly all right by myself. I'm grateful that you've stayed – but, Dulcie, I have to get used to the house. I can't be minded like a child.'

'Toby's fine. He comes over here for his supper and I make his crowst for him, he's not neglected.'

Rachel sat down by the kitchen table. With Dulcie it was impossible to pretend.

'Don't tempt me to be weak. I'd made up my mind – I *have* made it up. After Toby's had his supper this evening you're to go home with him.'

And she wasn't to be swayed.

The cottage was so quiet. A lamp was burning in the sitting-room, another in the kitchen. Everywhere else was dark and on the shelf in the passage was a row of unlit candles in their holders. Dulcie had only been gone about five minutes, she'd not even be home yet. To Rachel it seemed hours ago that she'd heard the iron gate shut behind her, heard Toby's voice growing fainter as they'd gone off down Fore Street.

Too early for bed. From the sitting-room she walked across the dark passage to the kitchen. She poked the fire in the range, lifted the lid on the kettle to make sure it was filled, moved the curtain to one side an inch or two and looked out onto the night. Darkness except for the ray of light from her

58

lamp falling on the granite wall of the chapel. No sound. Nothing. Taking one of the candles from the shelf in the passage she lit it and went up the narrow stairway. First to Patsy's room. Only Hodgkin was left there now, lying on the bed. Dulcie had done as she'd asked, taken all Patsy's things to the cripple girl in Howard's Lane, done it while Rachel had been in Helston seeing the solicitor yesterday. She peeped into the empty cupboard where her little clothes used to hang. Empty — everywhere empty. If only there were something! Something to touch, a garment that still held the shape of her ...

Turning away Rachel went out to the landing then into her own room, hers and John's. Then on through the door into the next, even smaller than Patsy's, where his clothes still hung. Trees in his boots that stood in a row just as he'd left them; his hats on the shelf above them. In the long mirror she caught sight of her reflection, a ghostly picture she made, candlelight casting shadows. She looked unfamiliar in her un-relieved black gown. Silence was all around her; it seemed tangible.

'I don't know what to do.' She said it aloud. How strange it was, no one to hear, no one to answer. If she shouted no one would know or come to her. Her fingers were moving on the cuff of one of John's jackets; she slipped her hand up the sleeve, holding the cloth against her cheek. If she sniffed there was the lingering smell of his tobacco. Again she spoke aloud. 'I'm glad about the house, John. I'd never have gone back there. Three of us came here. I couldn't go back. Don't know what to do ... no point in trying ... no one ... no reason ...'

The relief of her tears was a physical thing. There are limits to how long emotion can be stifled. Blindly she walked back through her own bedroom. On the landing she stopped. Upstairs ... downstairs ... it was all the same wherever she went. She blew out the candle as if darkness would banish the emptiness. But nothing could. With her arms clasped in front of her she rocked and as she cried, she moaned.

'Howl, go on, howl,' she blubbered loudly, 'no one can see you, no one can hear you, no one knows, no one cares.' Her voice was rising in a steady crescendo. Never in her life had she behaved like it, but then her life had never been like this. She found something akin to comfort in listening to herself, in breaking out of the mould that was familiar. She leant against the whitewashed wall, as if she were demented she banged her head against it and beat it with her fists; by now she was beyond controlling herself. How much later it was that she sank to her knees, weak and shaken, she had no idea. She was frightened, she couldn't stop crying and in the dark she was dizzy and not sure where the stairs were.

So it was that she didn't hear the door knocker. And when someone lifted the latch and came in she was beyond caring.

During the days the family had been with her Rachel hadn't spoken to Giles, but she knew he'd called at the house and talked to Dulcie. She supposed that during Richard's illness Dulcie had come to know him. Her own mind had been too removed to think about him, and Dulcie's loyalty wouldn't let her mention to him the cracks she'd seen in Rachel's armour.

It was quite by chance he should have been in Treddinock at this time on a Saturday night. A call to a cottage at the far end of the village, a cottage he'd visited each day recently trying to ease what he couldn't hope to prevent. This evening Hamish Oliver, a one-time miner, had given up the fight. Miners' disease, that's what Dulcie had called phthisis. To miners the country over it was the enemy but to none as much as those who worked in the granite rocks of Cornwall.

Giles must have left the cottage just about as Rachel blew out her candle to hide from the emptiness around her. He mounted his horse, his thoughts on the family he'd left behind him. Along Pellow Lane to the bottom end of Fore Street, then through the village past the row of terraced houses, past Traherne's grocery shop (where despite it being after nine o'clock the lamplight still cast a beam across the cobbled street). The Wesleyan Chapel was dark and empty. Then came Mulberry Cottage with its curtains drawn and the lamp in the sitting-room burning. What made him dismount he wasn't sure; a premonition that all wasn't well. If Rachel's behaviour was out of character, so surely was his, to open the door and walk into a house uninvited. He had no idea Dulcie had gone home, nor yet that the visitors had left. And yet he didn't hesitate. When no one answered his knock, he lifted the latch and went in to the dark passage.

In those first moments as he brought Rachel down to the warmth and light of the fireside he was doctor first, friend only a poor second. And as far as she was concerned he wasn't important enough to be either. In truth he was a safety valve, a voice to answer her. Tomorrow she might not be sure how much had been in her mind and how much she'd said to him.

He shovelled coal on to the fire, took off his coat and, as if he lived there, went to the sideboard in the adjoining dining-room and poured them each a small glass of brandy from the decanter.

'Here, drink this.'

She pulled a face as she swallowed. 'Horrid,' she gulped.

'It'll do you good. Take it slowly.'

'Do this! Do that! Doesn't matter if I drink it. Doesn't matter what I do, if I go or stay; doesn't matter if I live at all.' Her gingery eyes glared at him, she was full of hate, for him and for life.

'Then see that you make it matter.'

Her body ached from crying, her face was puffy, her eyelids so red and swollen that she could scarcely open them; wisps of hair had fallen from its pins. Looking at her standing there was a glass held in a hand that shook, glaring at him and glaring at life, he was moved with pity. He was no stranger to death, indeed he'd left a house saddened by it less than an hour ago. It was more than that that touched him. He thought of the little girl stepping out so proudly in her new boots — and hardly realising he did it, he put his hand to Rachel.

'I wish you'd kept Dulcie with you a little longer, given yourself a chance.'

'A chance for what?' The room was rocking, she put her glass on the narrow mantelpiece. Even with her eyes closed she could feel the floor rock. She was drifting, her head full of cotton wool and her legs too . . .

Had he not been there her day might have had a very different ending, standing by the fire as she was when she fainted. But Giles saw what was happening, his arms held her as she lost consciousness. The next thing she knew she was on the settee. She opened her eyes to find him bending over her.

'When did you last eat?' His voice was matter of fact as if he didn't appreciate what had happened. Never in her life had she fainted and here he was acting as if it were the most ordinary way of behaving.

'It's not that.'

'It's not only that. But you can't fight without food, it's your ammunition.'

'There's no way of fighting what made me faint. Nothing I can do about it. I'm going to have a baby.' There! She'd said it. Now it was real again, a truth she couldn't hide from.

'And you said just now it didn't matter what you did! Mrs. Treweek, it matters very much. You have more than yourself to be responsible for.' This might be his chance of helping her. 'Did your husband know?'

She nodded. 'When we found out about it we were pleased, excited, proud, oh so sure.' He could see how her spirit was fighting what fate had done. 'John was always satisfied with what we had. To him it was everything — why couldn't I have seen it, why couldn't I have been content?'

'But you wanted another child?'

'No, no. I don't mean that. I don't want it. I can't love it, I never will.'

'It's part of him, something of him still with you. Patsy's brother — or sister. You'll love it.'

She seemed to draw away from him, closing her eyes as if that way she could escape. But there was no escaping the guilt that haunted her and later she was to think back through the haze to these moments, never knowing how much of her thoughts she'd spoken aloud. She lived again how it had been when she and John had made love, he as tidy minded in that as in everything else. Christmas night magic had been in the air; she had used every wile that instinct had prompted, instinct and her own driving need. And for once he'd not been able to call a halt when the moment had come. It was because of what she'd done that she'd conceived this child, and over these last few days her troubled and confused mind had played one thing off against another. She ought to have been content, as John had been. But she'd always wanted more than he could give and now her punishment was that she'd been stripped of what she'd had. Patsy, her precious Patsy, was gone. How could she love the creature that had been given in her place?

She opened her eyes to find him watching her.

'Your family went today?'

'Yes.' There was no mirth in her laugh. 'Do this! Do that! I told her — I shall stay here.'

'You're serious?'

'Why not? Here is as good as anywhere else.'

'Here is a good deal better than many places.' His thin face smiled, the sudden warmth in his expression surprising her even while she felt too removed to be interested.

'Is it?' She shook her head, fright taking hold of her. 'I don't know what to do . . .'

'I felt like that too when I lost Anna. No point in anything. But you find there's still a purpose.'

'My life's so empty. Yours wasn't. I look at all the women around here, their work-worn hands. Don't you see? They're useful, they make their mark.'

'People do that in so many ways. It has nothing to do with being the breadwinner or running the home.' He held her gaze; somehow it was impossible for her to look away and yet she knew she was to receive a body blow. 'Patsy made her mark. A little girl of four years old. She made a mark that will never be rubbed out.' The only escape for her to hide from those penetrating brown eyes was for her to close her own. 'Now,' he went on in a businesslike tone, 'I'm going to make you a hot drink and you're going up to bed. Doctor's orders. Off you go while I heat the milk. I'll expect you to be in bed when I bring it.'

She didn't protest. Not that she wanted to go to the lonely bedroom, the long night ahead. But it was less effort to do as he said. She got to her feet.

'Can you manage?' Now he was gentle. 'I'll see you up the stairs. Come on, there's a good girl.'

She shook her head. 'Don't. Shout at me if you like. Just don't be too kind.' She held the corners of her mouth between her teeth.

Ten minutes later she was in bed, her hair unpinned and unbrushed, her clothes stripped off and thrown out of sight in a heap on the floor of John's little dressing-room. Giles brought her up a breakfast cup of warm sweetened milk spiced with the brandy she so disliked and he waited while she drank it like an obedient child.

'I'll put the bolt across on the front door and go out through the kitchen, then put the key in the letter box,' he told her. 'The fire guard is up and I've banked up the range and put the lamps out. Are you warm?'

She nodded. She ought to thank him but his manner made it impossible. He picked up the candle and opened the door, the shadows of the furniture making a moving pattern on the walls and ceiling as he went.

'Ah yes. I nearly forgot why it was I called here this evening. Rosalind sent a message,' he lied. 'She says will you have dinner with us tomorrow? I'll collect you at noon.'

'But why should she do that?'

Could it be he wasn't such a good liar as he thought?

'Ask her, not me. I'm seldom at home, she probably would like some company.'

'I can't. Please — don't you see? — I can't go to your house. Last time she was there with me. I'd see her — following the others up the stairs — holding her skirt up so that she could see her boots. I can't.'

'Yes, you can. And you must.' Because she and Patsy had been there so recently was why the sudden idea had come to him. The sooner she faced her ghosts the easier it would be for her to move forward. There was no arguing with him, even though he'd dropped his dictatorial manner. 'Don't run away from your memories. Your strength will come from them, and your comfort too.' Then, putting an end to the discussion: 'Twelve noon, then, and I'll tell Rosalind she may expect you. I shall leave this door open,' was his parting remark. Not 'Do you want it open?' or 'Would you prefer this closed?'

Then she listened as he went down the stairs, heard him push the bolt across on the front door. The sound of the kitchen door, then he was gone; just a clunk as the key came through the letter box and the clatter of his horse's hooves growing fainter as he rode away.

'Take a day at a time,' Hewlett had told her. And what other way was there?

She found no pleasure in her visit to Giles Derwent's home,

but in her present state she looked for none. He had told her to open her heart to memories, and whether she wanted to or not she had no choice. Almost she could hear Patsy's determined step on the carpeted stairs as she'd gone with the other children to the playroom. Last night she'd been terrified of the ghosts, yet standing in the small hall she found her eyes drawn to where Patsy had stood at the bottom of the flight, she saw again the quick look of panic as she'd turned to follow the others, her skirt held high. Sadness was a physical pain; but there was something else, something that caught Rachel unprepared. She stood gazing across the empty hall and, looking at her, Rosalind thought her mouth softened into what looked like a smile. Imagination, she told herself. For how could she know, how could anyone except Rachel herself know, of that brief and unexpected fusion of her spirit with Patsy's?

All day she made an effort and perhaps it was that that made her so tired by the end of it. Another day gone; another step taken. And so they went, adding up to a week, the weeks to a month. Snowdrops died, daffodils bloomed, then tulips and forget-me-nots. It was nearly the end of April and she'd done nothing but let time drift by. It wouldn't do! What must be happening at Harding's without John there? She remembered what he'd told her; how he'd bought into the business when things had been low. It could so easily happen again. He'd been pleased with the way the business had been going, he'd told her the order book was full. But for how long?

Even in grey Treddinock with its granite houses, so many of them without even a strip of garden, there was no doubt spring was here.

'I'm going out, Dulcie. I'm going to see Mr. Ross.'

'Mr. Ross? But why . . .? You mean . . .?' Dulcie's stammered answer surprised her.

'Yes, I'm going to Harding's. I've let all these weeks go by and I've done nothing.'

But that day she made up for time wasted. She'd started on that road to the summit of her hill.

Chapter Four

She'd seldom taken this road out of the village, the road that led, a mile or so on, to the sea. Not a safe gentle shore, but high cliffs, rugged rocks below. If John had made the mine out of bounds for Patsy, he certainly had the clifftop. Drawing her trap to a halt in the yard of Harding's she climbed down, turning to a man who came across to greet her.

''Morning, Mrs. Treweek.' It seemed he recognised her.

'Good morning,' she answered. 'Can you take my horse for me? I've come to talk to Mr. Ross.'

'Mr. Ross, here?' He sounded surprised. 'You'll not be finding him here, not 'n'ness he's expecting you. Then that's different.'

'If not Mr. Ross, then I'll see whoever does the book-keeping. Do I go through this way?'

'Ah,' he affirmed. But he wasn't happy about it. 'Jus' gi' me a minute and I'll take 'ee to Mr. Treweek's room. Get zome'un to come down to 'ee.' His missus had said she'd heard there was a baby on the way; no doubt about it and they didn't want any accidents with her slipping on those open-tread wooden steps up to the accounts room.

John's office smelt stale, it had had no air in it for weeks. On the desk were the pens he'd used, his rack of pipes, some of them still half full of burnt out tobacco. Near the window was a draughtsman's tall table. She sat at his desk, pulled open the drawer. Seeing his writing, breathing the dusty air where still hung the smell of his smoke, brought him very close. This — and other offices like it — had been his empire. Since he'd gone no one had worked in here. A business can't run itself. It was obvious Albert Ross seldom showed up here. Something must be done and it was up to her to see that it was. 'Not just for me, for all of us.' She thought of the assembly men, the clerks, the draughtsmen. 'We'll find ourselves all in the poorhouse if I don't do something.'

'It's up to me,' and this time she spoke aloud; she might have been explaining to John.

A tap on the door, followed straight away by it being opened far enough for a young man to put his head round it. 'They sent me down to see what you want,' he told her, his spotty face giving no sign of co-operation.

'Come in. Tell me your name and what you do.'

'Jack Hennesy. I help look after the books.'

'Good. So I want you to fetch me down the order books, from now back until Mr. Harding's time, and I want to see the up-to-date accounts books. I'll wait here. Thank you, Mr. Hennesy.'

Silently the youth might have been saying plenty, but aloud nothing at all as he withdrew. And left once more on her own Rachel opened John's drawer again, touched his things, even cradled the bowl of a dusty pipe in her hand, in the search for a confidence she couldn't find. What did she know of order books? Nothing. Nor of accounts either. But when Jack Hennesy staggered back bearing a pile of ledgers there was nothing to hint that this wasn't the most everyday occupation in the world for her.

'Thank you. Now you may leave me to go through them. I'll send for you to carry them back later.'

The morning passed. In the workshop the sound of hammering stopped, the machinery was stilled while the men ate their crowst — in most cases a pasty with meat or fish at one end and jam or fruit at the other. By now she'd made a sheaf of notes but she didn't send for Jack, nor for his superior. For it was very obvious he was only the junior. To send him down at all had been a clear indication of what they thought about a woman interfering at the works.

In fact she was glad to be alone, with no one to recognise how out of her depth she was. It would have been so easy for anyone who understood the trade, or who knew how the books were used, to work too fast for her and leave her floundering. At her own speed and forgetting all about food she checked the accounts that had been sent out, the money still outstanding; she compared this year's figures with last, the months when John had been here with the months just before and since. She went through the order book, more than half expecting that since the accident it would have been empty. But that wasn't so. A Treweek engine was being built for Tressider Mine out beyond Camborne; driving machinery for a Man Engine at Wheal Bertha; a stamp engine for Wheal Govier. The new life John had breathed into the company was still paying dividends, work was guaranteed for some months ahead.

Closing the last ledger she stacked her papers and rolled them, taking a piece of ribbon to tie around them. Carefully she left John's desk tidy, just as he would have, his pens put away, his blotting pad straight, the ledgers piled with their corners at ninety degrees. Only when she stood up did she realise how long she must have sat in that one position. More than three hours! No wonder her back was stiff.

'Will you send Jack Hennesy to carry the ledgers back please, Mr. . . .? I don't think you told me your name? she called to her original acquaintance.

'Westlake. Blackie Westlake. I'll see he fetches them back vor 'ee, missus. You're ready vor yur trap? I get un vor 'ee.'

The others kept their heads down. She felt their resentment. A few hours ago it might have bothered her but now she had far too much on her mind to worry whether the workmen considered she'd overstepped her role as the guv'nor's widow.

For more than two months she had mooned about and done nothing. Today she was making more than a step, more than a stride; indeed it was nearer a leap. Because everything about the day was so different she was prompted to turn to the right as she came out of the gate and head towards the sea, to the highest point on the cliffs.

A hundred yards or so from the cliff's edge was the site of old surface workings, disused for many years. Here she climbed down from the trap, not to look at the ghostly remains of times gone by, but because a broken vertical pole, all that was left of what had once been a horse whim, presented itself as somewhere to secure her reins while she climbed to the top of the grassy slope on the cliff's edge. Inexplicably there was a new feeling of hope in her today. She filled her lungs with the crystal clear air; the sea, so far below, sparkled like a jewel. The tide was out and how tempting the golden sand looked down there in the bay amongst the exposed rocks. From here there was no way down; the only path was on the other side of the bay, steep and rough. She sat on the grass gazing at the water. Soon she'd go back, she knew just what she meant to do next. But not quite yet.

How still it was. Not a breath of wind. There wasn't a tree anywhere about and if there had been there wasn't enough breeze to stir the branches. Further along the cliffs she could see the buildings of engine houses with their tall chimneys, the smoke going straight upwards, shafts of grey against the bright sky. She watched, too far away to see the wheels turning, only imagining the lifting gear, the stamps. Just a few moments more and she'd set out; if she needed anything to prompt her to action, the sight of the headgear of the mines was enough.

A movement far below on the sand caught her attention. A courting couple came into view, arms around each other. Only for a moment she glimpsed them, then they disappeared out of her vision, somewhere on the sand behind a great rock. Some of her newfound optimism evaporated. She averted her gaze, looked out to sea. The clifftop was empty, except for her; the sea was empty, except for one sailing ship so far out that it seemed not to be moving at all. Another of life's special moments, the sort that leave their indelible mark. Everything around was suddenly vivid, she felt sure she'd come to a milestone and yet why should she have, alone here on the cliff? The stillness of the air, the vastness of the sea and the sky, the silence; and it was then, when every nerve in her was aware, that she felt the first flutter of that new life within her.

Today she was making a great effort to look to the future. It was as if the child was reminding her she had more than herself to care for. The hint of a smile relaxed her mouth, her hands rested on her lost waist. She ought to go. On the way through Treddinock she'd call at Mulberry Cottage and find something to eat. No one would have worried that she'd not come home at lunch time, for today Dulcie had been going off

69

at mid-day, visiting a relative of Richard's.

Seconds turned to minutes, still she didn't move. Ah! There was the man from the beach, on his own now, he'd left his sweetheart behind. She'd not really looked at them before, but now she saw that he was wearing a pink coat, a huntsman's coat. Backview she watched him start to climb the steep path, but still there was no sign of the girl. Rachel was worried. Ought she to go down and make sure nothing was wrong? But what could be? Dreadful pictures crowded into her mind as she started to walk briskly along the cliff in search of the top of the path. But before she reached it she saw a shadow; the girl was coming from their hiding place. That's when for the first time she really looked at her. It was — oh, but it couldn't be! She'd gone visiting. But there could be no doubt, she even recognised the cloak. As the young woman walked towards the bottom of the path she was smoothing her dark hair, taking a pin out here and pushing it in there. Dulcie! The pink-coated man must be the relative of Richard's. But that couldn't account for the way they'd been behaving. Should she wait at the top of the path, give her a ride home? Something warned her not to. What had happened to the man she didn't know, the top of the path was out of her vision; but she heard the sound of horse's hooves, growing distant.

The sun was just as bright, the air as clear, but the magic of the spring day was gone. Unlooping her reins from the post Rachel got back into the trap and started towards Treddinock.

A brief call at Mulberry Cottage, then, fuelled by determination and a slice of bread and cold beef, she took her sheaf of papers and started on the road that led in the direction of Redruth. At the house with the long stone wall she turned through the iron gates. In all these months she'd never called on Elizabeth Ross; any invitation had been conspicuously lacking. Today she'd made her decision and if Elizabeth was less than hospitable she didn't care. Rachel hadn't come to see her, it was Albert she must talk to.

'I'm sorry, Madam, the mistress isn't at home,' the footman told her when she announced herself.

'It's Mr. Ross I want to see. Is he here?'

'I'll enquire whether he's returned if you'll step inside.'

His enquiries took a little while, but at last Albert was tracked down in the stables.

'Forgive me for keeping you,' he greeted her. 'I've been with the hunt all day. I'm sorry Elizabeth isn't in.' Handsome at any time, he was especially so in his hunting pink.

'And I've been with the books at Harding's for most of the day. That's why we must talk.'

It seemed their interview would be better suited to the study so he ushered her across the hall. Once on the other side of his desk (the desk that used to belong to his father-in-law) he was ready for whatever it was she'd come to say.

'Is something troubling you, Mrs. Treweek?'

'A great many things are troubling me. John did a lot for that business but we can't live on it forever and neither can the men who work there. That's what's troubling me. You aren't an engineer, and certainly I'm not. So what are we going to do about it? Put in a good manager? Or sell up now while we still have a viable business to sell?'

He'd expected a different approach, tears even, her wanting to keep everything as John had known it. For a moment he was at a loss, she'd moved too fast for him. And in that moment the door opened; Elizabeth had returned.

'Harding's have been in Treddinock for a quarter of a century,' she interrupted without as much as a 'good afternoon' to Rachel. 'Last year, after my father died, your husband was keen enough to come into the business. You've no doubt reaped the benefit over these months. Well, Albert, if Mrs. Treweek needs her capital, then we'll co-operate.' Her tight-lipped smile held no warmth. 'Indeed, I believe we have a duty to help her in her present circumstances.' Then to Rachel: 'You must be anxious to put this unfortunate period behind you, get back to your own people.'

'I'm anxious to ensure that the work John did isn't wasted – and it very soon will be. You couldn't run a restaurant by employing women to clean the vegetables and wash the dishes, you'd need a skilled cook. Assembly men and clerks can't run an engineering business.'

'I can understand your feelings.' Elizabeth's voice was smooth as silk. 'I do believe we should be prepared to help you. We'll buy you out, see that you lose nothing. We'll buy you out on the same terms as your husband came into the company.'

'You're not serious!'

'My dear Mrs. Treweek, it's the least we can do. You've had troubles enough, no wonder you want to put it all behind you.'

'John came into that company when it needed him. He gave it his designs, he gave it new life. And whose work is it that fills the order books now? I'll tell you — it's his. If you buy me out you'll do it at a fair price, based on the trade John brought to Harding's.'

Albert looked from one to the other. The gentle sex? Not these two!

Rachel went on: 'But I don't care who buys me out as long as the terms are right, whether it's you or someone else.'

'It amazes me that you can have so little regard for the things your husband cared about.' Elizabeth played a different card.

'John cared about the machines he designed. He always looked to the future, to improvements, new innovations. And so will someone else, just as he would have, had he been here. We can't live forever on the designs of 1883. What you do with Harding's isn't my concern, at least it won't be. But if you don't do something soon you'll be left with a dying business. If you want to buy me out, at a fair price, then we'll come to some arrangement. But it can't go on as it is. You'll need someone to run the place.'

'Give us a few days to talk this over before we decide.' Albert put a hand on Elizabeth's arm as he spoke as if to stay her. 'At an agreed price, based on the final year's figures. Will you agree to that? I'll see you aren't kept waiting for our answer.'

So it was left. It was Albert who invited her to take tea, an invitation not supported by his wife. Rachel refused, glad to get away. She felt she had carried the day; she was sure John would have been proud of what she'd done.

Driving home her mind went back to Dulcie. Until now what she'd seen had been pushed to the back of her mind, her business with Albert had had to come first. Perhaps tomorrow Dulcie would tell her ...

Coming up behind her was the sound of a horse being ridden hard. As it went by the rider raised a hand in salute but didn't slow his pace. Giles Derwent. There must be trouble somewhere for the doctor to be travelling so quickly without even the time to slow down and speak. They were on the road leading into the village, but he didn't carry on straight ahead, he turned up the narrow lane that led to the mine.

At the head of the shaft they waited. Men and women who worked on the dressing floors, men from the crushing house, the mine's blacksmith and the cooper, people from the village, the group growing all the time. It was almost an hour now since the alarm had been raised, thirteen strikes of the bell telling of an accident; then again four strikes, a break and five more, signifying that the trouble was far down on the fifth level below adit. Straight away a rider had been sent to fetch Giles, but that wasn't an easy matter, he'd had to be tracked down as he made his calls. That's how word reached the village, something wrong on the fifth level at Wheal Marston. In Treddinock trouble for one at the mine was trouble for them all, here where the dangers of underground working were a part of life.

The Man Engine was bringing the men to the top, a steady file of them appeared, each squinting as he came into the bright light of day. Toby was the first to notice Sally Pendleton as she hurried up the hill and broke into a run when the ground levelled towards the head of the mine.

'Is he out yet?' she panted.

'Not yet. They're only just beginning to come through. I haven't heard yet what's wrong down there.'

'Will you wait with me, Toby, until I see him come through?'

As she asked it she recognised the man who'd been the last to appear. 'Chummy' her father called him, he lived in the road behind them. In the royal welcome he was getting from his fat wife and four plump children 'Chummy' hadn't noticed her, so still holding Toby's hand she went over to them.

'Is Pa soon coming, Mr. Chummy?' For she knew him by no other name.

73

'It's Salleena Pendleton, is that right? I didn't see you waiting there.' He was playing for time while he found the right words to answer her.

'Waiting for your Pa, dear?' His plump lady sensed his unease. 'Where's your Ma? Is she about somewhere?'

'You mean his wife.' There was a pathetic attempt at dignity about the elfin child. 'No. just me.'

'I'm with Sally.' Toby didn't want anyone else taking her under their wing. 'I shall wait with her.'

'Here comes the surgeon now,' Mrs Chummy forced her voice to sound bright, 'he'll soon see to things down there if anyone's got hurt.'

As Giles dismounted he heard what had happened, for now that some of the men had surfaced the story was breaking. On the fifth level a working party had been blasting — three men, the usual number to work in a team. First they'd drilled a hole in the rock to a depth of two feet or more. This was done with what they called a 'boryer', a steel-capped rod which one of them knocked in while the second twisted. In theory it wasn't a difficult job, but theory takes no account of the narrow close they were working in, of the dust they breathed as they ground their way into the rock. When the hole was deep enough it was cleaned out with a wooden scraper and the blasting powder pushed in, driven home with tamping irons. Then the hole was filled with tamping pushed in around a slim steel nail, only then the nail withdrawn and replaced by a reed filled with gunpowder which would be fired with a touch paper — or snuff of a candle. In theory nothing could go wrong; in practice this wasn't so. There were the occasions when the men hadn't time to retreat to a safe distance before the powder exploded, or when one fall of rock would bring another.

The Mine Captain walked with Giles to the drying-room where he would change his clothes, talking as he went so that no time was wasted.

'Exploded too soon most likely — but can't be sure. No one was that near them when it happened.'

'Have they been moved?'

'No. They say they need attention before they can be shifted.'

74

In the drying-room Giles stripped off his clothes and put on a drill jacket and trousers, then the hard hat with a candle fixed to the front with clay, such as all the underground workers wore. Down there the temperature would rise perhaps to the eighties, he knew from experience what it would be like. Then, his big bag carried in a canvas sling on his back, he was ready.

As far as the second level he was carried down on the Man Engine, standing on a small platform attached to a moving rod which at each stroke of the engine descended twelve feet. Here he alighted on to another platform and while the first was raised again he was lowered another twelve feet on the next stroke of the engine. Then change again, the pattern continued, twelve feet at a time. So he passed the first adit, being lowered steadily, finally to reach solid ground on the second level. From here he had to climb. Ladder after ladder, down the old crooked shaft, in places hardly wider than the ladder itself. The air was dank, putrid with the stale mineral and rock dust and by now all hint of daylight was gone. Level five at last, where he was met by a party of men who waited for him. Six of them, each with the candle in his hat casting an eerie light, while all around was black. The sound of water dripping was constant.

'They're this way, doctor. We've not done ought but raised their heads out of the mud. Ted Prendergast, he's not gone unconscious, reckon he wishes he had from the sound of him. We left his old feller to keep an eye.' Father, sons, grandsons, one after another they made their living bringing the rich ore of copper – and, recently, more often tin – out of the ground.

It was another hour before word went round the crowd at the top of the shaft. The injured were being brought 'to grass' in the iron kibbles, the great buckets that were hoisted full of ore or waste. The springlike day had turned into a chilly evening, the moon was riding high in the pale sky and even so early the first stars were visible. It was going to be a clear, cold night.

Dulcie had come to join Sally and Toby. She noticed that the child didn't once look round to see if her step-mother was anywhere about, but stood white-faced and silent, her hand in

75

Toby's. The rattle of the moving chains told them the kibble was being raised. When it came into view they saw it brought Dr. Derwent and Ted Prendergast. A wagon was already waiting and Ted was lifted on to it and, with his wife with him this time, it set out for the Infirmary in Truro. As it rolled away a woman tugged at Giles' sleeve, asked him something. They couldn't hear what was said, but whatever it was she took no comfort from it. He led her towards a girl in the crowd, people moved a few feet away as if they didn't want to intrude on them; then women and girl together went to stand waiting at the head of the shaft. The moving chains rattled, slowly another kibble was being lifted.

Giles' clothes were grimy, drenched with water, mud and perspiration. Out here the temperature was nearly forty degrees lower than at the bottom of the mine. He scanned the faces for Clarry Pendleton but couldn't see her. If she wasn't here he must ride into the village to their cottage, and thinking on these lines he turned towards the drying-room realising for the first time how cold it was.

It was then that he saw Sally. Even in this light he could see her frightened expression. He pictured her home, he called there often enough when her father was sick. Home — that's where the man ought to have been today instead of down there in that dust, forcing himself to work. Rest, pure air, neither could have saved him — but what now for the child? Clarry Pendleton couldn't make a home for a cat, let alone a girl whose life would be shattered. He'd seen the bond between Sally and her father. All these thoughts flashed through his mind in less time than it took him to cover the space between them.

Later, the crowd dispersing, he rode down the hill towards the village. He knew he must call on Clarry, but he couldn't bring himself to pass straight by Mulberry Cottage. What it was that made him stop there he didn't ask himself. It had something to do with the lost look on Sally's face; with the way her hand clung to young Toby Caldecott's; with the memory of that glimpse of Rachel driving back towards the village this afternoon, sitting erect and alone in her trap.

Times enough he'd been called for to go down into the mine, it was part of his work. What was it he'd said to Rachel that first time as they'd watched the men come back to the surface? 'It makes one humble.' Today they'd looked to him for help and he'd been able to do nothing. How could he just ride away, back to the comfort of his home, and forget? That child's silent acceptance, the fear in her eyes; the woman who waited at the head of the shaft for her German husband's body to be brought up, for here, here amongst strangers, how this bright day had changed her life . . .

Rachel saw him coming through the gate and had the door open for him. He must have come straight from the mine. Living as she did on the main road anyone going to or from the mine had to pass her window. She'd seen how, one after another, the women had hurried towards the hill — and men too, those who worked a different core and had been off duty. She'd seen them come back. But she didn't know what had happened. She was an outsider, she couldn't go there to watch.

Closing the door behind them she led the way into the sitting-room. Only then did she really look at him.

'It was bad?' she asked gently. Not curiosity, he knew that. She asked because she cared.

'Oh, Rachel,' he slumped on to an upright chair, 'it's always bad. One man or half a dozen. Ted Prendergast — I doubt if you know Ted.' He shrugged, his voice bitter. 'Oh, Ted's going to live. Poor devil. Is it a life if you can't move? I couldn't do anything. Nothing. If it's what I believe, no one will do anything, even at the Infirmary. The spinal cord is severed just below his neck. But Ted'll live.'

'Here,' she passed him a dose of his own medicine, a tot of brandy, 'drink that. Are you cold?' For the glass rattled against his teeth as he drank.

'Suppose I am. The little girl from next door to Dulcie Caldecott — Sally Pendleton. Do you know her?'

'Patsy's friend.'

'Was she?' He seemed to be digesting what she'd told him. 'Rachel, what's it all about?'

'Tell me, Giles. What happened at the mine?'

'Arthur Pendleton was killed in the blast, he and one of the German workers who'd come to Cornwall for work and married a woman from somewhere up country. It was Sally's face ...' He took another gulp of the fiery liquid. 'Forgive me, Rachel, I've no business to come here, burdening you with other people's troubles. Thank you for listening.'

'Sally's father, you say? Giles, what do you know about them? About her family?'

'There is no family, just a step-mother.'

'From what I've heard of *her* she's only tolerated Sally because she had to. Dulcie tells me things.'

'I'm on my way to see her, I can't leave her to hear from anyone else. I was on my way when I stopped here – I don't know what made me – I saw the house, wanted to talk to you.'

'Are you warmer?'

'Warmer? Don't you mean less frightened by my own inadequacy.'

She smiled at him, surprised to realise how fond she'd become of him. Arrogant, bossy, authoritarian, all those things she'd believed (and would believe again, she had no illusions even now), but over the weeks they'd come to know each other so much better that now he could let her see this other side of his nature.

'Wasn't Mrs. Pendleton at the mine? I saw most of the village going up.'

'No, just Sally. Dulcie has taken her home with them. I don't want her to have to tell her step-mother about it.'

'If she wasn't at the mine, she probably wasn't even at home. Gone off to Helston or Redruth, I expect. She often doesn't come home until quite late, Dulcie has told me. Why don't you stay and have some supper here first? Nothing grand. I've been out most of the day and so has Dulcie.'

'Oh?' Which she knew really meant: 'Where have you been?'

'Will you stay? I know it's early to eat supper, but to be honest I'm starving. I didn't have time at mid-day.'

What had happened at the mine had upset Giles, she knew that. He was a doctor, birth and death were part of his day, but what he'd seen this afternoon had touched a raw nerve. She was surprised at how much she wanted to help him. Why else was she inviting him to stay, throwing out hints about her day having been too crowded to spare time for food?

'I'd like to. Thank you,' he told her.

'I'll have to leave you a few minutes while I go and find some food. I shan't be long.'

'I'll come and help you.' He followed her across the passage to the kitchen. 'You're looking well, Rachel. Not doing too much, dashing about and neglecting your meals?' A hint that he was waiting to be told.

'There! Cold game pie. Can you carve us some beef to go with it, Giles, while I carry the things through.'

'Let's eat out here.'

In an excited voice, a voice not quite her own, she answered: 'Will we do that, Giles? Will we?'

He gave her a curious look, not understanding.

'Sorry. You wouldn't have heard her, I suppose. Patsy always said that.'

His smile was warm. How good it was to hear her talk about Patsy like that, bring her presence close.

'You didn't answer me just now. Are you feeling well?'

'Yes, I'm well. And, Giles, you remember what I said to you − about the baby − well, it's not like that any more. I'm not fighting it.' She stood still, poised with the bread knife in her hand. 'I'm glad it's coming.'

He nodded. 'I'm sure you are. Enough beef? Shall I stop carving?'

It wasn't a royal spread: cold pie, cold meat, home made crusty bread, chutney, all washed down with cider from the barrel that stood on a table in the corner (supplied and delivered by Mr. Traherne). It's not the food that makes for a feast though; both of them were aware of the comfortable companionship that had grown between them.

'It seems I'm not to be told if I don't ask, so I'm asking. What have you been doing that has kept you too busy to have time for food?'

'I've been to Harding's. I've gone over the books, the orders, the accounts. I was afraid that since John hadn't been there there would have been no work coming in. But that's not true. They have new orders − Treweek designs, but new orders all the same. So I went to see Albert Ross. I told him I intend to sell out while the business is still worth selling. What John did for it can't last forever. I'm going while the going's good.'

'Going! You mean you're leaving Treddinock, Rachel?'

Something warned her. Perhaps it was his voice or the look in those intense brown eyes; the way he put his knife and fork down, seeming to bend closer towards her across the kitchen table.

She laughed, to her own ears it sounded forced. 'Going? In my state? By the time the business is sorted out I'll be in no state to go anywhere, at least for a few months.'

He nodded. 'And then?'

'Oh, Giles, let's not try and probe too far. A day at a time, that's what my father-in-law told me. It's good advice.'

'And for you this has been a good day. I can see that.'

'It's been an important one. The others I've lived though – this one I lived. There's a difference. And something else too.' Then she hesitated.

'Yes?'

She needed to share it with someone and there was no one else. In any case Giles was a doctor; she supposed that when the time came that she needed one it would be him.

'Today, for the first time, my baby moved. It's alive.'

Across the table her gingery eyes looked at him, wide with the wonder of what she'd told him. His Adam's apple seemed to fill his throat. He didn't mean to reach out and touch her hand. Neither did he mean to fall in love with her. For him that was one of life's special moments, indelibly imprinted on his memory. Did she feel the stillness in the room, the silence except for the steady ticking of the clock on the wall and the splutter of sparks in the grate as the coals slipped?

'A very important day for you,' he said softly. Then, after a long moment: 'Yet for that woman with the German husband, for Ted Prendergast, for poor young Sally ...'

But she knew he was more ready to face the visit he had to make than he had been an hour or so before.

'They said he couldn't have suffered, Sal, it was all over too quickly.' Toby tried to give her the comfort she needed. He felt helpless. He wanted to carry her away from all the misery. But he couldn't, no one could, she had to live through it and with a step-mother who didn't want her.

They sat together on a granite boulder, between the western

edge of the village and the cliff; it had always been a favourite place. As children they'd climbed it; it had been their castle, their meeting place. Its craggy face was familiar to them and now they were sitting on the bottom ledge, his hand holding hers.

'I know they say that.' Her voice was small, expressionless. Her face was pale, he knew it was even though it was too dark to see her properly.

'Sal — you've got me. I know that's not much —'

'Yes, 'tiz. 'Tiz, Toby. It's jes' I can't seem to take it in. Pa not goin' to be there any more, not coming up the street with the men back from the core.' She felt his arms around her. 'No Pa to meet up at the mine ...' she sobbed. He held her tighter, thankful that she would cry. That was something he could understand. 'Why did God have to take him? Why couldn't it have been her?' She was crying, great, gulping sobs. ''Tiz cos she's bad, that's why. He don't want her sort up there. An' I don't blame him either!' Another snort.

'You've got us, Dulcie and me. You know we shall always be there.'

'What am I gonna do, Toby?' She sniffed, making an effort for control. 'I'll get work. I'll go off somewhere. I won't stay with her, she can't make me stay.'

'No, Sally. Don't talk about going. Not without me. Stick it out. As soon as we're old enough we'll be together. I'll take care of you.'

She leant against him.

'I'm so ashamed,' she sniffed, 'crying like that and it's for myself, crying cos I lost my Pa, cos I'm left with her and I hate her. I never thought about him, about his life being taken away from him. He hadn't had much of a time either. His life all gone — and he'd not done much with it. Now he's got no chance to see anything, do anything. Poor Pa ...'

'Not done much? Why, Sal, he was a happy person. He married your Ma, he got you. And I dare say if we try and see it from his way, he must have got some sort of happiness with her — your step-mother — or why else would he have married her?'

'She had a sort of hold on him. When it was just Pa and me it was fine, it was different. Even after she came, when it was just us at home, he was like he used to be. Then she'd come back and spoil it all.'

'Perhaps now you'll get closer to her, both of you sad without him.'

'Her! She didn't even know him. Not the Pa I knew. I tell you she had a hold on him. It was horrid to watch them together, sort of offering herself to him, teasing – then off she'd go, out. To other men, so people say. I heard them. Pa must have heard them too. He wasn't happy – but he couldn't talk to me about her, or he wouldn't. And anyway soon as she sidled up to him like she does – did – she got him eating out of her hand.' A long silence. 'Grown ups are so funny sometimes.'

'We won't be. We know what we want and I'll see we get it.'

'Do we know?'

He put his hand on her silky hair. 'We know the things that matter. We'll be together. I'll take care of you. Try and put up with things for a while. I can't think you'll get a living-in job in Treddinock.'

She sat bolt upright. 'Doesn't have to be Treddinock. Pa's gone.'

'Don't say that, Sal.'

''Tiz only a pipe-dream. I've nowhere else to go anyway.'

The next day Dulcie's mind was taken up with Sally's troubles.

'If they were both a few years older Toby would marry her.' She laughed when she said it, knowing the suggestion quite impossible, yet there was an underlying seriousness in her voice. 'It's almost frightening the way he loves her, you know, worships her. Richard said he always did, right from when he first knew her.' All the time she talked Dulcie worked; her hands seemed to do their job independently. 'But that dreadful woman, her step-mother! You'd never believe the beastly things she says about them. I'm sure she expects that before Sally's much older she'll be in the family way by him. It's hateful. She's just a child and Toby wouldn't hurt a hair on her head.'

Her words triggered off other thoughts in Rachel's mind. 'Did you have a good day yesterday?' she asked, and following what Dulcie had been saying, surely that must have given her a perfect opportunity for confidences.

'I'm glad I went,' was all she answered — and that told Rachel nothing!

Each day Dulcie talked of the Pendletons. Sometimes it would be that she'd heard Clarry's raised voice ('It's the gin talking, that's her trouble'); or Sally not wanting to go home; Sally spending hours waiting on the hill near the assayer's house knowing that Toby would always be pleased to find her there when he came out of the laboratory; or men coming and going to the house next door. But all this was over a period of weeks, weeks during which Rachel had other things on her mind besides the Pendletons.

It was about a fortnight after her call on him that Albert paid her a visit. He told her that an engineering firm from the Midlands had showed interest in Harding's, no more than that. These things take time. So she waited. He made all the contacts with Gilbert Walkham of Jenkins and Walkham (a name so familiar to Rachel that she trusted them to make a fair offer, she'd heard John speak of them and always with respect). The smallest excuse would bring him to the cottage. Over the weeks from the middle of May, when first he told her of Jenkins' and Walkham's interest, scarcely a day went by when he didn't find some reason to come. Sometimes she was in, but more often during those days of early summer, she wasn't. She'd return home to find his horse tethered outside and Albert in the kitchen with Dulcie. Certainly he never failed to produce a plausible excuse for calling, but Rachel became more and more certain that he'd not been following the hunt on that April day when she'd seen Dulcie on the shore.

The day came when she went to her solicitor in Helston and signed away her share of the business. Jenkins and Walkham had been keen to make haste, Rachel certainly had, and, as for Albert, he'd known that any delay would have given Elizabeth a chance to find a spanner to throw in the works. By the 15th June the deal was done.

At last Rachel had some capital coming to her.

*   *   *

83

Rachel looked critically at her reflection. She stood as tall and as straight as nature would permit. There was no pretending the baby didn't show. She knew very well that what she was doing was flouting the conventions — but she intended to do it all the same. For a woman to go to a Count House Meeting was unheard of, even a woman who wasn't six months pregnant. She took a hand mirror so that she could examine herself sideways on.

'I don't care.' She said it aloud. 'I'm as much an adventurer as any of them, my money's as important as theirs.' So why should she be expected to sit quietly at home and have no say in the running of the mine?

Custom decreed a period of at least six months for the sombre black of mourning. For twenty-three years the Queen had mourned Prince Albert, a widow from the top of her lace cap to the soles of her black shoes. Rachel would wait until September when the baby was born and her shape was her own again.

If John had been there, he would have gone to the Count House Meeting. She saw the uncertainty in the ginger eyes that looked back at her from the mirror, and turned away. Perhaps she ought to wait ... miss this meeting ... she could go at the end of the year ... But, no! John had believed in Treddinock Mine, he had invested in it. She wanted to know what had been going on there since he put his money into it (their money, her money), since his engine had driven the pump that had kept Wheal Dovey in fork. She wanted to know what was planned for the next six months. She hadn't sold out of Harding's just to sit at home and count her gold.

They wouldn't want her there ... a woman, and an outsider at that. 'They can't stop me.' To give herself confidence she said it aloud.

To go to Harding's and work through the books at her own pace in the privacy of John's room was one thing; to face a room full of men, many of them who'd lived their lives amongst the mines, spoke the language, some of them financiers ... She sank on to the edge of the bed. Today she found no comfort in the movement of the child; she felt cumbersome, at a disadvantage.

Resolutely she stood up, reached for her hat and jammed the pins through her hair to hold it in place, secretly glad of the thin black veil that covered her face. Then, her cape around her shoulders, she was ready.

Chapter Five

The sight of Patsy's 'nodding giant' gave a boost to Rachel's flagging confidence.

'Do you look to the horses?' she called to a lad at the stables.

'I'll zee t'un,' he answered. He showed no surprise that she should be there; indeed he showed little interest at all and didn't attempt to hand her down from her trap.

'Good,' she told herself, 'I want to be treated the same as the rest.'

By the side of the stables were piles of ore, placed good side out. To her it all looked the same – copper, tin, arsenic pyrite. Best side out or no would have made no difference to her. But that was *her* secret. She inspected it, trying to assume an air of knowledge; she took a notebook from her purse and wrote something down. All she wrote was: 'Piles of ore put on show.' But *that* was her secret too.

With her head high she crossed the space to the Count House, a large stone building, the main room high-ceilinged, a hall rather than a conventional office. At the far end were the ante-rooms, the Purser's private sanctum, the kitchens. As she approached it she was aware of curious glances from the men who worked in the dressing sheds, but, most of all, she was aware of the roar of the stamp engine, the thud of the stamps. She mustn't slacken her pace. As if she were an awaited guest of honour she opened the door of the Count House and marched in.

With the noise of the engines shut out, a sudden silence fell on the assembly at the sight of a woman amongst them. Not for the first time. Rachel was grateful she could hide behind the shelter of her black veil. Some two dozen pairs of eyes were on her: curious, guarded – did she detect a snigger of amusement? – surprised, awaiting an explanation, even hostile she suspected; certainly none of them with any sign of welcome.

'Captain Bowen?' she asked, looking at the sea of faces.

'I'm James Bowen.' Normally the mine captain would have been recognisable in his workaday white coat and stove pipe hat. Today he was attired for the meeting, indistinguishable from everyone else.

She held out her hand to him: 'I'm Mrs. Treweek.'

'Ah, th's who I reck'n you t'be. Gentlemen, this lady's Mrs. Treweek,' as if the rest of them hadn't heard as clearly as he had. He was playing for time while he decided what to do about her. 'Th's no call vor a lady to ha' to attend here, we'll watch out for her rights. Ain't that zo?'

'Ah' ... 'Not the thing' ... 'We'll see to things' and so it went, they were all agreed the presence of a woman cast a damper on their day, curbing their tongues and spoiling what was always a convivial affair. Already before the meeting was underway there were smells wafting from the kitchens, evidence of the dinner that was to follow.

'Thank you, Captain Bowen. I do appreciate your kindness but, like all of you, I'm here because I want to be.' There! That should show them she wasn't to be ousted!

'Then, Madam,' a portly, ruddy-faced man got to his feet, 'come and take this seat next to me. A good day's never any worse for the company of a pretty woman.'

Under her veil she felt her face and neck grow hot. A pretty woman indeed! She pulled her cloak forward in a vain attempt to disguise her figure. Once seated she regained some of her assurance; she even took out her note book and put it on the table in readiness.

'Dinner's got a good smack to it,' her florid neighbour said, more to himself than to her. 'Reckon I'll go and have a look at the cookery 'fore we get started on the business of the day.' And he wasn't the only one. It seemed that for some of them the dinner had been a more tempting reason for attendance than the accounts.

87

'Mrs. Treweek! I'd not thought to find you here.' She recognised Albert Ross's voice as he came through the door behind her.

'I'd hoped I might see you,' she replied honestly, 'a familiar face, I mean.'

Unlike the others he didn't suggest that she needn't have come. Her spirits took an upward turn. Albert had had business dealings with her and he accepted that she should be here. When he brought another chair and put it next to hers she was glad; in that sea of antagonists she had a friend.

'Why have so many of them gone out to the kitchen?' she whispered. 'It'll be ages before they get their dinner.'

'It's all some of them come for,' he laughed. 'A few guineas invested and a right to come to the Count House Dinners. "Knife and Fork Shares", that's what theirs are.'

She laughed. 'I remember John telling me about the dinners there used to be when he was a boy. Drunken orgies more than business meetings.'

'Some of them still aren't so very different. Captain Bowen makes a very fair punch. Depends on the figures how the hospitality goes.'

'You mean if the mine's done well, they celebrate.'

'I mean that if the mine's done less than well they try to sugar the pill. Here come our friends, wiping the grease from their chins.'

'Shall we get the work done before the meal?'

'Before the dinner, yes. It could depend on whether Bowen wants us to have clear heads what time the punch comes out. Sometimes he likes to wash the figures down with a jar of something.'

'I shall go when the meeting ends. I don't want to spoil their day out. But I must understand what's happening.'

'Mrs. Treweek, you are a truly remarkable woman.'

'To be honest,' she leant towards him, speaking confidentially, 'I am a truly frightened one at the moment.'

'Then don't be, you've no need. In that little book of yours write down anything you want explained — I mean, if you don't want everyone to know you don't understand. I'll gladly come to Mulberry Cottage tomorrow and go through it. How's that?'

Really the day was taking shape remarkably well. She'd discovered that if you didn't let yourself hesitate, if you jumped right in and grappled, there was usually a way over the hurdles.

The meeting opened. Captain Bowen, the Mine Agent, read his report.

'The work of forking Wheal Dovey has gone ahead unhampered. The heavy investment in the Treweek engine' (with a courteous nod in Rachel's direction, somehow making her not quite one with the rest of the investors) 'is already paying off. Altogether there are thirty-five tribute pitches working, seventy-nine men and eight boys varying from sixteen shillings down to seven and sixpence in the pound. From the Marston Shaft at one hundred and fifty fathoms we're driving west. Twenty ends are being driven by fifty-two men and seven boys; and there are eighty-five men and four boys working in winzes and stopes.' Today the purser was having an easy ride, he was able to declare a one pound dividend.

So confident was he that he didn't bring out the punch. A mistake perhaps. Some of those 'Knife and Fork' shareholders could have been made more manageable with a little lubrication. Rachel's ruddy-faced neighbour, who since his visit to 'the cookery' smelt of the dripping he'd been dipping his bread into, was only one who might not have been so eager to find the weak spots if he'd had a glass in his hand.

'You tell us the two hundred fathoms is in fork in Wheal Dovey. You say thirty-five pitches are being worked. I note you don't spell out to us to what avail. What about that rich copper lode that was there before the landslip? You don't tell us they've hit on it.'

'I've given the figures. Surely no one disputes we have reason to be pleased by this quarter's result?'

'Copper? That's what I asked.'

'I was coming to that. No, the copper lode we're looking for at the two hundred fathom hasn't been found. There are good seams of tin –'

Two dozen men, all talking at once. Somehow Captain Bowen made his voice heard even though he didn't shout. Rachel had the impression that even though they were disgruntled that the two hundred fathom hadn't produced the anticipated copper lode, they knew very well Captain Bowen was as good a man as they'd find, and they knew when they had to listen.

'I suggest we set this to the tributors at £10 a fathom, with an extra, say, £3 if they can get the work done by Michaelmas. 'Tis my belief that we'll come to it if we go down another ten fathoms. I've looked at all the old charts.'

That set the tongues going again. Albert hadn't said a word but Rachel admitted it was him she watched for guidance. She remembered John's faith in him — nothing of an engineer but none better with finance.

When the time came for those in favour of the extra investment to raise a hand, she lifted hers. So too did Albert. She told herself that she'd followed his lead, but in her heart she knew it wasn't the whole truth.

She'd made a £1 dividend in every £100 John had invested. And what had she done with it? Put it straight back. ('Wasted it down that damned hole in the ground,' was the observation from her red-faced neighbour, whose sideboards showed evidence of his dippings into the dripping pan, and whose hand hadn't been raised as a sign of further investment.) Today she'd put back what the mine had provided. But as yet she had no money for anything else. What would happen next time? She was sure now of the road ahead of her. By next time she would have the money coming to her from Harding's.

The work of the morning was over, the glasses were being charged. The air was thick with tobacco smoke and the smell from the kitchens was making her feel less hungry than sick.

'Is it over?' she whispered to Albert.

'All bar what most of them came for.'

She stood up to leave.

'There's dinner waiting, Mrs. Treweek,' Captain Bowen made it his duty to remind her.

'No. It was the meeting I came for.' She could imagine the relief they all felt at hearing her answer. 'It was interesting.' And she couldn't help adding, for John's sake: 'It's good to know that the pumps have forked the two hundred level so quickly.'

''Tis a fine engine your husband made.'

There were grunts of agreement, then silence. If, in years to come, she looked back on that first Count House Meeting this surely would be the moment she'd remember. Two dozen men, their talk suspended as if in tribute to John. She saw them all, yet individually she saw none of them. They were a part of the whole scene as they sat around the table in the huge room with its tall accounts desks at one end, the windows set so high no one could see out of them, the bare holystoned floor – and, as a backdrop to it in the sudden stillness, the clatter of pots in the kitchen and the overpowering smell of food.

As she opened the door the noise of the stamps met her. The fresh air was lovely beyond belief. And the curious glances didn't bother her this time as they had when she'd arrived.

Albert came to Mulberry Cottage the next morning just as he'd promised. He must have expected Dulcie to open the door to him, but today there'd been no sign of her.

'Come in, Mr. Ross,' Rachel invited him, 'I hoped you'd remember your promise.'

He followed her into the sitting-room, casting a glance through the open doorway of the empty kitchen. Rachel noticed, memory taking her back to the scene on the shore.

'Dulcie hasn't come today. I shall walk down and see what's the matter if I don't hear from her soon.'

'Has she ever let you down before? Servants aren't always reliable.'

'Dulcie is far more than a servant, as you call her.' She'd said much the same to her father-in-law, but she'd not favoured him with the glare that she threw at Albert.

'I beg your pardon. Perhaps you'd rather we postponed our talk about the meeting if you're anxious about her. Better still – I'll tell you what we'll do. My gig's at the gate, get your bonnet and I'll drive you to see what's amiss.'

Rachel forgave him. Didn't that prove he was as anxious as she was herself? Or had she dreamed up the whole thing? What real proof had she of the identity of Dulcie's pink-coated companion? Still, as they started down Fore Street, it was obvious he knew where the Caldecotts lived.

When the gig pulled up outside her cottage, Dulcie came out to them, a finger to her lips in warning.

'I'm sorry,' she whispered to Rachel, 'it happened after

Toby left otherwise I'd have sent a message.'

'What did? What happened?' Rachel whispered back. 'Have you hurt yourself?'

'No. It's Sally. Saleena Caldecott. I can't tell you here. There was trouble. Sally and —' she nodded her head in the direction of the cottage next door — 'her — that woman. She's gone off to sleep now, poor little soul. I couldn't leave her.'

At that second there was the sound of the upstairs window of the Pendletons' cottage being thrown open and a woman leant out. It was the sight of her that decided Rachel what she meant to do. Unkempt, her untidy hair hanging around her shoulders, her face painted — Clarry Pendleton was a coarse-looking woman. As if by contrast Rachel pictured Sally's elfin features, her smooth honey-brown hair.

'Mrs. Pendleton?' she called up. 'Can you spare me five minutes?'

'Me? What for?'

'May I come inside? We can't talk out here. Dulcie, look after Mr. Ross while he waits, will you?'

'Door's open. I'll come down.' Which she took to be Clarry's invitation for her to step inside.

On one or two occasions she'd been to Dulcie's cottage which was identical to this. The same and yet so different. The door opened straight into the kitchen. Water had to be fetched from a communal pump, and disposed of into a ditch, but in that it was no different from any other. The range was small and, at Clarry's, the fire was out. Leading out of the kitchen was an alcove into what Dulcie termed 'the sitting room'. The Pendletons had no such thing. The small floor space housed three horsehair mattresses, the blankets on them as dishevelled as everything else in the place. Also from the kitchen was a narrow, steep flight of stairs which Rachel knew led to two small bedrooms.

'You may know who I am — Mrs. Treweek, from Mulberry Cottage. I have met Sally. She may have mentioned me to you.' Rachel was surprised to hear how pleasant she made her voice; it gave no hint of the repugnance she felt. In an age when women were tightly encased in stays, the necks of their dresses high, decorum the accepted behaviour, every curve and bulge in Clarry's plump body was obvious. Her shirt was unbuttoned low at the neck, her sleeves rolled up above her elbows. At a glance Rachel understood so much that she'd heard about her. But her voice didn't alter as she went on: 'As you can see I'm soon to have a baby and I'm wanting to engage a girl to help me. That's why I want to talk to you. I'd want this girl to live in. I've not met many local girls, but Sally —' No, to this woman she couldn't bring herself to say what was in her mind: 'Sally was Patsy's friend.' So she changed it to, 'Sally must be ready for work. Before I ask her I felt it right to have your permission. It's expecting a lot of you to spare her. Like me, you're alone.'

'Like you!' The face came within inches of hers. 'No, I'm not like you. Where could I get the money to pay for help? You don't know what it is to scratch and scrape to keep a roof over your head.' Clarry rocked unsteadily from heel to toe.

'One mouth less to feed, Mrs. Pendleton.' Rachel stepped back as she spoke. 'Will you agree to her coming?'

'Just you keep an eye on what she gets up to, that's all. That Caldecott woman's at your place, she and her fancy ways. And the boy, I wouldn't wonder he gets his knees under the table there too. I don't want him having a chance to be at Sally — you know what I mean. Can't take his eyes off her. Child, that's what her next door says. Child! She's no child and neither is he. You understand me ...'

'Oh I do, Mrs. Pendleton, I understand you perfectly.'

And under the make-up Rachel was sure Clarry Pendleton's colour rose.

'If she's willing I'd like her to come home with me today.'

'Willing! Not for her to say whether she's willing. If I say she's to work for you, then that's it. Yes, take her today. I'll throw out her things. Save her coming creeping back here spying on everything I do.'

Permission gained there was no need to keep up the charade any longer. Rachel turned to leave, throwing out her parting words without so much as a glance.

'I'll go next door and talk to her. You'll please parcel up her things and put them on the seat of the gig.'

Dulcie heard of the suggestion — by now it was more than

a suggestion, for already Clarry was bundling up Sally's few clothes.

'You don't know how relieved I am. It's no place for her there. I've been dreadfully worried ever since her father was killed, hearing the way they carry on.' She was the complete opposite of Clarry. They were as different from each other as were their houses. Dulcie's dark hair so smooth and glossy, her complexion as clear and fresh as a child's, her small hands as well cared for as any lady's and showing no sign of the hours of housework they did. Nature can be cruel. Clarry made no effort to scrub and clean yet her hands were rough, her nails broken.

'I'm awake, Dulcie.'

They turned to see Sally at the top of the stairs. Albert's first reaction was shock; Rachel's was fury. Had that woman done this to the child? The pale face was changed, one eye almost closed, swollen with the greeny-yellow bruise already visible.

'I say!' Albert blurted out thoughtlessly. 'Whatever have you been doing?'

'Sally, I've come to talk to you. Shall I come upstairs or would you rather hear what I have to say down here?' Rachel tried to ignore the black eye.

'Down there. With Dulcie.'

So Rachel told her what she had in mind. Dulcie nodded agreement and encouragement. Through the window they saw Clarry putting a bundle on to the seat of the gig. It was relief that made Sally's mouth tremble so. She wouldn't let herself start crying again, she wouldn't. She was old enough to do a job of work, and she'd do it well too. She wanted to tell Mrs. Treweek how hard she'd try, but she was frightened to attempt to talk. She blew her nose, then bit hard on the corner of her handkerchief.

'Will you come, Sally? The baby won't be here for a few weeks, but you'll be able to help get things ready for it.'

She nodded her head furiously, her teeth gripping the none too clean handkerchief. Who could have imagined this morning that the day was to bring such a miracle? Often enough before she'd been shouted at, even before Pa had died, she'd been used to that when he was at work at night and just she and her step-mother had been there. But it was the first time she'd ever had a fist lurched at her. She didn't want to remember any of it, not the smell of the stale drink and that face forced only inches from hers; not the man still in her father's bed; not the tears she'd bottled up for so long that once started were impossible to stop. Dulcie had appeared, she recalled the relief of being with her, of feeling herself being led out of the house and in here, away from that awful scene. Yet even when Dulcie had brought her in and closed the door behind them she'd not been able to stop crying. Sleep had been her salvation.

'We can't all get in the gig, Albert,' Dulcie was saying, 'you two ride, Sally and I will walk. It'll do us good, won't it, Sally.'

Her casual use of his christian name had escaped her unnoticed. But Rachel heard it — and if she'd not been sure before, she was now.

That day, the 30th June, saw the beginning of a new era at Mulberry Cottage. Because Sally was there, a third person and one so much younger, some of the intimacy that had naturally grown between Rachel and Dulcie disappeared. Perhaps it wasn't so much that it was gone as that it was buried beneath their effort to involve Sally. Each evening Toby called in on his way home and usually he, Dulcie and Sally had their supper together while Rachel ate in solitary state in the dining-room.

Upstairs what had been John's dressing-room had been taken over for the baby. It housed a crib in readiness, the drawers were getting steadily full as the layette grew. And day by day Sally's adoration of Rachel increased. She'd known Dulcie for years and loved her dearly; Toby was her rock, he always had been. But to Rachel she gave the adulation of a young girl in the throes of first love.

As the weeks went by and September loomed nearer they were all poised in readiness for the new life so soon to come among them.

It was almost the end of August. As usual at this time of evening Rachel was in the sitting-room, Sally, Dulcie and Toby in the kitchen. When a knock came on the front door

Rachel looked out of the window and recognising Giles'
chestnut mare tethered outside went to open the door to him
herself, surprised just how pleased she was at the unexpected-
ness of seeing him.

'Giles! Come in.'

'Only a brief call, I'm afraid, but I couldn't go away without seeing you.'

'Away! Now! But where to, Giles?' She had little more than
a fortnight to wait. How could he talk of going away?

'My mother has been taken ill. You remember she lives in
Salisbury. I have to go, I'm afraid things don't look good for
her.'

'You'll be back soon . . . ?' Later she might be ashamed, but
now her thoughts were only of herself.

Giles read the fright in her eyes and reached out to take her
hand. 'There's a Dr. Cleighton coming, I'm meeting him at
Redruth late this evening. Rachel, I hope I'll be here with you.
But Dr. Cleighton comes from a London hospital, he won't
fail you.'

'I'm sorry about your mother, Giles.' She was beginning to
collect her wits. With him here she felt safe. Surely he would
be back. A fortnight was a long time. She knew just when the
baby had been conceived, she couldn't possibly have it until
then, probably even later. Giles would be back, of course he
would. Sometimes she'd wake in the night, sick with fright as
she'd remembered how it had been when Patsy had been
born. A hell she believed she'd never forgot, and one that now
she was frightened to remember. What if things went wrong
again this time? She was miles from the Infirmary — and if
Giles wasn't here . . . but he would be, he wouldn't fail her.

'You've a long time to wait yet, Rachel,' he was reassuring
her. 'See that you rest, and no more of that climbing down to
the shore.' Not much more than a week ago she had done just
that on one of her solitary afternoon walks, and as a result of
it in the evening Toby had had to ride to fetch Giles. 'Promise
me.'

'I promise. I shan't do anything that might get my baby
born before you get back.'

'I shall ask Dr. Cleighton to come in to see you. No, don't
panic,' as she opened her mouth to protest, 'I want him to

96

watch that you're behaving yourself.'

'Of course I shall. You'd think I was a child, not to be trusted.'

'Early to bed and a rest each afternoon. Doctor's orders.'

'Just you wait until I get myself to myself again!'

'I shall be back long before then. Oh yes, and Rosalind said can she come to tea with you tomorrow if you've nothing more exciting in your diary?'

'As if I would have. Tell her to bring the children too if they'd like to come.'

Occasionally Rosalind had been here but never the children. That she should suggest it pleased him. He didn't ask himself why, whether it was because they were *his* children or whether because it was the first time she'd suggested having young folk about the place again. But all he answered was: 'I'll tell her.' Giles had had plenty of practice in keeping his feelings to himself over these last few months while he'd watched over her. Now he left with a light touch of his hand on her shoulder and a promise to be back as soon as his mother was out of the wood.

The next afternoon Rosalind came, bringing the three children, Oliver, Trudie and Peter, all dressed in their best and with their visiting manners. Oliver had just had his eleventh birthday. Already he was taller than Sally, Rachel noticed, as the girl opened the door to let them all in.

Digging in her mind for something they could do to keep them amused, Rachel got out John's backgammon board. For a while they persevered with it, but it was playing havoc with their instructions to 'be good and mind your manners'. Peter and Trudie combined to play against Oliver, but Peter couldn't understand the rules and Trudie discounted them. The exercise tested visiting behaviour beyond the limits and after half an hour or so Peter rebelled.

'Do you know what I think?' he asked in a clear, ringing voice.

'No, what do you think?' Rachel walked straight into it, while Rosalind fixed him with a warning look. No good ever came from that tone of voice!

'I think you should chop those stupid trees down. This is the most miserable room I've ever been into. It's dark and horrid.'

Rosalind was mortified. 'Peter! How dare you speak like that. You're to apologise to Mrs. Treweek. Come along now, this very minute. Rachel, I'm so sorry. He's being naughty because he's too little to play the game properly.' She too could hit below the belt.

Rachel laughed. Funnily enough his outburst had endeared him to her as a show of good manners never could. 'He's speaking the truth. The thing is that I've got so used to it I hardly notice. But I'll be thankful when the leaves come down. Why anyone planted trees so near a house I never could understand.'

Oliver was looking out at the mulberry trees.

'The trunks are quite thin, you know. They wouldn't be difficult to get rid of.'

'I can't think what's got into the children!' Rosalind wished she'd come on her own.

'They're right, though, Rosalind. In the winter it's cosy in here, but the summers are dreadful.' Rachel went to the window too, for a moment looking out and saying nothing. Then, in a voice of decision: 'I shall have them taken away, chopped down. By the next time you come they'll be gone.'

'I could do it for you,' Oliver offered.

But the thought of him let loose with a saw — and without his father's permission into the bargain — stopped her taking up his suggestion. Instead she promised that if they'd come to tea again on the same day next week, and in their play clothes, they could have a bonfire. The thought of it restored their good humour, that and the cherry cake that Dulcie had made for their tea.

It was Toby who set to work on the mulberry trees. Bough by bough he stripped them, and as each fell Sally dragged it off to a pile behind the stable at the back of the cottage.

'Mind your head, Sal,' he called from high up on his steps, 'this one'll be too heavy for you. I'll take it in a minute.'

'I can manage.'

But he came down from his perch and added his strength to hers. Watching them Dulcie said: 'She's growing up. I wonder if she realises how responsible she is for Toby.'

'That's not fair, Dulcie. She can't be blamed if he thinks he's in love with her. He'll meet someone else before long. It's all part of growing up.'

'You don't know Toby like I do.'

'Anyway, Sally's a dear. She wouldn't hurt anyone.'

'She might not mean to. But he's her friend, that's what she thinks, her special, dearest friend. Another year or two she'll wake up to feelings she's never known before — and will she want her faithful friend?'

'We don't know how either of them will feel by then. Who knows what's around the corner for anyone. My bet is that they'll not meet anyone else living here in Treddinock; they'll just stay together quite naturally. When do they ever meet any outsiders?'

'They're worth better than that, never to know what might have been.'

'You're gloomy this evening, Dulcie. Whatever happens to them they'll get their good moments and their bad, the same as everyone. If they've got friendship that's the best to build on, surely.' Rachel thought of John; dear, unchanging, unromantic, loyal John. Strange how since he'd been gone she'd forgiven him for never understanding a need in her he couldn't meet. Not forgiven — she'd tried to pretend it hadn't been so.

Dulcie didn't answer. Into the silence the clock on the mantelpiece chimed and struck seven.

'It'll soon be too dark for him to work with that saw.' Rachel changed the subject.

'Yes. But I shan't wait for him. I've finished everything outside and banked the fire.' She seemed anxious to be off.

As she went out of the gate she stopped to say something to Toby then walked at a brisk pace down Fore Street. Rachel still stood by the window watching Toby and Sally working, seeing new glimpses of the sky as the branches were cut. They were obviously enjoying themselves, so engrossed in their job that neither of them noticed the rider go by. Only Rachel recognised him and knew why it was that Dulcie had been in a hurry to be gone this evening.

The following Tuesday afternoon Rosalind again brought Giles' family, this time attired for working in the garden. From the huge pile they took enough to make a smaller one; it would be dangerous to light it all at once. Rachel set it going, the black smoke curling upwards, the smell of burning leaves a hint of autumn so soon to come. 'A prapper dirty aul smitch' the women of the village would call it. A year ago Rachel wouldn't have understood; a year ago there was so much that was different.

'May I come through to the garden?' a voice called to them down the path at the side of the cottage. 'Roland Cleighton. Dr. Derwent asked me to come and see you, Mrs. Treweek.'

'Oh yes, he said you'd be calling. But there was no need. He'll be back any day.'

Giles had told her his locum was well practised, but how young he looked! She wondered if he'd ever brought a baby into the world at all. Nature had given Roland Cleighton the appearance of eternal boyhood. Giles was somewhere in his forties, early forties she supposed if she thought about it, which she didn't; this man wasn't that many years behind him. Giles' craggy features would stay unchanged, with him she never considered age. But this man looked untouched by living, he might have come straight from the teaching hospital in London. There wasn't a child in Treddinock Giles hadn't helped into life (unless it had required no help and Mrs. Tresawna, the midwife who'd learnt by experience, had managed the job without him).

'It's good of you to call but really there was no need. Dr. Derwent will be here, he'll be back before I have need of him.' She wanted him gone. Standing there with his black bag in his hand his presence threatened her.

'I'm sure he will.' He smiled. Such looks were wasted on a man; in his case they often proved a decided disadvantage just as they had today. His complexion was smooth, not a line, perfect cupid bows to his mouth. Handsome? Beautiful would have been nearer the truth. Looking at his small, white hands, how could Rachel fail to compare them in her mind with Giles' — long, bony, capable.

Roland had the perception to realise his presence wasn't wanted. Wherever he'd called in Treddinock his patients had been civil enough, glad of his attention, but always he'd seen that Giles was held in high esteem. With this woman he was wasting his time with her repeated insistence that 'he'll be back'. Let's hope she was right!

So he left them, the first dirty smoke of the fire giving way to tongues of orange flame and the four children (for by now Sally had come out to help them) dragging more from the big pile stacked behind the stable to where the fire burnt further across the garden.

Branch after branch, the flames leapt high. Peter jumped with excitement, doing a wild dance around it, jabbing at its burning heart with a long pole. This afternoon more than made up for backgammon, best suit and best behaviour expected of them last time.

'You big ones are in charge,' Rachel called to them. 'Don't feed too much on at a time. We're going indoors.' She wasn't going to admit to an aching back. Instead she told Rosalind: 'Dulcie will be getting the tea made. The children can have theirs later in the kitchen. They'll come in smelling like chimney sweeps.'

The sitting-room had been transformed now that light could shine into it through the windows. It made it appear bigger too. Everyone who walked by stopped to look at the twin stumps.

'Mulberry Cottage, without a mulberry in sight,' Rosalind said, watching as two passers-by slowed down, made no secret of their curiosity, pointed at the smoke, peered up the side path, then walked on, still turning, still talking. In Treddinock no man was an island; the mulberry trees had been part of the village − now, it seemed, their going was part of it too.

'Let me see the baby's things,' Rosalind urged, 'Dulcie says you've all been busy with the room.'

'So we have and she busiest of all. She's trimmed the cradle so beautifully.' Then hearing Dulcie in the passage she called to her that they were going upstairs, to come with them and show Rosalind all their work.

The little room had just one small window facing towards the blank wall of the chapel. As a dressing-room it had been adequate and for a baby the outlook didn't matter; but in truth it was a depressing room. They'd chopped down the trees to let the light in to the front of the house, but there was no way of improving on the chapel wall.

Each small garment was shown and admired; the cradle draped in white lawn brought the praise it merited. Withdrawn from the other two Rachel half listened. Dearly she would have liked to have laid her aching body on the bed, yet even there she'd not be comfortable. Had she felt like this last time? Perhaps it was a warning to her, a sign that she was to follow the others, John and Patsy. Heaven knows, it happened to women often enough, the battle to give life proving too much.

Rosalind and Dulcie were enthralled with the layette. Rosalind as pretty as any young girl still; Dulcie with a serene beauty such as Rachel had never before encountered. Quietly she withdrew into her own room, slumping on the edge of the bed, for a moment letting her eyes close. The voices from the little ante-room followed her. She thought of Rosalind, so open in her hope, her expectation even, that one day Giles would realise his need of her. And Dulcie? She must have loved Richard. Rachel thought of the affectionate way she always spoke of him, her devotion to his son. So where did Albert fit in? And what about Elizabeth? At the memory of her Rachel pulled herself up short, put an end to her reflection. She opened her eyes. What was that? What was going on outside? She listened.

'Jis' chillern,' one woman was calling. 'I'm gwain t' gi' 'em a hand.'

Footsteps, coming this way. Forgetting her two friends and the preparations for the baby, Rachel moved heavily to the window. It must be the late summer day that stifled her. Her hand pressed against the small of her back. It felt as if it were broken in two.

Then all her personal discomfort was forgotten.

They were coming into the garden, Mr. Traherne running to join them, two carpet beaters in his hand.

'The bonfire! It must have got out of hand!' she yelled to the others. 'Quick!'

They would have been faster on the stairs but she went ahead; clumsy though she was, she ran. Smoke was creeping from under the closed door of the stable, flames were shooting upwards from behind it. In a second they saw what had happened. Something – perhaps a flying spark – had set the main pile alight, the pile that had stood against the wooden stable. The children had tried to drag the burning part of it

102

away, but all they had managed to do was to make a wall of fire joining the large pile to the small and trapping themselves on the other side of it, between it and the hedge. Dulcie rushed back into the house, coming back with brooms and another carpet beater. Already one of the women was filling a pail from the pump. But the flames were taking a hold on the back end of the stable, the end where the hay and straw were kept.

The little garden was full of people, unfortunately mostly women all in long skirts. Rachel didn't follow the others to fight the fire; instead she went to the stable. While they beat at the flames she must get the pony out. The smell of smoke was in his nostrils. As he neighed and tossed his head, he showed the whites of his eyes.

'It's all right, old fellow,' she soothed, her hand on the side of his velvety nose. Time only for a leading rein — and that wasn't easy to put on him in this stable. With the door open the draught was giving the fire the grip it was wanting. Any second the straw must catch unless outside they could beat down the flames that licked at the wooden side of the stable building. Holding the rein firmly, her hand near the pony's head, she led him out. But the garden was full of smoke. He jerked away from her; he bucked. Still she persevered, slowly she was winning. They were safely away from the straw and the door closed behind them.

The firefighters had come in through the little gate by the front path, along the sideway between the cottage and the hedge by the chapel. The pony would never be coaxed along there, it was too narrow, there was too much excitement and noise. She would take him to the wide gate, the one that led to a side lane, just as she always took him with the trap. A mistake! If she'd led him down the little passage at the side he might have been frightened by the people but he wouldn't have seen the flames. At sight of them his temporary obedience was gone, catching her off her guard. Dulcie saw what was happening and ran to her aid, her sudden movement doing nothing to restore his confidence. With a neigh that sounded as if all the hounds of hell were at his heels, he stood on his hind legs, thrashing the air.

Rachel felt herself being hurled to the ground.

*   *   *

The men who'd worked the early core at Treddinock Mine were coming home. At two o'clock they'd started the long climb to grass, then they'd changed their clothes, put the wet underground things to dry for the morning and set out down the hill to the village. It was about half past three. Today they'd be there earlier than usual, for they'd seen the smoke. Something was afire down Fore Street way! Dr. Cleighton had seen it too and wondered if he might be needed. He'd seen the bonfire in Rachel's garden (although not the huge reserve pile standing behind the stable), but strangely he didn't expect the trouble to come from there; that had seemed a well-ordered affair. When he arrived the men were beating the flames that by this time were raging inside the stable. Someone had managed to hold the pony and had finally persuaded him to be led away to be tethered out of range of the smoke. One of the miners had broken a gap through the back hedge so that the children could escape, for by now all attention was on the stable and the danger it brought to the cottage. No one was bothering any longer about an out-of-hand bonfire.

'Where's Mrs. Treweek?' he called to Dulcie.

'Oh, thank goodness you're here. They've taken her in to Mr. Traherne's — you know, the grocery shop just down the road beyond the chapel.'

'Thank goodness, you say? Is anyone hurt?'

'The pony knocked her down, knocked the senses out of her.'

'I'll go down there.'

As he went with his black bag in his neat little hand he heard the distant clang on the fire bell. He was a stranger here, but any of the others would have known how to alert the men to bring the fire cart. Tom Sowden, who worked for the cooper, kept the horse in a field at the other end of the village; Jimmy Tresawna (husband of the midwife) looked after the cart, made sure it was always filled with water and ready even though it very seldom had an outing. Treddinock was proud of its firefighters and at the sound of the bell those who weren't already at Mulberry Cottage soon came. A wooden stable stacked with straw would have taken a better appliance than this to douse and in any case by the time the cart arrived

104

the fire had already reached out to the wooden window frame of the kitchen.

All those hours of stitching for the coming of the baby! And now the smoke was filling the nursery, not so much as a vest was left untouched.

Baby-faced Dr. Cleighton may have been, but appearance can be misleading. He was experienced as a gynaecologist (an unusual attribute for Giles to have asked for in a locum for a mining practice).

All that evening trade was brisk at the counter of Mr. Traherne's shop. One after another women remembered something they needed as they waited for news from upstairs. 'Oh lou-ard, po-er zoul, an' no man t'be waitin'.' Some made the excuse of wanting 'jes' a vew taddies' or 'a zmall paice o'cheeze'; some found they could produce a tiny garment still lying by, unworn any longer. ''Tiz jes' summat over fr' when maine were zmall.' Not the layette Rachel had expected for her baby, but what better evidence that these people were indeed her friends?

And up in Ada Traherne's spare room above the grocery shop the struggle went on.

'Dearee, dearee,' Mrs. Tresawna, the local midwife, muttered. ''Tiz no nearer, an' the po-er zoul's worn out wi' the struggle.'

She was going to die. The world was slipping away, she knew it more certainly each time the pains of labour gripped her. Vaguely she heard the words; confirmation if she needed it: '... no nearer ... worn out ...' Just for a moment the pain eased and she opened her eyes far enough to know she was in a strange room, the only familiar face Dulcie's.

'Dulcie,' she tried to call her. Then it came again, catching her breath and cutting her off from all reason.

'Is this a first child?' Dr. Cleighton asked.

'No. There was a daughter, about five years ago,' Dulcie told him.

'Was it a normal birth?' He expected her to know.

'I know it was difficult.'

'Umph.' His soft hands explored. 'There's an obstruction. She has some sort of a tumour in the uterus.' He stood up. 'I shall need you both to assist me. I intend to operate.'

'Oh dearee, dearee, the po-or zoul. An' no man by her zide to see her through it.'

'Then we shall have to see her through it without one. At least we'll do all that's in our power.' Dulcie's anxious eyes asked their question. 'How can I tell you?' he answered. 'There's a better chance for her with an operation than without one.'

Dulcie nodded.

'Tell us what you want of us.'

Rachel didn't hear any of it. She didn't know she screamed and threshed her head on the pillow as if to throw off the torment that tore her.

'Mrs. Tresawna, will you ask for something I can use for bandages? And tell them I'll want hot water, lots of it, so keep the fire going. And bring a powerful lantern. I want an empty bucket, towels . . . I shall need you to give her the ether, Mrs. Caldecott. Hold the pad to her nose and mouth. Keep her just the other side of consciousness. I'll work as fast as I can. It's not a thing I like to do outside a hospital, but we have no alternative.'

Through the mists Rachel knew preparations were being made. It hadn't been like this last time. She reached back in her mind to those hours while Patsy was being born. They'd given her something to bite on, stood by her side and bathed the perspiration from her, tried to encourage.

If only Giles would come. Her mind was still rational enough every now and then, enough to believe that her trouble would be over if this wishy-washy doctor could be transformed into Giles. Then the pain came again. The mists grew thicker.

There was a clattering noise, it sounded like pails. Muffled voices. Her face was wet, drops trickled into the corner of her mouth. Tears or sweat or both? Oh God, let it end. She was dying, she wanted to die, for it to be over. Something had gone wrong with her baby. She'd believed she'd been given it, the promise of a future. But she hadn't. It was following John and Patsy. Where were they? Why couldn't she reach out to them? She was dying, surely they must be waiting for her. She just wanted it over. She didn't want to live. She wanted just to die . . . just to die . . . to die . . . die . . .

Holding the ether pad close, Dulcie watched her, watched the struggle weaken and fade. She was asleep. Now the doctor could begin and it was up to her to see she didn't wake too soon.

'Dearee, dearee, her po-or flesh, cut right through un, vair turns y' to look on un —'

'Quiet, woman. Just hold the lamp steady.'

On the landing Mrs. Traherne listened. There wasn't much to hear now that Mrs. Tresawna had been silenced. The doctor spoke only in brief instructions . . . 'bucket' . . . 'towel' . . . 'scalpel' . . . 'gut' . . . Then the grocer's wife heard something else, something that sent her rushing down with the news. The baby had cried out, a good lusty yell.

They expected the door to burst open now and the triumphant tidings to be told. But the baby was only half the story. Dr. Cleighton's night wasn't over yet, nor Rachel's battle won.

But at last the final stitch had been knotted, the bandages tied. Dulcie's job was done and it was only a matter of waiting until the ether-inflicted unconsciousness was broken by the pain. For even now that the baby was bathed and wrapped in his various hand-me-downs, her mutilated body still told her something was wrong, it hadn't been like this last time. That was her first thought . . . but it was shortlived. Mercifully sleep overcame her.

Many hours later she opened her eyes. Where was she? The room was unfamiliar . . . she must be dreaming. And because her senses were still only half with her she accepted that she should be lying in a strange bedroom, Giles bending over her. She closed her eyes again. And in the dream she believed he kissed her forehead. That didn't surprise her either, but then in dreams nothing does.

The next time she woke the sun was pouring through the window. Mrs. Tresawna was leaning over a makeshift crib, a drawer taken from the chest and padded with blankets. Her baby! Her hand went to her stomach. Memory stirred. But why was she bandaged like that, and why was her stomach so sore?

'The baby . . .?' she asked.

''Tiz a bootie of a zon vor'ee, Mrs. Treweek, m'dearie.'

'I don't remember —' She wanted to sit up, tried to prop herself on her elbow.

'Doctor says yo'n t'kape yersel' lying vlat. I'll get un over vor'ee to peek at.'

And peek she did. She touched the tiny hands, their fingers curled like unopened petals. With wide empty eyes he stared at her. It had all happened before. Just like Patsy had gazed ... her baby ... this tiny innocent. Tears of weakness, tears of sadness and of joy. Which they were, who could tell?

Later Mrs. Tresawna filled in the empty gaps in the story, told her where she was, how she'd got there. The pieces were falling into place, right up to the moment the pony had knocked her down was clear to her now.

'The stable. Did they get the fire out before it took the stable?'

''Twaz burnt, m'dearie.'

'Not the cottage?' For now she was aware of the acrid smell of charred wood.

'Nowt but a bit. Now dunnee be worryin'. Tidden naw gawd ver me t' be tellin' 'ee bout things I don'no. Th' 'indereside dairtied wi' smitch — but nort tha's beyond righting, zo I'm told. Doctor be comin' zoon, he'll tellee.'

'Doctor?' She remembered the nightmare she'd been through, those small, soft hands. 'Doctor?' she repeated.

'Dr. Derwent 'izzel'. Got awm las'night.'

Chapter Six

'So you didn't wait for me to get back.' Giles sat on the edge of the bed in a most unprofessional manner.

'Have you seen him, Giles? John Patrick.' Then, with the ghost of a smile on her pale face, 'Over there in the drawer.'

'He's a grand boy, Rachel. Perfect in wind and limb. I saw him last night, and heard him too.'

'Is your mother better?'

'Not better, but she's over the worst. I shall try and get up to see her again in a week or two. Rachel,' and she knew from the way he said her name there was something important to follow, 'I don't know how much you remember, how much you were even aware of.'

'I don't want to remember any of it.'

He took her hand in his and instinctively she gripped it. As if by contrast she thought of Roland Cleighton's slim, white fingers.

'Young John Patrick was in a rush, you probably realised that. But there were complications. You couldn't possibly have had a better man than Cleighton – far more experienced in cases of this sort than I am, a mine surgeon in Treddinock – but, Rachel, there will be no more children for you.'

She was silent. The seconds ticked by, he didn't hurry her.

After Patsy had been born she and John had been advised not to rush into any more family. But this was different. What Giles said now was final. But what difference could it make to her? There was no one, for her it was an empty statement. Her left hand moved under the blankets, she touched the

109

bandages. There was so much she still didn't understand – but did any of it matter?

'Cleighton will be in to see you later in the morning. He'll explain to you what he did. We must be thankful he was here to operate. A lesser man couldn't have done it. You're going to be well, Rachel – and you've a fine son.'

The echo of those prayers came back to her, when first she'd known this baby was to be born. Prayers that it would be a boy. John could never have given the love to a second daughter that he gave to Patsy. Her throat was tight.

'Can you help me to sit up,' she spoke resolutely. 'I ought to be able to do it, but I feel as if I've been whipped round my middle.'

With that gentleness she'd seen in him sometimes before he helped her. Then without being asked he lifted John Patrick out of his drawer and passed him to her.

Later, though, his bossy side came to the fore. When the baby had been put back into the drawer (upset by the disturbance, if his screams were anything to go by), he told her: 'Tomorrow I'm having you moved to my house.'

'That's ridiculous! Dulcie and Sally will soon scrub up the cottage.'

'I shall fetch you tomorrow morning. I've already arranged for an ambulance from the Infirmary to carry you. You'll stay until you're completely strong again. Rosalind has already gone off to Helston.' He smiled, thinking of her excitement in the trip. 'She's off buying small garments.'

'But I have everything.'

'Rachel, the cottage was smoked out. Scorched, too, part of it.'

'You mean my home's gone? But the fire was in the garden – the stable –' Today her face had no colour except for the red swelling on her forehead where she'd hit the ground when she fell, that and the brown freckles across the bridge of her nose. Even her lips were pale. The sight of her tugged at his heart, but there was no indication of it.

'Not gone, my dear,' he answered, 'but it'll need work, it'll need thought. And for a while you're not ready for it.' He called her 'my dear', spoke kindly enough, just as he might to any patient faced with trouble. But he didn't expect his decisions to be questioned. Today she hadn't the fight in her to argue with him; she'd say nothing, just wait. Later on Dulcie would come. They'd work something out together.

The day brought the promised visit from Dr. Cleighton who explained why it was that she would be incapable of conceiving any more children. He made no mention of the fact that she had no husband. Rachel was glad when he left her. He may have been a cleverer doctor than she'd supposed but she liked him none the more for that.

Then Dulcie came, but she did nothing to raise Rachel's spirits.

'Sally and I will do all we can there, but the kitchen is quite bad. The woodwork is bad, it's a blessing the floor is stone; the window has gone, the frame burnt; the ceiling is quite black and the walls. Oh, it's horrid, the smell is everywhere.'

'But the rest of the house? The furniture?'

'Most of it will be none the worse by the time Sally and I have worked at it. Smoke has been the worst trouble. It's in the upholstery, and the curtains, even in the bed things and the clothes cupboards. But we'll wash everything. We're taking it back to my place, bit by bit. Sally's going to stay with us too for a while; she can't go back to that dreadful woman (not that Clarry wants her, she's filled the house with what she calls "lodgers"). Dear Toby, he's given her his room. He's going to sleep in the sitting-room. But I was saying — the cottage — Dr. Derwent has been in with a carpenter, he's having the back doorway and the window boarded up, we don't want pilferers. Sally and I will go in and out through the front.'

So Rachel had to accept.

The next morning the ambulance arrived, a large enclosed wagon pulled by four heavy horses, Giles already on board. On a stretcher she was carried out and laid on the bench inside it; Mrs. Tresawna and John Patrick, still in his drawer, followed.

Once they were deposited at Perleigh House the ambulance went on its plodding way back to the Infirmary. Giles handed the drawer back across the counter of the grocery shop in Fore Street that same afternoon and by then Rachel was lying in the comfort of his high-ceilinged guest room, the crib that had

111

been used by all the Derwent children by her side.

'Johnny, you darling,' Rosalind cooed, gently touching his tiny fingers. 'Johnny, you little love.'

And from that day he was Johnny to them all.

Rachel may not have been fully aware of it, but Dulcie had stayed at the Trahernes' until well into the night that Johnny was born. By the time she finally reached home dawn was breaking. And during those hours no one had given a thought to what would happen to Sally — no one except Toby.

'The fire's out, I can stay here.' She wouldn't go back to her step-mother! They couldn't make her go back! 'My room's only just been smoked, nothing got hurt.'

'Don't be silly. As if you could stay here all by yourself.'

'You seem to think I'm a baby. I work here. It's my job to be here.'

The firefighters had gone, Jimmy Tresawna to re-fill his cart with water and be at the ready, the others because there was nothing to keep them now that the fire was quenched. It was late evening already, the lamps had been alight quite two hours when Sally and Toby came back to the cottage with a lantern, anxious that all was well.

'Anyway,' he played his trump card, 'it's not safe for you to sleep upstairs. You can't be sure something isn't still smouldering, it might start up again. Up there you'd never know. Of course you can't stay here.'

'Oh, Toby, you say we should go away and leave Mrs. Treweek's home with no one watching!' It seemed his trump card had turned out to be the joker.

'Then I shall stay here too.'

She smiled at him, her eyes bright in the light of the lamp he held. The night stretched before them, suddenly a great adventure. The sitting-room still smelt of lingering smoke but Toby was fearful that if they slept upstairs — or even if just Sally did and he was caught off his guard if the fire broke out again — they'd not get out. So they decided to make do as best they could in the sitting-room.

'Best turn the lamp out, Toby,' she said. 'Folk'll wonder who's in here if they see a light. They'll think someone's got in round the back to see what they can help themselves to.'

He did as she suggested, throwing the room into almost complete darkness for tonight there was no moon. They were both hungry, there had been no tea and no supper today; nothing in the larder would be edible after the smoking it must have had. A stomach rumbled loudly, neither of them sure if it had been their own.

'You have the settee, Sal. I'll be all right on the rug.'

'Smells awful. Put your face down, makes you feel quite sick.'

'We could cover it with a blanket from your bed. That mightn't be so bad. Could you find one in the dark.'

'Suppose so.' Her voice was small. He suspected that for her some of the adventure was fading.

'What's up, Sal? You're not scared are you? I'll look after you.'

'Don't feel very well ... cold ...' She shivered. But she wasn't going to admit even to Toby that the atmosphere in the cottage upset her.

'I'll make you warm.' He drew her to him, rubbing his hands clumsily up and down her back. 'Here, I know, you put my jacket on.' He released his hold of her and slipped it off, grateful for the chance of doing something for her. 'Better?'

'Will be, soon. Toby, there's some brandy on the sideboard. I could feel for it in the dark. We ought to have something and there's nothing else.'

'Good idea.' He kept his arm around her while she groped her way into the adjoining room for the decanter.

'We'll have a big glass,' he heard her rattling amongst the glasses in the cupboard as she spoke, 'we'll share it.' How strange it was that they should whisper. Mulberry Cottage had no neighbours, an empty chapel on one side, a lane on the other. Yet instinct kept their voices low. 'It'll be easier to pour it into a big one without spilling.'

He steered the decanter, she tipped it. They heard the splash of the liquid but weren't a bit sure how much she'd poured.

Soon she was warm again. He sat on the settee, she laid on it, leaning against him.

'Feeling better?' he whispered.

'Umph,' she muttered, busy with the brandy. She took another gulp then held the glass towards his lips. 'Your turn.'

113

His young heart was bursting with love. His blessed Sally, leaning against him, looking to him for warmth and protection.

'I was frightened you were going to make me go home, Toby – back to *her*, I mean, my step-mother. Not home, this is my home now.'

'I wouldn't have done that, of course I wouldn't. I meant to take you home with me.' Whether he'd thought that far at the time or whether her nearness and the brandy had given him his newfound masterfulness he didn't question. She heard the firmness in his voice and wriggled closer.

'Don't know what she'd say if she knew we were going to spend the night here together.' Sally was smiling, he was sure of it even though he couldn't see her. 'Or rather, I do know. She'd say –'

'Don't, Sal. Don't say it. You know it's not true.'

Only a slight movement, hardly a movement at all, yet he felt she'd pulled away from him. He couldn't guess at her hurt that he should regard Clarry's suggestion as so unlikely. He must see her as the little girl she used to be when she'd made a hero of him. Another gulp of brandy, that might help. It didn't occur to either of them that the glass was taking a long time to empty. Only by daylight would they realise that they'd pretty well emptied the decanter.

'I suppose you think I don't understand all that sort of thing.' And this time he heard the pout in her voice.

'The things your step-mother says? I don't want to know about them. You know it's not true. Not with us. Sal, I'd never hurt you.'

'But I do understand. Toby, I'm grown up. Can't you see I am? I'm a woman.' And at that moment she believed it was true.

'I know you are. My beautiful, precious, beloved Sally, you're my woman. You always will be.' At sixteen, rising seventeen, he wanted to hold her on a pedestal, write sonnets to her. Only the brandy had loosened his tongue this far. First love, first strong drink and first opportunity could so easily have sent reason out of the window, but Toby was determined it shouldn't. He mustn't frighten his precious Sal.

And Sally? Desperately she needed to know that she was

114

wanted. She said she was grown up; she knew it wasn't quite true. But soon they would be and the world was waiting for them; together there'd be nothing they couldn't do. She expected that he would kiss her, after those wonderful things he'd said surely he must kiss her. Until now he never had, but tonight was different. In the dark she turned towards him.

'I'll work hard for us, Sal, I'll always look after you,' he was whispering as her mouth found his. It was a clumsy kiss, she felt let down. Perhaps for all his fine words he still thought of her as a child, not ready for love. She pressed her skinny body to him, moving so that he might feel the hint of her breast. 'The things I'd like to do . . .' his voice was masterful. 'If you were just any girl. But not to you, Sal, you're too perfect. That's how I want you to be. That's why I hate to hear you talking about your step-mother, the things she says. It musn't be like that, Sal. Not now, not yet. One day . . .'

A minute or two ago she'd felt rebuffed, rejected. Now the whole situation took on a new emotional quality that in some way satisfied her quest for she didn't know what. His voice was thick with unrequited desire. He needed it to be, and so too did she. That the brandy had anything to do with it didn't occur to either of them. Her cheeks were wet with tears, she needed the release of them and he rejoiced in them.

The whole thing was like a wonderful dream, never had they been so close. The air they breathed was like nothing they'd known before, a combination of the aftermath of the fire and the lingering smell and taste of the spirit. This time it was definitely Toby's stomach that rolled, he felt it.

'Am I too heavy?' She pulled away, a sudden movement, just as sudden as his as he clutched her back to him. The room was rocking — it must have been, they could both feel it.

Again she moved, putting a hand on the arm of the settee to hold the world steady.

'Stay still.' She could tell from his tone that he could feel it moving too. Even in the dark the motion was there.

'Feel a bit sick.' She tried to swallow. The fiery liquid was rising in her throat. 'Bit sick . . .' and by now her maudlin tears had nothing to do with that strange new emotion that had consumed them.

Gently he swung her feet to the floor, then stood up. 'I'll

115

help you outside into the air.' Valiantly he tried to maintain charge of the situation. His foot kicked the glass; he could have done without a reminder. The next few minutes were a sure test of his love as outside amongst the ashes of the bonfire he held her. Time and again she bent forward, empty except for the brandy and soon empty of that too. Only later when she was asleep did he creep back outside. She never knew he wasn't man enough to hold his liquor.

The Derwent children did more to restore Rachel than all the bed rest. So many years younger than her only sister, she'd always lived amongst adults; noisy romps or sudden unexpected shrieks, these were new to her.

There was the first time she heard that high pitched 'Whee!' followed by Oliver's warning: 'Careful, Father's just ridden in, better not let him catch you.'

'Who's that?' she asked Rosalind.

'Oh, I'm not supposed to have heard. That's Peter taking the quick way down from the playroom sliding on the banisters.'

That was on her first day at Perleigh House. Soon she was as familiar with his 'Wheee! Here we come!' as any of them. Then there was that other mode of transport, the large tin tray. Even Oliver wasn't above riding the treads of the stairs on that, his knees pulled up under his chin. She'd hear it bumping down the linoleum-covered flight from the top, then the more muffled sound as it covered the carpet. It soon became apparent that when Giles was out his off-spring did much as they liked. It seemed Rosalind tried to make up to them for his unbending discipline.

Each morning the three of them were driven in the direction of Helston, but before they reached the town they turned into the wide gateway of Ipsden Grange, the home of the Nesbetts. Years before, Graham Nesbett had been a tutor when Giles was still a student. Even then he'd been elderly, or so he'd seemed to the young men he lectured. Quite by chance they found themselves living near each other and by that time Graham was undoubtedly elderly, his working days behind him. It had been during Anna's final months that Clementine, his wife, had suggested Oliver and Trudie might come to her for the occasional day. 'Poor mites, there in a house full of sadness.' She'd enjoyed their young appetites; to feed hungry children made cooking worth while, life had found a purpose again. As second nature, Graham had read with them, taught them their numbers. And from there the rest had followed naturally. Rather than teaching the young Derwents (and Peter too as soon as he was old enough to join them) being a strain, he found new life in their company; while at mealtimes Clementine came into her own. Together they all came to the table, Graham at the head, she at the foot, Oliver to her right and Trudie and Peter at her left. Giles was a disciplinarian but he could have found no fault in his children's behaviour with the Nesbetts. He might have been forgiven for taking the credit to himself, believing that he'd done a good job in his training. But in truth they learnt much from the example of the gentle old couple.

Rachel knew none of this, only that they went somewhere for their lessons and when they came home the house reverberated with the sound of them — until they heard their father ride into the stable yard.

She listened too, but not for Giles. She listened for the carriage that brought the children home.

'You musn't let them tire you, Rachel. Giles would be so displeased if he thought they were worrying you.' Rosalind made a token protest, her attention on Johnny, her little darling, bending over his crib. 'Who's my darling baby, then, yes you are, come on then, my pretty . . .' and so on. She never tired of it, sure that at two weeks old already he recognised her.

'Do I hear the carriage?' Rachel asked unnecessarily, for there was no mistaking the sound of wheels on the gravel driveway.

Rosalind went to look out. 'It's too early for them. It must be a visitor. Why, Rachel, it's Dulcie! Giles has brought Dulcie to see you.' She tried to make out what was going on by the front door. He appeared to be reaching for something from the floor of the trap. 'I can't quite see what he's doing . . .'

'We shall soon know. Rosalind, do I look all right? My hair? Is it tidy? Pass my brush quickly.' She was biting her lips to put colour into them.

'All this for Dulcie?' Rosalind laughed.

'She hasn't seen me since just after Johnny was born.' Somehow it was important that she looked ready for life again. She sat straight, holding her stomach in – not that anyone could see it, but it made her feel better!

Footsteps up the stairs. Eagerly she waited for the door to open, like a conjuror about to thrill his audience with some act of magic. And while Rosalind had her back to her, putting the hair brush away, she pinched her cheeks hard to give them a healthy glow. But her efforts were wasted on Dulcie, who returned her hug of pleasure then immediately turned to the crib. Rosalind bending over it on one side, Dulcie on the other, tongues clicking, heads nodding, they paid homage. The only person to appreciate Rachel's appearance was Giles.

'I'll put the box over here,' he said. 'Dulcie has brought you some clothes.'

'Thank goodness. I'm dying to be dressed again.'

'You aren't to get up until I tell you you're ready.'

'Giles, I am ready! I've been ready for –'

'Until I say, you're not to attempt to put your feet to the ground.'

She opened her mouth to argue, but his expression quietened her. His brown eyes were as sharp as always, but lurking there she knew there was a twinkle. He was leading her on purposely, teasing her.

'Yes, Giles. I'll lie quietly here and wait until you say . . .' So sweet, so docile, her gingery eyes wide, her expression demure – demure as he knew Rachel could never be! For a moment his eyes met hers, it was a game. It was a secret game. His mouth was first to twitch into a smile. Once before she'd told him: 'You know, you are a very bossy man.' This time she said nothing, but the message was the same. When the corners of his mouth tugged into a smile her answering laugh bubbled up of its own accord.

He wasn't going to wait up here while the women talked. He moved towards the door and watching him she wriggled back against her propped pillows. She didn't look for a reason for this feeling of well-being, she wasn't ready even to analyse exactly what she felt in those seconds. For so long now she'd battled, a step at a time, a day at a time. Just for a moment she

118

let herself indulge in being cared for. And there lay the difference: for a fortnight she'd been 'taken care of', but in that moment she felt 'cared for'. She looked away from him, then heard the door close behind him.

'Who did you come to see, Dulcie, Johnny or me? Come and tell me what's been happening.'

'And while you do,' Rosalind put in, 'I'll go and tell Edith to send up some tea.'

'The clothes I've brought have all been washed. Little by little we're getting on. But you'll need to have work done on the kitchen — you'll need a joiner to see to the new doors, and to the dresser. I've tried to scrub it but the wood is quite scorched.'

'When I get back we'll get it seen to.'

'Oh, but you couldn't possibly bring Johnny back into that! We couldn't have his little lungs taking in the stench of all that charred wood.'

'I'll ask Giles —'

'I know it's not for me to say. But, well, actually it was Mr. Ross. Of course he's been to enquire about you, he was so concerned at what happened.'

'You'll be able to tell him you've seen me, how well I am.'

'Yes, I will. I did say I hoped to be seeing you soon, so perhaps he'll call again one day to enquire.'

'I'm sure he will.'

Dulcie gave her a curious look, but said nothing.

'Mr. Ross . . .? You were going to tell me?' Rachel prompted.

'What do you mean? Telling you? What have I to tell you?'

'Something about the work to be done.' But Rachel reached out and took Dulcie's hand. 'Oh, Dulcie, we're friends aren't we? Why can't you talk to me?'

'I don't understand what you mean.' And she didn't wait to find out. In the same breath she rushed on: 'I was going to tell you that Mr. Ross says there's a joiner he'd be glad to recommend, he's done work for him. You need have no fear leaving him alone in your house.'

'I see.' Rachel knew she had no right to pry into Dulcie's life but she was hurt at the rebuff and wanted to strike back, let Dulcie realise that she'd noticed it. 'When Mr. Ross pays

119

you his next visit perhaps you'll ask the man's name. You often see Giles in the village, you can pass a message to him.' Her glance fell on the wicker box, the clothes Dulcie had got ready for her, and she was ashamed. What if Dulcie didn't want to talk about whatever was between herself and Albert Ross? What sort of a friend was she to try and prise their secret from her? 'Dulcie, I'm truly grateful to you. Soon we'll get the cottage put right. I can't laze my time away here much longer.'

Before Giles drove their visitor back to Treddinock, tea was brought up to the bedroom. Conversation was back on a smooth track again. They talked about Sally, about Toby; Dulcie delivered good wishes from the Trahernes and from various women in the village; she gave a report on the pony, temporarily housed in the stable at the Copperhouse Inn. She passed on a snippet of news about one, and of gossip about another. It seemed life was going on in Treddinock, the fire already belonged to yesterday.

As Dulcie was on her way downstairs Rachel heard the children's carriage arrive, then the trap bowling off down the drive.

A rush of footsteps on the stairs, then: 'Hello, we're home, can we come and see you?' An everyday ritual. She supposed they liked to see a friendly light from the upstairs window when they got home from their lessons. It was a novelty, and so it was to come up here into a room where the fire burnt brightly giving out the sweet smell of lavender that Rosalind threw on to it. It wasn't like a sickroom at all, they couldn't understand why Rachel was in bed for there seemed to be nothing wrong with her, but they were glad that she was. Once she was downstairs with the others she'd be distant again. Here, with her hair hanging loose, wearing a nightgown, they felt they knew her better. She wasn't buttoned up and private like grown-ups always were.

On a table in the corner was a large framed board and on it a half completed jig-saw puzzle. This half hour was part of the daily pattern. A true gentleman, Oliver carried the board to the bed and rested it on Rachel's legs, the picture facing her. Then they climbed on to the bed, Trudie kneeling on one side of her, Peter on the other and Oliver sitting further down, working from the wrong side of the puzzle.

'That bit of sky goes in there. Look, it's got a bit of the gull's wing on it ...' and so on. The fire crackled, Johnny sucked loudly on his tiny fist. They were all three of them so different, these children. Without touching the puzzle Oliver would decide the exact sort of piece he was looking for, its shape, its colour. Then his eye would methodically search. When he believed he'd found it, he'd turn it over to check that the grain of wood ran the way he hoped, and only then he would slot it firmly into place. 'Got it!' He liked his success to be seen and appreciated. Trudie worked quietly, always hopefully but without a method. She'd pick a piece up at random, try it in one place, try it in another, then another. 'That can't be right! Which way does the grain go?' big brother would jeer.

'I'm not looking. That's cheating.'

''Course it's not. It's common sense, stupid.'

But of the three the quickest was Peter and with each piece he slipped deftly into place he'd send up a whoop of triumph.

There are few quieter pastimes than a jig-saw puzzle, or so Rachel had believed until she saw one attacked by the three young Derwents. Today the room was full of noise, laughter, jibes, cheers. No wonder they didn't hear Giles come home.

'What in the world do you suppose you're doing on that bed?' His voice silenced them.

Oliver stood up. The other two who'd been kneeling started to move to get down but Rachel put an arm around each of them.

'We're having great fun, Giles. Come and try your hand. The piece with the end of the dog's tail on it is foxing us, we can't find it anywhere.' She could feel the children relax, or perhaps it was nearer to say she could feel they were preparing to relax.

Peter and Trudie waited, their eyes on their father, ready to jump if he said jump.

'You're not fit to have children climbing all over you.' But the sharp tone had gone. 'Are you children being careful?'

'Yes, Father.'

'They never climbed all over me, we know just how we have to sit so that we can all see, don't we.'

Peter nodded, wide-eyed and ready to see fair play was

done. Trudie bit her lip and didn't quite look at anyone.

'We're very careful, sir.' Oliver stood to his full height and a little bit more with his chin held high.

'Good. Now then you must put the puzzle away. Rosalind says it's time for you to go and get your tea.'

'May we come back later?' Trudie whispered.

'Yes, of course,' Rachel answered, then, feeling she owed some sort of loyalty to Giles, she added, 'if your father and Rosalind say so.'

It was after they'd gone, walking sedately down the stairs, that she told Giles: 'They do me more good than all your bottles of jollop.'

'They like you being here.' Now it was his turn to sit on the bed. 'We all do.'

'You've been very kind, you, Rosalind and the children.' She was ashamed at the unexpected sting of tears. 'You, Rosalind, the children' ... so complete.

He pretended he didn't notice.

'Dulcie tells me she's heard of a joiner. She's going to let me have his address if I call there tomorrow teatime.'

'Yes, she mentioned it to me.' Once more she was in control. 'Now, Giles, about me getting up. I've languished here too long.'

'Don't imagine you can leap out of bed.' He leant over and looked at Johnny. 'How he could sleep with the noise going on in here I can't imagine. Well, it seems he doesn't need your attention for the moment, so let's see how you feel with your feet to the ground.'

'Now?' It was more than she'd hoped for.

'We'll make a start. Push the covers back and let's get your legs over the edge.' Gently he helped her. She'd expected to stand up, but her legs were alive with needles, thousands of them pricking and tingling. She rested her bare feet on the carpet, she pressed against the ground. Neither feet nor legs seemed to belong to her.

'Just sit there. It'll pass.'

'It'll pass, everything does.' Her voice was flat. What was the matter with her? This was the moment she'd so looked forward to. Five minutes ago she'd been laughing with the children, not even knowing she was to get out of bed. Now faced with the prospect of getting up, what was the matter with her?

'... back into bed ...' she mumbled, frightened to try to speak any louder. She wanted him just to go away and leave her alone.

'No, you're not getting back into bed.' He stood up, then bent to hold her firmly under her elbows. 'You've two good feet, you've got to stand on them. I have your weight.'

She obeyed him, at least she didn't resist. The second passed, they stood quite still. The life was coming back into her limbs.

'Now, just a step or two. I've got you quite safely. One foot forward, then another foot forward. Good girl.'

The black misery was lifting, hope was coming alive again.

'Giles ...'

'Umph?' Progress was halted, they stood still, he still supporting her.

'About just now – I'm sorry.' A strange thing to say, when she'd tried not to let him see the battle she was having to fight and he'd pretended not to notice it.

'You're doing well, Rachel. Tomorrow perhaps you'll be able to see what Dulcie has sent you to wear – just for an hour or two.'

So that day saw her on the road back, and if the children were disappointed they didn't say so. Mrs. Treweek dressed could never be the same as any other grown-up visitor. She may wear her hair pinned up in a thick coil but they knew exactly how it would fall in a big wave if she took out the pins.

To them she was someone special.

It was like an interlude, living here at Perleigh House; it had no meaning in her real life. In a strange way she was happier than she had been for months. Happier? No. Happiness is a positive emotion, just as misery is. With determination she looked to the future, but she obeyed 'doctor's orders' without arguing, for that was the way to get back to being in charge of her own affairs. By degrees Giles extended the time she was allowed downstairs each day, but he'd made it quite clear (and none knew better than he how to do that!) Rachel would be at

Perleigh House until Johnny was eight weeks old and her own strength restored.

She saw very little of him, and one evening she said so to Rosalind.

'He's always the same,' Rosalind told her, 'never spends an evening at home. He's been like it ever since Anna died. To start with he seemed to fill every waking hour with work — and there are always patients glad to have a visit from the doctor. And of course he has friends, he needs more companionship than we can give him. But, Rachel, I do try and make his home everything he wants.'

'And I'm sure it is.'

Rosalind snipped a length of silk thread and held her needle towards the lamp to thread it.

'Sometimes I think he'll never marry again. I used to believe he would. I've tried to fill the gap in the children's lives, I've loved them all since the day they were born. But they need a proper feeling of family, like there used to be. It's as if, when he lost Anna, his ability to love — to love in that sort of way I mean — died with her.'

Rachel didn't want to probe into what losing his beautiful Anna had done to Giles' life. As if any of them could possibly know, or had the right to know. So she turned the conversation back the way it had come.

'Well, at any rate,' she said. 'You've made sure the children have never lacked love.'

'They've been my happiness. I don't think I could love them more dearly if they'd been my own.' As they'd talked she'd been stitching at the smocking on the bodice of a dress for Trudie. 'Look,' she held it up for Rachel to see the effect, 'doesn't that soft pink blend in perfectly.' Then, not waiting for an answer, she gathered the material on to her needle for the next stitch, going back to her work and to the conversation as if nothing had broken her train of thought. 'Anna would never grudge him, I'm sure of that, she'd be glad if he could find happiness again. Our families were friends, you know, hers and mine, that's how it was we were so close when I was a child although she was quite a bit older than me. I used to try and model myself on her.' She smiled as she talked, remembering. 'She was so lovely. I must have been about

124

fifteen when Giles came on to the scene. You know what fifteen-year-olds are.'

Rachel watched her as she sat with her fair head bent over her sewing, a loose curl falling over her forehead, her cheeks flushed pink from the fire. If she had loved him all these years, could he be so blind that he couldn't see it? Was someone to run the house and take charge of the children all he needed? Memories of John nudged at her. Kind, unchanging, undemanding ... a coal slipped on to the hearth and she stooped forward to take the tongs and set it back.

'You must watch the clock,' Rosalind reminded her. 'Don't forget Giles said you were to go up not later than nine o'clock.'

Obeying orders she said goodnight and went upstairs just as the hall clock chimed the hour. Snuggling down into the soft feathers she let her mind wander back over the fireside conversation. Was Rosalind in love with Giles? Would they drift into marriage? She'd given her best years to caring for him and his children, hadn't she the right to expect that if he ever took another wife it would be her? And, if they did marry, would that give him the happiness he seemed to lack? Or perhaps he didn't need anything more than he had already, work that interested him, an orderly home ... Rachel lay staring at the ceiling, the shadows dancing on it from the flickering lamp and the fire that had been lit in readiness for her nine o'clock retirement.

In his crib Johnny set up a loud smacking noise, sucking hard on his tiny fist.

How could Giles not see Rosalind's devotion to them all? '... I was ready to make him my hero ...' – and didn't he realise how much more complete the family could be if she were his wife? Rosalind, Giles, the children – perhaps more babies, their own.

A loud protest from the crib. Whatever Rosalind's future might hold, the next half hour or so of her own was certain. 'Johnny their darling' was master. Taking him in her arms she settled comfortably as he nuzzled against her, then found the prize he wanted. She clenched her teeth, every nerve in her tingled, yearned for something ... for something ... for what?

125

'Oh, Johnny, Johnny,' she mouthed silently, 'what you do to me.'

He fixed her with his unblinking stare, this son of hers she'd once believed she'd never be able to love. Already his eyes were changing colour, in this light they looked gingery as her own; and the new hair on his scalp would one day earn him the nickname 'Carrots'.

'Just you and me,' she whispered. 'Johnny, I want ... I want ... Oh, sweet Johnny, I want you.' He held his head away from her, a dribble of milk running from the corner of his mouth, then surely that was the flicker of a smile. Then back to the job on hand, drawing on her with all his might as if to make up for the seconds he'd wasted. She closed her eyes, the past and the present merged. Patsy ... Johnny ... Patsy ... her hand moved on the warm, tiny head.

She heard Giles return, riding up the drive and round to the stables at the back of the house; she heard the side door open as he came in. Then voices, Rosalind had come to the hall to meet him. The sitting-room door closed behind them. Silence.

Always she'd sought something, something that had eluded her; she'd never known what it was, and still she didn't know. She had Johnny, she had the cottage, she was an adventurer in Treddinock mine and now that her part in Harding's had been sold she had capital.

Resolutely she reached for the glass of water on her bedside table and took a long, cold drink.

Chapter Seven

Preacher Ezra Tresize's life was spent travelling the counties of the West Country, spreading the word to town, village and hamlet. He had no parish of his own, no local flock. Sally had read the sign on the board outside the chapel; he was coming to Treddinock today, the second Thursday in November.

'Seems everyone'll be going to hear the preacher,' she said as she and Dulcie made up Rachel's bed with sheets and blankets that had been airing on the tall fireguard in the kitchen. 'Do you wish we could go, Dulcie? People say he's a great talker.' Then she giggled as she plumped up a pillow. 'Great talker – or do they mean he talks for a great long time!'

'You go if you'd like to. I'm busy today. There's more to do than listen to his threats of damnation.'

Sally cast a curious glance at her, it wasn't like Dulcie to use that tone.

'No, I'm not that bothered. 'Twas only that it would have been an outing. Now, just 'fore Christmas the travelling players are coming to the Copperhouse, so folks say. That's where I wanna go, Dulcie. They say there'll be plays that make you laugh, and singing too. No, I'm not bothered with the preaching man. I'd rather be here this evening with little Johnny. My, but doesn't the room look pretty? You'd never think it had been all sooted up to see it now. 'Tis a shame we ha' no vlowers to put in a vase vor 'un.' Her brogue always took over in moments of excitement.

A loud banging on the front door interrupted them.

'I'll go.' Sally was already out of the door while Dulcie

craned her neck at the window to try and glimpse the caller. Whoever it was was already out of sight in the porch.

'Your mistress isn't home, I believe,' she heard a woman's voice.

'No, ma'am. She'll be home later on, though, her and the babe too.'

'It's not her I want. I'll wait in the sitting-room. Fetch her serving woman, Dulcie someone or other.'

'Mrs. Caldecott, ma'am.' Sally resented her manner.

It seemed the visitor had been here before. She swept past and went into the sitting-room where already the fire was burning brightly in readiness for Rachel's return.

''Tiz vor you, Dulcie.' They met on the stairs, Dulcie coming down, Sally going up with her message.

'Who?' Dulcie mouthed, to be answered with a shrug.

'Dunno,' Sally answered with a whisper. 'I zeen 'er but dunno for zure. Hoity-toity she is, seems cross about something. D'yer want me to come in with you?'

'No, silly, why should anyone be cross?' But for all that her heart was banging. She wasn't familiar with the voice, but she had no doubt who the caller must be.

'Mrs. Ross, I believe?' Instinct kept her tone low and controlled as she faced the stranger, just as instinct made her stand tall, hold her head high. She may be only a 'serving woman' but she had nothing to fear nor yet to be ashamed of. Albert and this woman had no proper marriage, it was her he loved. And so, confident of that, her bearing was proud. In that first moment as she met Elizabeth face to face she was aware of a surge of joy. At last the subterfuge would be over, what she and Albert felt for each other would be brought into the open. Her imagination was rushing ahead.

'You'll be surprised to see me?' Elizabeth's smile was no smile.

'Indeed, yes. Mrs. Treweek isn't expected until this afternoon.' Dulcie was playing for time, letting Elizabeth make the first move.

'And when is Mr. Ross expected? Eh?' She came close, her thin face only a foot or so from Dulcie's.

'I think you should ask him that. Or perhaps you already have?'

128

'Ah! Have I? You'd like to know, wouldn't you.' Again that sneering smile. Her breath made Dulcie turn her face away.

'What are you saying, Mrs. Ross? Are you suggesting I've lured Albert from your side?'

'Albert — so it's Albert, is it! And from a skivvy!'

'No husband looks outside marriage if he finds what he wants in it.'

'You talk like a fool. Since time immemorial men have looked outside marriage. A wife is someone to respect, to put on a pedestal. Lust, licentiousness, appetites that would debase marriage, these are kept for some strumpet. Yes, missus, a strumpet, that's what you are to my husband. Well, I've had enough of it.'

'And Albert? Has he had enough of me?' While Elizabeth's voice had risen, Dulcie's was even lower, colder. For a moment they said no more, like cat and mouse they watched.

Then Elizabeth flopped into a chair. Before Dulcie's quiet assurance she floundered. 'Leave him alone, can't you? Aren't there single men enough without setting your sights on *him?* You say if he had what he wanted in his marriage he wouldn't have looked outside it. What chance do you think I have? How can he find it? Always there's you. Leave him alone.' Her plain face was pale, only her nose pink, that and her eyes, swimming with unshed tears. 'If it's money you want, I'll pay. Why can't you go away, give me a chance?'

'I think you should go home before you say things you'll regret. Whether you really love Albert I've no idea, or whether he's a possession like everything else, to be bought and paid for. Me? I'm not for sale. I may be only a skivvy as you say, but—' she paused, then spoke slowly as if she were driving her words home — 'but Albert loves me. Do you hear me? He loves me — for myself — not for what I have.'

Silence hung between them as the seconds ticked by. Half an hour ago neither of them would have imagined that a meeting between them could have been like this. Dulcie looked at the thin, plain woman; she recognised the misery and was shocked with herself that she could feel no pity. She'd never known that she could remain so unmoved by the suffering of another human being. And certainly Elizabeth hadn't expected her interview with Albert's paramour to end this way. She'd come here confident that she could use her authority – and her money if necessary – and come away the victor. Yet before Dulcie's quiet dignity she was thrown off balance. Lust? Licentiousness? Was that what Albert found in this beautiful woman? In her simple grey dress with its white collar and cuffs Dulcie looked as demure as any young girl. It was that that frightened Elizabeth. Faced with a rough prostitute she would have held the trump card.

'You'll never have him!' It was she who broke the silence.

Dulcie's answer was to raise her brows, a sardonic smile playing with the corners of her lovely mouth. 'Never have him, do you say, Mrs. Ross?' The way she spoke the name was an insult. 'I have him already.'

From where she'd been listening outside the door, Sally crept away into the kitchen. She wanted to be out of sight. She could tell the interview was at an end and she didn't want to be found eavesdropping. She heard the front door close behind Elizabeth and was thankful that Dulcie returned upstairs; she wasn't ready yet to come face to face with her. She wished she hadn't listened, yet she'd had to. She felt guilty, soiled by what she'd heard. Now so much fell into place. She understood the times she'd been sent on some errand or other, eggs from the farm, a pan to be mended at the blacksmith's, anything to have her out of the way; and she'd come back to find Mr. Ross had called 'to enquire after Mrs. Treweek.' Dulcie, always her friend, so good and pure, ready to listen and understand ... yet was it so different from her own step-mother? Yes, of course it was. They loved each other, she'd said so. But he had a wife ... What about his wife? Dulcie was so lovely ... Mrs. Ross couldn't help it that she was thin and unattractive. Hardly aware of what she was doing Sally went on with her tasks. She raked the fire, shovelled on more coal. Her idol had been shown to have feet of clay. For Sally was still young enough to see the world in terms of black or white.

Upstairs Dulcie was glad to be alone too. This must be a crossroads in her life for Elizabeth would face Albert with what she knew; the truth was out. She sat on the edge of Rachel's bed and let her imagination have full rein. In her mind's eye she saw a room that would belong to her and to Albert, part of a home they'd make together, part of their life. No more clandestine meetings, no more stolen hours in her cottage, always listening for Toby to come home. She was thankful they could hide it no longer; her excitement was a physical thing.

And while Dulcie sat and dreamed, Elizabeth was driving her trap along the road in the direction of Redruth. She gave up the struggle to hold back her tears, she even found some sort of relief in behaving in a way so alien to her nature. She cried as a child might, gulping and snorting. It wasn't until she was almost level with him that she noticed a man on the verge, a man holding out his arm as a signal for her to stop.

'Whoa . . .' she hiccoughed.

'My dear lady, you have great trouble.'

'Are you asking for a ride? Is that what you want?' she said through her tears.

'I am asking that I might help you. I'd intended to take the road towards St. Just out of Redruth, yet my steps brought me this way. The Lord was my guide, He has sent me to help you.'

She saw now that he was a preacher. 'I've never looked at any man but him,' she began. And so her story was told.

In the afternoon Giles brought Rachel and Johnny home, and from the moment they arrived there was too much activity in the newly renovated kitchen to allow Dulcie time for dreaming. Fires had been lit in every grate in the cottage, the baby was laid in the little ante-room now exalted to the position of 'the nursery', and tea was brought into the sitting-room for Rachel and Giles.

'It's just about time for the children to be arriving home from school. I'm going to miss them, Giles.'

'Certainly they'll miss you. We all shall. I've enjoyed these weeks, Rachel, it's been a pleasure to come home — to see that you toe the line,' he added with a twinkle in his brown eyes.

She didn't take him too seriously. 'One less for you to boss.'

But the look he gave her now was changed, the laughter was gone.

'Having you and Johnny there seemed to bring the house alive, make it a home.'

She ought to say: 'It's Rosalind who does that, who's like a mother to your children, who could make your family complete.' She knew she ought to — but she didn't.

'You all made me very welcome. And Rosalind would soon spoil her "darling Johnny".' She laughed.

'Nothing pleases Rosalind better than babies.'

'Giles, I've never really, properly said it to you,' she rested a hand on his arm, 'but you do know, don't you, how grateful I am to you? You helped me back on my feet — I don't mean just over these last weeks, but all the months.'

She felt confused. Her memory was playing cruel tricks on her, sending up pictures of moments she didn't want to think about. A night when she'd been at rock bottom, when she'd been beyond knowing or caring how intimately she'd confided; an evening when it had been he who'd come to her out of some need of his own, after the accident at the mine; and another before that when he'd driven her home, the first of the snow blowing into her face under the hood, Patsy clutching her package containing her old boots while her scarlet-clad legs were stuck out proudly before her; a wintry afternoon by the lakeside, John gone, Patsy gone, her own hold on reality almost gone — through it all Giles had been there.

'Rachel,' he was saying now, 'I realise it's not long since you lost John' (almost he might have been reading her mind) 'but there can be no merit in living through years on your own. Let my home be your home. Johnny knows no other, why should he need to?'

'Share your home?'

'I'm asking you to marry me. Why come back here at all, why not stay where you were? You'd made a place there for yourself, you were part of the family. My children are fond of you, Johnny need never be without a father, I promise I'd care for him as if he were my own.' His voice was steady, unemotional, he might have been making her the offer of a business partnership. His gaunt face gave nothing away, except for the tic he couldn't control. 'I swear I'd be good to you. I'm not asking that you should love me. I know what you suffered, suffer still.'

'Giles, don't.' She wished he hadn't said it. His words came between them, made a stranger of him. 'I'm grateful — for this — for the months — I wish I could explain, but I can't. I don't even understand what it is I want. Perhaps it doesn't even exist, perhaps I wouldn't recognise it if I found it.'

'I could help you find it.'

She shook her head. 'No. Whatever it is we look for, it must be found within ourselves. Don't you see?' If only she could find the words to explain to him — or to herself? 'I was only eighteen when I first met John, you know. Always so much the youngest at home, then I fell in love with him, the first man I'd known. I'm not sure what this has to do with what I'm trying to say, if it has anything at all. I told you you helped me back on my feet. But that's just it, Giles, I've never really stood on my own feet. Never. But I'm going to. Johnny will depend on me, he gives me a purpose, a need —'

'Life isn't easy for a woman on her own. Let me help you.'

'No. Don't you see what I'm trying to say? I *have* to learn to steer my own ship, I *must* be able to take my own decisions, be mistress of my life. And thanks so much to you I'm ready to set sail — or I believe I am. Even if I don't know what course I'm going to set!'

'I shall always be there to help. I believe I saw it from the first, that day when I found you trying to hammer your wheel on with your boot.'

His words hit her unexpectedly. She shut her eyes. Patsy was standing in the trap, absolutely still, eyes wide with fright; Patsy still excited by her shopping trip: Patsy with life ahead of her: Patsy . . . Patsy . . .

'Giles, does it ever get easier to bear? When you said that — I can almost feel the warmth of her, feel the shape. Sometimes even now I can't believe it.' She didn't have to explain.

'Hold on to those moments, Rachel. Don't be frightened of them.'

No one had seen into the hidden recesses of her heart as he had. All the sadness of her yesterdays she'd shared with him. So how could he suggest she should share her tomorrows?

'Think about what I said. At least promise to do that. Rachel, I'm not asking that you love me. But we could bring up the children as one family. We're friends, aren't we? My

133

children would welcome you — and surely it would be to Johnny's advantage to be one with the others.' He put his hand under her chin and turned her face towards him. There was no avoiding his eyes. 'Would you find marriage to me — abhorrent?'

She didn't duck the question. 'You mean, going to bed with you?'

'What I'm trying to say is — if it's just that that prevents your accepting, then I promise you I'd not expect it.'

Only a few moments before, clearly and unexpectedly, Patsy had been near her. This time what he said conjured up other memories. John, the familiar sounds from his dressing-room as he prepared for bed, unhurried under any circumstances; boots carefully on trees, suit hung away in the cupboard. Order, routine, a pattern with everything in its place. And what had made her so sure that Giles was different? If he were, would Rosalind be left to weave her dreams in solitude by his fireside?

Rachel felt let down; she didn't dig deep enough to ask herself why it should matter. One thing she was sure of, though. Whatever it was she was looking for in life, it certainly wasn't marriage for the sake of security.

It was a relief to hear a tap on the sitting-room door, then to see Sally's head peep round it.

'Johnny's crying. Can I vetch un down, Mrs. Treweek?'

'It's time I saw to him. You can go up to him, Sally, take him out of his crib. I'll be there in a minute or two.'

Just what Sally had hoped.

'And I must go.' Giles stood up. 'This evening you're to go to bed early, eight o'clock. No, don't argue. You've had a tiring day.'

'Yes, sir.'

Sally's interruption had put an end to what went before it, yet it still hung on the air. Rachel knew Giles' brusque manner was his way of putting it behind them, just as was her obedient and teasing 'yes, sir'. She need say no more. And yet . . .

'Giles, despite all my brave talk about standing on my own two feet, I'm sure I shall lean on you just as I have for months.' She was standing in front of him; her hands reached out to touch his shoulders and her lips brushed his cheek. She

134

hadn't meant to kiss him, wasn't even sure why it had so suddenly been the only way she had of telling him how much his friendship had meant. For a second he stood quite still, then she found herself pulled towards him to be held close, his grip like steel. She'd kissed him lightly; she wasn't prepared for his hold on her. He didn't attempt to kiss her, but she knew that if she should turn her head towards him his lips would fasten on hers. Her heart was pounding, it took all her will-power not to turn to him. 'I would never expect it.' ... Rosalind devoting her youth to him ... a man content to live with no partner, no love ... the sudden passion, the strength ... She was confused, one thought chased another through her mind. Just as suddenly as he'd pulled her into his arms, he released her and turned away.

'Remember, bed by eight.' This was the doctor speaking. 'I'll look in sometime tomorrow to see you're both settled.'

'Yes, Sir Giles.'

This way they glossed over the unguarded moment.

Now that there were no trees to block the window, she watched him go, down the short front path that had taken Patsy three giant leaps, out of the gate, then climb into his carriage. Her little sitting-room seemed dingy despite the flaming coals, the hours until eight o'clock long and empty. Her gaze followed him as the carriage disappeared into the early dusk, home to Rosalind and the children. Resolutely she closed the curtains and went upstairs to Johnny.

So it was that she didn't notice when some minutes later a man came in, this time to the side path where the light shone out through the kitchen window. Sally let out a stifled yell when she saw his face pressed to the pane, but it wasn't her he'd come to see, and a second later he opened the door and walked straight in.

'So!' Just one word, his eyes on Dulcie; a word that held no affection.

'I saw on the notice on the chapel that you were coming. How did you know I was here?' There was no emotion in Dulcie's voice as she looked at her father. Sally looked from one to the other. She didn't understand but she felt the undercurrent and knew Dulcie was on her guard.

'There can't be so many women calling themselves Dulcie

Caldecott. I met a lady — a *lady,* you hear me. I was led to her, not by my own design but by the will of the Lord. What she told me left me in no doubt.'

'And what did she tell you?'

He ignored the question. He came very close to Dulcie, standing so that his face was only inches from hers. 'The Lord's work, you hear me? You had a mission. I brought you up through your childhood with a mission. You travelled with me, listened to the Word. Listened, did I say? Nay! You heard it, day after day you heard it, but you never listened. Never! Your heart never heeded it. You were prepared to cast out the Lord's work to chase after the lusts of the flesh.'

'Father, we've been over this before. I'll not listen to you again. It was all years ago. What sin was there in marrying a man who loved me, in caring for a child who needed me?'

He went on as if she'd not spoken. 'Your life — yours and mine — were pledged to God. But his wrath came upon you for putting earthly pleasures before the work you owed to His service. Did He let you keep this man you'd chosen before Him? Did He? No! He took him from you.'

'He took him because he was ill beyond curing. You're steeped in superstition. Evil! That's what you called me for loving a good man, for looking after his child. It's you who are evil. Have you no humility, no love in your soul for your fellow men —'

'How dare you!' Even from the pulpit Ezra had never spoken with more venom. 'All your life I taught you where your duty lay, to serve your God through me.'

'What was it grieved you? That I put another man before you and your comforts?'

Ezra's thin face, always a high colour, was purple with fury. 'I care nothing for my comfort and well you know it, missus.'

If he'd stopped to consider it he might have realised that Dulcie was fighting for time. After this morning's encounter she was sure who 'the lady' had been and the tale she'd told him.

'Evil!' he spat at her. 'The evil that has been woman's primal sin. You have beguiled a man into adultery, done the Devil's work for him. My daughter!' His mouth was working,

136

his fury was nothing compared with his own guilt that somewhere he had failed, he should have kept her with him. As a child she'd travelled the circuit with him, she'd read aloud from the Good Book to the crowds who'd come to hear him; she'd never complained at their poor lodgings, nor at the lack of regular meals that was part of an itinerant preacher's life. It must have been because of some sin of his own that she had rebelled against him. Now, though, the Lord had pointed the way to him, had guided him to that poor woman who'd cried out to him for help, and so back to Dulcie. 'Tonight you're to pack your bag. We'll leave Treddinock together, I'll help you find the path back. We must praise the Lord, daughter, that you're to be given a second chance, not everyone is so blessed in the sight of God. Don't you see the workings of the Almighty?'

'You'll be late. People are going in to the chapel.' He might not have spoken, his words had been wasted.

'The lady told me everything. Repent of your sin. Here, now, down on our knees,' he gripped Dulcie's wrists, 'put your hand on the Book, beg forgiveness for the sin you've committed. Beg forgiveness for my sins. I failed you, I should have kept you with me. Pray that your heart may be cleansed!' His voice rang out loud and clear, it throbbed with the only passion he knew.

'Father, my heart has no hatred in it. It has pity, pity for you, pity for Elizabeth Ross. I'll never love the God you pray to, the God you preach about with his threats of hell and damnation. What of love, compassion? Go away, Father, forget you've seen me.'

'How can I forget it?'

'You think I'm a scarlet woman because Albert has a wife. It's not true. I'm not going to explain, I'm not going to talk about it. My God isn't your God. I'm sorry you came. It's opened old wounds. Go and talk to your flock, perhaps they'll heed your warnings of the slippery slope to damnation.'

'May the Lord have mercy on your wicked soul,' was his parting shot, but his tone made it quite clear he saw little hope of it.

Only after the door had shut behind him did she let her

shoulders sag. The room was still, quiet. She'd forgotten all about Sally until she heard a suppressed sniff. The girl was hiding in the larder, snivelling.

Often enough in the past Dulcie had comforted her when her step-mother had used her badly. It had been natural to Sally to turn to her. They'd worked together cheerfully and happily restoring the cottage, they'd grown close. But not close enough for this. Dulcie knew that what she'd heard would have been beyond Sally's experience, beyond her youthful understanding.

'There's no need to cry,' she made an effort. 'One day I'll tell you about my father, perhaps. But not now. I'm sorry, Sally, that his ravings upset you.'

''S not that.'

'Then don't weep for me, Sally. One day you'll understand. I'm happy — I'm relieved.'

Another sniff was Sally's only answer.

Upstairs in Johnny's little room Rachel hadn't heard Ezra's arrival. But before long she'd heard raised voices — at any rate, his — for he was practised in rallying the crowds. From the room above the kitchen she'd understood enough to guess who the visitor was. The notice on the chapel rail had caught her eye when Giles had brought her home; a preaching man was expected here today; she remembered what Dulcie had told her briefly of her years on the circuit with her father. When the kitchen door closed on him she went to her own bedroom window and watched him leave, then went down.

'Can you go up and keep an eye on Johnny for me, Sally? He may settle all right, but lift him if he has wind.' That the girl was upset was obvious but Rachel pretended not to notice it.

So Sally escaped. 'Johnny you darling' did more to wipe away the image of the scene downstairs than all the explanations could have.

By now Dulcie was seated by the kitchen table, for once her hands idle in front of her.

'Why can't you talk to me, Dulcie? Surely you know I'm your friend.' Rachel pulled a chair to sit near her.

'He's been here. My father. Did you hear him ranting?'

'He's the visiting preacher next door? Yes, I heard him — and quite a lot of what he said. But it's not him, it's what *you* say that matters to me. Dulcie, is it serious between you and Albert?'

'What do you know about us?'

'I believe you're in love with him. And Albert?'

Dulcie turned to look directly at her. This was no woman bowed down by guilt, there was an inner glow shining in her eyes. 'Oh yes. For months he's been trying to find a way of breaking it to his wife. It's so difficult, he knew she'd be hurt, she has no one else, you see. But it seems she knows already, there's nothing more to tell her. Anyway, surely it's kinder in the end to be honest than let her believe a lie. Nothing can come between us, Albert and me.'

'He'll not be a free man. Do you care for him enough for that?'

'As if that matters! As things have been we've had no more than stolen hours together, meeting outside the village, careful never to be seen. Or sometimes he'd come to my home, but we'd have to listen in case Toby came home. It wouldn't be fair to Albert if people guessed, not even Toby. Now everything will be different. What the world says won't touch us, we'll be together.'

Listening to her, seeing her radiance as she talked about Albert, Rachel envied her. Giles had proposed marriage, a marriage that would make no demands, would give a home to her and to Johnny. Dulcie would have no marriage, but she would have what mattered. 'I must stand on my own two feet,' Rachel had said. Oh, but what would that matter, what would anything matter if one could find whatever it was her lonely heart craved?

'Will your father come back here when he leaves the chapel?'

Dulcie shrugged. 'I shouldn't think so. He believes he's right, he's so sure there can be no way to heaven except his way.' It was as if she pleaded for Rachel's understanding, as if she owed at least that much loyalty to the preacher with his threats of hellfire.

'And for him I don't expect there can be.'

'But for us?' Dulcie needed reassurance.

'I suppose we all trust what our conscience tells us, to each of us that has to be the right way. We think we try to keep to the rules; but often enough we bend them, find excuses.'

'He'd say there can be no excuse for what I've done.'

'And you'd say the excuse is in showing Albert the meaning of a true love.'

'That's right.' Dulcie looked at Rachel, undecided whether or not to say any more. Rachel waited. Then: 'You see, Albert's had a dreadful time. It was before he met the Hardings. His father got into financial trouble, lost nearly everything at the gambling tables. What should have been Albert's was gone. Then he met Mr. Harding, got on well with him; Mr. Harding was obviously quick to recognise Albert's use to the business, he's so clever. I don't know the business side of it, not all the details, but he's told me how Elizabeth's father persuaded him to marry her. He wanted Albert in the firm, I suppose, and, as a sort of bribe, he gave them part of the firm when they married. You remember that's when it became Harding and Ross.'

'Gave it to Elizabeth, do you mean?' For Rachel remembered that interview when she'd told them she wanted to sell the share John had left to her. There had been no doubt of the sway Elizabeth held.

'To Albert, I imagine. Anyway that can make no difference now. You know they sold out when you did.'

Rachel had had no liking for Elizabeth but for all that it was impossible not to feel pity for her. They'd never talked of Mr. Harding, but she'd been conscious of Elizabeth's affection for him, her pride in the firm he'd built up. Yet Albert had sold it − or persuaded her to sell it. And now he was to cast her aside too. Had she set out on marriage with hopes and dreams, or had she known Albert's prize hadn't been her so much as a hold on the business?

'" . . . with some skivvy," she said. 'That's what she called me. A skivvy!'

Rachel concentrated on what Dulcie was telling her, until now she'd not known that Ezra Tresize hadn't been the day's first visitor.

'Put it all behind you. Go home early, Dulcie, now, before Sally comes back down.'

'Yes, I think I will.' Dulcie had already made up her mind that this wasn't the time to make a bid for Sally's understanding. 'He may come for me this evening. When she faces him with it he won't go on living under the same roof. I can't believe it's really happening, it's been a distant "one day" for so long. "One day", "this day".'

'Does Toby get on well with him?'

'Toby hardly knows him at all. He's grown up now, isn't he? At sixteen he doesn't need me to mind him. If Albert wants to leave the district — and I'm sure he will — then I shall go. Is that wicked? Haven't I waited years enough?'

'Tell Toby he is always welcome here. If you go I'll have to find someone else, Sally can't do everything. But she'd always have a welcome for Toby, wouldn't she?'

They both stood up and Dulcie took her bonnet off the hook on the door and tied it on, then wrapped her cloak around her.

'I want nothing more than to go with Albert when he's ready, but I shall be sorry to leave you and darling Johnny.'

'Hark, here comes Sally. Off you go.'

And without more than a quick nod, off she went. As she opened the kitchen door they could hear hymn singing from the chapel. Any minute Ezra would start his oration; for an hour or more the congregation would be held in silent awe as he expounded on the frailties and temptations against which they must for ever be on their guard, and the retributions that would come to them if they let the Devil overcome them.

Much later, after Rachel had gone to bed and upstairs the lamps were out, Sally stood outside the kitchen door to listen. She couldn't forget his face, the vein that bulged on his temple, the dreadful things he'd shouted at Dulcie. The truth was that while she dwelt on all that, she didn't have to think of Dulcie's part in it. In the still, dark November night she could hear only the one sound — his voice raised as if by its volume he would imprint his words on the minds of the congregation. She was mesmerised by it, so much so that she didn't notice when the front gate was opened.

'Oh!' Visibly she jumped when a young man appeared only feet away from her in the beam of light thrown by the kitchen lamp.

'Sorry, did I gi' yer a scare? Message here for Mrs. Caldecott, the master says.'

141

'Who's your master?' she wanted to know.

'Mr. Ross, he sent it. Urgent, he says.'

'She's gone home. Do you know where she lives?'

'Ah,' he winked, 'I know where she lives right 'nuff. I'll take 'un on down there then. How's it you're not next door having yer soul saved, eh? Or can you hear 'un well 'nuff from outside?'

'I just came out for a breath of air. I'll be locking the door now. Good night.' She hadn't liked the way he'd grinned when he'd spoken about Dulcie; she hoped her tone had put him in his place!

By midnight a steady rain was falling, fine needles that dropped gently with no breath of wind to promise that the clouds might be blown away. Rain like this usually lasted for hours and morning showed no sign of it easing. The cobblestones rose out of a sea of water, the caves dripped, and the notice that had drawn the crowd to hear Ezra Tresize was a sorry sight, the lettering smudged, the ink running down in blue 'teardrops'. Johnny had been restless in the night, perhaps he'd taken his mood from his mother's, for her mind had jumped from Giles to Dulcie, to Rosalind, to Giles, to Dulcie, to Albert, to Elizabeth, and constantly to John and to Patsy, the even tenor of her yesterday and the challenge of tomorrow. About six o'clock she slipped into a heavy sleep and knew no more until she woke to see Dulcie making a wet and miserable Johnny comfortable enough to face his breakfast.

'Dulcie! It must be late!'

'It's just after nine o'clock, you were in a deep sleep.' From the look of her that was more than Dulcie had had.

'I hardly expected you here at all today.'

'Albert has had to go away on business.' Did she imagine it or was Dulcie avoiding her eyes as she spoke, concentrating on Johnny with just that bit too much show? 'He sent me a note last night. You see, he wouldn't have known about any of it — her coming to see me — my father — he wouldn't have known, would he?' Now she did look up, her huge dark eyes (this morning with shadows under them that told their own tale) seemed to plead with Rachel to support her.

142

'No, she couldn't have told him. Anyway, Dulcie, he wrote to you, he made sure you weren't worried at not seeing him.'

'That's right.' Dulcie smiled. 'And I've been thinking — to be truthful I've spent half the night going over and over it all — it seems to me that just supposing she had told him, that would be the very reason he had to dash away. I mean, he wouldn't just go on as things had been, and he'd need to get his affairs settled before he and I could go away anywhere. That's right. You think that too, don't you?'

'That's right,' Rachel echoed her words. 'You'll hear as soon as he's arranged things. And you don't know how glad I am to find you still here with me.'

'So's Johnny, aren't you, my little love?' And she was rewarded with a dribbly beam, whether at the sight of her or the feeling of a warm dry napkin only he knew.

That was Friday. The weekend came and went; the next week followed ... and the next.

There could be no returning to the old routine at Mulberry Cottage, for there had never been a young baby in the house before. But in the shaping of a new pattern, at least on the surface, memory of Ezra's visit faded. And Rachel was so busy standing on her own two feet and, indeed, learning to walk on them, that she didn't consider the suffering hidden under Dulcie's habitual calm.

It would soon be time for the next Count House meeting, but now that she had 'herself to herself' once more, Rachel wasn't prepared to wait. No need now for a trap, she could sit a horse. Alone in her room she dressed in her riding habit, she actually did the buttons of her skirt up and had room to spare! And if her spirit had needed a boost what better one could she have found than that! The newly built stable smelt of fresh wood, somehow it suited her mood on this day that was to see a new beginning. 'A day at a time,' her father-in-law's voice echoed and she was struck with something like guilt that she could have come so far in these months that she was excited by the next step forward.

'Well, bless my zoul,' Captain Bowen greeted her, 'I heard zay that you were back home in Treddinock.'

'I missed the last meeting, although Mr. Ross sent a message telling me how it went.'

'Mr. Ross, you say? Means to get rid o' part of his shares. He told you, I dare say.'

'No. He said that at the meeting, Captain Bowen?'

'Bless you, no, not a hint of it.' And she knew then just how frightened she'd been for Dulcie. What was Albert meaning to do? The Captain went on: 'I was telling un bout our need for a bigger calciner, and of the lot of them, 'twas Mr. Ross backed me. Now he wants his share to be cut.'

'The calciner was what I wanted to talk to you about. But first, Mr. Ross. When did you hear?'

'Not an hour since. Post brought me this. Here, you read un for yersel'. Going abroad he says — something about his wife.'

She read. Albert and his wife had been staying in Bath. He'd been persuaded that her health would benefit from a warmer climate and they were travelling to Italy to stay indefinitely. Their house was to be closed up. His stake in Treddinock reduced. He ended with the hope that the business could be conducted soon and the address of his solicitor in Redruth who would handle his affairs in his absence.

'I don't believe it . . .' But it wasn't true, she did believe it. It was as though she'd been waiting, expecting it.

'Oh, 'tiz true all right. Wants his capital, I dare say, if they're to set up home in foreign parts.'

'Captain Bowen, I sold out of Harding's too, remember. What money would I need to take the holding Mr. Ross wants to sell? Do your sums — and I'll do mine.'

'Add that to what you got . . . why, Mrs. Treweek, you'd have more than any other adventurer in Treddinock, far and away more.'

She knew now without a doubt the course she had to set. Harding's had been a stepping stone leading her to this. Treddinock village . . . Treddinock mine.

She walked to the window. The whole scene before her was exciting, it fulfilled a primeval urge in her. Massive columns on the stamps, their ever steady rise and fall, rise and fall; a thud that seemed to shake the ground when the iron shoes crushed the ore. Too far away to hear it, yet in her mind she knew just the roar of the engine with its rocking beam that moved the stamps, each at the same pace as the other. Then, beyond that, the lifting gear raising the laden kibbles so that the ore would be tipped into wagons on the elevated tramway and from there to the floor of the stamping house. Everywhere was movement, industry. Just as she had seen it on that day when John had brought her to admire his engine. She'd been struck then by the purposeful way the men — and women, too — went about their work. But then she'd felt herself on the outside, she'd watched without understanding. From one stage to the next the process of dressing the ore fitted into place. It was like one of those jigsaws she'd worked on with the Derwent children, gradually building up a picture, until now it was complete.

Beyone the boundaries of Treddinock there were other mines. She looked out at the whole magnificent panorama: cliffs, engine houses, tall chimneys, each minehead a replica of this, set against the wide expanse of gleaming, empty sea. This was the outward sign of the industry, while under those cliffs, under the sea itself, men battled to wrestle the riches from the ground.

Captain Bowen came to her side. 'There's good tinstuff being brought to grass. But as for copper ...' He shook his head.

'Copper is there. It was there before the landslip, it can't have vanished.'

'With Wheal Dovey in fork we've found nothing but the one narrow seam. I'd stake all I got that that lode weren't worked out when the fall came, yet there's not a sign, not a smell o' it.'

'You mean the investment in John's engine was for nothing?'

'Now, did I say that? Wheal Dovey is sending up good ore. Treddinock is healthy, make no mistake. Here, see the figures I've got out ready for the meeting.'

She went to his table with him and together they leant over the books.

Four thousand eight hundred and fifty tons of tinstuff had been raised; seventy-four tons of black tin sold realising £4016.6s. Labour had cost £2,950.12s., coal £390.10s., carriage £198.7s., stannary assessment £3.19s. There had been two hundred and ten fathoms of tram road laid.

'To me it reads well, Captain Bowen.'

'But we're missing a point. Look out there at the chimney on that calciner.'

'Well?'

'Belching out its fumes, losing 'em in the air.'

'That's really why I came to see you today. Mr. Ross told me that you'd raised the question of a new calciner. I know you must have your reasons, but I didn't understand. What's wrong with that one? Just look at it, smoking away merrily enough.'

'Jes' you let me explain. You're familiar with what goes on on the dressing floors. You know how the ore goes on from being broken in the stamps to be buddled.'

'Yes, I've watched. The waste is washed away — the slimes, isn't it, you call it? And the black tin is left behind.'

'Not quite that simple. First time through the buddle it's not pure black tin, Mrs. Treweek.'

'Oh no, I know that. You explained that to me,' she laughed, 'that was Lesson No. 1, remember?'

'Ah, so you'll remember right enough that amongst that black tin there's iron, arsenic pyrite, maybe even a percentage of copper.'

'And that's when it goes into the calciner. I know. In the burning process it separates, so that when it's buddled the second time the iron — and copper if there is any — can be taken off. Then we're left with pure black tin.'

'Hah, zo there y' have it, Mrs. Treweek, m'dear! Iron and copper, you said it yersel. And what about the arsenic? Where's that got to? Let me tell 'ee where 'tiz. Up that chimney there and gone, lost in the vapour and the smoke. An' you know jes' as well as I do, there's good money to be got for arsenic crystals. Refine it, powder it, then ship it off to the New World. You read your newspaper, you're not the sort to shut yer eye to what's going on in the world. Think on't, Mrs. Treweek. In the cotton growing lands o' North America they're crying out for the arsenic we're wasting on the breeze.' He was in his stride now, and seeing he had her interest he warmed to his subject. 'There it goes, you see it, up that chimney and away. Ours for the taking. And there's something else — it don't jes' come from the good ore. We'd

146

find it in much that's being wasted as things are, in the deads, the rubbishy stuff that gets used to fill up the old shafts, in the poor stuff that as things are we'd find so little tin in we don't bother wi' it at all. But arsenic pyrite is there zure 'nuff, waiting for us, jes' waiting.'

'So why don't we put it through the calciner now?'

'Like I said, m'dear, what goes in is lost up that chimney. Now, let me show you this, let me explain what it is we're wanting. I've got it all drawn out ready for the meeting, try 'em again. See here − five kilns, each one of 'em three foot across. See here, this is the cross-flue, it leads to the main flue. And see here, a zeries,' he checked himself, 'a series of these arched chambers. Sixty-six of 'em there are, openings in the connecting walls.' As he talked he'd got more and more excited. Now, looking at her puzzled expression, he knew he'd left her behind. If he wanted her support he must go at her pace, make sure she understood. Already he'd come to recognise that she'd never give lip service to anything she didn't agree with − but she'd never refuse her backing when she knew he was in the right. 'Y'understand, in this area the scorching mundic and arsenic fumes would have three hundred yards where they'd deposit their crystals as the vapour condensed.' Captain Bowen peered hard at her as if that way she'd better appreciate what she was hearing. 'Three hundred yards! Crystals, deadly white crystals worth gold to us these days. Arsenic is fetching £6.10s. a ton. That's what we're wasting up yon chimney, £6.10s. a ton! Ours for the taking.' He blew out his cheeks, shaking his head at the folly of men, then expelled the air through compressed lips in a high-pitched squeak. 'Well, there 'tiz, Mrs. Treweek, m'dear. Takes money to make money. We'll ha' to see what the meeting has to say.'

She nodded. 'You're quite sure, Captain Bowen, about it being there in the poor stuff, in the deads.'

'Oh ay, I'm sure 'nuff.'

'You'll have my support, that I promise. Now then, Captain, do your sums for me. Tell me what money I need to find to take the whole of Mr. Ross's holding. More than fifty percent share of Treddinock, you say. If I had that, then we could begin to talk of new calciners!'

From her first visit after only one Count House Meeting she and the purser had talked the same language. Now she looked at him, her expression one of exaggerated helplessness, a mischievous twinkle in her gingery eyes. 'Am I mad, Captain?'

'That I can't rightly say, Mrs Treweek, m'dear, but if you are, 'tiz a madness there's no cure for.'

She looked again through the window. The huge wheel of the lifting gear − in her mind she seemed to hear its creak as it turned laboriously, bringing full kibbles up, sending empty ones down; the beam of John's engine, Patsy's nodding giant − its movement constant, day and night. ''Strordinary.' Rachel knew a strange peace. Reason and logic had nothing to do with what she intended, but she had no doubts.

'I feel I'm starting to understand. I do want to, to feel that I'm some use . . .' Not to many people could she have been so honest.

'Don't you worry, Mrs. Treweek, m'dear. There's some o' the Knife and Fork lot, they'll never get the feel o' the place. But with you, 'tiz different. You're a natural.'

She had to stand on her own two feet. Today it seemed she'd started to run.

148

Chapter Eight

The end of year meeting refused investment for a new calciner. Had there been some sign of the promised copper, that would have put a different complexion on things but Captain Bowen believed in telling the truth. In this case Rachel thought he would have done better to keep his thoughts to himself.

'I hate to say it, gentlemen, but 'tiz beginning to look like the lode was nigh on worked out when the land slipped. Tinstuff is good, but as for copper, not a hint of it.'

With nothing to report surely it would have been wiser to do just that, report nothing. But that wasn't Captain Bowen's way. Around the table the adventurers muttered amongst themselves and the one who finally spoke out glowered at the purser as though the recent good fortune at the neighbouring workings of Wheal Vardin were his personal responsibility.

'I hear there's a rich lode being brought out at Wheal Vardin. Not a quarter of a mile from where their sett meets up with Wheal Dovey. You'll be telling us next that when that land moved it gave what was ours to our neighbours.'

'At what level are they finding it?' Rachel asked.

'I'm not that much in the know — just that copper's coming up.'

'It's around the two hundred level,' Captain Bowen told them. 'A diagonal seam, so I'm told, running north west and dipping.'

'Dipping this way. Doesn't that show it must be part of the same seam that we lost!' Rachel was sure. 'And if it is, doesn't it prove to you that it must be only a question of time before we find it again?'

No one answered her. The sound of their silence told her just how much store they put in any thoughts of hers! Wealth so near at hand and here they were with a dividend of only five shillings. After that the calciner didn't stand a chance.

To find the money she needed for the part of Albert Ross's holding he was selling took everything she could raise, everything that had come out of Harding's and out of John's efforts for the company he'd helped back on its feet.

'I must be mad,' she said to Captain Bowen. 'Perhaps it would have been a good thing if we'd found enough copper that the price would have been out of my reach.'

'Seems to me, Mrs. Treweek, m'dear, the copper held off purposely.'

'You mean I've done the right thing?'

'You've done what you had to do. And I'll tell 'ee zumat — I done the same thing myself. Oh, not that many shares, hadn't the gold to do it with. But what I'd got saved — well, like you, I put the lot down that mine. Seemed to me this was the time to do un.'

'Captain Bowen, it's not how much money, it's how much faith you put in that matters.'

'Oh, I've plenty of that, never you fear. If we don't find that copper, there's good tin. And now you hold the king share we'll get that calciner burning, and soon there'll be arsenic too.'

'Pour a glass of something for us, Captain. Today deserves a toast.'

He blew out his cheeks, whistling through tight lips as he poured the Madeira.

'To the copper we both know is there.' She touched his glass with hers.

'We'll drink to it. But who's to say, Mrs. Treweek, that the seam won't get narrower as it comes our way? A wide seam they say in Vardin, but as it comes nor' east it might ha' been thinning down even before the slip came.'

'It might. But there again it might be getting wider. It was Dovey where it was first found.' Today nothing would destroy her optimism. She had no spare capital, she was following a hunch that owed nothing to reason, and yet she'd never felt so certain.

At the Lady Day meeting approval was given for building to start on the calciner. Work commenced mid-way through April. Before autumn came they meant Treddinock to be shipping arsenic.

Through all those months, on the surface time passed smoothly at Mulberry Cottage. It was a strange life for Rachel. There were days when she felt she belonged nowhere, had no one. The villagers had shown her friendship, sympathy, given her help; but they were a close-knit people and she was outside their normal day to day living, her background so different from theirs. All the love that was in her she lavished on Johnny. He was like a safety valve; she needed to nestle him against her, feel the warmth of him. When he opened his mouth in a wide grin she felt weak with the need to respond to him, to draw him into herself. She didn't question the yearning in her, didn't dare to analyse the moods that came and went. Beyond Johnny she wouldn't let herself look.

Almost she might have imagined Giles' offer of marriage, he never referred to it. Yet because of it, something between them had changed. Up until that point their friendship had grown and flourished, but now they were both guarded, careful not to allow emotion to creep into their relationship. Yet without it, even friendship can't grow, becomes stunted. Just as she put Johnny between herself and her need for a physical expression of love, so she and Giles used his children, a wedge that allowed them to be together and yet held them apart.

'Here's the children, Mrs. Treweek, ma'am. Miss Huntley's brought them.' Sally was busy trimming the wick of the lamp on the table by the window but still she managed to have an eye for anything that went on outside.

Mulberry Cottage was almost a second home to the young Derwents these days. A visit no longer called for best clothes.

'The front door isn't bolted,' Rachel called through the open window. 'Let yourselves in.'

'We're off for a picnic. We've called to collect you to come with us.' That was the gist of what they said, but they all spoke at once, Rosalind and the children too.

'We've food enough for a regiment.' This time it was

Rosalind. 'We're going to the shore. And where's my pet?' She was down on her hands and knees by Johnny's side on the carpet. First Peter joined them, then Trudie. It was a game after Johnny's heart; he chortled in that uncontrolled way only babies know how, crawled a few feet, stopped, turned his head and peeped at them, his gingery eyes teasing, begging them to chase him. Another chortle, then off again at a furious rate.

'We'll get you! Here we come!' Part of the fun of the chase was the way they brought their hands down, banging the carpet as they crawled after him, exaggerating the noise and speed too. He shrieked with glee, then his giggles turned to hiccoughs. Swooping him into her arms, Rosalind turned back to Rachel. 'Come on, get your bonnet. It's such a beautiful day. We've brought a big blanket to sit on and towels so that we can paddle.'

Somehow they all wedged into the governess cart, even making room for Sally. Only Dulcie was left at home. Not for the first time recently, Rachel was conscious of a suppressed excitement about Rosalind. She was reminded of that evening by the fireside. She told herself that she didn't want to know — but she had to ask.

'You're very cock a' hoop these days?' By this time they'd tethered the pony on the grassy cliff top and walked, one behind the other, down the steep path to the sandy beach.

'And why not on such a heavenly day? There, Johnny my pet, what do you make of that?' Rosalind set Johnny on the blanket that Rachel spread. He made very little of it, it seemed, for he scurried straight on to the golden sand.

'We've had other heavenly days, as you call them.' Rachel looked at her keenly. Perhaps after all this time Giles had seen that any warmth and love his home had, stemmed from her.

'You're right, of course. Every summer we have days just as lovely.' Rosalind stood upright, very still. 'Don't ask me about it, Rachel. One day I hope I'll be able to tell you, but not yet. It's too new, too fragile. And yet, I do know. I have a deep inner feeling of the way I'm heading.'

'Then I'll just have to wait.' Rachel heard herself laugh, and turned away to catch Johnny who was making a bee-line for the water.

'Oliver is to go off to Rugby in the autumn. It's where Giles went, you know,' Rosalind told her when she carried him back. 'Dear old Mr. Nesbett can't be expected to have the children every day for ever, I think Giles might look for a tutor for them — unless he sends them to Helston to school.'

Dumping Johnny again on the blanket Rachel heard herself answer casually: 'My word, changes ahead at Perleigh House.'

Rosalind nodded. She'd be drawn no further.

They'd all taken off their stockings, and today with her skirt hoisted and tucked into the leg elastic of her drawers, Sally was more child than woman. In and out of the sea the children dabbled, then, together, they all collected driftwood. No picnic was complete without a fire, even on a day like this.

Today should have been magic; to Rosalind it seemed it was. But though Rachel could see the beauty, the happiness around her, it only served to throw her own loneliness into even deeper relief. Changes at Perleigh House ... too fragile yet ... Desperately she clutched at memories of John, but he was as far out of reach as the high, clear sky.

On her own she wandered at the water's edge, the rippled sand firm under her bare feet.

'Mrs. Treweek, come with us, it's warm as anything in the rock pools. We're finding crabs.' Trudie's voice offered her an escape and holding her skirt out of the water she waded through the shallow water, sinking her toes into the soft sand.

'Look at this one. Here, Sally, look at this, what a big 'n. Here, Mrs. Treweek, come over here, come and look!' Peter was jumping with excitement, what did he care that his sailor suit was getting soaked, the sun was warm.

'Peter, there's Father!' Trudie's expression was of near disbelief.

'Doesn't your father usually come?' Rachel probed.

'Gracious, no. Father on a picnic!'

'Come on, Mrs. Treweek, do come and see my crab. He's 'normous.'

So at last Giles had come to appreciate all that Rosalind meant, not just to the children but to him too. When he asked *her* to marry him, that proposal wouldn't be made out of kindness, sympathy, friendship. Following Trudie, she clambered across the slippery rocks towards Peter, her mind far removed from crabs, large or small. The moment had come when she was faced with the truth that she'd been running away from. When did a day pass that she didn't watch out for him — in the village, at the mine, perhaps tying his chestnut mare outside her cottage? Friendship? If that had been what she'd wanted from him would she have refused his offer of marriage so positively? 'If that's all that prevents you accepting, I'd never expect . . .'

'Careful!' Trudie shouted.

But it was too late. Rachel's foot slipped on the green slime. She tried to save herself but the other foot had nowhere firm to step. The jagged rock scraped the skin down the front of her leg. Not a deep cut, but a wide patch that bled profusely. The wound had sand in it, her leg was green with slime from the rock and the blood trickled down to her foot.

'I can't clean it here,' Giles said after examining it. 'I shall take you home.'

'You'll do no such thing! I can tear a strip off my petticoat. That'll wrap it until I can see to it later. It's not deep. There's no need to fuss!'

'Am I fussing?' He raised his brows. 'Leave Johnny with Rosalind, he'll be perfectly safe with her.' As he'd talked he'd been bandaging the leg with a napkin, but this was a makeshift affair. Rachel would have liked to have argued. She knew she must be spoiling their day for them – and the children had said what a rare thing it was for Giles to join them. He'd come to be with them and with Rosalind. She bit hard on the corners of her mouth, determined to keep her lips steady. She'd learnt though that to argue with Giles was useless; she'd tried it before. If he said he was taking her home, then take her home he would.

'Giles is quite right,' Rosalind was saying, 'you must get that beastly dirt out or you'll have a poisoned leg.' How could she smile so warmly? The magic of her day must have gone yet she showed no sign of her disappointment. Rachel was ashamed of her own self-pity, angry and ashamed.

Giles helped her to the saddle, then mounted behind her. His grip was firm, she felt safe and as she leant back his hold tightened. Surely she was entitled to this much? She didn't try

154

to fight, she let herself indulge in the nearness, in his strength. Uninvited came the thought of Rosalind. What must Giles be feeling, having to leave her on the shore? Instinctively she pulled forward, sat straighter.

It was a few weeks after the new calciner had been brought into use that she chanced upon him at the mine. He came to lift her from her saddle as she rode to where he and Captain Bowen stood talking.

'Is there trouble? Or is this just a routine call, Giles?'

'I've come to make a random check of the arsenic processing. We have to be extremely careful, you know.'

'Oh, you won't find anything wrong, will he, Captain? We know it's dangerous stuff to handle, the men always wear hats and gloves,' she said confidently.

'There's more to it than that. That fine dust is deadly.'

'We're *most* careful. Each barrel is lined with paper first, not a single particle could leak out and the men have no cause to handle it.'

'It's in the air, a powder so fine one's hardly aware of it. I'll come back and talk to you when I've had a look. I want to see the men who shovel the crystals, but most of all I'm concerned about the packing sheds.'

'May I come with you? I've not seen them working.'

Just for a second he hesitated. 'You can come as long as you do as I tell you.'

'Yessir,' she laughed.

But this time Giles wasn't playing games. There was no answering twinkle in his eyes. In the outer sheds, where the men donned their working garb, he said: 'We won't be able to speak. You're to plug your nostrils and ears with this, then to make sure that you don't inhale any dust you're to push some into your mouth and breathe through it.'

He passed her a wad of cotton wool then, without waiting for her to argue, took another wad from his bag to use himself. Next he checked that her boots were high enough to protect her ankles and her sleeves pulled over the cuffs of her gloves, before leading the way into the packing shed, the end of the line for the arsenic workers. Here the full barrels had been stacked ready to be taken to the railway station where

155

they would be transported in a closed wagon; the empty ones were waiting, already paper lined, their lids secured, with only a bung hole in the top where the powder would be poured in through a funnel. Question after question came to Rachel's tongue and there hit upon the protective cotton wool and remained unasked. Giles said not a word. How could he, gagged as surely as she was herself! The men who were shovelling the fine powder into the funnels had their noses plugged, they breathed through the filter of cotton wool and were rendered equally speechless.

Giles led the way through the arsenic refinery. Even with cotton wool up her nose Rachel found the smell revolting, reminding her of the wild garlic that grew in the hedgerows. And how hot it was! The kilns gave out great heat, and difficulty in breathing had the effect of making the temperature seem even higher than it was. They went through a long, narrow building, where along the length of one side was a series of openings out of which men were shovelling the snow-white arsenic crystals, the end result of the vapour condensing in the labyrinth of brick built chambers. Even here, where the material was so much coarser, dust hung in the air. There was something sinister about it. Involuntarily Rachel shivered. The deadly poison seemed a far cry from tin and copper, the reason for the mine's existence.

From there they went on to the washroom where Giles pulled off his gloves, then took his cotton wool filters and threw them into a bucket that appeared to be used for that purpose.

'Open wide,' he said, and with relief Rachel took a gulp of fresh air.

'That's better!'

'You mustn't lick your lips. Here,' he ladled water into a bowl, 'wash your face, especially around your mouth and eyes.' Then, sharing the bowl, he did the same.

'Giles, what a dreadful way to have to work! You feel you're choking with that stuff filling your mouth. And it was so hot!'

'It's that that concerns me.'

'We had more clothes on, I suppose, but imagine being there all day. You found it dreadfully hot too?'

'They must be made to understand how important it is to wash, frequently I mean.'

'You mean the heat's bad for their health? Underground it must be far worse — in the eighties in the lower levels.'

'It isn't just the heat, that wouldn't matter if it weren't for the arsenic. That's the danger. If they perspire, the dust gets into their pores. I must make Captain Bowen impress on them that they need to keep their skin clean at all times, avoid sweating — if not, there could be serious skin problems.'

'I hadn't realised. I knew the stuff was poisonous but I hadn't realised it was like that to work.'

'We're new to it here in Treddinock. I've been visiting one or two refineries, looking at the safety standards, seeing how they protect their men. I've talked with other mine surgeons.'

They might have been business acquaintances, nothing more. Not for the first time in his presence over these last months, Rachel was conscious of a feeling of disappointment.

'How are the children? Rosalind hasn't brought them to see us lately.' She asked it purposely, a reminder that Rosalind and the children were part of his world, the 'us' at Mulberry Cottage, hers.

'She's been spending money like water. Oliver is off to school at the end of next week, and the others begin their new classes in Helston on Monday.'

She nodded. 'And is Oliver still looking forward to it?' She might have been the children's maiden aunt, interested but restrained. What had happened to the easy flow of conversation they used to know?

'Yes, and ready for it. The rigours of a boys' school will be a new life for him, but the rough and tumble won't do him any harm. It's not good for a boy to be cosseted and protected.' Then, with an indulgent laugh: 'But it would be no use expecting Rosalind to understand that.'

'And you'd have her no different.'

'Rosalind could never be any different.' His tone had altered. He hesitated as if he were turning something over in his mind, undecided whether to say more. As she waited Rachel gave all her concentration — and more — to re-pinning her hat. Then he went on: 'Although, over these last months —'

'Ah, so that's where 'tiz you are,' Captain Bowen's voice interrupted as he appeared in the doorway, casting a long shadow in the bright afternoon sunlight.

So Giles was cut short. But she needed no telling what had happened over these last months. Hadn't she seen it for herself time and again, felt the repressed excitement in Rosalind? She and Giles would marry, and how pleased the children would be. The hat pin had found a will of its own and gave her an excuse to hold back from the men as they discussed the refinery. Giles was explaining to the purser, just as a few minutes ago he had to her, that problems could come if the dust got into open pores of the skin. He said he intended to visit the mine next day prior to the beginning of each core, to spend a few minutes talking to the men before they started work. It was easier to prevent damage than to cure it.

Rachel walked away to stand by the open doorway. What sort of a creature had she become that she could feel so dispirited at the thought of another woman's happiness?

Together the three of them walked back towards the Captain's office, but Giles didn't come in.

'Already I've been longer than I'd intended. I'll be here early tomorrow morning.'

'Tell Rosalind to come and see me soon,' Rachel called after him as he went to meet the lad who was bringing his mare to him. He assured her that he would pass on her message, climbed into the saddle, lifted his tall silk hat in salute to them, then rode away.

'Now then, m'dear, let's go and look at the books, see the figures I've been getting out for the meeting.' For it was almost Michaelmas.

Resolutely Rachel collected her wits and pushed Giles from her mind. The atmosphere of the purser's office never failed to restore her when her spirits flagged. The pile of old ledgers on a table in the corner, the lamp hanging over the wooden table where he worked. The very smell of the place was its own; she could close her eyes and know exactly where she was. And in the background the constant sound of work outside, the dull thud of the stamps. She had never been underground – she was ashamed to admit even to herself the horror the thought of it held for her. A day seldom went by when the

Captain didn't go below and because she was so familiar with his surroundings here and because he talked to her of 'levels', 'shafts', 'adits' as part of his normal conversation, she felt she had an understanding.

She was aware now that he was looking at her keenly. There was very little escaped him.

'Tell me then, Captain, are we going to afford to be able to eat this next quarter?' Metaphorically she rolled up her sleeves. The mine was her life, she'd made it so. And more than that, it was her bread and butter — hers and Johnny's too.

The Captain made his mood match hers. 'Reckon you'll manage your goose for Christmas. Can't say it'll be the one that lays the golden egg, but things could be a lot worse. We're still managing to pay a dividend and that's more than can be said for many a mine.'

'The world is becoming so small, isn't it? Steamships make foreign trade so easy. Tin gets shipped here all the way from Australia — and we see mine after mine being closed down because the imports have brought our prices so low. And what do we do? We send our arsenic all the way to America to help our budget.'

'Ah, times change right 'nuff. Even some of the old smelting houses are having to make way for big companies. I'd not have believed it if someone had told me two decades or so ago when first I came to Treddinock, that ore would be brought in by boat to Cornwall from Bolivia, be smelted here, because not enough is brought to grass from our native ground to keep the smelting houses in business.'

'But that's not true with us. Our output is as high as —'

'Ah, I tell 'ee, Treddinock's health is good. But for all that, with tin at today's prices 'tiz copper we want.'

'And it's copper we shall find, never doubt it.'

They were interrupted by a pounding on the door.

'You there, Cap'n?' And in burst a wet and be-grimed miner, clad in his underground clothes and hard hat with the candle on the front still burning. 'Where's the doctor? They told me he was here.'

'Left about five minutes ago.' Instinctively Captain Bowen reached for his own hard hat that hung on the back of the door. 'Send the lad from the stable after him, let him take my horse. Doctor'll be down in the village. Then come back and tell me what's the trouble.'

The message was passed and in no time they heard the horse being ridden hard towards the lane that led down to the village. Then the miner came back.

'It's young Dougie Philips. Not got used to the ladders yet, he missed his footing on the last stage to the two hundred foot. Says he can't feel what he's done, doesn't seem to have pain so much as he's shaken up — but I reckon he's hurt himself all right, can't move his legs, nor sit up. We'll have to give him a lift to grass in the kibble. But we can't touch him till the doctor's had a look at him. I'd best get back down. I'll take a strip of canvas and some poles to carry the lad on.'

Within minutes they heard Giles arrive but he didn't waste time coming to speak to the Captain. Instead he went straight to the drying sheds where the men changed from their own clothes into the working drill suits and hard hats they wore below ground. 'Drying room', because when their daily core ended they came back to surface wet through with a combination of sweat and moisture from the walls and roof of the mine. Here, their working clothes were hung until next day.

From the open doorway of the purser's office they saw Giles emerge a minute or two later, looking neither to left nor right. Dressed as any of the miners except for his bag which he'd slung on his back, he looked a very different man from the one who'd doffed his silk hat to them little more than a quarter of an hour before. And yet, watching him, Rachel felt she saw further into him than ever she could with the public face. He looked expressionlessly in her direction and she was sure he purposely avoided meeting her gaze. To look at him now was to remember the evening when he'd come to her after the accident in which Sally had lost her father; how he'd shaken as he'd drunk the 'medicinal' brandy she'd poured for him.

'Giles — ' She ran towards the head of the shaft, but he gave no indication that he'd heard. Then he was gone from sight into the entrance of the dim incline where he'd step on to the platform of the Man Engine.

All this time the work of the mine went on.

'Sorry about the lad.' Captain Bowen blew out his cheeks, giving vent to his feelings in that long high-pitched squeak through closed lips. 'Bad business. His father works down there, and his grandfather too. Young Dougie only started underground last week, when he had his thirteenth birthday and was old enough.'

Rachel let her gaze wander over the scene that had become so familiar, men and women hurrying about their work ... and down there, deep in the ground, lay a child, his childhood over. Next week Oliver was to go off to Rugby. Two boys, the same age. In that moment she came near to hating Treddinock — not up here where the industry was under God's high sky, but below in the bowels of the earth. She tried to imagine what it must be like. For all that Captain Bowen talked to her of the work that went on down there, it was something in the way Giles approached the Man Engine Shaft, his pace never slowing, his expression giving nothing away, that brought home to her the dread she'd never admitted, even to herself.

Almost two hours went by before the kibble was hauled up bringing Giles, Arnie Philips and, strapped securely to the improvised canvas stretcher, his son Dougie. By this time the boy had lost consciousness. He knew nothing of being shifted from the kibble to the floor of a wagon for the bumpy ride to the Infirmary.

Someone had been to the village to fetch his mother, and one after another neighbours and friends had come to join her in her wait.

''Twas a bad fall, Mary, young Dougie's hurt,' Arnie told his wife. His voice was low and level, everyone who heard knew that he was understating the injury. 'The doctor says we're to ride with them to the Infirmary.'

Mary Philips was a tall, powerfully built woman. All her life she'd been a worker — and a fighter too — for those she cared for. Looking at the pale, still form of her son she was helpless, she could do nothing but obey the doctor's word. She'd never been the sort to find relief in tears. Now she glowered at those who stood by, she had to hit at someone.

'Learn a lesson from our Dougie — keep your boys out of that hell-hole. An extra one and sixpence a week, that's what Dougie was to get. Was to! Hasn't had so much as a week's

161

work and look at him! Jes' look at him!' Her wild-eyed glare rested on Rachel. 'Well, he'll not go down there again, that I promise you.' But even in her despair, she didn't guess the truth of it.

'Come along, Mary,' Giles took her arm, 'you sit where he can see you. If he wakes, it'll be you he'll need.' His voice was gentle, so different from hers.

Rachel was ashamed to be within earshot, watching. She'd not gone home because she'd wanted to know the boy was safely raised to surface, that's what she told Captain Bowen. There was more to it than that, though. It had to do with the way Giles had walked towards the shaft head. The other people gathered there were friends of the Philips', she was an outsider – a curious bystander to their misery. She felt degraded. Giles didn't look her way at all, he probably didn't even notice she was still there as he helped Mary into the wagon and climbed in after her.

That afternoon (by now it was evening and at home they'd be wondering where she was) had shown her a new side to Treddinock, a harsh side, experienced by the men who worked the arsenic and those who risked limb and health underground. She was in a despondent mood as she rode home.

She looked ahead to the Michaelmas meeting next week, imagined the adventurers, all hopeful for a good dividend, greedy for more. The lesson she'd learnt this afternoon had to be thought about. There was more to being an adventurer than worrying about how many shillings the dividend would be. A seed had been sown in her mind. It was too soon yet for her to know what would grow from it, but it was there, and once planted the root would take hold.

Once the children started lessons in Helston and Oliver was settled at Rugby, Rosalind got back into the habit of dropping in at Mulberry Cottage. Johnny's excitement at the sight of her was a great pull. No announcement came of an engagement, no confidences either; and yet her bubble of happiness held. Of course she'd known Giles for years, she must understand him and recognise the signs of his affection. And anyway, Rachel chided herself, why should it matter one

162

way or the other? What interest could she possibly have, herself, in a man content to let month after month drift by when the woman he supposedly loved (if, indeed, he was capable of it!) was patently eager?

She and Giles had been friends, never anything more than that. She wondered now if she'd ever really known him at all. Not so long ago it had been a natural and important part of her days to watch for him in the village, to look forward to his visits. Now she instinctively avoided him as she spent more and more time at the mine. Here she knew she was welcome; Captain Bowen was her friend and her mentor.

So through the months of autumn and winter Oliver adjusted to the rigours of public school and Dougie Philips to the restriction of life in a bath chair, for the Infirmary had been able to do no more than Giles had to help him.

It was Dulcie who told Rachel about the chair.

'Dr. Derwent gave it to him, actually bought it for him from his own pocket. Mary said so herself so I know it's true.'

'Dougie's just Oliver's age, you know.' Somehow Rachel was glad to know that Giles' mind must have followed the same track as her own, made the same comparisons.

The gift of a wheelchair was better than no wheelchair at all for a boy who would never walk. But independence is sweet. The roots of that seed sown the day of his fall took hold more firmly.

When Rachel arrived at the Count House for the Lady Day meeting there was already a hum of conversation, a pale mist of tobacco smoke drifting towards the high ceiling, and smells of the dinner that was to follow wafting on a cloud of steam from the kitchens. By now the scene was familiar to her, just as her presence was to them. There were those who, because she was a woman, would never accept her; there were others who welcomed her for the very same reason. Neither way was what she wanted. She strived to earn respect for her business acumen. But, for all that, she always took particular pains over her appearance for these meetings. One can fight one's corner with more confidence while looking one's best!

'So there y'are, Mrs. Treweek ...' Captain Bowen never failed to watch out for her and make sure she was brought into the otherwise all-male circle. But today she didn't even notice his greeting.

'Rachel, I've put my chair next to yours.' It was a year and a half since she'd seen him yet he spoke as though it were yesterday and he'd never been away. Albert Ross, as elegant as ever and surely even more handsome. 'I'm told you're an important personage here these days,' his eyes shone with teasing laughter, 'and me, I'm no more than a Knife and Forker.'

'I'd no idea you were back. How is Mrs. Ross?' And silently, although she was sure he 'heard' the question: 'Have you seen Dulcie?'

'I shall be here for a while at any rate. I may stay, I may go back. Elizabeth died last month.'

'Albert, I'm sorry. I didn't know — about her being ill, I mean. I thought you went . . .' She wished she could learn to think before she spoke!

'Her health has been poor since she was a child. I didn't imagine sunshine would bring her a cure. In fact she found it very trying on the Adriatic coast.' His tone conjured up a picture of Elizabeth, her view on life as jaundiced as ever — as well it might have been! 'The end was very sudden. So I've come back. There are things to see to, business to be settled. One has to make a life — I don't have to tell you that.'

Captain Bowen rose to his feet. The quarterly meeting started. He made his report, read out the figures that Rachel already knew, and was able to declare a dividend of six shillings. Not a fortune, but these days even the most hard-nosed adventurer realised he must be thankful that no call was made on his capital.

Opposite Rachel sat Mr. Nankerwin, regularly to be relied on to raise a note of discord.

'And what about the profit we were promised for our investment in that calciner? Smoking its head off out there! And whose money is going up in its stinking smoke? Ours! Where's the profit, just tell me that.' His blue eyes stood out like organ stops.

Albert leant towards Rachel to whisper in her ear: 'I see friend "Bluster" hasn't lost his touch.'

She kept her head down to hide her smile. It was good to

have him back, he'd always been her ally at these meetings.

'If it hadn't been for the arsenic, gentlemen, there'd scarce be a dividend. 'Tiz that that's keeping us afloat wi' the price of tin down to £50 a ton.'

'Tin! Arsenic! Was copper we'd expected, and before this too.'

Token rumbles of discontent; the Captain musn't be given to think they were satisfied too easily. But they mostly had the wisdom to know that it was his good husbandry that made even a six shilling dividend possible in these days.

'Now, gentlemen, may I offer you a glass of my punch?' His sign that the business of the meeting was concluded.

Rachel was surprised when she took her leave to find that Albert did the same.

'You're not staying?'

'I'll ride with you if I may.'

'I'd be delighted.' She was thinking of Dulcie, just as she was when she added: 'If you're not rushing off somewhere else, why don't you come back and eat lunch at the cottage?' Out of the corner of her eye she watched to see the effect of her invitation.

'Now that's much more my idea of pleasure than the gorging they were getting ready for back there. Tell me, is the lovely Mrs. Caldecott still with you?'

'Thank goodness, yes, she is. She'll find herself lonely when Toby goes. He's off to college soon.' That should give him something to ponder on.

When they reached the cottage she led the way into the sitting-room, then left him on the pretext of taking her hat and coat upstairs.

'Dulcie,' quietly she closed the door of the kitchen behind her as she went in, 'can you stretch lunch for an extra? There's someone here ...' She paused, uncertain what Dulcie's reaction would be.

Whatever she expected it certainly wasn't what she heard.

'I know. I saw from your bedroom window when I was taking Johnny up for his rest.' Dulcie's voice was controlled. Albert might have been nothing more than the most casual visitor. 'An extra, Sally. Will you go and set a second place.'

When they were alone Rachel tried again. 'He's come back

165

– things to see to, he said. Dulcie, his wife died last –'

'I heard. Word travels fast in the village, I've known for days.' She looked hard at Rachel, seeming to weigh her words before she went on: 'If someone steals from your house, you aren't going to invite him in a second time.'

'I must go back.' Rachel felt piqued on Albert's behalf by Dulcie's lack of interest. Of course, it was no more than he deserved and yet as they ate their lunch it was impossible not to enjoy his company. How long since she'd laughed, finding humour in simple everyday things, laughing not because they were uproariously funny but because of the light-hearted mood that held them both.

When he left she walked with him to the gate. It was almost the end of March, the early spring sunshine full of promise.

'If I were a cat, I'd purr,' she murmured. She might have forgotten he was there, been speaking her thoughts aloud as she held her face towards the sun, her eyes closed. Unprepared for the brief touch of his mouth against hers, her eyes shot open. But already he was standing straight, his hand reaching to take hers in parting. Almost she might have imagined it. Almost? She wasn't even sure that she hadn't, yet that twinkle in his eyes must be telling her something.

'I want to see that son of yours, you know. I shall come again, if you'll let me.'

She was surprised just how much she looked forward to it. He made her feel carefree, attractive, young; he made her want to look around the next corner even though she had no idea what it was she hoped to find there.

Chapter Nine

Even before he'd gone away to school, Oliver had considered himself too adult to make a habit of being brought to Mulberry Cottage with Rosalind and the two younger children. But, for all that, he wanted to see Rachel; he was sure she'd be a receptive audience for his tales of adventure in his new all-male environment. The Easter holidays had begun to drag, his pony could do with the exercise, he'd ride into Treddinock and call at the cottage.

She was gardening when he arrived.

'May I come and help you? I've tied Cinders up by the side of the stable.'

Rachel got up from her knees. 'If you've nothing more exciting to do, I'd like that. There's plenty to occupy you here. I've been tidying up the edges of the grass.'

'You'd never think this place was just scorched earth eighteen months ago. You've worked wonders.' Every now and then his voice took a dip, landed somewhere between his knees and ankles, then jumped back into place again.

'Last year it was dreadful, the plants were all new and tiny and the birds seemed to think the grass seed was there for their pleasure. But it's shaping up. Did you come on your own?'

'Yes. Rosalind's got things on her mind,' he chuckled at the thought, 'she must have told you all about it. If I use these clippers I'll start the other end, shall I, and work towards you?'

'She hasn't told me anything. But she seems very pleased with life these days.'

'The infants keep their eyes open. Trudie says Rosalind's in

167

love.' He giggled, child enough still to have presumed that at her vast age of twenty-nine she would have known better!

'She deserves to be happy. And your father does too.'

He gave her a curious look then mumbled something which she took to be his agreement. 'Anyway,' he didn't slow his vigorous clipping, 'she hasn't told us anything. Perhaps it's having me at home that puts her in such a jolly mood! Actually I'll be quite glad when term starts. Did I tell you ...?' And he launched on a series of anecdotes of life at school. He always liked talking to Rachel. She treated him as an equal, realised he wasn't a child like the other two.

'Funny, isn't it,' he said presently, 'here we are, scratching away at the surface — yet do you ever wonder what's down below you? Are there any deep workings from the mine in this direction? Perhaps there are seams of ore no one's found yet way down below this very spot.'

Rachel sat back on her heels. 'It's exciting, isn't it, Oliver! There's something about wresting mineral wealth from the ground ... and yet this is something I've known and yet never put into words, I'm ashamed to hear myself say it but it's the truth — the idea of going down there, wet, dark, airless — even talking about it gives me a tingling feeling from sheer fear.'

'You'll never have to, that's one sure thing. In any case, women — even working women — aren't allowed to be taken on for underground labour, are they?'

'What are you going to do with your life, I wonder, Oliver? Have you any thoughts yet? A doctor perhaps like your father.'

'No, not for me. I suppose Father's not paying my school fees so that I end up down the mine, or even managing a mine. But it's fascinating — exciting too. I'll probably be a mining engineer or a metallurgist. Something connected with the industry anyway. Isn't it funny how different we all are? I was thinking of what you just said about going below ground; Father has never told me so, but I'm sure he hates it too. I've been with him sometimes when he's been called down. He doesn't say a word, but I'm sure I'm right. Now the thought of going underground, the narrow tunnels, the rocks all around, the structure of the earth, *I* find it exhilarating. Yet when it comes down to it neither of us has tried it. We may both be wrong, you and me.'

'Well, as far as I'm concerned, I've no intention of finding out!'

They went back to their work, an easy silence between them. He was growing up well, this eldest son of Giles'. Johnny was let out into the sunshine to come staggering, feet wide apart, across the grass. A slow mode of travel, using hands as well, doubled the speed; two hands, two feet and knees bent, he made a bee-line for Oliver. For a while the grass edging was forgotten. Oliver, who wanted to be looked on as an adult, had infinite patience as he and the little boy pushed a soft ball backwards and forwards to one another. Yes, Giles must be proud, the very gentleness was proof of a new confidence.

Later, when Oliver led Cinders out from the side gate, Rachel walked with him along the track to Fore Street. They both stood still, listening. The sound of a horse being ridden so hard down the hill from the mine boded no good; it probably meant someone was looking for the doctor. But it was Albert who came into view at the bottom of the hill and crossed to them.

'I went up to talk to Bowen — was there when the news broke. Copper! Bowen's gone down to inspect. They were driving an end to the northeast on the two hundred level.' His voice changed to a remarkably true copy of the locals: 'Ne' 'er zeen the like, gurt nuggets o' native copper.'

'We must be there when the Captain gets back to surface.' Rachel looked up to him, sitting above them in his saddle. Her face was alive with excitement, her eyes bright. Albert watched her; not that she noticed. Copper! So they'd been right to have faith! It was seldom that John came close to her, but in that moment he did. The Treweek engine, the biggest engine Treddinock had invested in, keeping Wheal Dovey in fork. John had had trust in the engine and in Wheal Dovey too.

'We'll ride up together,' Albert agreed, and to his credit didn't protest when she suggested Oliver should come too. For this was the sort of thing the boy's dreams were made of, it was right he should be there at Treddinock's moment of glory.

At the mine head men who'd come up from the morning core still hung about, not wanting to go home until the Captain brought word that this find was all that was rumoured.

'No doubt on't. I zeen the colours — reds, greens, black, bronze — never ha' set my eyes on a lode wi' the promise o' this one.' Those who waited were grouped around the man who spoke, the man who'd brought tidings to the Captain, for he had actually seen the find. Again and again they pressed him to tell them, his words varying but never his message. Whether they were tributers or tut-workers, copper meant extra money for any of them who worked it.

'I heard it was where they were blasting in an end to the northeast. How much could you actually see? Were you in the end? Are you sure the lode is wide?' Rachel wanted to know.

'That's where the blasting was, ma'am, but you could see plenty once the dust had settled. Not just the three who were in the end. The roof fell, seemed to crack and fall away right from the seam itself.'

'And no one was hurt?'

'Reckon Tom Hawkes got his leg broken. Doctor's down there seeing to him. Nothing that won't mend — by the time they get the roof shored up, he'll be hobbling about.'

By his side stood a tall, thin man with stooping shoulders and a long, thin face that looked as though it didn't know how to laugh.

'May be but a broken leg,' he spoke for the first time, his words falling into sudden silence, a confirmation of superstition and misguided religious fervour, 'but 'tiz a token and we should heed it.' Not knowing why, Rachel felt a cold shiver run down her spine. 'Remember the time when the seam were lost to us? Plenty of men hurt then — some mortally hurt. That should have been warning enough to have lasted. 'Tiz the knockers decide where we should take the riches.' He started to cough, the familiar, hollow cough of the miners, then cleared his throat and spat on the ground, looking hard at Rachel and Albert. 'Jes' try telling that to the men who sit round the table wi' Cap'n, you tell them o' the folly of not heeding the knockers.' He might have said 'men' but she knew she was included.

She didn't want to listen to him, but she had to ask.

'What are the knockers?'

'You think you know Treddinock, and you ask that! If you went down there quiet, on your own, especially at night-time, that's when you'd hear them. Then you'd know, then you'd see why we should heed what they tell us. Spirits. That's who they are. Part o' the very mine itself, trapped there these many years. There are those who say they're the ghosts of the Jews who crucified our Lord, got sent here to be slaves to the Romans and worked down the mines. After what they'd done no wonder their spirits can't get free of purgatory. Ah, they know things we mortals can't tell. 'Twas the knockers moved the earth back in '80 when the land slipped and we lost that seam o' copper — then again today. Jes' a broken leg, you say, and ain't that reason enough to show us 'tiz time we let well alone. I been down there plenty of times and heard them. Ain't that zo?'

The silence was almost tangible. The men looked uncomfortable, but no one had the courage to dispute his word. There was no reason in what he said, but what has that to do with superstition? Was it the same with all the men who worked below ground, did they all pin their faith to anything so illogical?

'Hark, the kibble's coming. Must be Tom Hawkes.'

On its clanking chain the great bucket came into view from the shafthead to be raised beyond and above them and come to rest at a platform by the upper storey of the stamp sheds. She saw Giles climb out first. To be honest she saw only Giles and looking at him she remembered what Oliver had told her about being sure his father hated going into the mine; she remembered too the way he had walked towards the Man Engine shaft the day Dougie had been hurt. Yes, he hated it, he dreaded it — but he did it. Looking down at the waiting group he saw her too, and he saw Albert Ross standing close, his hand on her shoulder as if to protect her in the mêlée. Then he turned away.

'I'm not waiting for Captain Bowen,' Rachel told Albert. Never before had she wanted just to get away from the mine.

'I'll stay here and go home with Father,' Oliver called to her. There had been a time when she would have waited for him too, have found sanity and confidence in being with him. She felt Albert take her elbow and steer her through the jostle of men.

'You musn't take any notice of the rubbish they fill their minds with,' he said once they were out of ear-shot. She was surprised that he'd felt the undercurrents and had known what she was running away from. For of course that *was* all she ran from. Yet her eyes wouldn't obey her, they turned again to the platform — and, timed to the second, Giles looked down at her.

'Come away,' Albert piloted her forward. 'You look quite pale. Let's ride along the cliffs, get some clean air.'

'Albert, do they all think like that?'

He shrugged. 'Superstition plays a big part in their lives. They're uneducated men, they look for signs, "tokens" they call them, something bigger than themselves.'

'But he talked of the Jews, the men who crucified the Lord, being sent here. How could they believe that, how could they know?'

'There were Jews brought to Cornwall, that's true enough. They were slaves to the Romans, working the smelting houses. You've heard of a place round the coast called Marazion. "Bitterness of the Jews", that's what the name means.'

'And they build their superstitions on that?'

'Men will build superstition on anything. A smattering of truth and there's no stopping them.' Then he laughed. 'Of course, if we had a ha'porth of wits we'd play their own game, spread some good omens down at the two hundred level to give them confidence.'

'I'm serious, Albert. There was something sinister about it. They truly don't believe we control our own destinies.'

'And do we, I wonder?'

'Whether we do or not, no ghost from the Roman age is going to tell me what to do with my life.' There was a swagger in her voice.

'One thing I'll vouch. When they hear what there is to be earned bringing that copper to grass, their wives won't listen to talk of warnings from the "knockers".' Albert laughed.

She was determined to put the incident at the mine head behind her — and neither would she let herself think of Giles.

172

He'd watched her walk away, Albert holding her arm. And she was glad.

Only later, lying alone in the darkness of night, did she face the truth. He may have watched but it wouldn't have mattered to him. Why should it? Even the children knew where the romance between him and his faithful Rosalind was heading, albeit slowly!

As Dulcie had said, news travelled fast in the village. Before nightfall there wasn't one who'd not heard of the exposed seam of copper ore. And something else too — it was already evident that Albert was to be proved correct. Womenfolk who'd never heard the sound of silence nor the unaccountable bumps and creaks their men listened for down in the deep workings in the wee, small hours, had less faith in 'tokens'. Copper meant extra shillings coming into the house, new shoes for the children, enough oil in the lamps to light upstairs as well as down. And against the power of the wives what chance had the 'knockers' of being heeded?

'I rode out there with Albert, you know.' Rachel watched for Dulcie's reaction next morning.

But she watched in vain. It was as if he'd never been more than a stranger to her. Rachel might have imagined that brief spell when Dulcie had opened her heart.

The seam was strong and wide. Treddinock trembled on the brink of 'copper fever'. Even before Captain Bowen showed her the written report from the assayer, Rachel heard in the kitchen of Mulberry Cottage the wealth of the ore.

'We took various samples,' Toby brought the good news, 'so it wasn't just a lucky streak. Upwards of twenty percent copper. That's high, very high. Most ore in this region hasn't yielded more than twelve percent copper.' Such a serious young man was Toby. Sally gazed at him in open admiration for his learning. Already as far as she was concerned he was as able as any master Assayer.

Rachel remembered Dulcie's anxiety about them; by now she'd come to know both of them well enough to understand her reason for it. Sally hung on his words now, but would she still when she'd tasted life for herself? Toby was the sort whose loyalty would never waver. Before long he would go away to college; for years he'd saved for it and now Mr. Dowty was helping him. His course was plain before him, he had no doubts: college, back to Treddinock a qualified assistant to work with Mr. Dowty, marriage to his Sally, and perhaps one of these days in the distant future to replace Mr. Dowty as Master Assayer. So simple, nothing to stop everything going to plan. The only unknown was whether the woman Sally would want what the child Sally had chosen. Somehow Rachel doubted it. Small, eager to please, gentle — yet there was a restlessness in the elfin creature.

Up at the mine Captain Bowen had made another trip down to the two hundred level, this time to decide what timbers must be brought in, huge timbers that must support walls and roof. The only ore to be taken before these were in place was that that had been sent to Mr. Dowty. It would be weeks yet before the first kibble of copper ore would be raised.

Oliver had been looking forward to the start of his new term, in a way he still was. But watching the great pieces of wood being eased down the shafts, each one bringing them that much closer to gaining the copper, he felt he was seeing history unfurling. By the time he came home again that hidden wealth would be being brought out.

He had a lot to learn of the uncertainties of mining; so too had Rachel.

Through all the time since that icy winter's afternoon more than two years ago when the thaw had come to Whems Pond, there had been one ghost Rachel hadn't had the courage to face. Not once had she been back to Manns Wood. Today she'd been shopping in Helston and, driving home alone, as she passed it she saw how the sun glinted between the trees, highlighting the carpet of bluebells. For a moment she drew to a halt; the silent wood seemed to call to her. To be frightened to remember that last afternoon was robbing her of so much else. She could never hold on to all that had been happy if she was afraid to hold on to everything. There was no dividing line between then and now, then and what was still to come. There musn't be.

With a flick of the reins she started forward and drove the rest of the way at a brisk trot. She'd go back there this very day, before her courage failed her, and she'd take Johnny with her. She couldn't carry Patsy and John with her into tomorrow unless Johnny was allowed to be part of her memories of yesterday.

So, that afternoon she pushed her young son to the outskirts of the wood, parked his perambulator by the side of the track and lifted him out. His head was uncovered, his carroty curls vivid. A tall boy for not quite twenty months, yet with much of the baby still about him.

'— ook, — ook!' He held his head right back to gaze straight upwards at the sky through branches where new leaves were starting to show the first promise that summer would soon be here. Then, as if looking weren't enough, he stretched both arms high. '— ook, up. — ook.' He laughed delightedly, showing two rows of milk teeth.

She stood quite still. Everything was quiet, no sound but the call of the birds rejoicing in spring. Then a whisper of breeze through the branches. There had been another day, these same trees heavy with snow, the wood shrouded in silence. Patsy's first awareness of a beauty beyond her understanding. 'Magic,' she'd said.

'— ook, — ook.' Rachel held Johnny close, her face buried against his curls. He wasn't aware of what the moment meant to her, but Johnny always enjoyed a cuddle so he wrapped his arms tight around her.

Now she could go on, down the track until the pond came into view.

'We'll bring a boat another day, Johnny. Patsy's boat. You'd like to sail her boat.'

He had no idea what she was promising him but, his hand firmly held in hers, he made his uncertain way along the water's edge.

Today they stood on a strip of coarse grass. That day it had been covered with slushy snow, churned up by the rival gangs who'd been snowballing. Sally and Toby, children then, neither of them children any longer. At their ages two years saw great changes. And for her? What changes for her? It must have been somewhere by this very spot where she stood now that Giles had come to her. She closed her eyes, even now she wasn't strong enough to re-live the anguish of that hour.

Without him what would have become of her? He'd been her strength, her lifeline, her sanity. And afterwards, for months as their friendship had grown. A sob caught in her throat and she felt hot tears on her face.

Something tugged her skirt. She looked down at Johnny, her hand still tightly gripping his; she tried to hold her face stiff in an effort to control herself.

'Up ... up me.' His gingery eyes pleaded. How could a chap make his mother feel happy when he was right down here, so far away!

She dropped to her knees and held him close. The last time she'd given way to such a paroxysm of crying as she did now had been the night Giles had let himself into the cottage. Again it had been Giles.

'Johnny ... don't know what to do ... love him ... all the time ... right from then ... just kind to me ... that's all it was, Johnny ... kind to me because I had no one.'

This time it was Johnny who helped her find her grip, although he didn't know it. He was upset and frightened; in his baby world grown-ups didn't cry. Too young to reason, he wanted just to make this person he loved happy. So he squeezed her. But all his hugs and squeezes were getting him nowhere.

'Uggh.' He wriggled away from her, planting his feet wide. 'Uggh,' he whined. And a wet nappy did more for her than any dose of sympathy. She blew her nose, wiped her face, straightened her hat and picked him up.

Today was a day for echoes. She seemed to hear Hewlett Treweek's: 'One step at a time.' How long since she'd consciously built her days around his words? Walking back to the perambulator, Johnny in her arms, she thought about the step she'd just taken. Just for a second she stopped, looking around her at this place she'd come to so often. What can there be to fear in any memory of those you've loved, those who've loved you? None. Sadness that they're gone? No, even that wasn't true. They weren't gone, they'd never be gone, not from her. John, who had loved Patsy above all else; Patsy whose life had been snuffed out before it had been tainted with living.

She walked on again. She'd come here because of John and

Patsy. And in taking that step she'd stumbled upon Giles. He belonged to Rosalind, even if it had taken him a long time to realise it. Rosalind had loved him for years, he'd accepted her love and all the care she'd lavished on them, it was no more than justice that at last he should have come to value her as she deserved. Rachel knew it was her own fault he'd stopped coming to the cottage. Frightened of her own feelings, she'd put a distance between them. On the occasions they'd met they were pleasantly amiable. But where was the man she'd turned to in her unhappiness and, not meaning to, fallen in love with?

Johnny was wet, cross and grizzly as she pushed the perambulator as fast as she could back towards the village. She knew her eyes were bloodshot, her eyelids stiff and swollen, her hair a mess. The last thing she wanted was a visitor, but outside the cottage was a pony and trap. Like salt rubbed into her wound she recognised it; the visitor was Rosalind.

'I'll just run upstairs with my things and see to Johnny,' she called from the passageway as she came in through the front door.

'Let me take un for you, Mrs. Treweek. Miss Huntley's come to see you. She's in the kitchen talking to Dulcie till you got back. I'll tell 'un you've come.' Sally lifted Johnny into her arms. 'What a wet boy! Yes you are! Who's my sodden boy, then?' By now he'd forgotton his fit of the miseries and was beaming his pleasure. Whatever he'd done, it seemed to be earning him Sally's admiration. 'Slip your hat and coat off, Mrs. Treweek. I can carry them up at the same time if you lay 'em on my arm.'

Rosalind came out of the kitchen just at that second. The passageway was always gloomy and for that Rachel was glad but there was no escape. She led the way into the sitting-room. Following her, Rosalind closed the door behind them.

'Rachel, except for Giles, no one knows. I've been just bursting to tell someone. I thought you'd never get home!'

'I took Johnny to Whems Pond,' Rachel said. It was no use, she couldn't keep her back turned forever; so round she came, her face set in a bright smile. 'Tell me, indeed! Do you think I don't know? Rosalind, I'm so pleased, so happy for you, both of you.'

'But how could you know? I've never mentioned it. I was so afraid all my dreams would turn out to be made of cobwebs.'

'Ages ago you told me, when I was staying at the house. Don't you remember? And in any case, how could you have cared for his children like you do if — '

'*His* children! What ever have you been imagining?' She giggled. Only on a day so full of excitement could Rosalind giggle. 'You've thought I was in love with Giles! Oh, Rachel, how could you have!'

'But you told me so. You said he was your hero right back when you were no more than a child, when Anna first knew him.'

'And so he was. He was so grown-up and dashing. But can you imagine Giles — the Giles of today — wanting that sort of emotion in his life? When he was younger, when Anna was alive, he was so different. Dear, kind, sombre Giles; he's as reliable as the days of the week. But to be honest, Rachel, he does worry me. He seems to have forgotten how to laugh. I shall hate leaving the children. He means to take a house-keeper, but they need more than that. One blessing, though, he wants me to find someone I consider suitable. It'll save him the trouble and I honestly don't think he cares. I'll have to be sure it's someone who'll bring a smile to the house. It's the best I can do — but it's not enough.'

'Never mind about Giles. Tell me about yourself.' Rachel sat with her back to the window, hoping to hide the ravages of her afternoon. 'If it's not him, then who is this Romeo who's swept you off your feet behind our backs?'

'Oh, but it wasn't a bit like that. He's Hamish McGregor, the Reverend Hamish McGregor, he's just been given the parish of St. Mary's in Pentreath on the far side of Truro. His induction was last week, but I didn't go. We thought it better, because of the Bishop — '

'Slow down, I'm getting lost.' Rachel laughed. 'What has the Bishop got to do with it? There's no rule that the Rector of Pentreath can't have a wife, surely!'

'No, it's not that. Hamish used to be a curate quite near Helston. That was ages ago, ten years and more. I met him when I was staying with Anna one summer. We saw a lot of each other, we were really good friends, Hamish and I — but there was no thought of anything more than that.' Again she giggled. 'I'm not saying I didn't think of it, but we both knew that he was about to set off for East Africa doing missionary work. It was just one glorious summer holiday, I never even expected to see him again. It was chance that I met him in Helston one day last year.' Her disinterest in anything except herself was giving Rachel confidence. She still sat with her back to the light but she was less conscious of the tell-tale eyelids.

'That must have been in the spring. Before the picnic?' She turned her head towards Rosalind. 'You remember that day on the shore when Giles came, the day I hurt my leg — before that?'

'I don't remember when that was. But I know exactly when I met Hamish again. It was the 8th May, Furry Day. I took the children to Helston like I always do, they joined in the dance — and suddenly, just as if he'd never been away, there he was.'

'But why didn't you say? What was so secret?'

'I did mention it to Giles, but he'd forgotten him. I couldn't tell anyone else, not even you. To me it was so important, how could I say "I bumped into an old acquaintance" when seeing him mattered so much?'

'But all this time ...'

'I know this sounds horrid ... when you meet him you'll know he's not the sort willingly to hurt anyone. You see, he'd been home from Africa for more than a year, he was only a curate still, in the north of the diocese. He'd heard that the elderly incumbent of Pentreath would soon be leaving; it's a lovely village, he says, not just lovely to look at, but the right size so that he'll know everyone there. Then he met the Bishop who had a niece living with him.' Only for a second did she hesitate. 'When I met him he was engaged to her, you see. But we knew, even after that one morning we knew. Is it so wrong of us, Rachel? Ought he to have gone ahead and married her, feeling as he does?'

'There's only one proper reason for marriage. Doing the honourable thing is no basis for it. Friendship, kindness, even they're not enough. You might learn to run smoothly on two parallel tracks, like the lines of a railway, but that's not what a proper marriage should be. Like grafting a cutting on to a plant – the wedding is just the beginning. It's the growing together that counts.'

'Oh, Rachel.' Rosalind looked at her friend and saw now what she ought to have seen before. With a swift, spontaneous movement she was across the room and on her knees in front of her. 'Here I am, prattling on ... Whems Pond, you said. You've been to Whems Pond on your own.'

'No. Johnny and I went together.'

'I would have come, you know I would. I do wish you'd told me you were going.' She was ashamed that she could have so much to look forward to and Rachel so little.

'If you want to cheer me up, tell me your plans. And tell me when I'm to be allowed to meet Hamish.'

Rosalind sat back on her heels. With so much to tell it was hard to know where to begin. So she took up the story at the end.

'Hamish was given the parish of Pentreath, his induction service was last week.'

'And the girl he was engaged to? The Bishop's niece?'

'He didn't make up any stories, he said he must be honest with her. I had a letter from him this morning. He'd visited her, told her all about me. Truly, we've wrestled with it.' She spoke so earnestly, she might be twenty-nine but there was much of the child in Rosalind still. Certainly too much for Rachel to suggest it might have been more honest if he'd told her months ago and risked the Bishop's anger.

It was later, Rosalind was just leaving, when she referred again to Giles.

'I suppose when one's circumstances alter, so do one's hopes. I know Giles would never look for a romantic sort of relationship. But I was thinking of what you said – about running smoothly on parallel lines. But now, for him, a companion, someone really to take an interest in the children, share things in a caring way – how much better that would be for all of them.'

'Find them a housekeeper you think fits the bill. If she could be pretty too, who knows what might follow!'

'Giles wouldn't notice a pretty woman if he fell over one. But I'm serious. It's the one cloud for me, leaving them all.

180

He must know it's what the children need — not just some person to look after them for a wage.'

Oh yes, he knew it. The twin devils Mistrust and Self-pity nudged Rachel's memory.

Yet, after Rosalind had gone, she sat on her own, her mind adjusting itself to a new view of things at Perleigh House. Rosalind must be right; she'd watched the change in Giles over the years. A just man, fair-minded, autocratic, reserved, he'd expect unquestioning obedience from family and patients alike. She let her mind wander back to the day he'd asked her to marry him. 'Think about it,' he'd said, 'at least promise me you'll do that.' An unpaid housekeeper, someone to give the children the permanence of a mother. The offer had been made partly for that, partly for Johnny. What other reason could there have been? He'd made no more reference to it, he seemed to have shied away from her company as much as she had from his. And yet ... and yet ... a shared supper in the kitchen ... his hand reaching out to hers when she'd told him of the first flutter of Johnny's life ... the grip of his hands on her arms as he'd supported her, weak from weeks in bed ... supported her then and so many times. She remembered his mask-like expression as he'd walked towards the shaft head; Giles would allow himself no quarter. Kind, reliable, wasn't that what Rosalind had said? Love, that sort of love, was over for him, she'd said that too. And yet ...

May the eighth, the day Helston celebrated the victory of light over darkness, the return of life after the death of winter, the beginning of summer. It may have been based on pre-Christian rites, but the passing of the centuries had done nothing to diminish the festival. Each year that Rosalind had been looking after the children she'd driven the governess cart to town, first of all so that they could watch, then as they grew bigger so that they could join the long serpent of young dancers, the boys dressed in their best and bedecked with sprigs of lily-of-the-valley, the girls in white with wreaths of lily-of-the-valley in their hair. On the day of the Floral Dance, or Furry Day as they called it, the grown-ups wore their finery to welcome spring. On this special morning it was easy to get up early, while dawn still coloured the sky.

181

This year for the first time Oliver wouldn't be with them and it was Rosalind's suggestion that Rachel should drive with them in the cart, and why not Sally and Toby too? Mr. Dowty would give Toby the time and a day like this should be enjoyed by the young people.

At Mulberry Cottage there was a small patch of lilies in the front garden, by the stumps of the trees, and before it was quite light Rachel was out there picking them to make the sprays.

'There!' She stood back to admire the effect of Sally's on the shoulder of her dress. 'We ought to make Saint Michael proud.'

'Have we to put our cloaks on? Musn't squash 'em.'

'Sally Pendleton! The very idea! Today we let vanity keep us warm. As if we could herald the season of light with our winter cloaks rolled up under the seat of the cart!'

Dulcie and Toby arrived, she to look after Johnny, he to escort his pretty Sally on this day of holiday. Even Johnny was downstairs, beaming his delight in the excitement around him. Scowls might well follow later when he realised that an early start meant an early rest and he found himself back in bed by mid-morning. For now, though, he crowed with pleasure as he and Dulcie waved them away, Toby in his Sunday suit, Sally in a cream dress with a frill round the hem (a good thing she was slow to grow, for it was still her 'best' even though she'd had it since Dulcie had made it to try and cheer her up soon after she'd lost her father), and Rachel in a soft shade of light green, a symbol of the season they heralded.

In Helston the dancers were already assembling although the day was so young. By the time they'd taken the governess cart to the yard of the coachhouse and handed over sixpence to the lad who'd look after the pony for them, the hands on the Guildhall clock were moving through the last few minutes towards seven o'clock.

'You'll have to run, you two. The band's all ready.' Trudie gave Sally a push. But she needed no prompting as, her hand in Toby's, she darted off towards the throng of young people. The first dance of the day was for the 'lasses and lads'. From where the others watched they saw Sally and Toby get into line, faces alive with excitement. On Guildhall the clock's hands pointed to the magic hour, seven o'clock. Boom ... boom ... Twice the big bass drum thundered. Then, they were off! Da da de da da da — even watching from the roadside it was impossible to stop one's toes tapping. The band led the way up Menage Street, the serpent of dancers followed.

'Just look at Sally! How she dances!'

They weren't the only ones to watch her as the long trail of lads and lasses went by. She was part of the rhythm, not possibly could she have made a wrong movement. It was as if the music and the mood possessed her. To Toby the joy was to be dancing with her; to her the joy was simply to be dancing.

Next it was the children's turn. Da da de da da da ... Musicians of Helston with trombones, cornets, all of them blew out their cheeks swelling the sound. Everyone knew the tune. Their fathers and grandfathers had known it. They'd never seen it on a printed music sheet, but that was all part of the wonder of their day. It was something inherited from yesterday, they were handing it into tomorrow. Their tune. From oldest to youngest, this was their tune, their dance, their day. But into it they welcomed those who'd ridden in to join the fun, those like Rachel's party and the Derwents — and halfway through the morning a fresh-faced young man wearing black, relieved only by a clerical collar.

It must have been because all this time Rachel had believed Rosalind's admiration to be centred on Giles, a man so different, that Hamish came as a surprise. He must be older than he looked, he'd been a curate more than ten years ago, but about him was the innocence of a fun-seeking child. In the throng of merry-makers there was no serious talk, just the occasional question and answer, a short remark here, a laughing rejoinder there. That was the sort of day it was. And yet because it was all thrown into the atmosphere of carnival they came nearer in an hour than they would have in a day of polite drawing-room conversation.

The main dance of the day was at noon. Ladies and gentlemen, the local hierarchy, professional people, county folk, the men in their tallest silk hats, the ladies in their prettiest gowns. The same tune, the same rhythm, yet this time it would be slower, even the bass drum wouldn't destroy its dignity. Already couples were lining up for it with about six minutes to go before the clock chimed the hour, noon and the sun at its highest. Rosalind, her hand on Hamish's arm, was heading for the steps of the Guildhall.

'I'm in time to lead you into the dance.'

Rachel turned in surprise to see Albert just behind her. 'How did you know we were here?'

'I was in Treddinock, I saw Dulcie – the lovely Mrs. Caldecott. Madam,' taking off his tall grey topper he gave her an exaggerated bow, 'will you honour me with the dance?' For a man so recently widowed he sounded in festive mood.

The rhythm had set Rachel's feet tapping from the first drum beat, now she faced him eagerly. Surely he must be quite the handsomest man in Helston and certainly the most debonair, his silk hat the highest.

'This is my first Furry, I don't know the step.'

'You'll find no better teacher this side of the Tamar. It's a stately affair, none of the skipping and jumping you've seen so far. Our procession moves with fitting dignity.' But his expression mocked his words.

The highlight of the afternoon's entertainment was the play, when the mummers acted the age-old tale of Saint Michael slaying the Dragon. Trudie and Peter wriggled their way to sit on the ground at the front of the crowd, determined to hiss and cheer even louder this year than they had last. Sally would like to have done the same. She was pulled two ways, half wanting to join the children and half rejoicing in the fact that she'd moved on to the next stage with new and exciting temptations beckoning.

'Do you really want to see the mummers?' Albert kept his hand on Rachel's shoulder as the crowd jostled and pushed for position. 'Come on, leave Toby to see Sally home. They'll have more fun on their own anyway – and I promise you, so shall we. Let's go and look at the springtime we're here to welcome.'

She felt that only now was she getting to know him; and yet they'd sat side by side at the Count House Meetings often enough, he'd always been her ally there. He'd treated her

184

fairly over Harding's; he'd guided her first steps at the mine. But a silent voice reminded her: John had never respected him. 'Good with finance,' he'd granted, but as a man she'd always known that Albert had fallen short. Then there had been the way he'd treated Dulcie − or was it the way he'd treated Elizabeth? Mentally Rachel shrugged. Her eyes were wide open. In her he'd find he'd met his match.

She willingly agreed to Albert's suggestion. The day took an unexpected turn, and what could be better than that when the sun is shining and the countryside new and fresh? Settling by his side on the bench of the trap John's words still came back to her: 'Talents relate to success with the ladies.' No doubt of that! But what sort of man would John have admired? Giles? Yes, of course he would, and so he should. Good, reliable, calm, unchanging ... was that Giles she meant or John himself? John and Giles: purposely she bracketed them together. She held her face up towards the warm, spring sunshine; the pony trotted briskly taking them on the Penzance road out of town.

'Did you mind coming away?' Albert asked presently. 'You weren't disappointed at not seeing the play?'

'What a funny question,' she laughed. 'If I'd minded I wouldn't have come, would I? There'll be other years for the play. I like things just to happen − like this did. Where are we going?'

'To be honest I've no idea. Just that if it's the coming of spring we're heralding, then the country is surely the place to do it.' He turned to look at her. 'Although it's a sin to waste you on the sheep and the birds when you look so delightful.'

'It seems I'm not being wasted.'

'Indeed you're not.'

After a while they came to a high point where the view was spread out before them, a place that begged passers-by to stop.

'I remember when I met your husband,' Albert drew the pony to a halt as he spoke. 'I don't believe he'd thought of coming into the firm at Harding's until that day. Didn't think much of me, you know. A hanger-on, no good to the company.'

'He respected your advice about the mine. He put all he could get together into Treddinock.'

'Ah, Treddinock. Pity I sold out as much as I did, now that that elusive copper has been found. I lost faith — and I wanted my capital for something that would pay me a better dividend.'

She smiled. 'I don't doubt that. John said you were wise about investment — no engineer but a good man for finance.'

'And which pays better, eh?'

'They each depend on the other.'

Another silence.

'There was another occasion too.' Albert seemed to be in a reminiscent mood. 'You, shrouded in your widow's weeds, facing all those strangers at your first meeting. A remarkable woman, I remember calling you that. And you are, Rachel, truly remarkable. With your drive and my cunning we'd make an unbeatable team.' He bent a little nearer as he spoke, not attempting to touch her but somehow accentuating what he said. The heady smell of lily-of-the-valley was strong.

'I don't know about *my* drive, I think it's about time *you* drove.' She laughed his remark away, wondering where his cunning was aimed at leading her. She had the measure of him. The cunning wasn't all his.

He didn't keep her out late, in fact she was home long before Sally. The early morning 'serpent' danced again at five o'clock and it wasn't much later than that that Albert deposited Rachel at the cottage, declining her invitation that he might come in. By the time the party of revellers were wending their way back up the hill to collect their governess cart, Rachel's spray of lilies was already in water on the kitchen windowsill.

'Albert came to join us,' she told Dulcie.

'Yes, I know. He called here and I told him where he'd find you.' Her voice gave nothing away.

'Dulcie — ?' Rachel started. But she wasn't given a chance.

'Johnny had a good sleep this morning after being up so early. I put him down before ten and he didn't wake for his dinner until nearly two o'clock. If there isn't anything else you want me for, I'll get home soon. I did nothing at all before we came out this morning.'

It sounded reasonable enough. For all of them the day had started before the night had finished.

It was later, she'd just put Johnny to bed in the little nursery and was coming back through her own bedroom. The sound of someone riding down the road made her glance casually out of the window. Recognising Albert she wasn't surprised, she'd seen him going that way before. A piece of the puzzle she'd not been sure about slotted into place. Watching him disappear down Fore Street, knowing just where he was heading and the game he was playing, understanding why Dulcie had wanted to be away in good time, all these things brought home to her the truth of her own feelings. Albert might be setting the rules, but he'd find that she could play the game quite as well as he could.

Her lips twitched into a ghost of a smile as he disappeared from view.

The Count House meeting at the end of June showed great promise but not profit. A dividend of only eight shillings was paid. It had taken money to get the level ready to be worked. As he always did, Captain Bowen broke the bad news before the good, so today he ended by telling the adventurers what Rachel knew already, that the assayer's report showed the samples of ore to have had a copper content of twenty percent. This boded well for the future.

'Tomorrow! Always tomorrow!' Daniel Nankerwin's reaction was predictable, but this time he grumbled alone. There could be no doubt that this year the Michaelmas dividend would be worth having. They'd waited so long, what was another three months!

And through those months of summer the haul started to come to the surface, it was everything they'd hoped for. The lode had been struck to the northeast of an end being worked on the two hundred level, but it was in a northwesterly direction that the seam ran, under the bed of the ocean. And where the seam led, so the tributers would follow. Treddinock wasn't the only mine on that coast to take its wealth from under the sea.

'This disease we suffer from,' Rachel said to Captain Bowen, 'it's a fever, a raging fever.'

He watched her affectionately as she read the report he'd prepared for the Michaelmas meeting. He'd taught many a

187

Treddinock man his craft and not one had been more eager to learn that she was.

'Those figures should meet with even Mr. Nankerwin's approval.' He rubbed his hands together with satisfaction.

'Oh, never! I don't believe it.' She laughed. 'He'll find something, you see if he doesn't. I'll see you on Thursday for the meeting but not before, Captain. You know there's to be a wedding.'

'Ah, the young lady from the doctor's home. You'll be going, of course.'

'Yes. I'm what is called a Matron of Honour — it sounds like a maiden aunt, doesn't it? I'll look forward to the meeting.'

'This time I'll have no call to soften 'em up wi' the punch bowl.'

That was on Monday afternoon. The morning core had come to grass, changed out of their wet underground clothes, but seemed in no hurry to go home. As Rachel rode out she saw them gathering together, waiting. But for what? For some unaccountable reason she was uneasy.

'Wait for me, we'll ride down together.'

She recognised Giles' voice and turned to see him astride his chestnut mare hurrying after her. The men were forgotten.

Chapter Ten

Rosalind had done her best for the children. She'd found a Miss Grimshaw, a woman of about forty, plain of face, but with a gentle humour and a kind heart. Her build was 'average', by which it might be implied that it was something to be covered with the clothes she wore and yet gave no hint of anything as intimate as a body beneath them. And Rosalind hoped that she'd done her best for Giles too!

'How is Miss Grimshaw settling in? Have the children taken to her?' It was the first time for weeks that Rachel and Giles had been alone together. She clutched at the first thing that came to mind to make conversation.

'I've not heard of any trouble. Rosalind thought her suitable. She interviewed five or six, I believe.'

Rachel had met Miss Grimshaw only very briefly but it did occur to her now, in view of Rosalind's hopes, that the applicants must have been a singularly plain lot!

'I hope Trudie and Peter will still come to see me when Rosalind's gone. Surely they're big enough to ride along on their own now, they manage their ponies well and what possible harm could they come to? Johnny loves it when they're there.'

Between them hung his offer that the children should be brought up as one family. In all this time they'd neither referred to it until now, when Giles answered her.

'If things could have been different there needn't have been a Miss Grimshaw.'

'Miss Grimshaw, Mrs. Treweek, Mrs. Derwent . . . No, Giles, with or without a wedding ring, I don't see me as Rosalind's replacement.'

'You know very well Rosalind didn't come into it.' His mouth was set in a firm line.

'I'm sorry, that was a horrid, shrewish thing for me to say. I know you suggested it out of kindness.' Then, taking all her courage in her hands: 'We used to be friends, proper friends. What happened to us, Giles?'

'I spoilt it. But of course we're friends.'

'No, it wasn't just you who spoilt it. It was me too. I was so anxious to prove myself.'

At that he smiled. 'Well, you've certainly done that. Our friend Captain Bowen thinks you're worth the rest of them put together.'

'Captain Bowen has been a real friend.' A bad choice of words, she realised it as soon as she'd spoken.

'*Touché.*' But this time he laughed.

She felt light-hearted, as if a burden had been taken from her.

'Come in and see Johnny, you've not called at the cottage for ages,' she invited. By now they were at the foot of the hill, almost into Fore Street. He might have given a different answer, but they both recognised the black horse tethered outside. Albert Ross was waiting for her, or so Giles supposed. Only Rachel wondered: where had he called, to the back door or the front? She'd never know.

Giles made his excuses and turned towards the village and she rode down the side lane to the stable. It took a minute or two to unsaddle Dancer, then she went through the back door to the kitchen, only to find it empty. She heard the front door close and Dulcie come back down the passage, humming softly.

'Oh! You did give me a start! I didn't hear you come home.' Was there just a little too much surprise in her tone? 'I wonder if we might be in time to call him back — Albert Ross was here to see you.'

'Never mind, Dulcie. He knew I said I'd be at the mine.'

This afternoon it would take far more than Albert Ross and his games to bruise her new found glow of well-being. 'Of course we're friends . . .' And if friendship was all he had to give, that she must take and be thankful.

'Here comes Sally with Johnny. I asked her to walk over the

190

hill to Mentreith Farm. We needed eggs and a fowl.'

This cunning that Albert had spoken of, it seemed they all had their share of it. A walk to Mentreith Farm and back must have taken Sally two hours or more, and on an afternoon when Rachel had said she'd be busy with Captain Bowen.

More than ten years ago Hamish had fallen in love with the exquisite fair-haired girl he'd met in Helston. Now she was nearly thirty, but the same innocence and purity radiated from her. When he turned to see her walking towards him up the aisle on Giles' arm, he would willingly have considered the world well lost for her — the world and even the Bishop! She was attended by Trudie and Peter and, behind them, dressed in a crinoline gown of deep rose, came Rachel.

The familiar words ... the vows ... the grafting of the plant. Rachel moved through it as in a dream. She daren't let her eyes rest on Giles, yet she couldn't keep them away. The service was long, the Reverend Hamish McGregor wanted to begin married life by sharing Nuptial Mass with his bride. So Rachel and Giles found themselves side by side kneeling in front of the altar. It was all too much to be absorbed in these short moments, yet she knew it was indelibly printed on her memory, a feeling of peace, a sense of union. Coming from the church she walked by his side, her arm linked with his.

The hour had been too crowded with emotion, she couldn't take any more. She felt she was being hurtled forward and had no power to stop herself, not even to slow down. She wanted just to get away, frightened to think where she was heading. The solemn service was followed by the wedding breakfast at Perleigh House. For Rosalind and Hamish the excitement, the tension and emotion, would build up, they'd be hurtled forward too. But for them would come the release they'd find in each other.

Rachel and Giles drove back to the house in the same carriage, sharing it with Trudie, Peter, and Rosalind's widowed mother. How would it have been if they'd been alone, no one else to hide behind? How could one follow what had gone before? At the reception she was too cowardly to try. She talked to the guests, Rosalind's relatives and Hamish's, she spent some time with Miss Grimshaw. She helped Rosalind to change into her travelling suit. And then it was over. Still only four o'clock but the bride and groom had gone, and some of the guests were leaving.

'I'll take you back to Treddinock.' Giles must have known she'd been holding a distance between them.

'No, honestly, there's no need. It's broad daylight, I have my trap. You have house guests.' She threw in one reason after another, then ended: 'Let me drive home alone, Giles. I'd rather. I can't say why.'

He nodded.

Her eyes filled with tears; she musn't blink or he'd notice. Not tears of sadness, but so much emotion had to find an outlet somewhere. She lowered her head and pretended to fiddle with something at her cuff.

'It was a wedding we shan't forget.' His voice was level, it told her nothing.

She didn't dare look at him. 'I'll get my cloak.' One blessing — she may have tears stinging her eyes but there was no hint of them in her voice. Thankfully she escaped.

He was her friend, her true, faithful, special friend. Over and over she told herself that as she drove home.

Captain Bowen was already in his place when she arrived for the meeting. Her warm smile of greeting received only a nod in reply then, looking somewhere between her and the ceiling, he gave vent to his feelings in his customary way, cheeks bulging, lips compressed. Something was wrong. She knew him too well to misread the signs.

'Gentlemen,' as the hands of the clock moved to the hour of eleven he got to his feet, 'this is the meeting you'll have been waiting for. Copper ore is being brought to grass. 'Tiz too soon yet for a full quarter's copper out of the two hundred level, you'll understand me, gentlemen, but already we've sold near one hundred tons o' the ore — and that's but the beginning. Signs do bode us well in that direction. Already it has credited us £942.15s. And another thing I'm able to tell you — a slight rally in the price o' black tin, risen it has to £81 a ton this quarter, and we've sold sixty-seven ton 4½ cwt., giving us a yield of £5,223. Labour has stayed steady at £3002.8s. Arsenic has brought us £396 — and that figure,

192

gentlemen, is more than the £382 we've spent out on coal. So you'll see how the benefits from that new calciner have more than covered the cost of powering our other workings.'

Satisfaction. All around her Rachel was aware of it. To her there was nothing new in the figures, she'd heard them already. Yet, still there was something in the purser's manner that worried her. It was evident there was more to come.

''Tiz my custom, gentlemen, as well you know, to give you any bad tidings first — get them to one side afore we come to the good. This time I knew what it was you'd come to hear, the results of the new lode on the two hundred. So that's the way I've told it. But now we come to another matter, one which ain't so straightforward as profits and losses, one that could have grave consequences if we handle it badly.'

Rachel watched him intently. They all did.

'There's a feeling of disrest amongst the men. I've felt it for some months, but 'tiz only now things ha' come to a head. Was on Monday, late in the afternoon. The men thrashed out their grievances and one o' them, Arnie Philips by name, been here all his days and his father before him, he came to me with their discontent.'

Monday! Hadn't she seen it, felt it amongst that group of men gathering silently?

'Money! They think we're getting rich, that's what's behind this. Is that it?' This time the spokesman wasn't Daniel Nankerwin, it was the florid-faced man who regularly took his place on Rachel's left — and took his share of dripping from the cooking pot in the kitchen too!

'In a manner o' speaking 'tiz money, you might say, but not as simple as that. With more wealth coming to grass the tributers aim to make more, the tut-workers too. A good dividend for you, gentlemen, means better pickings for them that work below ground too. It's those who can't work, those who are sick, those who get no share of this new wealth we're all looking to. That's where trouble lies.'

'If they don't work for it, man, what do they expect?' Daniel Nankerwin's eyes shot open wide as he glared along the table. 'Think we're one o' these new-fangled philanthropic societies, is that it? Well? Speak up, man, speak up.'

'Gentlemen,' the purser ignored his outburst, 'I've taken

the liberty of inviting Dr. Derwent to speak to you. Not until now, of course, now that the business side of the meeting is done. And while I go and tell him we're ready for him, may I offer you a glass of refreshment?'

The punch was passed, the ripples of unease spread, each man bolstering himself by asserting that the workers had no cause for complaint ... many a mine was closing down, best they remember that before they ask for more ... the future of Treddinock looked good.

'Like children who've been called in from their play,' Rachel whispered to Albert, 'just when they were having such a lovely time.'

'You can see now why Friend Bowen works the other way round, bad tidings first and then the sweetener.'

Captain Bowen had already come back in through the door directly behind Rachel, ushering Giles ahead of him.

'Gentlemen, this is Dr. Derwent.'

Like petty thieves caught red-handed, the men were silent, sentences half finished.

Taking his place next to Captain Bowen at the head of the table Giles addressed them.

'Mrs. Treweek, gentlemen, I have no doubt that your meeting today has given you reason for satisfaction, but before I say anything else I want you to understand that that is *not* why I have been asked to put the miners' case to you at this particular time. The injuries I deal with from this mine could be sustained at any level, deep workings or shallow.

'However, I do believe that one particular accident which occurred some months back exacerbated the feeling of grievance; it didn't cause it, it was there already. Like a wound it's been festering in men's minds. Some of you may remember the accident I'm referring to,' and here he looked directly at Rachel, 'a boy of thirteen, thirteen years and five days, with less than a full week's work behind him. Unused to the vertical ladders, he slipped. A boy of thirteen with his back broken, no feeling in his body below his chest, no control of bowel or bladder.'

At this some of the men tut-tutted, not out of sympathy so much as disapproving that he could speak of such things, especially in the presence of a lady.

'Lower him into a tub of boiling water, his skin would be scalded, he'd feel nothing. A legacy of the mine to last him as long as he lives! Some of you will have sons of your own. I have a boy exactly the same age; he's enjoying the rough and tumble of the sports field. He'll grow to manhood, please God, and he'll marry, and father children. But what is young Dougie Philips' future?'

His opening words had riveted the men's attention on him, but by now they were starting to shift uncomfortably; fingers drummed on the table; throats were being cleared, noses wiped. A most unfortunate business. What did this doctor think they were? Brutes? Most unfortunate. But not their concern, accidents happened at all levels of life.

But Daniel Nankerwin meant to fight to the last. 'I fail to see, sir, what we can do for the young man. A broken back — bad business, very bad business — but no one can hope to cure him. You're a doctor, you know that better than we do.'

'I do. Dougie will always be paralysed. He'll have no hope of earning a living. And what does Treddinock do for him? Let me tell you. Nothing! His father still works, his father keeps him. His father won't always work. Gentlemen, you must believe, as I do, that the mine has a responsibility.'

'Wait ... woah there ... not so fast, young man,' a portly, white-whiskered man stopped Giles. 'There's a sick club. Nothing to do with us — but if we know about it I'm sure you must. Dammit man, we put our money into this show. If 'tweren't for us the tinstuff would stay where it is, tinstuff and copper too.'

'If it weren't for the men it most certainly would. Who amongst you has ever been carried down on that clanking Man Engine, filled his lungs with the stale, foul air? Do you know, any of you, what those men do to bring out the tin and copper?' His voice was cold, controlled. Perhaps only Rachel knew the effort it cost him. She recognised it from the tic in his cheek, from the white knuckles of his clenched hands. She wanted to applaud, to call out to him. Her heart was thumping. 'There are men who are hurt in accidents,' he went on, 'and, as well, there are men who carry on working when they are too ill, when they should be in their beds. They know that either way there will be no cure for their diseased lungs.

Another legacy from the mine. A club, you say, sir. Yes, a club they pay for themselves. From every thirty shillings of their wages they pay back sixpence to the club and sixpence for the doctor's salary.'

'Seems you're on a safer wicket than we are, answering every call on our pockets the mine makes.' The white-whiskered man was determined to have the last word.

Giles ignored him.

'If a man is laid off because of sickness brought about at work — accident or illness — then he gets from the club a basic wage: one shilling a day for a man, sixpence a day for a woman or boy. That is always supposing his absence from work is temporary and he'll be back to his job and making contributions once more into the club funds. In the case of his death his widow gets a single payment of £10. Those are the facts, and in telling them I'm getting away from the cause of discontent amongst the men — discontent to which I give my whole-hearted support. What of that child, thirteen years and five days old? He'd paid not a penny into the club. He has no entitlement. And even if he'd worked longer, paid his share, he'd still have no entitlement for his is no temporary illness.

'There are others, men who have finally had to give up the struggle. For them there is a payment of a few pounds — based on the number of years they've subscribed, but £10 is the limit. And then what? An act of God would you call it? No, sirs, it is the injustice of our society. And, by God, it's time it was righted.'

'Very altruistic sentiments, Doctor,' one of the Knife and Fork brigade — whose looks implied that his digestion wouldn't stand up to what would shortly be expected of it — gave a withering glare to this troublesome surgeon who seemed intent on preventing them getting to their food, 'but Treddinock is no better and no worse than anywhere else. These things are facts of life.'

'And we subscribe to it.' For the first time the ice in Giles' tone cracked. 'Is that what you believe to be right? Any of you? Haven't we a duty? In God's name, how can we fill our stomachs knowing there are children going hungry, children of men who've given their youth to bringing wealth out of that hell-hole.' He paused. He seemed surprised at his outburst.

196

Then he went on, more quietly, the tone level again: 'That's what I've heard it called – that's what it is. Go down there – if you dare – feel your clothes heavy with sweat in the heat, breathe the choking dust, smell the stench of excreta, men's and ponies' too – '

'May God forbid that we ever have to.' Rachel could stay quiet no longer. 'What should we do, Doctor? How can we change the rules of a club which isn't ours to control?'

'You can't, Mrs. Treweek. But given the financial backing the club needs, the men would change the rules themselves. I've no doubt at all of that.'

The meeting wasn't going at all the way the adventurers had expected. One of them, a rotund, bald man whom, until now, Rachel had never heard utter a single word, had been listening to Giles with curious interest.

'Nothing in this world will ever be perfect, Doctor. But there are always some, like you, who have a vision of justice. Justice? Foolhardiness might be nearer the mark. Tell me, sir – I'm curious, that's all – in this Utopia you're striving for, what changes would you bring about? How do you envisage a perfect society?'

'No matter how much goodwill, nor even how much finance, was given to support these people who are my patients, Utopia would be a long way off. There will always be the risk of accidents, I don't need to spell out to you the sort of thing that could happen. Then there's the ever present danger of phthisis, miners' disease, some call it, more prevalent in this part of the country than others. Given all that, though, I'd like to see that a man whose health puts him off work for good is paid the same amount as the man who is absent through illness for a mere week. I'd like the club to have sufficient assets that in cases like Dougie's, special consideration could be given. Utopia, you say. I wish you could come with me on my visits, you'd know just how far we are from anything resembling it. Cottages where men share a bedroom not just with a wife, but with the children too. Imagine for yourselves what it would be like to live in such cramped conditions; add to that the worry of no wage at the end of the week, nothing but what is granted out of the charity of the Parish.'

It would have been so easy to go on talking. The many times he'd called to examine a patient only to find there was no-where to see him alone; children sleeping on the bed upstairs, children underfoot downstairs, and in the midst of it all a man weakened by the cough that wracked him, needing rest and care, quietness and nourishing food. He did what he could, he gave every hour of his day; but none knew better than he how heavily the odds were weighted against these men.

Yes, easily he could have talked. But today he'd come to fight a different battle. Fair treatment for those who worked at Treddinock, a few shillings a week for men who could no longer work, so that they could keep their self-respect. Wasn't every man entitled to that much? Their living would be scant but at least it would come from that fund they'd paid in to. These were proud people, they asked for justice, not charity.

'Gentlemen,' and from his tone they knew he'd said what he'd come to say, 'you've heard me out and I'm grateful. Any decision you make must be your own. My last word is this: the men in this village, at this mine, have a pride in the part they play, each one of them. Of course it's the wage they work for, how else do they feed and clothe their families? But whatever Treddinock is, it's because of them; whatever your dividend is, it's because of them; whatever my salary is, it's because of them. And this is something we must none of us ever lose sight of. They don't shirk their labours, they treat us fairly, they give of their best. Have you ever watched them come to grass at the end of their core, grey with dust, wet with sweat, the ore they'd loaded into the kibbles down there in the black laby-rinths brought up to the dressing floors?' As he spoke his finger pointed downwards, a reminder to those who sat around the table waiting for their dinner of what was happen-ing under this very spot. 'They are fine men. Those men *are* Treddinock.'

There was nothing cool in his voice now and whether they wanted to or not every man listened. Albert saw clearly the effect of Giles' words on Rachel; she seemed to lean towards where he stood, her bottom lip caught between her teeth, her eyes shining. As he finished speaking she brought her hands together, two loud claps. It was her safety valve, just as that familiar high-pitched squeak was the Captain's. Plainly he had *her* support and what she said held great sway.

'Now, gentlemen, it's out of my hands. You'll want to talk about what you've heard. Sixpence out of each thirty shillings is what they pay; any increase in their wage would mean a proportionate increase in the club's funds.

'Thank you for listening patiently. I've done my best to make the position clear to you — done it because I believe most sincerely that their cause is a just one. Now I'll leave you, Captain, you'll talk more freely without me and I have patients waiting. Mrs. Treweek ... gentlemen ...' He inclined his head first to her and then to no one in particular.

She wished she could run after him, find words for the emotion that surged through her. Giles, always calm, dependable, unchanging — the same adjectives that had so perfectly described John. Surely she'd known that beneath that reserved exterior was a fire lying smouldering, dormant but not dead. Around her it seemed that every man had an opinion to voice and was doing so, the room hummed.

'Gentlemen.' She stood up, there would have been no chance of anyone paying attention or even noticing she was speaking if she'd remained seated. 'The doctor should be listened to. He knows the people here as none of us do, probably not even you, Captain. He visits their homes, tends their families — for there's one thing he omitted to tell you. Sixpence a month from each thirty-shilling-wage covers wife and children too.

'Dr. Derwent would tell us nothing but the honest truth. If thoughtlessness has led us to overlook anomalies, now that we've been made aware I'm quite certain you must all feel as I do. A fair worker should have a fair master. May I ask that we spend a little time examining our labour costs, see if the daily rate can't be increased. Let's take a figure and work it from there. Say an extra threepence a day for each man, tuppence for each woman or boy. What do you say, gentlemen?'

Mr. White Whiskers was doing his sums.

'Threepence a day ... say there are twenty-six working days in the month ... why, that's fifteen and tuppence,' he blustered. Whatever it was he meant to say next, he didn't have the chance. For the man with the jaundiced expression — Mr. Dyspepsia, Rachel had silently christened him — put his oar in with a splash.

199

'That would give another threepence to the club, ah yes, and I see it would give another threepence to our high and mighty surgeon. Small wonder he fights their cause for them.'

'That's not fair!' Rachel jumped up again, her gingery eyes ablaze. 'You'd not dare to say it to his face. Now I'll tell you something — something I heard outside, the doctor has never mentioned it himself. That lad he told us about, the boy who'll never walk. Who was it bought him his bath chair, paid out of his own purse? It was Dr. Derwent.'

'With the sort of money he must have coming in, I dare say he was well able. Well, if this matter comes to a vote, I'll tell you here and now I'm against the proposal.'

Up until this point Albert had said nothing, said nothing and missed nothing. Now, slowly, he pushed his chair back and got to his feet. There was something in his deliberate movement that made the meeting stop squabbling and listen.

'The doctor has brought things to our notice that I believe all of us here would wish to see righted. Whilst I applaud Mrs. Treweek's suggestion, I don't feel it is the best way of correcting the injustice. Any extra money paid to the fund would be insufficient to cover invalid pensions, however small.

'I propose that for every sixpence a man pays to the club we contribute an equal amount. The average tut-worker is paid about £3.15s a month, one and threepence of that goes to the club; we add a further one and threepence, enough to be of some value to the fund. With respect to Mrs. Treweek, her suggestion of a wage increase direct to the men would benefit the fund only threepence as you've already said.'

Nods of agreement, grunts of satisfaction.

'I second the proposal,' came from the florid man on Rachel's right. 'Let 'em sort out the rules for themselves. They won't be able to say their masters haven't given 'em a fair deal. Are we all agreed?'

'Aye' . . . 'Best we can hope for' . . . 'That'll surprise the doctor; didn't like his tone, didn't like it at all'.

'Cost us a deal less than a rise in their wages, I'll say that for it.' Daniel Nankerwin nodded affably to Albert.

'It wasn't wages they were aggrieved about, sir, it was fair treatment for the sick. And this way I'm confident everyone will be happy.'

Rachel turned to him with a smile. In backing Giles he'd earned her approval and so done himself a good turn.

'I'm not staying for the dinner,' he whispered to her as the meeting started to break up. 'I left word at the house that I might possibly bring a guest home.'

'A guest?' she asked, knowing very well who he meant.

'You will come, won't you? Please. It's been a long meeting.' Somehow he brought her mind round to his way of finalising it.

'A long one but a satisfactory one. Yes, I'd like to come.' Partly she agreed as a way of showing her appreciation for the support he'd given Giles; partly she found herself looking forward to the visit. She'd not been to Newark Hall, as the house with the long wall flanking its garden was called, since that day when she'd called to say she meant to sell out of Harding's.

Riding out towards the Redruth road, she was prepared to enjoy herself. Later on she'd think back to the Count House, to Giles' appeal, to her own silent response to the latent passion she'd sensed in him. Later on, but not yet. When Albert had taken up the cause she'd gratefully turned her attention to him. Here was something she could handle. Willingly she threw herself into the pleasure of the moment.

She accepted Albert for what he was. She knew that like every other woman, she was a game to him; she didn't take his attentions seriously. She'd seen how he'd treated Dulcie — and perhaps was well on the way to treating her again. John had considered him a 'ladies' man' and so he was. But he was good company and, although Rachel might not have consciously considered it, being with him she felt herself to be attractive. Because she recognised him to be a philanderer, and never let herself forget it, she felt she was safe; no hearts would be broken, nor even bruised.

After their meal, they strolled outside in the late September sunshine. At Newark Hall the landscaped grounds merited the term 'gardens'; there was little resemblance between them and the patch behind the cottage where she pulled up her weeds and tried to keep the small square of grass a tidy lawn where Johnny could play.

'What shall I do, Rachel? You tell me. Shall I settle here in

201

Cornwall, just an occasional trip to London on business? Shall I sell all this and go to London, put my heart into making money? Or shall I say goodbye to it all, go back to Italy, lead a life of indolence in the kinder climate of the Adriatic coast?'

'Tell me about it — Italy, I mean.' She ignored his question.

'I'd like to do better than that. I'd like to take you there. The house is delightful. Not sombre and dark like this one. It's light, bright, the windows are large, the view from the western side magnificent. It's built around a small courtyard, so sheltered that even in winter there are plenty of days you can sit outside. But telling you about it can't give you any real idea. You have to sniff the perfume that hangs in the air on a springtime evening, see the bougainvillaea that clings to the walls.'

'But however lovely it is, would it really be home to you? It's a big decision, to pull up your roots and go to live amongst people who aren't your own. It's quite different from going on a visit.'

'One can make a home anywhere. But not alone.'

'It must hold many memories, Albert. You weren't alone last time.'

His shrug was so slight it was hardly a movement, yet she knew he brushed her remark aside.

'Elizabeth never cared for it. She found our existence there pointless.' His lips twitched into a smile that held all the intimacy of a shared secret. 'Elizabeth wasn't given to the indolent life.' Then, more seriously: 'She could never resign herself to the fact that we'd no longer an interest in Harding's, you know.'

'She was proud of the business, wasn't she? After all, her father had founded it.'

'She'd have been proud of anything he'd done. No man could hope to compete with Father Harding.' She made no answer and after wandering on in silence for a while he surprised her by saying: 'We get on well, don't we, Rachel? I felt it from the first time I met you.' His hand gripped her arm, holding her back.

'We understand one another.' She smiled at him, a

mischievous twinkle dancing in her eyes. 'You know me for what I am — a hard-headed business woman. And you don't pull any wool over my eyes, Albert Ross. I know that you're more than a bit of a roué.'

'You're a business woman, yes, an intelligent and quick-witted one. I doubt if you're as hard-headed as you like to think. As for me, I've probably been all you say. But, Rachel, we are what our circumstances make of us. Let's both forget what we've been in the past, let's look at us now, today. There's something about you and me, you say we understand each other, I say it's more than that. We're alike, we chase the same rainbows, laugh at the same jokes.' His hands rested on her shoulders, he was standing close to her now.

Against her will she felt a rising excitement. She was on uncharted ground. John had never looked at her as Albert was now, saying more in his silence than he did in words. He had treated her as if she'd been Dresden china in those far off days before they were married. She'd loved John; she didn't love Albert. Yet her heart was thumping and her lips, only inches from his, parted slightly, invitingly. She hardly dare name the rainbow she chased at that moment, she who'd been so sure that she could handle him, play his game and beat him at it. For so long she'd been starved for love. His kisses, his caresses, were arousing sensations that tingled through her every nerve, sensations she couldn't fight. Pressing close against him she returned kiss for kiss, thrilling to the know-ledge that he was as aroused as she was herself.

In those seconds she was lost, willingly and eagerly she was lost. Wherever the afternoon might have taken them, at that moment she didn't question. It was Albert who made the wrong move. Up to that point she'd looked no further than the minute.

His lips almost touching hers, he said: 'We'd make such a team, you and me. There's more to the world than Treddinock, my beautiful Rachel. Let me show it to you. Give my home a mistress again. For our honeymoon I'll take you to Italy —'

'Albert! Slow down!' She forced a laugh. She'd come here to enjoy herself, to escape from emotion. What he was saying brought back to her all she'd been running from. Yet his kisses excited her, not because she was in love with him; rather to the contrary, because she wasn't. With Albert sentiment didn't cloud her vision. His talk of marriage pulled her up short. Instinct was her guide. She didn't want to hurt him — although she didn't honestly think it was in her power — she didn't want their relationship to end.

In fact, her feet still weren't quite on the ground, her heart was still pounding, she wanted to feel his mouth on hers . . . only with difficulty could she collect her wits.

'I'm not the man for single blessedness. And neither, my dear, are you, business woman or no.'

'You seem to know a good deal about me,' she made herself answer lightly, still not strong enough to pull herself away from him.

'I know this much. You want the same things from life that I do. We'll work the future out together.'

All this time she'd not given a thought to Dulcie. Now, quite clearly, she pictured her, that night when her father had been preaching in the chapel next door, the night they'd sat together at the kitchen table, Dulcie with stars in her eyes and certainty in her heart.

'My immediate future is going to take me home.' Her eyes smiled — or did they laugh? — into his, her words no answer to what he'd suggested. She felt that she'd handled the situation well, put herself in control again; yet she wasn't happy about it. That Albert had talked as he had must have spoilt their old camaraderie. Perhaps she did have no respect for him, but he was good for her. She liked that streak in him that made him less than a gentleman, that laughed at life.

'Running away?' This time his mood matched her own. Once again they were on safe ground.

'I was getting worried, I thought something must have happened to you,' Dulcie greeted her. 'You've never stayed for the dinner before.'

'I can just imagine their faces if I said I was going to do that.' Rachel laughed. 'No, I've been to Newark Hall.' She said it casually, it might have been an everyday occurrence.

'To the Harding place! I wonder what Mrs. Ross would have said to that! She never went out of her way to make you welcome, if I remember.' Dulcie's answer plainly told that Rachel's friendship with Albert mattered to her more than she'd admit. 'I was afraid that you'd forgotten what tonight is. You remember you promised you'd manage without us for Toby's last evening.'

Tomorrow Toby was to go off to Plymouth. He'd saved hard for the training he must have if he were ever to be a Master Assayer.

'I'd not forgotten. You get home as soon as you like, Dulcie — both of you. Toby's sure to finish early. Have a lovely evening for his send-off.'

'They're going out. I shall be busy making sure he's got everything together ready for tomorrow. The travelling players are in the village this evening, you must have seen the notices. Down at the bottom of Fore Street, just beyond the horse trough where the road widens, that's where they're going to be. Last time they came here was the winter, nearly two years ago. Too cold then for people to stand about out of doors, they came to the Copperhouse.' While she'd talked she'd raked the ashes and shovelled more coal onto the fire in the range. Now she opened the damper. 'Give that ten minutes or so, it'll draw up beautifully, then close the damper or it'll burn away too fast.' Dulcie never stood idle, she was one of those who could give all their attention to one thing while doing another. 'Sally!' she called up the stairs. 'Bring your cloak when you come down. I'm off now and you can come with me, Mrs. Treweek's back. Just finish seeing to the lamps first.'

For months, years, Sally had known the day would come when Toby would go away. He'd not be gone forever — and yet her imagination stopped short when she thought of his not being here. This would be their last evening, nothing would ever be quite the same for them again. Put like that it was exciting! This was a step towards something new, different. But even so she had a hollow feeling in the pit of her stomach; he'd been her one proper friend for so long.

It wasn't this evening she dreaded, it was all the others that would come after it. This one was full of romance, emotion. She relished the drama of the hours ahead, the promises, the sadness, the pain of parting; all experiences new to her.

'Have a lovely evening,' Rachel said to them, busy securing Johnny into the long-legged chair that raised him to table height for his supper. 'Dulcie, I've written a little note wishing Toby well. It's on the dresser. Give it to him with my love, will you?' She didn't mention the three shiny golden guineas she'd put in with it.

Soon they'd gone. She and Johnny were left alone. Like any other cottager she prepared his supper of breadcrumbs and warm milk, sprinkled with sugar, then sat down by his side to help him. Independent though he was, a spoon had a habit of turning upside down just before it reached his mouth. Newark Hall with its regiment of servants seemed miles away, as distant as that sheltered courtyard where the bougainvillaea clung to the walls. With each spoonful of bread and milk Johnny blew, it was the way Sally had taught him to cool his food. An extra vigorous puff sent a spray, enough that he abandoned himself to the huge fun of the game. If she'd had anything but an empty evening ahead of her, Rachel's patience might have given out. Supper over, he was delighted to find himself the centre of her attention. They went into the sitting-room and played his favourite game of chase, still on hands and knees despite the fact that he'd been walking for months. It was hard to say which of them enjoyed it more. His face was pink with excitement, her hair falling loose by the time she reached out and caught him, both of them collapsing into a giggling, hugging heap. Gathering him into her arms she stood up.

'No more, Johnny my lad. It's time to find your nightshirt.'

'More. Down gen, more p'ay, more down.' He beat his little fists against her shoulders. He hadn't that fiery head of hair for nothing!

'Oh, you rascal. Would you beat your poor Mama! Ouch ... ouch ... boo-hoo.' She pulled her face into a look of agony. His momentary fit of temper was forgotten, the game on the floor was forgotten too — this new one was better by far. She held him high, nearly to the ceiling; his clenched fists could no longer reach their target. He chuckled, he laughed, he giggled, he dribbled. It never took long to restore Johnny's good humour.

Like any other cottager she put her son to bed, then washed

his supper plate. Her instructions about the damper had been completely forgotten in the excitement of the game but she did her best to save the fire that had burnt through too quickly and banked it up, closed the damper so that it would do no more than smoulder slowly, then decided to go to bed. If she leant out of her bedroom window she could hear music coming from the other end of the street.

Except for her, all Treddinock must be there — or so she thought.

But in that she was wrong. A black horse was tethered to the post outside the Caldecotts' cottage. In the tiny sitting-room the lamp was turned low, in the soft glow of its light 'the lovely Mrs. Caldecott' was quite exquisite.

There was a mystique about the night. Men held flaming torches that threw their light on the players and cast strange and wonderful shadows; above them the stars were high. This was no ordinary evening, there was a feeling of unreality. Or perhaps it was that Sally couldn't bear that it was real, that by morning it would be over and Toby gone. Each minute that ticked away was one nearer to the time when he would take her back to Mulberry Cottage for the last time ... the last time. As long as the music and dancing went on, as long as the tumbling man fell about and the soprano screeched beyond her limits, then it wasn't over. And yet it was only then that they could be on their own, away from people who crowded and pushed round them.

The final chorus was swallowed in clapping and shouting. People were already starting to move in the direction of the Copperhouse.

'Let's go,' Toby whispered. He held his arm tightly around her. She felt drunk with emotion as only a sixteen-year-old can. There was no question which direction they'd take; out of the village on the western side, towards the cliff, to the boulder that had always been their special place.

'Sal, I hate going, I can't bear to leave you.' Wordlessly she shook her head. 'Promise me, while I'm away, you'll always be my girl, my sweetheart. There won't be anyone else.' Again she shook her head. 'Then, when I come back we'll be married. I've got some money by me, I'd got it ready for college — well, not enough for me to start as soon as this, but

I was getting on. Then Mr. Dowty said he wanted to pay the fees. They've been wonderful to me, Sally, all the time I've been there. Today when I left — well, it was strange leaving them. She said I was like a son to them. We'll have them to see us when we have a home.'

This wasn't the passion and drama she'd been ready for. He must have sensed it, for he went back to what he'd been saying before. 'The money I'd put by will be a start for us.'

'You'll need your money, Toby. There'll be lots of things to spend it on in the city. Not like here. Nothing here . . .' Her voice croaked.

'Don't cry, sweetheart. I'll soon be home.'

'You'll have your qualification, you'll be able to go anywhere.'

He laughed softly at her wild talk. 'I'll be back to Treddinock, don't you worry about that. One of these days, Sally — not for ages, I hope, but one of these days — Mr. Dowty will give up. Why do you think he's helped me all these years, and insisted on paying my fees? I'll come back, don't you fear. And when I do, Sal, I'll matter here in Treddinock, a proper qualified assayer.'

Sally bit her lip. Never had she felt so without hope. She loved Toby, she dreamed of the day she'd be his wife, the wife of an important assayer. But why couldn't he see the world was full of promise? Dull little Treddinock, the same this year as last — and next. But tonight they musn't argue, nothing must spoil this last hour.

From the boulder she slipped to the grass, kneeling in front of him. Their eyes were accustomed to the dark, he could see her face clearly.

'Grounds dry 'nuff,' she whispered, 'come down here, Toby, nothing wrong in that. Lie close to each other. Like we will one of these days when you come back, when we're married. Mrs. Tobias Caldecott, that's who I'll be. Sounds grand, doesn't it?'

He wouldn't hurt a hair on her head, wasn't that what Dulcie had said? Not quite a woman yet, yet with all a woman's instinct, Sally wanted so much to be crowded into this hour.

'Can't be wrong, Toby. How can it be wrong for you and

me?' Her hands were warm, her voice was warm. 'We've only got each other. We could really belong ...'

He gave up the struggle. Of course they belonged, now, always ... How often he'd stared blindly at the ceiling of his dark bedroom and dreamed of this moment; in his imaginings it presented no difficulties, he never fumbled, was never at a loss. But this was real, this was Sally, his beloved Sally.

Later, before they started the walk back to the village, he peered hard at her, holding her by the shoulders. 'You're not sorry, Sally?'

'No, no, I'm glad. I couldn't have borne it if you'd gone away with us not belonging properly.'

'Oh, Sal.' In the last half hour their parting had almost been forgotten.

She'd wanted drama, passion, emotion; she hadn't bargained for feeling like this. He drew her into his arms so gently, his face wet with her tears.

They were nearly back to Mulberry Cottage when he said: 'As soon as I get back we'll be married. While I'm there, you get your bottom drawer together, collect up the things we shall need, then when the time comes we'll look out for a place. It's not difficult nowadays, so many people are going off abroad with work getting hard here.'

'Won't be hard for an assayer to find work, Toby. Not here or over the sea either. Once you qualify there's nowhere you couldn't go, you'll be a real important person. We could go – '

'Sal, don't talk like that. Mr. Dowty's helping me through college, he's looking to have me for his assistant.'

'Like you are now! Don't see what you're going away for if that's all you're going to do when you finish. And what about me? What about what I want? Treddinock! You never see further than Treddinock!'

'As long as you and me can be married, Sally, I'd live anywhere. And Treddinock's better than lots of places, I bet.'

'How would I know? I never got to going anywhere else, except that once when Pa took me to Truro. You'll be seeing the city, talking with men from the ships I expect.'

'Never mind all that. We're nearly there, Sal, never mind the city, talking with men from the ships, I expect.'
Sal, you're so wonderful. I can't tell you ...'

And she forget everything but that he was going.

In bed she cried, her head buried against her pillow. She couldn't picture her life here without him.

Sleep was a long way off. Lying in the dark she re-lived so much they'd shared. They'd neither of them be quite the same after this evening. She stopped crying.

The world was full of exciting places and once he got used to being away from Treddinock, Toby would start to see things differently; especially after this evening. She stretched her slender body, turning on to her back, her feet reaching towards the end of the bed. Her eyes were wide open; there was a hint of a smile playing with the corners of her mouth. Yes, Toby would see things her way.

Sleep eluded Rachel too. Here in the quiet bedroom memories of the day marched before her. Dulcie: so, that disinterest in Albert had been no more sincere than the 'game' Rachel herself had been playing with him. And from Dulcie her mind went back to the 'game' itself and, this afternoon, his unexpected change of the rules she'd thought she'd been sure of. Then on back to the Count House, to Giles standing before them fighting for the things he believed to be right. She tossed and turned. Out in Fore Street she could hear the familiar sounds of night, people being turned out of the Copperhouse as they prepared to bolt up for the night, hobnailed boots on cobblestones. Giles ... her friend ... if it hadn't been for Giles, would her answer to Albert have been different? Then back to Dulcie ... She heard Sally come in and creep upstairs to her room. Tomorrow was already here, it was past midnight.

Rachel was determined to be mistress of her own life and, lying there in the dark, didn't doubt that she could sort other people's out for them too. Albert Ross wasn't going to break Dulcie's heart twice over!

Chapter Eleven

'Copper fever' raged. Even the warnings of the knockers, the tokens that played such an important part in their lives, went unheeded, seemed to be forgotten, as more and richer ore was hauled to grass. For over a century men had mined these cliffs at Treddinock, mined with hope and with steady profit. But never had there been such a lode as this. Superstition was bred in the miners, but as they drilled further out under the bed of the ocean, seeing no end to the seam they followed, so their fears of what they'd believed to be signs from the spirits faded.

'Copper prices are good,' the Captain told Rachel, 'peaked at the highest for a long time. Tin's realising no better, though, 'tiz a mercy for us we don't ha' to depend on that or there'd be nothing in the kitty for a dividend at year's end.'

'Is arsenic holding?'

'Ah, but I smell trouble, Mrs. Treweek. We'll need to give consideration to a complaint from – ' he sifted through his papers until he found what he wanted – 'ah yes, here 'tiz, a letter from Cuthbertson and Cribbins, solicitors they are, m'dear, and they're acting for Mr. Nicholas Kumley. Would you know the gentleman, I wonder? Seems he took Cradleigh Farm last spring.'

'Which is Cradleigh Farm?'

'The fields there across the valley, they belong to him. And now we come to what the pother's all about. Do zeem he got us wi' our backs to the wall, m'dear. Here, you read what these solicitor people ha' to zay.' Clearly he was worried, his speech alone was evidence of it.

She read. It seemed that harvest had failed at Cradleigh Farm, the crops had been lost. The mine was being held responsible, the calciner and its poisonous fumes.

'But is it possible? Captain, is he trying to use us to make up for a bad season? Surely it's bunkum.'

'Has been a good summer, no reason for a bad harvest as far as weather goes. No way o' being certain, he can't prove 'tiz our concern any more than we can be sure 'tizn't — but you've noticed it for yourself, you know how the fumes hang. He's jes on the same level as we are, straight across the valley. I don't know the man, but honest or no, I believe it to be possible. Wish I could say different. Mrs. Treweek, m'dear, looks to me as plain as the nose on your face, 'tiz a claim we can't ignore.'

'How much is he asking?' She scanned the letter again. 'Why, it's a huge sum, £79.10. That's what he says is lost to him in ruined crops. And it'll happen again! What if he isn't as honest as we hope? What if next year his harvest is bad again? Are we expected forever to carry his losses?'

''Tiz my belief that the calciner chimney should be raised, enough to carry the smoke over the brow of the hill. And 'tiz my belief too that we'd be wise to let him see us doing it, let him realise we mean to play a fair game.'

'And the claim?' But she didn't wait for his answer. 'We'll have to pay it, to fight him over it would be to make an expensive enemy. Suppose, Captain, that we tell the solicitors we're having the chimney heightened in view of this farmer person's problems, high enough to ensure the fumes get carried above the level of the hill. Ask that he draws up an agreement: in future we'll pay a regular amount of £20 an annum as long as we are producing arsenic from that calciner, whether or not he experiences any further trouble. Subject to his agreeing to those terms — and putting his signature to them — then we'll pay his claim.'

'You know what some of them will think to that. Madness! That's what they'll call it. Paying away good money without a struggle.'

'Then, Captain, I'd tell them to come to the village any day except when there's a good south easterly blowing. If the fumes can ruin a harvest, I daren't think what they must do to we folk who have to breathe them.'

212

He still expected trouble from some of them at the next meeting, but they couldn't wait until the end of the year. And Mrs. Treweek was as smart a thinker as any man, she would make sure they stayed one jump ahead of Farmer Kumley.

'Cheer up; Captain, with the sort of figures you'll have to put before them — and plenty of Yuletide over-indulgence behind them — we'll be able to manage them, never you fear.'

The friendship between the two had rooted and grown as naturally as a wild flower in the hedgerow. Somewhere hidden in the depth in every relationship sex must play a part, just as it does in each person's personality. To the middle-aged purser she was the sister, daughter, niece he'd never had, for his experience of women had been limited. To her he was much more than a mentor; their minds worked the same way, their humour too. Had he been a different person, her path would have been a stonier one here at the mine.

'Weather's coming in,' he said as he walked with her to collect Dancer, ''bout time we expected a break in it. You'll jes get yourself home ahead o' it if you're lucky.'

She did. By afternoon the rain had started, not a sudden heavy shower but rain that fell straight to earth from the over-laden clouds, heralding an autumn and winter the wettest in memory.

'I went to hear the state of the figures as I shall be gone before the meeting. The good Captain has been telling me about the Farmer Kumley affair. 'Tiz plain as the nose on your face he thinks the world o' Mrs. Treweek, m'dear.' Rachel felt herself bristle. The laughter in Albert's voice, his mimicry of her friend, annoyed her.

But she preferred to ignore it.

'Looking to the trouble that could be in store in years to come, what choice was there?' she answered. 'And let's hope the taller chimney does the trick, not just for the sake of his crops. The smell of the fumes gets in everywhere — even when the doors and windows are closed it finds cracks. There's no wind, that's the trouble, hasn't been all the autumn. Just this everlasting drizzle.'

Ah, now, that played into his hands, gave him the perfect cue.

'It's not like this in Italy, Rachel.' He took her hands. 'Come with me, let's run away from it all. You've never given me a proper answer, you know. Have you thought about it?'

'Let things rest as they are, Albert. What's wrong with us being friends, colleagues?'

Oh no, my dear Rachel, he thought, You want more from a man than friendship, you don't fool me.

But aloud he was less outspoken.

'We make too good a partnership to be wasted.' He steered her to the window, driving her before him, then standing behind her with his hands on her shoulders. 'Look at it, just look at it out there. Rain dripping from the eaves, the road awash, mud everywhere, can't see to the end of Fore Street for this infernal drizzle. Look at the people, do you see a smile on anyone's face? No, of course you don't and do you wonder! Poor devils, what is there to make anyone smile about? Come with me, let me take you to where the sky is high, where gardens don't smell of cabbages but grow citrus fruits.'

'Albert — stop trying to tempt me. You could teach Eve herself her job.'

'And remember, against her Adam hadn't a chance.'

'Then more fool he! Another proof that you men aren't the master sex you profess to be,' she laughed. Then, more seriously, or did he detect a hint of fear: 'Forget it, Albert. You're wasting your time if you're still talking of finding a wife.'

Silence. The pressure of his hands on her relaxed, but he didn't move away.

'Then come with me anyway. Let's leave this land of mist and mildew, gardens overgrown with wet weeds. Forget about marriage. Come with me as a friend, let's just enjoy each other's company. I shall take servants from the Hall and the "lovely Mrs. C." could come with you to look after Johnny — young Sally, too, if you want. Now what could the gossip mongers find to complain of in that? A most respectable ménage. Just a holiday, moral and above board, I give you my word — the word of a reformed roué.'

She shook her head.

'I can see that you're ready to say goodbye to all this. But, Albert, I'm not. Even the weather, the people's stoic accept-ance — no, don't laugh at what I say, I'm serious — it's all part of what makes the place what it is.'

'Oh, come, no one really wants to be cold and wet, breathing in the stench of arsenic. Oh, they stay, of course, they stay. They don't complain, what would be the use? But offer them the chance of something better and you'd soon find it's not choice that keeps these admirable stoics here. And you, are you trying to say you would rather have this, that you don't long to see the clear, high sky?'

'No. You're right. Of course I'd love to and to feel the warmth of the sun. If I cared enough for you to want to marry you, then I'd come and I'd be thrilled at what we were planning to do. But don't you see, Albert? I can look at all this and know it's here I want to be. Isn't that proof enough that Italy and all the temptations you dangle before me aren't for me? It's not where we are, it's who we're with, whether what we do is important to us, those are the things that matter.'

Just then Mr. Traherne went by, pushing a cart load of vegetables covered with wet hessian. He'd been to the farm to collect stock for the shop. Raindrops dripped from the brim of his hat and round his shoulders, like his vegetables, he wore a covering of hessian as some sort of protection from the weather.

'Well, my dear, I'm afraid Traherne and his ilk don't appeal to me to that extent. I shan't be leaving for a week or two, we could arrive just in time for Christmas. Never fear, I've not done with you yet, I'll see you again before I leave. I have a bit of business to settle first, so you've time to think it over. Imagine, Rachel, how good it would be for the boy to get some clear, dry air in his lungs — and for Dulcie and young Sally too.' He smiled at her disarmingly. 'We'd have such a winter as you've never known. Don't we always find life good when we're together? You know we do.'

She nodded, but still she told him: 'It's no use, Albert.'

'I'll not try to persuade you, not today. Mention it to the "lovely Mrs. C." and to Sally, just see their reaction. And then think, unless we take them what chance will they ever have in their position of seeing further than the next town along the track?'

She moved forward to the window, pulling away from him,

and knowing even before he came into view that the rider approaching along Fore Street was Giles. He looked towards the cottage, saw her — and no doubt saw Albert just behind her — doffed a hat that appeared every bit as wet as Mr. Traherne's had been, then rode on, turning up the hill to the mine.

'There goes our worthy doctor,' Albert observed. 'Oh well,' he gave an exaggerated sigh, 'we can't all dedicate our lives to good works. Here's one, off for a winter of lotus eating.' The way he said it conjured up a picture of Johnny, running away to hide, looking back at pretty well each step to make sure he was being chased, desperate for a game and frightened that playtime might be over. She laughed, she couldn't help herself, as she turned to face him.

'Oh, Albert, I wish it could be different, I wish I could want to do as you say — or that you could take Dulcie and Sally. You're right. What opportunity have they? Sally's so eager for life it's cruel to take the chance from her.' Then she paused, her eyes meeting his squarely as she added, speaking deliberately: 'And Dulcie — Dulcie would want to go with you.'

Momentarily he was disconcerted, but Albert never lost control of the situation for long.

'Perhaps they'll have more success in making you change your mind than I've had.' He dropped a light kiss on her brow, stood back to hold her at arms' length, his eyes as alight with mischief as ever young Johnny's were. 'And now, my friend Rachel, I must leave you. Your persuasions that I should stay must go unheeded. Be it as inclement as it may, I must forget my dreams of sunshine and battle my way to Helston. I have an appointment with my banker.'

The day seemed greyer after he'd left, the steady dripping from the eaves depressing.

What harm could it do to accept his offer — not of marriage but of a holiday for all of them? They'd have a winter of sunshine and laughter. Surely she'd made it clear that she wanted nothing more than friendship from him. The steady dripping of the rain seemed to be on his side, trying to add its own persuasion to his. So what was it that held her here? She'd miss the mine far more than it would miss her. A

216

few months and she'd be back, spring would have come — the mine wouldn't have so much as noticed that she'd been away. Not true! Her lips twitched into a smile as she pictured the look of satisfaction on the faces around the table when the end of year meeting assembled and her seat was empty.

'Mr. Traherne and his ilk' as Albert had said, the women in the village, the men who climbed the hill to work, even Captain Bowen — all of them would be just the same when she came back.

Trudie and Peter? Yes, they'd miss her. And, even more, they'd miss Johnny. Through this long rainy autumn they'd ridden here each Saturday morning without fail.

Ah, now she was coming nearer to the truth. Giles. He'd miss her and the habit that he'd grown into again of dropping in at Mulberry Cottage, often for no more than a few minutes when he was passing, and only ever when there was no trap outside, no black horse tethered to the post.

She knelt down on the rug in front of the hearth, taking the poker to break a smouldering lump of coal so that it sent a shower of sparks up the chimney and burst into flame. She bent nearer to it, the room seemed cold. The truth wouldn't be ignored. It was Giles who held her in Treddinock. Every hurdle that had faced her she'd overcome knowing that he'd been there to give her support. What if she went away with Albert, and Giles misunderstood? She couldn't be sure that it would matter to him. Oh, but surely it must matter. There had been moments, moments so brief that sometimes she wondered whether they'd been in her imagination, when she'd been sure their spirits had met and fused. And yet always he'd held himself a little distant; he was her friend, but never more. So what made her so sure that her going away with Albert would matter?

She sat back on her heels. Alone here in her little sitting-room, the sound of the rain a melancholy background to her thoughts, there was no ducking the truth. Nights when she'd lain awake, her body craving the love it was denied — and in those lonely nocturnal hours it was Giles she reached out for, always so sure that with him she'd find that elusive something she'd always sought. In her dreams she knew his lean body as well as she knew her own, and the strength of him ... the

217

desire that matched her own ... the hidden passion ...

''Xcuse me, Ma'am, here's the doctor come. Shall I bring your tea in?'

At the sound of Sally's words Rachel felt her neck grow hot. Purposely she stayed where she was kneeling before the fire to give a reason for her burning cheeks.

'Thank you, Sally. You can bring Johnny's chair in too. I'll give him his tea in here with us. Hello, Giles. Come near the fire, you look drenched.'

'And you look remarkably snug. I came in the back way and left my hat and coat in the kitchen,' he smiled as he spoke. 'I hoped I might be invited to share your pot of tea and steam by your fireside for a while.'

Johnny came in and, in the way of small children, completely ignored them, giving all his concentration to a small wooden horse on wheels that Mr. Traherne had obligingly found in the drawer with those 'vue odds'. Sally followed him, carrying his tall chair, and Dulcie came last bearing the tea tray.

It was a scene of domestic harmony in the low-ceilinged sitting-room. Giles lifted Johnny to this seat; Rachel poured the tea.

'I noticed you go by on your way up to the mine,' she said as she passed him his cup. 'Nothing wrong, was there?'

'I'd been out of Treddinock all day, so I went up to check I'd not been needed.'

'Where have you been to on a day like this?' she asked, busy making Johnny a jam sandwich and cutting it into 'soldiers'.

'Wheal Hamlyn, out near Pendyne. Do you know it? About an hour's ride and a wet one too. Arsenic is big business at Wheal Hamlyn. Despite the sort of care we all take, they've got two cases of arsenic poisoning. I went to talk to Dr. Cressey, find out anything I could. His experience might well help us prevent trouble here before it starts. You know, in all the time I've been here I've never seen the amount of water lying that there is this year and we're only in November, the winter is still to come. There seems to be no end to it.'

'Johnny, open your mouth, come along, open it properly.'

She concentrated on Johnny. Giles' words pushed her thoughts towards sunshine, sunshine that made winter feel like spring. She turned the conversation on to safer lines. 'Any news of Rosalind, Giles?'

'In fact I had a letter from her this morning. She suggests that we go to Pentreath for Christmas.'

Again his words pushed her thoughts the way she didn't want them to go. 'We'd be there in time for Christmas,' Albert had tempted.

'We've been invited away too,' she heard herself telling him. 'Albert has suggested we go with him to his place in Italy. He's crossing the channel to Cherbourg then going by railway.' She hadn't meant to say it. After all, she had no intention of going. Or had she? She watched him closely as she spoke, it was as if in him she'd find her decision. A burning coal slipped on to the hearth and Giles got up to take the tongs and put it back. 'Giles ...?'

'To Italy, you say. You'd take Johnny?'

'All of us. Dulcie and Sally too.'

'You've been invited, you say. And are you going?'

'Run away from the dreary months? I don't know.'

'I don't believe it's in you, Rachel, to run away from anything. If you run it's because you want what you're running to.'

'And you? Are you going to Pentreath?'

He shrugged. 'I dare say the children would like to. Christmas by ourselves would be a dull festival for them.' Giles wasn't running away, yet neither was he reaching out towards anything else.

Johnny discarded a piece of crust onto the floor.

'Do that once more and there'll be no cake,' she told him. In the last months his understanding had made great strides and now although he may not have followed her words, he got their message clearly. He was hanging over one side of his chair, another piece of crust dangling ready to be dropped. But Johnny was no fool, he knew that when one couldn't win it was better to look as though one hadn't realised there was a contest. He swung his arm backwards and forwards, the crust hanging low then, meeting his mother's glance with a mischievous twinkle, he sat up very straight and popped it in his mouth.

'Good lad,' Giles told him. And here he understood both the words and the meaning. Praise and cake too! No wonder he cooed to himself as he munched.

With the proposed holiday hanging between them it was easier to concentrate on Johnny than each other and he was prepared to enjoy the extra attention. Of course, it went to his head, he got over-excited as children do. He giggled, he swung his legs, he kicked the table, he pushed a too-large piece of cake into his mouth and choked on it and, recovering from that, took the mug of milk Rachel passed to him and slopped most of it down his front.

'That's naughty! If you behave like that you can eat in the kitchen!'

His bottom lip trembled, from the heights he dropped to the depths. Rachel frowned. She'd had to shout at him; she'd had to shout at someone. She looked at his face and wanted to cry with him, find relief in tears. Yet she'd nothing to cry about. She ought to be ashamed.

She lifted Johnny from his chair, hugging him tightly in her arms, her back towards Giles. All his life Johnny had been her safety valve.

'Rachel, you can't –' His sentence was left unfinished. From across the narrow corridor came the noise of a crash, glass shattering, a scream ...

They found Dulcie sprawled on the floor, the chair she'd been climbing on to reach up to the shelf where she stood the preserves lying nearby. She'd been putting away two large jars of pickles. One she'd dropped at the first lurch of the chair; the second she'd clung on to, evidence of that was a jagged piece of glass stuck deep in the palm of her hand. Broken glass, vinegar, pickles, two jars had spread themselves a long way. The vinegar was in puddles, the contents of the jars and the pieces of glass right across the room.

Rachel was still holding Johnny who by this time was screaming, frightened by the disturbance.

'Take the boy back in the sitting-room. Keep him there,' Giles told her as he preceded her into the kitchen and started to shut the door on her.

But she was having none of that! 'Sally, take Johnny. You play with him and I'll help the doctor.'

220

Gratefully Sally escaped, almost as frightened by the commotion as Johnny was himself.

Dulcie had been lucky, if it could be called lucky to have a piece of pickle jar sticking out of the palm of her hand. No bones were broken and, although she was going to be stiff and bruised, she'd put out her arms and warded off far worse damage. Even so a lump was already swelling over her right eye.

Without waiting to be told, Rachel rinsed out the bowl and poured hot water into it from the big iron kettle they kept permanently on the range, then added a large lump of salt and just enough cold water for comfort. Then she took a clean piece of cloth from the drawer in the end of the table.

'Good girl,' Giles said without looking up as she put them close by him. She'd told Sally she would stay and help the doctor, but apart from bringing him the water she felt she was surplus to his requirements. His black bag, which he had left on the dresser when he'd come in, carried all he needed and there was nothing for her to do but to re-fill the kettle ready for the floor scrubbing that would be Sally's job for this evening, then clear away the scattered splinters of glass and far-flung pickled vegetables. Every now and again she glanced at Giles, saw his gentle handling of Dulcie.

It was Dulcie herself who seemed remote. She was fully conscious, but the fall must have shaken her, and it seemed to have silenced her too.

'She needs a hot, sweet drink,' Giles said. 'Is there any water?'

'I'll soon stir up the fire.' She'd seen Dulcie do it often enough when she just wanted a drop of warm milk for Johnny. She took the lid from the range as if she were going to add fuel, but instead she put a small pan of water straight on top of the coals.

Dulcie's right hand was bandaged; arms, legs, ankles, checked and intact.

'A good night's sleep and you'll feel better,' Giles told her.

'I'm sorry. Must have been clumsy.'

'Try and drink your tea. Horribly sweet, but lots of medicines taste worse.'

'Aah!' The cry escaped her, the pain that cut through her

221

was so unexpected and so violent that it took her breath. Giles was watching her; Rachel stood quite still; no one spoke. The moment mattered. No limbs had been broken, but there was no doubt that Dulcie was hurt.

This whole evening was important, Rachel had felt it from the first, before Giles had come, before Dulcie had fallen. Later, perhaps for as long as she lived, she'd remember it. The long hours would be compressed into this: Dulcie's involuntary cry of pain and, as if the elements were aware, a sudden gust of wind lashing the rain against the window and howling in the chimney, a down draught that sent a billow of smoke into the room. So ended the steady, fine drizzle of autumn, giving way on that November night to a new fury.

'I'd like her to lie down. Which room shall I take her to?'

'On my bed.' Now what instinct made Rachel say that, when in an hour or so Johnny would be in the adjoining room? Wouldn't a rest on Sally's bed have been more sensible? Yet Giles didn't question it.

'I'll help you up the stairs.' He steadied Dulcie as she stood up. She took a step or two towards the door, then caught her breath again and bent forward in pain.

'Please,' she panted, 'help me get home.' Her dark eyes entreated him. 'Please. I'll be better there.'

'You're to rest first. I'll carry you to Mrs. Treweek's room.'

It wouldn't hurt Johnny to stay up late, Rachel thought. An hour or so and Dulcie would have had a sleep and got over the shock. Sally could take her home and stay the night with her, she might wake up stiff and uncomfortable in the morning. And now, while she rested, Giles waited, wanting to reassure himself that she woke with no worse after-effects than bruises.

Downstairs they neither of them talked of Christmas, although both of them felt the shadow of it. In the kitchen Sally didn't like it on her own, the horrid smell of vinegar was everywhere, a constant reminder of what had happened. She looked for an excuse to come into the sitting-room.

''Scuse me, Mrs. Treweek. I thought I ought to tell you – that chair Dulcie fell off, it do zeem wobbly. Perhaps that was why she tumbled.'

'I'll come and look at it for you, Sally,' Giles offered. 'Have you any tools?'

All of them welcomed his suggestion.

An hour or so beyond his bedtime, overtired and fractious, Johnny was undressed for bed downstairs by the fire, then carried up, Rachel whispering to him, 'Sshh, because Dulcie's having a sleep.' And seeing the still form on her bed she believed it to be true too — but it wasn't. Dulcie had heard them coming and kept her eyes closed.

'I'll check her once more and if she hasn't woken by then, you go home, Giles. I'll keep her here tonight, it's a double bed, we'll manage.'

So again she crept up the stairs and this time Dulcie didn't hear her. On the landing it was dark, so from where she stood at the top of the stairs Rachel could see clearly into the bedroom where the lamp gave out a flickering light. She stood very still. Dulcie's face reflected all the bottled-up misery she'd fought; she was making a strange sound, so softly that Rachel had heard nothing until she'd reached the doorway of the room, then she was reminded of the whimper of a dog who'd been whipped.

'Dulcie, don't. Tell me, where does it hurt you? Giles is still here, he's waiting to see you again. You're to stay tonight, I'll find you a nightgown to wear. I'm not having you go home feeling like that.'

'But I must,' Dulcie struggled to sit up, 'please, I must go home. I'll be better when I'm there, I know I will.' She swung her legs off the bed and stood up. 'See! Of course I can go home.' But her face belied her words, her lips trembled and with her hands on the small of her back she sat down on the edge of the bed, bent forward so that her head was almost to her knees. And again, that small sound, full of pain.

'Giles!' Rachel called down the stairs in a stage whisper. If Johnny was still awake she didn't want him to think he was missing out on anything! And there was Sally to think of too, she tried to make her tone sound cheerful in case Sally heard. Or was it to bolster her own confidence? 'Can you come up a minute.'

Two stairs at a time he came and yet not rushing, his first glance taking in far more than Rachel's had.

'I'm going to examine her thoroughly.'

'I'll help her into a nightgown, shall I?'

Dulcie had no fight left in her. She held her arms up when Rachel said; she wriggled out of her clothes and let the nightgown be put on her.

'Do you want me to go downstairs while the doctor examines you, Dulcie, or would you rather I stayed?'

'You can go down. Stay with Sally. Don't let Sally come up the stairs.' Dulcie lay back with her eyes closed.

'Call me if you want me, Giles.'

From the kitchen she could hear the swish of the stiff scrubbing brush on the stone floor. Vinegar, at least the smell of it, took a lot of shifting. Hot water, soda, and all Sally's effort, yet it still lingered. In the sitting-room Rachel waited, listening. Movements in the room overhead, then Dulcie crying out. She must have done more damage then they'd thought. Perhaps Giles had suspected it, that might have been why he'd been so insistent on staying to see her again.

And all the time the wind howled, blowing the rain to beat against the window.

Ah, he was coming down. She heard Giles' step on the stairs.

'Rachel, if Johnny's asleep I think it would be a good idea to carry him through into Sally's bed. I'll drag his mattress through for her to have on the floor.'

'But, Giles, why should it disturb him to have two of us in my room?'

'We're likely to have a bad night ahead of us — that's one reason. And the other is Sally. If she has Johnny to look after, she'll have her mind kept occupied.'

'What's Dulcie done to herself?'

'She's very shaken. A night's rest may settle her.' And that was as far as he'd say.

'What's the use of asking you! You talk to me as though I were a child!'

He ignored that. 'Go up and talk to her, Rachel. She needs a friend.'

She did as he said. Perhaps she'd get more sense out of Dulcie that she had him.

'Is there anything you'd like, Dulcie? I know you can't be

comfortable so I won't ask you, but can I do anything to make it easier? Where does it hurt, is it your hand?'

'I don't mind about that, it's not that. I couldn't explain to the doctor, he wouldn't understand what it can feel like. I'm afraid it'll start, then I'll flood, I know I will. I just want to get home. Be better at home.'

'But Dulcie, as if that matters. I've got everything you'll need. But you don't usually get pains like this, do you?' She sat on the edge of the bed. 'I'll find something for you in a minute, then you try and sleep and not worry about it.'

'You see, I'm late, ever so late. Perhaps if I lie still the pains will go. Do you think they will?' She drew up her knees, panting for breath as the pain tore at her.

'You'll feel better once it starts. I expect the fall has triggered it off. I'll find you your things. Then I'm going to carry Johnny through to Sally's bed. It'd take more than that to wake him when he first goes off. Giles said to shift him, then if there's anything you want in the night you won't be worried that we're waking him.'

'The doctor said that?' Clearly she didn't like what she heard, but she turned on her side, her back towards Johnny's room, muttering something about going to sleep. Rachel knew nothing was further from the truth.

Johnny was very obliging. He snorted a couple of times, thrust his thumb deep into his mouth without opening his eyes, snorted again, but stayed lost to the world as he was laid in Sally's bed, the covers pulled up around his little shoulders. Giles dragged the mattress through for Sally, then they came back to look at Dulcie. Her eyes were closed, her breathing even, but neither Giles nor Rachel were fooled. They left her alone and went downstairs.

'If I've got Johnny waiting, I might as well go up,' Sally said, soon after nine o'clock, 'or do you want anything, Ma'am – or the doctor?'

'No, you go on to bed, Sally. If we do, I'll get it. Anyway, the doctor will soon be gone.' It was said to reassure the girl and it seemed it did the trick. They heard her creeping up the stairs, then her bedroom door close behind her. Never before had she had 'Johnny their darling' in her bedroom for the night!

225

'Rachel, how much does Dulcie confide in you?'

'Confide? Dulcie's life is an open book. She's here from morn till night, she hardly has time for secrets.'

'Ah, so you know that she has a man friend – or men friends as she implied when I examined her.'

'Men friends! Dulcie! Why, that's ridiculous.'

'Time enough to worry about that later. I've examined her thoroughly. There's no doubt at all. Dulcie is pregnant.'

This was something Rachel hadn't for a moment considered, not even upstairs when Dulcie's desperate need to get home, to be on her own, bordered on panic. Men friends! But it was impossible, a lie to cover the truth. There was only one man in Dulcie's life. 'We're too good a team to be wasted' . . . 'We're two of a kind' . . . 'We'd arrive in time for Christmas' . . . 'Ask Dulcie and Sally, perhaps they'll be able to persuade you'.

'Are you absolutely sure? She told me she's very late, that's why she feels so wretched.'

'Absolutely certain. And so is she. Our immediate problem is that she may possibly abort after that fall. I'm afraid that all the signs are that she will.'

'You mean she told you?'

'I told her – and she admitted to it.'

'And the father? Didn't she tell you who he is?'

'No. She says she can't be certain. But I can't believe it. She must be protecting some married man. It made no difference how I talked to her, nothing would persuade her to confide. That's why I sent you up. I hoped that having told me a certain amount she might say more to you. She needs help. Oh, I don't mean that we could do anything if he's got a wife, but she oughtn't to have to bear it alone.'

'She told me nothing at all.'

'I'll go and take another look at her. If nothing's happened, I'd better ride home and let them know I'm having to stay with a patient. I don't want the children worried where I am. I shan't be more than an hour.'

He went up to see Dulcie, but this time she really was asleep.

He'd been gone about forty minutes when Rachel heard movements overhead. Dulcie was out of bed. She hurried up to her, determined that this time they'd talk about it openly. Knowing as much as she already did there was no sense in trying to fob her off with stories.

But the time for stories was over and for confidences too. Dulcie made a grab at her hand as she came in, panic taking over as she cried out to call the doctor to come up to her.

'He'll soon be here. Back to bed, we'll manage till he gets here. Lots of towelling, old sheets. I'll get them. We'll manage.' Rachel had no idea what to expect, nothing terrible, surely, it must be in the early stages. Yet Giles had insisted he should be here. She wasn't nearly as confident as she made herself appear.

Leaving Dulcie once more on the bed she went down to bank up the fire and fill pans of water, then she collected a pile of towels, old cot sheets, rags. And from then on her feet hardly had time to touch the ground as, crying with pain and unhappiness, Dulcie lost her baby. Rachel had borne two children, but as for abortions she knew nothing. All she could do was to answer each call as it was made on her. Towels, a pail, water and a cloth ... she looked no further than the immediate job.

And then she heard Giles' step on the stairs.

'Good girl,' he rested a hand on her shoulder, 'now, let's see where we've got to.' Off with his coat, up with his sleeves. 'Warm water and a brush to scrub my hands.'

That much she'd anticipated. 'Here, all ready for you.'

'Good.'

Then they said no more, the only sound that occasional whimper from the bed. Rachel had seen him with the miners, she remembered his reassuring gentleness after Johnny had been born. Tonight she watched him at work, her heart full.

How much Sally heard they didn't know. Perhaps nothing, certainly they tried to be quiet, each trip up or down the narrow stairway was consciously soft. Then it was all over, Dulcie, white and drained, was asleep.

There was only one way of disposing of the embryo that would have been her son.

'Go in the other room while I clean myself up,' Giles told her, and knowing that she had far more than himself to clean up, she did as he said. When she heard him raking the fire in the range then taking the lid off to make it up, she knew this was the final act. She shivered.

All these weeks Dulcie had said nothing, each day she'd carried on as though she'd had nothing on her mind. And tomorrow she'd wake to find it all over. Dulcie who'd once been so confident, so sure of Albert's love. She'd guarded her secret, so for her sake Rachel must guard it too. Did she love him so much that to have his bastard child would have been better than to have nothing of him? And Albert? He'd gone straight back to the 'lovely Mrs. C' as soon as he'd returned home from Italy. But marriage, marriage to a miner's widow . . .

'You're not going to have a very comfortable night.' From just behind her, Giles' voice startled her.

'And you're going to have a very short one by the time you get home again. Oh, Giles,' she turned to face him, 'how cruel life can be. Her little boy. She had nothing – and now she'll have nothing again.'

'You're sure there isn't one man friend? She needs someone to share the loss with her.'

'Of course there must be. But she's never told me.'

'If this hadn't happened tonight, life would have been very difficult for her no matter how you'd tried to befriend her. The best you can do for her is help her put it behind her, let her realise her secret is safe.'

But that wasn't all she could do, nor yet all she intended to do.

She went ahead of him into the narrow passage by the front door, carrying the lamp off the table. The northerly wind hammered and battered, finding spaces to get through and take shelter in the house.

'Will she be in bed long, Giles?'

'Probably only a day or two. But don't rush her. Sometimes women suffer depression – it's harder to recover from a miscarriage than it is a confinement.'

'Poor Dulcie.' They spoke in whispers. 'She needs a change, a rest, something to give her hope.' And strangely when she said it she had no thought of that courtyard with the bougainvillaea-clad walls, nor even of Albert.

Giles put his hat on, then opened the door.

'She should be fit to travel in a fortnight,' he said. 'I'll visit tomorrow.' A nod of his head and in less than Patsy's three big strides he was lost in the darkness, outside the orbit of her lantern.

Sally accepted that Dulcie should be kept in bed, it wasn't surprising after going such a crash on the stone floor. And there was a lot to be said for being 'queen bee' in the kitchen, especially when Mrs. Treweek said she was going out for an hour or two and leaving Johnny behind. She supposed she must be riding up to the mine, but fancy going on a day like this. The window panes were rattling, rain coming off the roof like a waterfall. Watching from the sitting-room she saw she was wrong. Mounted on Dancer, an oilskin cape over her riding habit, Rachel came out of the side lane, but instead of going up the hill to the mine she turned left, away from the village.

Sally shrugged. 'Come on, Johnny, you and me got work to do. Can't waste the morning standing here.' Apparently Johnny agreed. Pushing his wheeled horse and moving on hands and feet he preceded her to the kitchen.

Out of Treddinock on the Redruth road were two other mines, quite near each other, Wheal Alice and the St. Elmo. Rachel passed the first, then on towards the second, looking to neither left nor right but keeping her head down against the rain. So it was that she didn't notice Giles in the distance coming down the lane that led from the St. Elmo.

But he saw her ride by. What other woman would be out on horseback on such a day? He recognised her even from so far away and knew exactly where she was going.

Chapter Twelve

'My friend Rachel!' Albert held both hands to her as he came
into the morning-room where she was waiting. 'You've come
to tell me you've changed your mind! And who can wonder at
it on another day of this.' He nodded his head in the direction
of the window. 'You'll come with me? You don't know how
pleased I am.'

Didn't he so much as notice the way she ignored his outstretched hands — and his words too?

'Albert, I'm here to tell you that Dulcie had a fall yesterday.
She has lost her child — your child.'

She'd never expected that Albert could be so thrown off
cue. His face flooded with colour, he opened his mouth and
then shut it without speaking. But not for long; soon he
recovered his composure.

'I don't understand you. Dulcie, "the lovely Mrs. C",
expecting a child, you say? And she a widow, I believe.' His
eyebrows raised. 'But why should you connect me with her
indiscretions?'

'I didn't ride out here to play games.'

His eyes narrowed. 'You mean she's spreading rumours,
telling lies? You must see what it is, Rachel. She thinks this
could come between you and me.'

Rachel watched him. This was the man who had made her
laugh, who'd made her feel young and carefree. Look at him,
wriggling like a worm with a hook through its belly! All she
felt for him now was contempt, for him and for herself too
that she could have been so blind. She'd always known life
was a game to him, part of the enjoyment she'd found in

being with him had been that her eyes had been open to him; but not far enough open, she realised now, to see that a game is only fun so long as it's not in the rules to plunder and hurt.

'I've ridden here to tell you, because I know you'll hear of it no other way.' Surely he must have felt her contempt.

But no, it seemed he hadn't.

'She's jealous. Both of you widows and you with a second chance of happiness. We'd talked yesterday of taking her with us. Not now! Not if she can do this to us.' He reached to take her hand, but she recoiled from his touch as if she'd been burnt. 'You can't believe what she's saying! Why, down there where she lives, heaven knows what goes on. Look at that Pendleton woman next door to her.'

'I haven't come to talk about the morals of the Pendleton woman. And as for Dulcie, you're not fit to speak her name. You and your "lovely Mrs. Caldecott"! You broke her heart once. I believed that this time she was as wise to you as I was myself. You're a fool, Albert, a poor wretched miserable fool. You ask me to marry you, yet you know very well that I don't love you. But, then, my husband was a successful man, and I hold the largest stake in Treddinock. Is that honestly worth more to you than a woman's heart?'

'I asked you to marry me for yourself, not for what you have. We're two of a kind —'

'That we certainly are not! I'm going now. Dulcie is staying at Mulberry Cottage for the time being. Only Giles Derwent and I know about the child and no one will hear of it from us.' She pictured Dulcie, her face so pale; she thought of her empty future, even the child lost to her. The coldness left her voice, for Dulcie she could even plead. 'Albert, you *must* feel something for her. You walked out on her before, but then you had a wife. When you came back to Treddinock you were drawn to her. Isn't that the truth? I know Dulcie would never do what she did without love. Take her to Italy with you, marry for love — there's nothing else worth marrying for.'

He'd walked away from her, was standing gazing out onto the rain-beaten garden. Whether or not her words had made their mark she didn't know; he said nothing.

'I'm going now. Dulcie doesn't know I've been to see you and I shan't tell her. If you want to see her, you'll be made welcome at the cottage. But not if you make a pretence that your visit is for some other reason, there's been too much of that already. It's time we were all honest with each other.'

Still he didn't turn round. When he heard the door close he knew she'd gone.

Not even the wettest season is without its short bright intervals and when Rachel went to the stable to collect Dancer the rain had stopped. By the time she'd got half a mile or so along the road towards Treddinock a ray of pale sunshine was trying to break through the clouds. The area was a natural high plateau, the flat land almost devoid of trees. For so long the visibility had been restricted by the drizzle, it was a joy to look at the far distance. There, alone on the road, she stopped, sitting straight, taking in the scene that had become a part of her life. Memory nudged at her, recalling the autumn evening when it had all been new to her; John sitting opposite in the carriage with Patsy on his lap, their first drive from Redruth, her first twilit glimpse of a land so alien. She'd left Warwick with such expectations and this had been what she'd found. Flat, dull, drab; she'd seen it as all those things. More than three years ago; she'd been a 'foreigner'. Not being Cornish born, some might say she still was. She slapped her heels against Dancer and they moved on. No, she was no 'foreigner'. This flat land with its tall engine houses, its smoking chimneys, even the fumes from the arsenic, this was where she belonged. Many places were beautiful, but it was something more than beauty that tugged at her. It was its industry, its purpose, the pride and courage of its sons.

Again she stopped. The clouds parted to show a patch of blue. This was her day for clearing the mists out of her own life. Honesty. That was the only way forward. And honesty brought her thoughts to Giles. She wanted him and needed him, with her mind and with her body. Ah, that was honesty. But what was the use of sitting here dreaming? She'd been fast enough to tell Albert what he should be doing – so what about taking a hard clear look at her own life?

Why had she encouraged Albert all this time? No, no excuses, tell the truth. Laughter, flattery, feeling attractive, hadn't she told herself so often enough. But today was the time for truth. It had been in the hope that Giles would notice, would see her as Albert apparently had. And had he noticed, or had he cared? She was his friend, he was fond of her, he wanted her to find happiness. Honest? True? Only he could know.

Again she kicked her heels into Dancer's side, this time putting her into a brisk trot.

She arrived home to find that Giles had already called.

'Hope you'll say it's all right, Ma'am, but the doctor told me to say "Can Johnny share your bed?" You see, Ma'am, he's put Dulcie in mine.'

At her worried expression, Rachel laughed. 'He said that? Can Johnny share my bed? More likely he said: "Tell her Johnny will share her bed," wasn't that it?'

'Is that all right? Not waiting to ask you, I mean?'

'I think it's fine, and so will Johnny. Did Dr. Derwent say when he's calling again?'

'I think he told Dulcie he'd come tomorrow.'

Tomorrow seemed a long way off and, as if it shared her disappointment, the rain started to splash once more against the window.

It was late that evening. All day she had expected to see Albert arrive. With time to think about what she'd told him, surely he must want to be with Dulcie. For Rachel had no illusions: he might have proposed marriage to her, but whatever he might say to the contrary, he'd seen her as a suitable candidate, his head had ruled his heart. With time to think, he'd come to realise that what had pulled him back to Treddinock had been Dulcie. But the hours of the day had gone by and he hadn't come. By now Johnny was in her bed and asleep despite his determination that he and the ever favourite Hodgkin the bunny would stay awake and wait for her; Dulcie was in bed and not asleep; Sally was seeing to the fire for the night.

There was a knock on the front door. This must be Albert. She'd send him upstairs, make sure that Sally stayed out of the way.

'I'll go,' she called on her way to the door. But it was late for a casual caller, Sally was curious and opened the kitchen door to see who it was.

'It's late, I'm sorry. But I have to talk to you.'

'Giles! Is something wrong?'

'I don't know. That's what I want to find out. Rachel —'

She cut him short. 'It's all right, Sally, you get to bed when you're ready. You don't want to wake Dulcie up once she's got off to sleep. Goodnight, sleep well.'

''Night, Mrs. Treweek. 'Night, Doctor.'

'Come in, Giles.' It was probably nothing, perhaps he wanted to explain about his reasons for changing the sleeping arrangements, a problem about Dulcie, or to do with one of the children. One thing after another: she clutched at reasons for this late call. But in her heart all she knew was that this was the day for clearing away the mists, finding the truth.

There was an urgency about him. He followed her into the sitting room, dropping his hat on the table, regardless of the fact he'd come in out of the rain. A most un-Gileslike thing to do, a sign that something important was troubling him.

'Tell me?'

'I was coming earlier. Then I had to go down to the hundred and forty. Nothing serious, only a sprained wrist.'

Ah, so that's what made him so tense. He'd been down that hell-hole.

She put her hands on his shoulders and gently pushed him into a fireside chair.

'Just imagining it makes my heart thump,' she said. Certainly something did.

He nodded. 'I've done it for years. It never gets easier. Perhaps it never does for any of them.'

'Oliver finds the idea thrilling.'

'Oliver's a child.' She detected a trace of his bossy voice and smiled. 'But I didn't come to talk about the mine, or Oliver either. Rachel, I came to talk about you. I can't let you do it. You don't love that fellow. Aren't I your friend, can't you trust me enough to tell me?'

'You mean Albert Ross? Did I ever say I loved him?'

'I saw you — this morning. You were going to his house. Then, only hours later, I heard what he's doing.'

'I told you he's going to Italy. That's why I went to see him.' She stopped short. Where were all her high-flown ideas of honesty. 'No, that isn't the truth. He thought that was why

234

I'd come, that I'd changed my mind and would go with him. But I'd come for something else. I wanted to tell him about Dulcie —'

'You mean that she's told you — that it was Ross?'

'Dulcie hasn't told me anything. I know it was his. He knows it too. All day I've expected him to come to her.' She knelt down in front of the fire, her eyes level with his now. 'He hasn't come. Perhaps he won't as long as she's here. Perhaps he'll wait until she goes home.'

'Rachel — I've watched you with him —'

She turned to face him.

'Can you understand, I wonder? Albert made me laugh. When I was with him I felt carefree, attractive — I'm ashamed, put into words it sounds so paltry. "Two of a kind", he said that's what we were. But it's not true.'

'No, it's not true.' He took her hand in his and carried it to his mouth. Now, had Albert done that the act would have been elegant, flirtatious. Giles' eyes were closed, he held the back of her hand against him, she felt the hardness of his teeth, his jawbone; he clung to her as though she were his lifeline. Then, just as suddenly he let go of her, his eyes open and looking hard at her. 'Why are you telling this to me, why are you making me your Father Confessor?'

'Because coming home from Newark Hall I saw it all so clearly. Between you and me, always, there must be truth. All those dreadful months when we avoided each other — we did, you can't deny it — I chased rainbows with Albert. Then we were friends again. I'll always remember the relief, the — joy — yes, it really was, when I knew we were honest with each other again.'

'Honest? Oh, Rachel, is that what you want, honesty?'

She lowered her eyes. How could she pretend that it was honest to tell him she wanted just friendship? Kneeling so near to him, her hands seemed to have a mind of their own; it took all her will-power to stop them touching his cheek, the way his hair grew in that widow's peak.

'Then you shall have it.' He stood up, his hands gripping the mantelpiece. 'I am your friend, I shall be your friend as long as I live, but if it's honesty you're asking for then friendship isn't all I want of you.'

'Giles ...' Now her hands wouldn't be told, her fingers moved on his legs, his shin bone, his knee, just as she'd known. 'It was friendship that made you ask me to marry you, you said —'

'I know what I said. At any price I wanted you. But I was a fool, I made promises I could never have kept.'

She knelt up straight, those fingers of hers caressing his waist. Her head was back so that she looked to where he stood above her. If her hands wouldn't be told, certainly her eyes wouldn't; they spoke their silent story. She felt the touch of his hand on her head, then she was on her feet. Whether he pulled her up or simply willed her nearer to him she didn't know.

'Not just a friend?' She wanted to hear him say it.

'A friend ... a wife ... a purpose for everything I do. You asked for honesty.'

She wanted to laugh. She wanted to cry. Everything she'd ever dreamed of was suddenly hers. She leant against him and felt the banging of her heart — or was it his?'

'And you?' he cupped her face between his hands. 'Can a husband not be a friend?'

She nodded.

'And that ship you insisted you had to steer for yourself?'

He asked it lightly, purposely lightly. And in the same vein she answered him. Into the last five minutes had been crowded the reflected emotion of years.

'I've set my course. I've even seen land a'hoy.'

His mouth covered hers, she clung to him.

Later he sat in the chair, she on a footstool at his feet. The thought came to her that just so had she sat with John. The evening she especially remembered had been Christmas. Dear John. She looked at Giles. Her hands reached out just to touch him, to know that she had the right, that he wanted her.

'What you were saying about Ross not coming here, that you expected him to see Dulcie, my feeling is that we've seen the last of him.'

'He doesn't cross to France for another fortnight or so. He may come tomorrow.'

'Captain Bowen mentioned him this afternoon. Rumour travels like a bush fire. It seems he'd heard that Ross had given the staff of Newark Hall notice to quit. He's either closing it up for some time or, more likely, selling. He told the servants three days ago. At least that's what I hear.'

'But he said if I wouldn't marry him, to go just for a holiday.'

'Then, my dear, I expect he had enough faith in his charms to believe he'd persuade you to change your mind once he got you there.'

But Rachel still didn't lose faith. 'If he takes Dulcie – and he should do, not just out of duty but because with the sort of love Dulcie has for him he'd have a chance of finding happiness – then he'd probably not come back here. Why should he keep Newark Hall? He'll wait until she's in her own home, and then he'll come to her.'

'And I came here believing it was you who were going.'

'Then, Giles Derwent, you should have known better!'

'You've taught me to know better. Honesty clears the mind.'

She laughed softly, then knelt between his knees, leaning against him.

'Rachel, Rachel,' he was whispering, 'only hours ago I was schooled to accept an empty life. Now ...' His words were lost. So the seconds ticked away. They shovelled more coals on to the fire, they went to the kitchen and cut cold meat sandwiches and brought them back to eat by the fireside, not so much because they were hungry as for the pleasure of the intimacy of a shared plate. This hour (or two, they had lost count of the time) was made up of comfortable domesticity and unrequited passion, blended together with joy, relief and excitement. A brew sufficiently strong to go to any head.

From the start Rachel had held a very special place in the young Derwents' lives. There was no doubt that she – to say nothing of Johnny! – would be welcomed at Perleigh House. Oliver was expected home for Christmas on the 19th December, so they chose the 20th for their wedding.

It seemed their future held no single cloud.

Giles wrote to his mother. She was to come for the wedding and stay for Christmas. Rachel wrote to invite her sister and Hewlett Treweek too. He'd see where those steps she'd taken, one at a time, had led her.

Their replies came.

'Of course I shall be with your for your wedding,' Muriel wrote, 'and, bearing in mind the distance, I shall accept your offer of lodging especially at such an inclement time of year as you have chosen. I have no recollection of Dr. Derwent, but I trust you have made a suitable choice. It is as well you decided not to follow my advice and make your home here in Shrewsbury amongst my friends. We lead very full lives as I told you, but we are none of us husband hunting . . .' Rachel's lips twitched into a smile as she read. There had been a time when Muriel's words would have stung. But not now.

Hewlett Treweek wouldn't be able to travel to Cornwall. Anno Domini had made arthritis his companion. For John's sake he regretted it; he would like to have met the man who was to be her husband and take the place of the boy's father. It would have neatened off the odd ends. John always liked things to be kept in order. But he sent his sincere good wishes for her future and assured her that on the 20th December she would be in the thoughts of hers affectionately, Hewlett Treweek.

He was part of that life she was leaving behind. If anything could touch her with sadness in her present euphoric state, then his letter had the power to do it.

November gave way to December. Dulcie, pale and composed, insisted she was well enough to work; her hand was healed and the bump on her head disappeared. As for any wound to her heart, she didn't admit to one. But it was rare for any sound of chatter or laughter to come from the kitchen and when it did it simply meant that Johnny was there and Sally, reacting against the silence, was working him into a state of excitement.

There was nearly three weeks to go until the year's shortest day, but darkness was loath to leave them. Mid-morning and in the kitchen the lamp was still burning. Yet today there was no rain, simply a sky so low that it seemed to cover the village with a grey shroud.

'I let Johnny go with Sally to Mr. Traherne's,' Rachel said, coming into the kitchen where Dulcie stood at the table kneading dough with a monotonously regular motion.

'Dulcie, things will get better.'

238

'The Lord gives and the Lord takes away. Blessed is the Lord.' Dulcie's voice was harsh, but still her hands worked with the same pace as though they weren't part of her.

'I know.'

Those moving hands were still. Rachel had made a dent in her armour.

'Yes, of course you know. How could you bear it?'

'We don't get asked how much we can bear. Things happen and we have no choice. Dulcie, don't look beyond the hour. They all go by, hours and days. It'll get better.'

Dulcie re-started pummelling the dough. 'But you had Johnny. You had something.'

'At the time I found no comfort in that. I believe I hated the baby that was coming, because he'd been given and Patsy taken. It wasn't like that, though,' she sat on the edge of the table, 'not later, but I couldn't see that at the time. Johnny helps me to hold on to her. Patsy can never be gone, I'll have her as long as I remember. And I won't forget.'

'But how can you even try to hold on to something that was false?' It was the first time Dulcie had spoken honestly, acknowledging what they both knew. Now she looked directly at Rachel. 'Pride — that's a sin. You ask Father, he'd tell you what happens to you if you have the sin of pride. I had pride, conceit too. I was so sure. Oh, I knew his games well enough, I knew how he'd come creeping down to see me, not wanting to be recognised; yet he escorted you about, invited you to the Hall. I knew all that. I saw you as part of the game he played, someone to be flattered and flirted with. Me, I was different, I was outside all that, he really loved me. I didn't care that you might be getting hurt. Each time he left you here and came on to me I laughed. Yes, I did. I'd scored the point.'

She laughed now too, but it wasn't a happy sound. 'We don't score points in this world, we simply tot them up for the hereafter. Ask Father.' Her voice croaked, self-control stretched beyond its limit. 'If only I could have kept my baby, but not even that.' Rachel heard the heartbreak. She slid off the table to come and put her arm around Dulcie's shoulders, but she didn't seem to notice.

Her voice low now, she went on: 'The auctioneers are at the Hall, you know.' Once more the dough took over, the even

239

rhythm seemed to help her. 'Word gets around. There's to be a sale. Everything. All the furniture, carriages, horses, all Mr. Harding's books and things. Harding's. There wasn't another name like it round here at one time. People live and die, doesn't matter how important you think you are it's all the same in the end.' But her mind wasn't on old Mr. Harding when she said: 'Everything will be gone. This time he won't come back.'

'Albert Ross isn't worth a single tear, Dulcie. Not anyone's, and certainly not yours. Think of the sort of man Toby's father was, someone you could respect. We were both wise to Albert, we both knew what he was.'

'You don't love people just because they're good.'

There was no answer to that and from the sound of Sally and Johnny coming up the path it was a good thing for him that it was so. Johnny possessed quite the finest pushcart in Treddinock, a wicker seat where he could ride, holding the reins of a wooden horse, the whole thing on four wheels. Today he'd been fooled, something he didn't take kindly to. The pushcart had only been taken so that Sally had somewhere to balance her box of groceries. He'd anticipated a proper walk. He was at his least attractive.

'Behave properly or I'll put you in your room.' Rachel's tone meant business.

His look of thunder was for all of them. Then, deciding 'proper behaviour' was too high a price, he made for the stairs, his little feet banging down on each tread. They heard his door close — close? slam! — then all was quiet. He'd gone to tell his tale of woe to Hodgkin. Johnny's storms were vivid and short-lived. Ten minutes later they heard him coming back, taking one stair at a time, singing tonelessly as he came.

Giles might be at the mine, she'd not seen him go by on his way to the village. Captain Bowen would certainly be there. The low grey clouds of morning had built up into a mid-day deluge and then lifted to lure them into believing a fine afternoon was ahead. The watery sun tempted her out, just as it did Sally, Johnny and his 'horsecart' as he called it. Rachel's route was up the hill opposite and as she disappeared Sally stopped the 'horsecart' outside Mr. Traherne's shop and lifted Johnny out. He'd been caught this way before! He remembered the disappointment of the morning's jaunt and stuck out his bottom lip.

'More riding – c'mon, more walk.'

'Just got to get something.'

Her tone implied the interruption to the outing would be brief. He brightened.

'. . . weeties?' he asked, hopefully.

'Th li'l mas'er come t' zee un agen,' Mr. Traherne beamed his welcome, 'an' what 'ee wantin', Zally, m'luvver?'

'Have you any liquorice, Mr. Traherne?'

'Ah, I've good lumps o' lick-rish. Don' ee let the lad ha' too much. Only a li'l chap yet vor lick-rish. Why don't ee take a vuew aniseed balls? Better vor un, aniseed.'

'Give me twelve balls then please, Mr. Traherne. I know he likes them.'

'Better vor un. Here, laddie, open wide.' And he popped a bonus into Johnny's mouth.

The afternoon was turning out remarkably well. Back in his wicker chair, the reins in his hands, the sweet taste in his mouth, what more could he want of life? If he leant right back as far as he could and held his head so that his chin went towards the sky he could see Sally. His gingery eyes danced with pleasure. Johnny knew nothing of wedding plans – nor yet of bruised and broken hearts – but like all children he was susceptible to the mood around him. And there was no doubting Sally's – she was excited. He didn't question why, but was pleased to share the spirit of the afternoon with her.

Perleigh House was only a mile or two up the road, but it was away from Treddinock. No wonder Sally was excited. She was escaping the village, it was her first step towards freedom, she who'd been so frightened that this was to be all she'd ever know. This afternoon she walked fast, singing and keeping in step with her song. Johnny la-la'd too, shaking the reins to hasten his steed along the road.

Arriving at the head of the mine, Rachel got rid of Dancer then went to the purser's office. Empty. She saw that his hard hat wasn't on the peg and was disappointed but not anxious. Every day or two Captain Bowen went below ground, inspected what was going on. The working of Treddinock

Mine was organised from his office, based always on what he saw on these tours.

There was no sign of Giles either. Her journey might have been fruitless, except that no visit here was ever that. She watched the steady rise and fall of the stamps, breaking the chunks of ore; she walked over to the buddles, gazed fascinated as she always was to see them going round and round the circular bed, holding back the good metal, while the sludge was washed away into the slimes pool.

'Never seen the slimes so high,' one of the men told her. She couldn't know all those who worked here, but it was evident they all knew her. Something of a character they thought her ('a remarkable woman' had been Albert's way of putting it), dressed like a lady and with manners to match, coming here as if she were a man!

'Do we ever drain the pool?' she wanted to know.

'Been there as long as I have. Drains itself, works its way through the ground to the adit, drains out there on the west side, through the cliff face.'

There was something sinister about that grey pool, water so thick it was sludge. A man could fall into it and never be traced. Why they called it the slimes she could never understand, for there was nothing slimy about it.

The first heavy drops heralded the next rainstorm. There was no point in her waiting. She walked back towards the sheds to collect Dancer.

'Rachel, don't go!'

So he was here after all. Giles came towards her, approaching from the drying room.

'Damned weather. Does it never stop!' Not like Giles to be uspet by the weather.

'"Gi's uz vine tatties", or so Mr. Traherne tells me,' she laughed. 'How's that for a silver lining? There's usually something good if we look for it.'

'Like that mine! All they see is the good in it. They're like maniacs, take any risk —'

'Let's go into Captain Bowen's room.' She led the way. 'You sound very disgruntled, Giles. You wouldn't be getting cold feet?' she teased.

His only answer to that was a quick, firm touch of her

hand. 'Rachel, I was called down to a youngster, his people have just come from St. Just, I didn't know him. He'd slipped.' She'd known there was something and waited. 'They thought he'd broken his ankle, but it was only a nasty sprain. It was down on the two hundred and twenty, the deep workings.'

'You went under the ocean?' Her mouth felt dry.

'What's the difference? If it falls on you you're not going to care whether it's rock or water.'

She didn't like his tone, there was a bitterness that wasn't a part of him. The afternoon must have been harder to take than he meant to let himself admit.

'Rachel, at the Count, Captain Bowen reported that we were driving ten fathoms under the ocean bed, he told me so himself. I went along an end where they were working. You get a certain distance and the sound changes. It's a marked change, you can't miss it. Whether there's a dip in the sea bed I don't know. You can hear the ocean clearly. And the men are driving into the roof, tempted deeper and higher all the time by great bunches of copper. I hardly remember the climb back, I went straight to find Bowen and tell him. Rachel, the man's as mad, as copper crazed, as the rest of them. No one but he can stop what they're doing — but he didn't credit what I told him. Said he was there yesterday.'

'And so he'll be there again today, climbing down to it this very minute. They said he'd gone below about ten minutes before I arrived,' she defended her friend.

They had a long wait for the Captain to come back, but they went home reassured.

'I've been down to the two hundred and twenty,' he told them. 'To be honest, Mrs. Treweek, m'dear, I went on account of what the doctor here told me. 'Twaz he who opened my eyes — or my ears. Only yesterday I was there, nothing untoward then. They'd been boring since then, of course. I've stopped it now, though. There must be a decline in the bed of the ocean.'

'You mean they've stopped working?'

'Stopped in that end. And we'll ha' to go steady. Didn't care for the look o' things. Plenty o' copper still, ne'er you fear on that. They'd already started drilling two new ends,

243

working in a southerly direction. The lode's wide. Plenty o' rich ore. But mus' never be vor uz to vorget our roof is the ocean's floor.'

That was on the Tuesday. If they'd been looking for confirmation that they'd been drilling too high it came the following Friday. There was a suspicion that the water pumped from the two hundred and twenty level up Incline Shaft to the adit above was salty. The pump was keeping the deep working in fork; but any hint of salt water in the mine was enough to cause alarm. Captain Bowen instructed that observations should be taken at each stage of the tide. Their fears were confirmed. The pump worked at constant pressure but the water in the adit rose and fell with the tide. Work was immediately put in hand to shore up the roof where the sea's roar could be heard. Load after load of rubble and deads were brought down and piled into the end where the drilling had been called off.

Of all the adventurers at Treddinock, Rachel was the only one who knew what was happening through those anxious days. But her faith in Captain Bowen was firm – and not even the most critical would have found fault with the measures he was taking. Disaster had been averted.

At the cottage there was plenty to do. Rachel sorted and boxed her things to be taken to Perleigh House; each day the cottage looked less like home. She went on a shopping expedition to Helston, then, finding nothing worthy of her honeymoon there, had a long day's outing to St. Austell with no more success.

'I wonder whether I could leave Sally with Johnny for a couple of nights,' she said to Giles. 'If I could get to Plymouth I could find what I'm looking for.' He cared nothing for what she wore; he was surprised that it mattered so much to her, surprised and secretly pleased. 'Perhaps Dulcie could stay here with her.'

'Better than that.' He took a hand in the arrangements – and so settled them! 'The nursery is ready, let them move in before the wedding, give Johnny a chance to get settled. Enjoy your freedom,' adding with a tease in his voice, 'a few more days and it'll be gone.'

She'd steered her own ship, made her own decisions, but

244

what luxury to be told to go and enjoy herself, there was nothing to worry about. It was on the 15th December that Giles took her to Redruth and saw her on to the train. Two nights away from home and she returned, her purse a good deal lighter and a porter piling a truck with boxes, hats, gowns, shoes, gloves, petticoats; two days of self-indulgence made a heavy load.

Just as he'd seen her off, so Giles met her. It was as they left Redruth on the road towards Treddinock that she caught sight of the name on a notice. Ezra Tresize. She craned her neck to read it as they passed. The 16th December, that was yesterday, he'd visited the New National School at ... too late, the notice was lost to sight, but it must have been somewhere nearby. Well, she hoped that he wasn't planning to grace Treddinock with his presence again, it was two years since his last visit. That was something Dulcie could well do without!

'Mother arrived yesterday evening. Why don't you come home with me and meet her now, leave your shopping there, have some tea and see Johnny? He's settled in as if it were tailor made for him.'

'I'd like that. Dulcie doesn't know what time to expect me, so she won't get worried.' And of course she wanted to see Johnny, and to meet Giles' mother too. But suddenly she was being pushed along on a tide of preparation. She and Giles were the central players and yet she felt quite untouched by all the plans, the arrivals, the feasting. It must have all happened to her before. But at eighteen one accepted. The excitement of the actual wedding had seemed important; without it the first few days of marriage might have been more difficult. John, so caring and gentle with her ... Now all she wanted was that Giles could drive her straight through these hours until the wedding was over, all the fuss done and they were together at the beginning of the rest of their lives. In thinking it she realised just how far removed she was from the girl-bride of fifteen years ago.

Perleigh House buzzed with life. Miss Grimshaw saw that the wheels of progress were kept oiled, certainly the house-keeping arrangements were handled with an efficiency unknown in Rosalind's time. And, just as Rosalind had anticipated, she was kind to the children. But kindness isn't the same as loving them. They rushed out to meet Rachel; there was no doubt of their welcome.

And behind them stood Giles' mother.

'Well, so you're the young woman. Let's have a look at you. Umph, well, I've seen your boy so I might have guessed what you'd look like. You'd better give me a kiss, you're to be my daughter it seems.' Whether or not that was a sign of approval Rachel couldn't be sure. But she'd expected to be sized up, even if not quite so openly; after all she was doing the same thing herself, and surprised at what she saw. Not a bit what she would have imagined Giles' mother to be. A tiny woman, with eyes as blue as a child's and as clear; cheeks that were rosy, but close inspection showed that their colour came from the fine criss-cross of veins rather than from health.

'Well?' Small she may be, but not timid. 'And what do you make of me, eh? Will I do you? Am I what you expected?'

Rachel laughed, beginning to like her future mother-in-law.

'No, not a bit. He doesn't take after you, does he?'

'I had a brother like Giles, tall, gangling fellow, all bones. Now come over here by the lamp, let me get a better look, I don't see as well as you young ones, I dare say. You're a good-looking young woman. What's he been doing all this time? More than two years ago he was fidgeting to get back. A patient was worrying him, he said. Not just any patient! I wasn't silly enough to believe that. Waited with me just long enough to see my Maker couldn't be doing with me yet, then not a second longer.'

No wonder Rachel liked her more all the time.

Giles had been right. Johnny and Sally had settled into their new surroundings, it was quite evident her presence hadn't been missed. Then downstairs to hear about the arrangements for the wedding breakfast from Miss Grimshaw, who had everything in hand in a most practical way as if wedding breakfasts occurred every week.

'Get your cloak, Rachel. It's time we left.'

'Yes, Dulcie will be anxious.' They both knew that Dulcie didn't come into it. Like her, Giles wanted the next few days over. Had he felt differently last time too? A young bride-groom, an excited bride . . .

'Warm enough?' he asked as they bowled the last mile towards the village.

She nodded, wriggling closer. A few minutes and they'd be at home by the fire. They'd send Dulcie home, there'd be just the two of them. She realised that they'd never been truly alone in the house before, always someone had been in the kitchen or upstairs. The unmade lane gave way to the cobbles of Fore Street, the light from the lamps making shining patches on the wet ground.

But no lights shone from the windows of Mulberry Cottage, no smoke curled from the chimneys.

'The fire's burnt to nothing and the grate's quite cold.' Giles held his hand against the kitchen range. 'She can't have been here at all today.'

'But why? Giles, you don't think ...? We'll go and make sure nothing's wrong. She's bottled things up, I know how miserable she's been. I shouldn't have gone away and left her here with the cottage empty. You don't think ...?' But still she didn't finish the sentence.

'Don't you come out in the cold. I'll go and see her, perhaps she isn't well. And when I get back I'm going to take you home with me. I'm not leaving you alone in a cold house.'

'Wait!' It was only then that she saw the sheet of paper on the ground. It must have been left on the mantelpiece and fluttered down in the draught as the door had been opened. 'Here's something.' She carried it to the table where the lamp stood and together they read.

It was dated the 16th December, yesterday.

My mind is quite clear, I know just what I have to do. That he came today when I'm here alone is like a sign. All the misery and anguish is over, I have no doubts.

May God give you the happiness you so richly deserve. The Lord giveth, and the Lord taketh away — and I remember what you said, that nothing is ever finished as long as you remember. I think it's true too that what we live becomes a part of ourselves, those we love do too. Now I can see the truth, the truth and the way.

I shall remember you always, your kindness — and my

247

darling Johnny, and Patsy too. Wherever I go Patsy will be alive in my memory.

I hope you will forgive my going like this, letting you come home to a cold house, and that you will think sometimes of your devoted Dulcie.

Then on the bottom, as an afterthought:

'If ever my travels bring me this way I hope I may come and see you.'

'Oh, no!' Rachel stared at the single sheet. 'How could she do it?'

'If he's taken all this time to come for her, it's not something he's done lightly. I think we have to give our blessing to the alliance. Captain Bowen told me he was at the mine yesterday, but I somehow didn't expect this.'

'The mine? But why?'

'He wants to get rid of the rest of his holding. This time I think he's leaving the district for good.'

And then she understood him.

'You mean Albert! But is it Albert she's gone with? Her father was somewhere Redruth way, I saw the notice as we drove past. Ezra Tresize.' Then in the cold kitchen she told him of the preacher, the hold he'd had on Dulcie. 'There's only one piece of comfort in her note. She says one day she may come and see me. I was frightened for her. I shouldn't have left her.'

'Whatever she's decided to do, it seems her path is quite clear. It may not be the one we'd have chosen for her, but only Dulcie can know.'

'Oh, Giles.' She nuzzled her cold face against his neck and felt his arms go round her. 'She deserves better. I have so much — everything. If only —' He let her get no further; for both of them Dulcie and their cold surroundings were of no importance.

'I shall take you home,' he told her after a minute or two, 'I'm certainly not leaving you alone here.'

The soft sound of her laugh was like a caress. 'Good, I'm glad you're not. We'll light the fires. Come on, Giles, you're not above kindling a fire, are you? There's plenty of chopped wood, Dulcie always keeps a box of it. We'll be warm in no time. I'm warmer already, just thinking about it!' As no doubt he was too.

First the kitchen range and with the wind blowing so fiercely from the west it drew up quickly. By the time the first yellow flames were taking hold in the little grate in the sitting-room the coal was turning to a red glow in the range and the kettle had been put to heat. There's nothing like the flickering of a fire to bring life to a house.

Rachel had lit the lamps. The cottage was strangely quiet, no one here but the two of them. At Perleigh House the wedding, only three days away, was uppermost in everyone's mind. Here it had no place; the marriage, but not the wedding. Giles' mind must have been following the same track as hers. He sat down on a fireside chair, watching her as she poured two glasses of port wine.

Then he said: 'Do you know when I made my vows to love you — forsaking all others — as long as we both shall live?' He spoke it softly, his words held her quite still, a glass in each hand.

'Did you? At Rosalind's wedding. And so did I.' The glasses were put down on the table, she needed her hands as she went to kneel in front of him. 'Every word, every second — but I didn't believe you could ever want me like that.'

'Not want you! Rachel, if you knew how I've wanted you.'

She rested against him. Rested? No, not that. There was nothing passive in Rachel.

'In three days we'll be making those vows for everyone to hear,' she whispered, 'but, darling Giles, all those people, family, friends, the wedding breakfast, the congratulations — it's all a part of the conventions. We've already made our vows. We made them before God on that day when we knelt together.'

'What are you saying?' He knew very well what it was she'd left unsaid, but there was a stillness about him. Only Rachel could make the next move. She'd never been afraid of the truth, and it had never been more important than now.

'I'm saying that I want us to be together, I want you now, tonight.' She lay with her head against his neck, he could feel the soft warmth of her, her weight. 'You said just now, Giles, "as long as we both shall live". It's more than that, it's this world and beyond. You know that and so do I. You'll always love Anna, I'll always love John. When I married him I was an innocent young bride — and that bride will always be John's. I'm not a young girl now, wanting to find out about love. I'm a woman, and whatever I am, my heart and my body, I'm yours.' She sat back on her heels, her expression serious. It was so important that he understood just what she was saying. 'When I come up the aisle to you, Giles, when we make those promises, I don't want to come as — as —' For a moment she was lost.

'You'll come as the answer to my every prayer.'

'I hope you still think so.' And for a second her eyes danced with silent laughter. Then she took his hands in hers. 'I want us to make our vows not as two separate people but as people who are already one. Can you understand? Stay with me, here on our own. Nothing can disturb us, nothing can come between us.'

'Not tonight, not ever,' he pulled her back into his arms. The fire had burnt through and the coals slipped. She knelt up again, her gingery eyes tender in the lamplight.

'There's no hurry, the night lasts until morning.'

In another seventy-two hours they would be on their honey-moon but this night was secret and their own. She took the tongs and put more coal on the fire, then reached for their wine. Rachel, who had always craved a passion that had eluded her, knew that at that moment both she and Giles wanted just to rush ahead. She longed for his touch — and yet she wanted to savour the solemnity of the hour.

Then she told him: Dulcie always has the kindling in the bedroom ready so that the fire can be lit during the evening.'

'I'll do it. And you go and find us some supper.' It was almost like playing a game, the 'mothers and fathers' of every generation of children. To both of them it was necessary, it steadied them, held them back, gave reality to what they were doing.

The night lasts until morning, she'd said. It must have been almost morning. By her side Giles slept. Rachel pushed her

250

feet to the bottom of the bed, her knees straight; held her arms above her, her fingers spread wide. So a cat might stretch on waking. Memories of the hours that had gone crowded in on her. Last night she had loved him; this morning she loved him even more. Her eyes were wide open and full of peace. Only she could know the thoughts that made a smile play with her lips.

Outside she could hear the first clatter of hobnailed boots on the cobblestones, the early core setting off for the mine. Too dark still to see the clock, but the sound told her that it must be about half past four. For them the beginning of just another day. But for her the start of a new life.

It was the 18th December, two days still until the wedding, but now she was prepared to enter into the spirit of it, for the children's sake, for the families' sakes — even for Miss Grimshaw's; she'd worked so hard to see the arrangements had no hitch.

Another group of men passing by, not talking, just walking together. Half past four on a cold, wet morning. Their pace didn't falter. 'Like the heartbeat of Treddinock,' she mused silently. Her smile this time was at herself. Such flowery thoughts weren't usual for her. But this morning perhaps she may be excused.

It was then, quite suddenly, quite surely, she knew what she had to do. The germ of an idea had been sown in her mind long ago: there should be a place in the village where the men could meet together, those who worked and those who were no longer able; a place, too, where Giles could have a surgery. And where better than here, Mulberry Cottage? She imagined them playing cribbage or shove-ha'penny on a winter's evening, somewhere of their own that belonged to the Miners' Club.

She wanted to tell Giles. She wriggled closer to him, hoping to wake him.

The start of a new day, their first together. As he pulled her into his arms the cottage was forgotten, everything was forgotten, except joy that was almost more than she could contain.

Chapter Thirteen

Dancer plodded up the muddy lane towards the mine head impervious to wind and rain, which was more than could be said for her rider. Rachel kept her head bent, turned to look at the ground to the left of them. That way the oilskin hood partially protected her face from the onslaught that hit her from the northwest. Her mind was travelling ahead of her. She urged Dancer on and the pony did her gallant best. But the hill was steep.

Rachel had been alone in the cottage when she'd heard that long blast on the hooter. It could mean only one thing. An accident! Hurry as she might, she'd had to change into her riding skirt, she'd had to saddle Dancer; by the time she rode across Fore Street to the hill, more than a quarter of an hour had gone.

'Come on, come on, good girl,' she urged, not that her words meant anything to Dancer who could do no more to improve on her pace.

'What's happened?' she called to the lad who looked after the horses before she even slid from the saddle.

'Couldn't say, Ma'am. I heard 'tiz trouble on the fifth level, but don't know what. Captain's gone down, o'course, and the doctor too.'

Work was still going on. Loaded trucks were being trundled along their tramways, kibbles being hoisted, the stamps never ceasing in their steady rise and fall. She pulled the hood of her oilskin cape further on to her head then, leaving Dancer with the pony lad, she went towards the shaft where she could see a small group of men.

In answer to her question they seemed to know little more than the boy had.

'′Tiz down on the fifth level, the bell told us that much. We're waiting for word to come up. Captain and Doctor are down there now.'

'Hi-up!' One of them pointed to the Man Engine shaft. 'Here's news coming.'

Always when men came to the surface at the end of their core, they would be hot and dirty, but this man was grey with dust and rubble, and with a smear of blood (possibly not his own) down his cheek.

'I need help,' he called to those who waited, 'can some of you carry the poles and splints with me? Roof's fallen in.'

'You mean the ocean floor?' The horror was beyond imagination. Wasn't this what Giles had warned!

'No. The fall is close by the bottom of Incline Shaft.'

She wanted to hear more, but he didn't stay and the other men had already gone. Trouble for one at the mine was trouble for them all. Yet she was outside it, helpless and waiting. Her feet were hardly on the ground yet from the hours of night she and Giles had shared − and now he was in that hell-hole.

'Let him come up soon, please, please, let me see him come soon.' She watched the way in to the Man Engine Shaft, her plea repeating itself over and over. Yet she knew he couldn't come, not as long there were injured to be cared for. It was about eleven o'clock, those men who'd tramped past the cottage while she'd lain warm and content, they'd be somewhere down there below the ground. Would they be amongst those on the fifth level? Would they be hurt? For some of them would this morning have been the last time they'd clatter along the cobblestoned street and turn up the hill? For them it had been the start of just another day, she'd supposed; and for her the beginning of a new life. How could one know? How could anyone be sure what waited? A cold shiver ran down her spine. 'The heartbeat of Treddinock,' she'd called the sound of their footsteps walking towards this.

Another group of helpers were coming, some carrying poles, some hessian, the makings of the stretchers Giles must be wanting. They disappeared into the head of the shaft. Out here the cold rain fell relentlessly, was blown straight from the northwest, cutting the visibility to yards. The mine head was near the cliff edge, but today the sea was lost.

The work of the mine went on, sounds that had become so familiar to her and always with the background of voices, men calling to one another in that rich Cornish brogue that had once seemed to her like a foreign language.

She walked to the entry of the Man Engine Shaft and alone she waited.

But she wasn't alone for long. News travels fast. The hooter had been the first sound of trouble and word of where it was had filtered down to the village. Wives and mothers of the men who'd gone to work on the early core in the two hundred and twenty fathom level soon started to appear, climbing up the hill, heads down against the weather. Some, like her, wore oilskins. But most of them topped their normal clothes with an extra covering of hessian or, in one or two cases, of canvas.

'No one up yet?' A fat young woman who had been one of those who'd contributed towards Johnny's layette came panting to join them.

'No. The stretchers went down an hour or more ago.'

'So doctor's with 'em.' She seemed to take comfort from that.

Rachel nodded. Like all these others, she was waiting for 'her man' to come safely out. There was a strange comfort in being one with them. Reason told her that for Giles there would be no danger, the accident had been over before he even went down there. But at the back of her mind, deaf to reason, was her own sick fear of those unknown dark passageways and the certainty that Giles' dread was as great as her own.

'Here comes someone.' They heard voices as the moving platforms of the Man Engine brought the first men to surface. In those next seconds each woman was an island, each waiting for one special person. No one spoke. Only when the men came from the shaft head did questions break: 'Have you seen Jimmy?' 'Is Josh Tyzack safe?' 'Is anyone badly hurt?' (And they all knew exactly what 'badly hurt' could mean.) 'When are the others coming?' They made up for their silence, all speaking at once. For them the vigil wasn't over, none of the five men who came out into the light, eyes half closed after the darkness even though it was a dull day, were theirs.

'Jethro Towse came off bad,' one said, 'and old Ted Pollard — '

'Don' you start setting the alarms like that,' another interrupted, 'things oft look worse 'n what they are down there. Lost the lights for a bit, what with that and the dust . . . but the doctor's there, ah an' plenty vor un to do too.'

'And who's to say it's all over?' Rachel would know that voice anywhere! Today, though, his face was grimed, his eyes bloodshot. Each breath he took broke in a strangled cough at the back of his throat as if his lungs were choked with dust. She expected to hear him tell them they'd brought it on themselves, they should have heeded the warnings of the knockers. 'Another load just came, could be jes' the tip o' the iceberg we've seen.'

'Caught the doctor a glancing blow,' a fourth took up the tale, 'near knocked the senses out of him.'

'The doctor? The doctor's hurt?'

'Says he's not. Threw him off his feet, and gave his head a bloody gash. Your Jimmy's on his way up, Nell.'

For one of them the waiting was nearly over and when a minute of two later the woman he'd called Nell, by now shrouded in dripping hessian, went off gripping her Jimmy's arm, for the others their own anxiety seemed heightened.

By now the news had reached those who worked different cores, those who had been underground all night or who were to start work later in the day. All the time more people came, men and women too. And from underground those who could were coming to surface. As each one appeared from the shaft he was borne off just as Jimmy had been.

One o'clock . . . half past . . .

Near where they were gathered was the building that housed the steam winding engine, the engine that hauled the kibbles of ore from below ground. Rachel heard the bell ring just inside the building, this was the way instructions came from the mine. The crowd listened, counting. Eight rings — that meant a kibble was ready to be hoisted. Five rings — that it was from the fifth level. The injured must be being brought to surface. Slowly it was raised, the chains rattling. This time the women watched, afraid of what they'd see. The relief was almost audible when the kibble was hoisted out of the Incline Shaft and the men came into view. One had a broken arm, one a broken collar bone, nothing worse than that. Giles had done what he could for them below ground and up on the platform of the dressing shed where the kibble came to rest they were helped out, one with his arm splinted and in a sling, the other with a sling.

The group moved to the steps of the dressing shed to meet them.

It was Rachel who called to the first of them: 'How much longer? How many more has the doctor to see?'

His answer was a silent stare. Pain and fright seemed to have robbed him of his powers of understanding. This time an oilskin-clad woman pushed her way through the crowd and bore him away.

Right from the beginning Rachel had been drawn to Treddinock, and had grown to feel herself to be a part of it. Yet how could she be? An inner voice whispered to her now. You don't know a man by his face and his build, by the colour of his hair; you only know him by understanding the working of his heart and mind. She thought of Giles. Indeed she thought of nothing else.

'I'm going down there,' she said to a man who stood next to her. How could she believe she knew Treddinock if she was frightened to look below its grassy surface? She had to find Giles. Somewhere far, far below the ground where they stood — dark, damp, what air there was full of dust — she had to go to Giles. 'You know where the things are. Please — find me trousers, a hat, candles. I must go down there.' She couldn't climb ladders in petticoats (Oh! The thought of it, burrowing into the earth, no air, no light. She musn't think), even the skirt of her riding habit would hamper her and make it dangerous.

The man hesitated. 'Don't see I can do that — er, 'tiz Mrs. Treweek, isn't it?'

'If you won't show me, I'll have to find out for myself. I'm going down there.'

'Have you ever been in a mine, Ma'am? And those ladders, straight against the side, some o' them, steep —'

'Please. Just show me where I can find the things I'll need.'

Less than five minutes later she came out of the drying shed where the men left their underground clothes to dry off between one core and the next. Skirt, petticoats, all of them gone. She wore the same drill trousers and jacket as the miners, the same as Giles would be wearing. But in her case they hadn't wasted time trying to find something to fit her, the legs were rolled up, the sleeves too. On her head was a hard hat, a candle fixed to it and already alight. She was ready.

'I don' like it. Don' know what the Cap'n'll say. And the doctor — and your wedding day almost here. But, if you must go down there, and I see you're set to do it, then I'll be a pace or two ahead of you.'

'You'd do that?' In her relief for a second she almost forgot her panic.

'Best we get a move on.'

Plenty of times she'd watched the men coming to grass from riding the Man Engine; Captain Bowen had shown her diagrams of the moving rod set with steps, he'd explained how it worked, and there in the light and safety of his office it had seemed so simple. Her guide went ahead of her, stepping from the platform at the side of the shaft on to a 'perch' on the moving rod. 'I'm jes' ahead o' you, there's nought to fear,' he said, and as he was lowered away from her into the dark hole: 'When un comes back, you jes' hop on like you saw me do. Change and down, change and down.' His voice and the glow from his candle was all that was left of him. The rod moved down twelve feet, she remembered that from what Captain Bowen had told her. Now here it was coming up again. With teeth clenched it took all her courage to grab the rod and step on to the 'perch'. Her next hurdle was to find the will-power to let go at the end of the twelve foot drop. But somehow she did it, helped by the voice below her: 'Change and down, that's it, change and down.' She alighted at the second platform and the rod moved back up, the one from below rising its twelve foot to her level. 'On we go, soon as 'ee comes to 'ee. I'm riding jes' below.'

So she travelled for fifty fathoms, helped by the steady rhythm of his voice. 'Change and down ... change and down ... that's the way.'

Then: ''Tiz ladders from here on. At the bottom o' the first we step to the side to come to the next. You'll soon get the hang o' it and I'll be right ahead of you. Jes' you ease yourself from one to the next, your candle gi'es enough light to see the way. But, missus, keep your eye on the rockface jes' afore you. Jes' you keep looking at that wall. Never look down. Now then, I'll go first, I'm right beneath you.'

She felt a trickle of sweat run down her side, not from heat but from fright. 'Please God, please, help me, don't let me think, let me do what I have to, just step, one step, another step, please God help me, make me do it.' One last frantic look upwards. Beyond the Man Engine the fading afternoon light was no more that a tiny grey disc now, far above. Facing the wall she moved, her toes reaching for each rung until at last she contacted a ledge of rock; then, holding her breath, she eased herself on to the next ladder. Her legs ached with fear, were weak; the dank smell from the rockface was getting stronger with each ladder she climbed down. And somewhere – it sounded far below – she could hear a steady dripping of water as if it were splashing into a pool. It must have been the adit.

It was no use, she couldn't move, she seemed paralysed, couldn't loosen her hands from their grip on the sides of the ladder.

'Jes' you hold steady a minute, missus, you'll be all right. Firm as a rock, you'll soon get the hang of it.' Desperately she tried to conquer her panic. 'Steady till you're ready, then a step at a time. Don't think beyond that, a step at a time.'

A step at a time! Hadn't that always been the way? She closed her eyes, she couldn't look at the rock only inches in front of her. In the light of her candle it was sinister, eerie. She musn't think of the ladder fixed vertically to it, nor the long drop below her, nor the darkness. A step at a time! The words brought memories crowding into her mind: the person she'd been; the hopelessness of being alone; the fight to build her future; the fight even to want a future. Then Giles – the feeling of being in safe harbour, of being wanted, loved, of loving – Giles, far below her, needing her now. The doctor was knocked off his feet ... gash on his head ... says he's not hurt.

258

'Will we go on now, Mama, will we do that?'

Here, entombed in the rocky ground, Rachel felt Patsy's spirit so close. Almost she heard her voice, half baby and half child. And John ... she felt his presence, calm, placid. The picture was clear. She saw him in his study in their house in Warwick, at his desk, his pipe in his mouth. John who never changed, never varied. 'You've brought them close, thank you, let me never lose them.' And as her garbled thoughts chased across her mind she moved on downwards, feeling for each rung until again she came to rocky ground. Then, opening her eyes just enough to follow her leader, she inched her way to the next ladder, hardly in control of what she did. Her hands were wet with fear, her arms and legs ached with it, yet as she moved on she made no conscious effort.

Minutes went by. Deeper and deeper they descended. She'd been warned not to look down, certainly she didn't attempt to. But just for a second she opened her eyes and peered upwards, she needed to see the last hint of daylight. But above her now was nothing but rock. They'd not followed a straight course; the shaft head was out of their vision.

At one point they heard a low, distant rumble. Involuntarily she cried out.

'Steady now, 'tiz nothing to fear. There's work going on still, remember. Sounds to be out to the south, some way, from the fourth level I'd guess. Get used to the noises when you work down here, y'know, get so that you can pinpoint them. That didn't come from anywhere near the doctor, don't you fear.' His voice was so unruffled, it helped her to hang on to her control. 'As you step off this ladder you can rest easy, you're on a firm stretch this time.'

'You mean we're there?'

'This is the third. This stope's been worked out, too dark to see, but 'tiz roomy. Now jes' you follow me, we get on again over this way.'

'I don't even know your name.'

'Gerard St. John Helverton.'

At his reply she had a wild desire to giggle. Just as a minute or two before terror had been almost more than she could contain, so now was this need to laugh. If she started she'd never stop! She fixed her concentration on the worked-out

259

stope, tried to take in what she could see of it. Her candle and Gerard St. John Helverton's each threw its own pool of light. They seemed to be in a gallery; but with no more than the light of the two candles she could get no idea of the area of it. At least the ground was firm. From somewhere not far away she could hear the plop-plop of water. Even here where the rocks weren't pressing in on her there was no movement in the air.

The third level. Only two more and she'd find Giles, the nightmare would be over. Ahead of them would be the climb back but she wasn't ready to think of that. And by then they'd be together, moving upwards, towards the air, the light, the cool, fresh rain.

'You're doing well,' came the reassuring voice of her friend, 'seems a long way the first time. When you get to —' The rest of his sentence was swallowed in a deafening roar, the very earth seemed to shake. Rachel cried out but she didn't know it, and no one could have heard. Her knuckles were white as she gripped the ladder, her head buried against it. Then, almost level with her, she heard a voice.

'We'll hold steady here. Safe enough here.' Gerard St. John Helverton had climbed back to where she was, she could feel him just behind her, standing on the rung lower than hers, his body protecting her, his hands gripping the sides of the ladder only just beneath hers.

'What is it?' Now the rumble was fading. She didn't need a reply. There was only one thing it could have been. Hadn't the thin, grey man, the 'friend of the knockers', said who could say there wasn't more to come?

'Best we get back up to grass, missus.'

A bell, far below them. Thirteen times it rang. The accident alarm had been sent to the surface. Where would it be? But in her heart she knew even before the five bells rang out.

"Tiz no good going on, I can't take you into that, missus."

'I shall go on. Please, I'll manage now if you want to go back. I must go down, I must!' Her voice was shrill, unnatural, the sound of it surprised her.

'It won't be a pretty sight. Dust, fair chokes you.' But he was moving on down.

But now she didn't even think of the darkness, nor of the consequences of putting a foot wrong. She wanted just to get

260

there; whatever was happening to him she must get to him. In her imagination she built a picture of what they'd find when they reached the deep workings: Giles tending the injured (her mind baulked at any other possibility), the light would be poor, the temperature high, nothing to stir the stillness of the air.

But whatever she'd expected, she was unprepared.

''Tiz along this way,' Gerard told her unnecessarily as they stepped off the final ladder, for what they heard was guide enough. The ground of the two hundred and twenty level was wet, water sloshed around their ankles. Their own candles gave light enough and as they came closer what they saw and heard was like a glimpse into hell. The picture she'd conjured up had taken no account of the cries, the moans. Someone was sobbing uncontrollably, a young boy's voice. Then there was the symphony of coughing; in the atmosphere of dust and grit she ought to have expected that there would be. The first thing she'd learnt about the mine had been from Dulcie, how Richard had died, the victim of phthisis, the lung disease that was the enemy of so many who worked underground. Somewhere amongst the rubble, the cries, the dust and the blood Giles must be.

She tried to hurry but now the ground was rough, uneven and pitted under her feet; and by her side her faithful guide quickened his pace. He must be with her until he handed her over to the doctor. Nearly all the candles had been extinguished, the only ones burning were those on the hats of other miners who'd already reached the scene of the disaster. For disaster it was. The air was thick, putrid; each individual candle gave its own small isolated hazy glow. Men lay trapped under the fallen rock and rubble, some cried like babies. It was like stepping into a nightmare, too horrific to take in. The sound of the coughing brought the tragedy alive to her, something familiar, part of a life she understood; but this was coughing such as she'd never heard, men straining and retching to clear the dust, vomiting grey slime.

'Where's the doctor?' Gerard grabbed the arm of a man who was hurrying in the opposite direction.

'Down yonder. But you'll have to wait, he can't work any faster. I'm off to fetch more help.' This was no time for climbing up by ladder. Eight bells to haul up the kibble, five to let them know in the engine house where it was to come from.

'Down yonder,' he'd said and Rachel waited to hear no more. She picked her way over the wet, uneven surface, through debris; she tried not to see the outstretched hands. She must reach Giles. But there was one lad she couldn't pass by, he didn't look anywhere near the thirteen years laid down by the law. Not that she could see much of him, he was lying with his face towards the ground, from his shoulders to his feet covered with debris. His crying was pitiful and it took all his strength to hold his face from the water. She squatted at his side and held her hands under his chin, feeling the sudden weight as he relaxed his head.

'They'll soon get you out. Here, Mr. Helverton, can you take your shirt and make a pillow of it.'

'Ah, that I can. Here, son,' tearing at the buttons, 'rest your head on that out o' the wet. Then I'll set about getting you free.'

She left them, her kindly friend working on lifting the stones carefully so that he wouldn't set up an avalanche.

Then she saw Giles. Stripped to the waist, grimed with dirt, rivulets of sweat leaving streaks; Giles, Captain Bowen, the miners, they all looked alike.

'I've come to help.' She said it as if it were the most natural thing. Later on she might think back and be surprised that her being there was accepted so easily. Captain Bowen's 'Ah'; the way Giles rested a hand fleetingly on her shoulder. 'There's plenty to help with.' And soon she was working as hard as any of them. Gently lifting off the rocks and stones, digging out the survivors, carrying bodies of the dead to be laid side by side out of the aura of the candles of the workers. There was one man whose shoulder was dislocated. When Giles touched him he screamed out.

'Grit your teeth, try and relax your body.' Amid the noise his voice was quiet, reassuring. She watched as his strong, bony fingers moved on the shoulder, then taking the man completely by surprise he manipulated the joint. She heard the sound of it, then the man's breath escape in a kind of whistle.

'Wheeoo!' And gingerly moving his shoulder: 'Why, you put un right, you put un back.'

By Giles' side she worked. She passed what he asked for — wood for a splint, bandages, scissors. She must have been down there about an hour when the bell alerted them that the kibble was coming down. Men went to meet it and came back with sheets, more flat pieces of wood for splints, more poles and sacks for stretchers. Until today Rachel had never made a bandage, never learnt to tie a sling. Giles gave his instructions as they worked: pass this, tie that, hold this, cut that; willingly, proudly, she did as he said. They were a team, she thought, as much a team as they had been last night. Some of the men had drifted into unconsciousness; some had fallen into their last long sleep; many, weak from coughing, had groped their way to the bottom of the Incline Shaft and been hoisted in the kibble; but there were others who were more comfortable and by the light of the lanterns able to look around and be reassured that life wasn't over after all. Continuously the kibble journeyed, carrying men up, usually two or three at a time, then back for the next load. There was no other way for them, most of them were in no state to climb.

It must have been evening, they'd lost track of time, only hunger made them realise the passing of the hours. Dr. Noall from the St. Elmo mine arrived to offer his services.

Hour after hour the work went on. Tiredness and hunger were part of it, to be accepted and overcome; Rachel found that there comes a point when one ceases to be aware. Giles had been here hours longer than she had; the wound on his head must be painful even if he didn't admit to it; under the dust and dirt that was embedded in his skin she knew he was pale. But who wouldn't be, breathing this foul stench all day? He'd painted the picture of it clearly to the adventurers — sweat, excreta — but he'd said nothing of the water under-foot. And here amongst the rubble, the water, fragments of rock and, as it settled, the dust too, combined to make a thick cloying floor to walk on. And yet, it seemed the dust would never clear from the still air. It hung like fog, coating her lips and her tongue.

The worst cases were hauled up to the surface, their stretchers strapped to the kibbles where necessary. Word came down that Dr. Robson from Wheal Vardin was there waiting for them, he'd sent for wagons from the Infirmary. This was something Rachel hadn't realised, this sharing of disasters, helping each other in time of trouble. And there was another truth she came to know down here in the heart of the mine: working close to Giles, being part of the horror, sharing with him and with Captain Bowen and the men, today she'd earned the right to feel that she belonged to Treddinock.

When Giles told her she was to go to the surface and wait for him there, she knew why he wanted her gone and didn't argue. They were going to move the bodies of the dead. To humour him rather than to spare herself she agreed. What to expect of riding up in the kibble she didn't know; by now she was beyond caring. It was over. Within the hour she would be back in the fresh air, Giles not far behind her.

Five men had died; five bodies had to be lifted to grass. Did their wives know? Or were they standing there still, waiting, hoping, praying?

The kibble was descending. In a minute she would start her long haul upwards.

'Stay well down,' Giles told her, 'sit on the floor of it, don't try and stand. Don't be frightened, it'll soon be over now.' He touched her cheek gently with his fingers. 'Rachel,' he said softly, 'bless you for coming.'

Alone here at the foot of the shaft, water sloshing around their feet, they could hear the clatter of the empty kibble getting louder. It was more than the dust that made her throat feel dry and tight. She leant against him, rubbing her cheek against his bare chest.

'I'm none too clean.' He gathered her close against him. She sniffed, dust and sweat.

'Giles, my beloved Giles,' she whispered, her lips against him. 'All this, today, it makes one feel so humble. I remember you said that the very first time we spoke to each other. Humble – and yet proud too, to be part of it.'

'Rachel, I love you so very much.'

The kibble was almost here.

'Come soon, Giles. I'll wait for you in the Captain's room.'

'I shall have to speak to the wives – the widows.'

She nodded.

'It must be well past midnight,' to her it was connected with what had gone before, 'Oliver will be home today. We're so lucky.'

He kissed her tenderly. It seemed he'd followed the way her mind had worked. Then he helped her climb into the great iron kibble. 'Sit down, right down. You've nothing to do but wait now, you'll be quite safe. A few more minutes and you'll be out of here.'

She sat, her knees drawn up, her hands clasping her legs. He rang the bell. Eight times, a pause, then five times more. The first jolt was violent, no wonder he'd told her to stay on the floor, then she was being carried upwards, rocking from side to side. Once or twice she felt a thud as they knocked against the side of the narrow shaft. As they ascended, so it widened; but she had no means of knowing that, for her world went no further than the four sides of the iron container that carried her, dirty from the ore that was its customary cargo. She could feel the atmosphere changing, the air was purer. Hurtling upwards through the dark, that was the only hint she had that she was almost at the surface.

Then she was out. The joy of opening her mouth and filling her lungs with the damp night air and of feeling the blessed pure rain on her face! Perhaps it was relief that turned her legs to jelly. When they helped her out of her 'carriage' and she stood on the platform of the dressing shed, she had to grab the rail to steady herself. At this time of night (nearly two o'clock but she knew only that it was sometime in the night) she'd not expected so many people still to be waiting. One of the women brought her a tin mug of warm, sweet tea and another a slab of apple cake. It hadn't occurred to her that what she'd done would make her something of a heroine. Gradually her limbs felt as though they belonged to her again, either because her fear was over or her appetite partially appeased.

She knew it was cowardly, but she avoided the small group still waiting at the shaft head and went straight to the purser's room. Cowardly? Yes, and yet what could she give them but sympathy? It was Giles who could tell them what had happened, reassure them of the last moments of the ones they loved.

The kibble disappeared down Incline Shaft. Soon they'd

hear the bells, eight then five. Giles, Captain Bowen, Dr. Noall and two men were still there, each of them would bring one body on the dark ride to grass. And Giles was sure to be the first, he'd want to talk to each of the wives who, on this day just a week before Christmas, had become widows.

She didn't light the lamp in Captain Bowen's room, but stood by the open door disregarding the cold nor'westerly, listening. Had it not been so cloudy there would have been a full moon. Even now it was light enough to see the silhouette of the lifting wheels, the great beams of the engines rising and falling, the tall chimneys. Always she'd loved this place; but now her love went deeper, not just what she'd known and understood at the mine head, but all of it. Treddinock had no secrets from her.

By now the kibble must be down at the deep level, they would be carrying the first man, carefully putting him on the floor where she'd sat. Giles would be climbing in. Someone would ring the bell. She listened. The minutes went by, five, ten, a quarter of an hour. No bell sounded.

No one watched the Man Engine Shaft, those they waited for wouldn't come to surface that way. The man who emerged unnoticed soon held their attention. From the doorway Rachel couldn't hear what news he brought, but even in the near-darkness she sensed the urgency.

'Oh, no, please, please, no ...'

Leaving the door wide open she ran to where they huddled together. 'What's wrong? Why don't they come up?' But surely this wasn't one of the men she'd left down there with Giles?

'Down in the deep workings. Not to be wondered at. They've had warning – then with today's fall, what else did they expect?'

Another, waiting in the crowd, added his bit: 'Sit around yon table, counting their gold.' He spat on the ground, a sign of his opinion. 'And what do buggers know o' the two hundred and twenty? I'll tell 'ee, they know jes' how much they'll get to put in their banks come next Count!'

'Nuff o' that talk. Remember who 'tiz you're speaking to, and 'tiz the doctor who's down there still.'

'Ah,' another put in, 'we should send up a praise-be that

the work had been called off. Or jes' think how many good zouls 'd be lost.'

'Stop it!' This time it was Rachel. 'Just tell me!'

'Weeks ago we knew they were driving too near the ocean's bed. Oh, they put in the timbers, filled up the end. Takes more 'n that to hold back the ocean.'

And suddenly she knew. All day as they'd worked the water and slurry at their feet had got deeper. Even then the sea must have been finding the cracks, forcing a way in.

'Are the pump's still working?'

'Full out, but a pump's no use against the ocean.'

'Where were you working?' she asked the man who'd brought the tidings. 'I don't remember leaving you down there?'

'On the fourth. Further to the south.'

'Have they gone from there to help? There are five men, they stayed to bring — '

'Help them? What help could we be against *that?* Sudden it was, like thunder — only it didn't stop, just come on rushing. Nothing could stop it. 'Tiz goodbye to the deep workings, copper an' all.'

Here in the dark she looked around her, desperate, not knowing what to do or where to start. But there was no one but her, here in the middle of the night. Giles ... oh no, please, no, don't let it be, please, please ... It would have been so easy to give way to the panic, the wild fears, that fought inside her. It took every ounce of her strength of will to speak as she did now.

'I want a party of men to go down, men who know the — '

She stopped speaking. No one was listening to her. There was something else. A strange sound, something they all heard yet none of them recognised. It started softly, then got steadily louder. Was it water? No, not quite. Was it a fall of stones? No, not that either. Then, what? And where? Underground? Somewhere towards the cliff edge? 'What's that?' With one voice they asked it.

'Sounds to come from the slimes ...' The slimes pool, the water and waste from the buddles.

From the dressing sheds men were coming with lanterns. Word spread, passing from one to the next. Following the lights of the lanterns they moved together in the direction of the slimes. There was no doubt, and yet even as they watched they seemed unable to believe what they saw. The ground beneath the pool had collapsed, the thick choking liquid was being sucked into the labyrinth below. They watched in stunned silence as the level went down, released into the honeycomb of passages.

No one had seen the mine without the slimes pool. Like all things it had come from a small beginning, had grown with the mine — and over these last weeks of autumn with the rains too. More than eighty years ago there had been an old disused shaft somewhere in the vicinity. It had been sollared over and filled with stones before anyone here tonight had even been born. The grass had long since grown over it. Its surface, and that of the land around it, formed a natural hollow, and so the pool for the slimes had developed. No one ever suspected any seepage, and if there had been any it must have been slow and steady, pumped out of the adit in the same way as the water from below ground. Today something had shifted in it, enough to let a greater volume of water filter through, and that extra force had been enough to start the movement of the stones. The pool had grown from a small beginning and now it had taken but a small shift of the stones to start the flow of water that rushed ever faster, carrying with it anything that got in its path.

In stunned silence, by the light of the lanterns, they watched it. There was no sense, no reason in what they saw.

'Naught to stop it till it reaches adit.' At last a man who carried one of the lanterns broke the silence, and with his words came realisation of what this meant. Between surface and adit level, men were working. As Captain Bowen had said, Treddinock was healthy, there was plenty of tinstuff coming to grass. These days prices were low, but the tide might turn and ore was brought steadily from the second and third levels.

The crowd moved towards the Man Engine Shaft. The early core was arriving but today no one attempted to go below ground. Their numbers swelled. They waited ... and waited ... What had been the pool was no more than a quagmire, and at last the noise was stilled.

'Can't get up that way.' In the dark no one had noticed the approach of a straggle of men, coming from the opposite direction. 'We got out up old Shem Shaft.'

''Tiz the slimes. Where's the slimes gone?' Someone wanted to know.

'Too dark to see. Black as the ace of spades. The candles all got snuffed with this great draught. We heard the roar — but not till now did we know what it was.'

The ladders of the old Shem Shaft hadn't been used for years. The men had groped their way to them in the dark, the only chance of getting to the air, away from the rush of wind that had knocked them from their feet, and a noise like nothing they'd ever heard before. Now they were safe, solid ground beneath them. With the relief, so reaction hit them. In the night air they coughed, they 'oh deared', one of them was bent double like a broken reed, all his strength drained.

'We need lanterns, stretchers ... Who's with me?' The disaster had thrown up a natural leader, a young man, his straw-coloured hair hinting at the fair skin hidden by the dirt.

'Who's that?' Rachel asked, then peered in the dark to see who the woman was she spoke to. It was the same fat girl who'd arrived at the first rumour of trouble on the two hundred and twenty level. It seemed a lifetime ago. And she was still here, still waiting. Was her man one of the two who'd stayed behind to help carry up the dead? Or was he one of the five?

'That's Harry Boscowen. Lives down by us. Harry'll think o' something, he'll get un out.'

'I'll come w'you, Harry.' 'Ah, I'll get and fetch the poles.' 'I'll see to the lights,' – and someone else the ropes. It seemed young Harry had everyone's confidence. Soon the rescue party set out, climbing down the old Shem Shaft. They had no idea what they'd find, but wherever the slimes pool had drained to, it had found its level by now, the damage was done and it was up to them.

With daybreak more women came from the village. They brought cans of warm drink, pasties, cake, bread, cheese — anything they could spare. Rachel found herself with a piece of crusty bread in her hand, topped with a chunk of fat salt bacon. And just like everyone else she took it thankfully.

How could she want to eat, not knowing where he was? How could any of them? Perhaps it was the only way to hang on to their reason as the wintry sun rose over the land behind them. Sun! For the first time in weeks the sky was clear of clouds.

More men were crawling out from Shem Shaft. In twos and threes they came, all with the same story: a sudden great force of wind that knocked them down and snuffed their candles; groping in the dark as they tried to find a way of escape. Only gradually would the full picture build up; how, breaking through the sollar, the sludge had forced its way down the old disused shaft, along an eighteen foot cross-cut, down another shaft, through the fifty fathom cross-cut, its force breaking away the base of the Man Engine. Then like a greedy giant it had reached even further to tumble down another shaft until at last it had found its way to the adit.

Strapped to stretchers the first of the injured men were raised, their colleagues risking their own lives on those vertical ladders as they found strength they didn't know they had, and managed to climb, one pulling the front, another bearing the strain behind. They would have said it was impossible, but there was no other way.

Reason ought to have told Rachel that these men were being brought from the higher levels of the mine. Below sea level it was flooded. And that's where he'd been, even lower than the level of the ocean's floor. If she shut her eyes, here in the winter morning sunshine, she knew again the warmth of his bare chest, the smell that would always bring back to her those hours deep inside Treddinock. 'Giles, my beloved Giles.' 'Rachel, I love you so very much.' She bit hard into the fatty, salt bacon, gripping her teeth together. 'Please God, please, I beg You, I don't know how You can do it, but You can, I beg You, bring him back. Don't let him be gone.'

What of those other women, wives and widows? What made her think she had the right to ask special favours?

She chewed. To chew was easy; to swallow, impossible.

Near her two women were talking.

'No, I'll stay a bit yet. If he comes he'll look for me. They're still coming out.'

'Come home, Jess. He was down in the two hundred and twenty.' The answer was spoken gently, but there was no

disputing it. The two hundred and twenty was under the sea.
A minute or two more, then the women moved away.

The kitchen of the Count House was running with steam.
Today there was no pot of rich dripping where the bread could
be dipped in anticipation of things to come, no rib of beef
either. But long before first light two or three women had the
fire going and had been chopping vegetables. Now, mid-
morning, a great black iron cauldron of broth was bubbling,
neck of lamb, every kind of vegetable they could find at this
time of year, and handfuls of pearl barley as a filler.

The never-varying pattern of the mine head was broken, the
huge wheel of the lifting gear was still. Only the pumps were
working. Come what may, nature sent the water to find its
way through the ground, water that must be pumped to adit.
If Treddinock had a heartbeat, surely it was the constant rise
and fall of the great beam of the Treweek pumping engine.
Smoke came from the chimneys of the engine houses, the
boilers were still stoked, but today no ore was coming to
grass.

The rescue work was slow and dangerous. Not only was the
Man Engine out of use but, far below them, the onslaught of
the ocean had torn away the kibble in this section of the mine.
Help came from ropes, strength, endurance and endless
patience. Men of Treddinock were short of none of these.
Reinforced with steaming gruel they battled on. In her early
days here Rachel had seen this as a close-knit community but
never had she been more aware of it than today. Friends,
relatives, colleagues ... 'Hold the rope steady' ... 'Right, I
got un' ... 'Ease it out, bit at a time' ... 'Care o' his head'
... It was a marriage of strength and gentleness as one after
another the men were brought out.

Dr. Robson was still here and by now he'd been joined by
Dr. Durloe from Wheal Alice. The Count House itself had
become a temporary medical station.

''Tiz the Captain.'

He was dead. Rachel knew it from the way the words were
spoken. Her dear friend Captain Bowen, his body tied to the
hessian stretcher, hoisted by ropes. All this time she'd not
shed a tear, but now as she knelt by his side she saw him

271

through a sudden mist. Her eyes stung. Fatigue and grief mingled at the sight of him, coated with grey mud, what hair he still had on his balding head matted. There was no hiding from just what the disaster meant. Nothing could ever be the same.

'Am I mad?' came the echo of her question.

And his reply: 'That I can't rightly say, Mrs. Treweek, m'dear, but if you are, 'tiz a madness there's no cure for.'

In that moment she believed she hated Treddinock.

'Is Father out yet? I came straight here as soon as I got home.'

'Oliver!' She fought for control. Oliver home for Christmas; home for the wedding.

'Is he?'

She shook her head. But still she wouldn't admit that hope was gone. 'They're still bringing men out.'

'He won't come until he's done all he can for them down there.' Oliver was growing up fast, but he still had a child's faith that his father was invincible. 'Tell me what happened. At home all they knew was that there'd been an accident.'

It was a relief to talk to him, repeating a sequence of events steadied her, helped her to find her control. He still had the blind confidence of youth.

'And the Captain was with him. Are you sure the kibble bell didn't ring?'

'Positive. I was listening for it.'

'Supposing just after the kibble was raised, bringing you up, the water started to rise fast enough for them to be warned what was going to happen. They wouldn't have stood down there waiting, now would they? They'd have started up the ladder. That must have been what the Captain did — and Father was with him, you said so yourself.'

It made sense; it had to make sense. Her heart was beating a wild tattoo. She didn't ask herself why if he was safe he hadn't climbed to the surface, or if he was injured he hadn't been brought out. Blind hope had been re-kindled. And she clung to that hope, not so much because she trusted as because she was frightened to admit that she didn't.

The kibble had carried Rachel upwards while Giles watched

until even the small glow from her candle had disappeared, then he'd turned back to join the others, to carry the first of the victims along ready for the journey to the top. It had been then that he'd realised that the water underfoot was getting deeper. He'd stood still and listened; he'd peered beyond the Incline Shaft to where the work had been stopped and the end filled.

'Captain!' he'd shouted, his voice echoing along the tunnel. 'All of you, quick, make to the ladder. The sea's breaking through.' The noise of water had been clear. Not yet a roar, but that could only be minutes away. It would take more than the deads that had been brought to fill the end to hold back the ocean.

One behind the other they'd started up the first ladder, and, as a background, had come the sudden roar as the sea took command, pushing the deads ahead of it as it claimed its victory. But they were safe! Up, up, their candles giving enough light. At the fourth level they'd stopped to get their breath, safe on firm ground. Then on again, the horror of the past hours behind them. They'd been nearly to the third level when there had come that great rush of wind. It had been all they could do to cling to the ladder in a world that was suddenly pitch dark. Then they'd heard that uncanny sound, a sound that none of them could recognise. 'Best you jes' stay steady, get the feel of the dark.' Captain Bowen had taken charge. 'Then when you're ready we'll go on again.'

'What is it, Captain?'

'Don' rightly know. But 'tiz trouble, no doubt o' that.'

The roar had been a constant sound; the shouts and screams hadn't, they'd heard each one as an individual cry of terror.

It had been then that they'd lost touch with the Captain. While they'd done as he'd said and 'stayed steady to get the feel of the dark', he must have been going ahead. And of course he'd had the advantage; he'd known every inch of these tunnels and galleries, the dark hadn't put him at a loss as it had them. He'd climbed on up, following the direction of the noise that none of them had recognised — the slimes rushing on its way through levels, down shafts, towards the adit and escape.

The remaining four had made their way to the next level, groping blindly as they'd changed from ladder to ladder. Then on the third level they'd found themselves in an old tunnel, long disused, its height no more than four feet. Crouched low they'd formed a human chain as they'd felt their way forward. This part of the old workings had been strange ground even to the two miners; instinct had drawn them in what they'd believed to be the direction of the Marston Shaft, conscious with each shuffling step that between them and the Marston were ventilation shafts. The tunnels had been barely wider than their shoulders, jagged rock had caught them unexpectedly and torn at their bare flesh. Fatigue had been their enemy, that, hunger and lack of air. A sudden crack on the temple and one of them lost the struggle to go on.

Only a few people still waited. As their men had reached the surface so they'd gone home, but for all of them was the shadow of friends injured, neighbours whose lives could never be the same again, wives this morning and widows this evening.

Treddinock had had its share of accidents in the past, but it had seen nothing like this.

'End o' the copper — end o' Treddinock too, if you ask me.' A man standing near Rachel voiced the thought that must have been in many a mind today. 'Good money coming out, so long as there was copper, but they'll not put their hands in their pockets to get things right after this lot.'

No one answered him.

'Treddinock is healthy.' Rachel seemed to see the Captain as she said it. His words, his faith never faltering. 'The Captain had no doubt on that. Even without the deep workings — and we can't win against the ocean — but even without that, there's good tinstuff in Treddinock. We'll get it back in fork again.'

She tried to hold out a hope for tomorrow, yet for this group of women who'd stood all day — and some of them, like the fat girl she'd spoken to yesterday, even longer — what hope could there be? For them? For her? She gripped the corners of her mouth hard between her teeth, her eyes closed.

Her silent plea had been repeated a thousand times in these hours. Hers? Theirs?

Oliver felt young and helpless. His father would want him to be taking care of Mrs. Treweek. Mrs. Treweek? This time tomorrow he would have to start calling her 'Mother'. His mind defied the alternative.

'You've been here for ages, right since yesterday. Why don't you go home? Honestly, I'll ride straight down to you the moment he arrives.'

She shook her head.

'I'll wait here,' he told her. 'Why don't you go to the kitchen and get some food?'

She was weak for want of it, yet the thought of eating made her feel sick. When she walked away, Oliver believed she was doing as he said. But she didn't. She went towards the buildings behind them, the only movement at the mine head coming from the rocking beam of the Treweek engine. There was a strange sort of comfort in seeing it, its steady movement never faltering. On her own she stood by the building of the engine house. In the last hour a breeze had risen; overhead a seagull swooped, its laughing cry seeming to mock her.

Only mid-afternoon but already dusk was starting to gather. Except for the rescue parties no one had been below ground today. Shem Shaft was far across to the right of where she stood – so what was she seeing? She peered into the gloom telling herself it must be tiredness, lack of food, making her imagine what wasn't there. Only Marston Shaft was in that direction, a mile at least from where the rescue work had gone on. Yet men were coming from that way . . . far along the cliffside . . . men were coming . . . three men . . . was it three? What were they carrying? She started to run towards them. And as she got closer she could see, what they were carrying was a fourth man . . . four men . . . yet how could she be so sure? At this distance they were no more than that – four men . . .

Then one of them broke away, was coming towards her.

She wanted to hold on to these seconds for the rest of her life, the relief, the thankfulness, the joy. Wordlessly they clung to each other.

And behind them the beam of John's engine rocked, its

pace steady and constant ... yesterday ... today ... tomorrow. Tomorrow, a new beginning.

'Am I mad?' the question echoed.

'That I can't rightly say, Mrs. Treweek, m'dear, but if you are, 'tiz a madness there's no cure for.'

Hannah's Wharf
Connie Monk

The enthralling story of a young girl who becomes heiress to a great shipping line.

When thirteen-year-old Hannah is left an orphan, she is sent to Devon to live with an aunt she has never met. But Aunt Louise is not fond of children, and Hannah suffers appalling loneliness. In time, though, she develops an interest in the family shipping business and sets about learning all she can.

However, the laws of Victorian England are strict with regard to property. Hannah may well be her aunt's heiress, but it will be Hannah's husband who effectively controls her considerable fortune on Louise's death. And when Hannah falls in love with a charming opportunist, Tommy Webster, she little imagines she will have to fight tooth and nail for everything she has worked so hard to achieve.

FONTANA PAPERBACKS

The Juniper Bush
Audrey Howard

Winner of the 1987
Romantic Novel of the Year Award

The passionate saga of a nineteenth-century Lakeland girl, her search for happiness in a web of conflicting emotions and loyalties.

Lovely Christy Emmerson is the only daughter of an explosives manufacturer and a fine catch for any man. But there is only one man Christy cares about, and when she becomes betrothed to the Squire's son, Robin, it seems that all concerned are happy.

But with only a few weeks to go before the wedding tragedy strikes the community, and the Emmerson family. Apparently abandoned by Robin at a time when she needed him most, Christy, heartbroken and confused, falls into a marriage with a local mine owner, the handsome but arrogant Alex Buchanan. As her family grows, Christy becomes increasingly wrapped up in her new life and almost succeeeds in forgetting Robin. Then, one day, she meets him again and her whole world is thrown into confusion.

Audrey Howard's other bestselling sagas, *The Skylark's Song*, *The Morning Tide* and *Ambitions*, are also available in Fontana Paperbacks.

FONTANA PAPERBACKS

Windmills of the Gods
Sidney Sheldon

Mary Ashley, a bright young professor and mother of two, is appointed US ambassador to an Iron Curtain country. But even before she takes up her post, unseen and powerful enemies – including the sinister Angel, assassin *par excellence* – plot her destruction.

From the White House to the romance of Paris, from Rome to the shady menace of Bucharest, the action races.

Two men are by Mary's side: Mike Slade, her tough deputy chief of mission and the courteous French doctor, Louis Desforges. But soon she comes to believe that one of them is out to kill her . . .

FONTANA PAPERBACKS

Yes, Mama
Helen Forrester

Bestselling author of
Twopence to Cross the Mersey and
The Latchkey Kid

Alicia Woodman was born into a home that should have been filled with comfort and joy. Her mother Elizabeth was bright and vivacious, Humphrey Woodman was a prosperous businessman. But Alicia was not Humphrey's child and he would have nothing to do with her, and before long Elizabeth, too, turned her back on her daughter.

It was left to Polly Ford, widow of a dock labourer, to bring Alicia up, to teach her to say 'Yes, Mama', and to give the child the love she so desperately needed. In a hypocritical society full of thin-lipped disapproval, Alicia would learn that the human spirit can soar over adversity, and that, though blood may be thicker than water, love is the most powerful relationship of all . . .

FONTANA PAPERBACKS

Fontana Paperbacks: Fiction

Fontana is a leading paperback publisher of fiction. Below are some recent titles.

- ☐ SHINING THROUGH Susan Isaacs £3.99
- ☐ KINDRED PASSIONS Rosamund Smith £2.99
- ☐ BETWEEN FRIENDS Audrey Howard £3.99
- ☐ THE CHARMED CIRCLE Catherine Gaskin £4.50
- ☐ THE INDIA FAN Victoria Holt £3.99
- ☐ THE LAWLESS John Jakes £2.99
- ☐ THE AMERICANS John Jakes £2.99
- ☐ A KIND OF WAR Pamela Haines £3.50
- ☐ THE HERON'S CATCH Susan Curran £4.50

You can buy Fontana paperbacks at your local bookshop or newsagent. Or you can order them from Fontana Paperbacks, Cash Sales Department, Box 29, Douglas, Isle of Man. Please send a cheque, postal or money order (not currency) worth the purchase price plus 22p per book for postage (maximum postage required is £3.00 for orders within the UK).

NAME (Block letters)_____

ADDRESS_____

_____

While every effort is made to keep prices low, it is sometimes necessary to increase them at short notice. Fontana Paperbacks reserve the right to show new retail prices on covers which may differ from those previously advertised in the text or elsewhere.